I0672369

It's only cheating if you get caught.

LYING, CHEATING
HEART

The Game of Hearts Series
BOOK TWO

mindy ruiz

This is a work of fiction. Names, characters, places, and incidents are the product of the author's imagination or are used fictitiously. Any resemblance to actual events, locales, or persons, living or dead, is purely coincidental.

Text copyright © 2016 Mindy Ruiz.
All rights reserved.
Cover design © 2016 Regina Wamba of MaeIDesign.com
Cover image by Mae I Design
Content edit by Tracy, Tee, Tate
Copy edit by Hayley Cruz
Proofreading by Deana Lathrop of D.L.Editing
Book design by Inkstain Interior Book Designing

No part of this publication, digital or print, may be reproduced, distributed, or transmitted in any form or by any means, or stored in a database or retrieval system without the prior written permission of the author or publisher.

Published by A.P. Press, LLC

The author acknowledges the copyrighted or trademarked status and trademark owners of the following wordmarks mentioned in this fiction: Converse, Plaza Hotel, Fremont Street, Fremont Street Experience, Frank Sinatra, The Rat Pack, Fremont Casino, Jimmy Choo, Manolo Blahnik, Caesar's Palace, Golden Gate Hotel, Club 1906, Prada, Chanel No. 5, Golden Nugget, Luxor, Bellagio, Jeep, Mustang, SlotZilla.

ISBN-10: 0-9904804-4-5
ISBN-13: 978-0-9904804-4-0

—To Dina Alcantar and Rochelle Spears,
For *always* being there.

LYING, CHEATING

HEART

PROLOGUE

JULIA ROTH WAS DEAD.

The beautiful redheaded actress lay in a coffin of white satin with a red rose in her hand. I stared at the up-and-coming starlet like she was a Disney princess waiting for some special prince to break the evil spell she was under.

But there would be no prince.

Julia Roth was dead.

And she was only a year older than me.

The sentence tumbled around in my head from the time we left the funeral and well past the two hours I'd given Mom to decompress. But if the panic that clawed my throat were any indication of peace coming, Mom wouldn't be back to her chipper, cooking-channel binge-watching self for a while.

I knotted my hair into a bun and sneaked out of my room to see how Dad was faring with Mom. We were so lucky. Mom barely had a scratch on her from the car accident that killed Julia. Guilt wormed its way back into my belly chasing after the feeling of relief. We could have been lowering mom into the ground today. It felt so wrong to be happy Mom only had a few scratches and a black eye, when a girl was dead. I tried to shake the sickening pit-in-my stomach feeling it should have been, not Julia. It would have been me if I hadn't bailed on meeting Taylor Swift at Dad and Mrs. M's latest movie release. I'd have to thank Malory the next time she was allowed visitors at rehab.

Another shuffle shredded the silence in our house.

One-Mississippi.

Two-Mississippi.

Three—

Dad taught me to count the seconds between card shuffles like it was lightning waiting for the clap of thunder, when Mom had her deck of cards out. Three seconds to shuffle a deck meant I'd be sitting on the top step well into the night. And Dad had much bigger things to worry about than a day's worth of missed meals. Something had Mom spooked. She usually saved this level of panic for all things Vegas related. My adoptive mother's past was as much a mystery to me as mine.

I undid my bun and started twisting it into a braid, knowing it would do nothing to stop the conflicting waves of guilt and relief washing through me. All I could do now was wait for the sign that Dad had talked Mom off the ledge, and she was hiding the playing cards back in the deep, dark recesses of the garage. Mom had banned playing cards from the house when I was seven, but I knew she still had a deck squirreled away in the top of the rafters in the garage. Drunks had their emergency bottle. Mom had her crisis cards.

Muffled voices snaked their way into the foyer.

"You have to get a grip, Sassy."

I did a double take at Dad's use of Mom's nickname from high school. Forgotten nicknames and card shuffling—something hadn't just frightened my mom, it had straight up crawled down from the Welcome to Vegas sign and terrified her.

Another shuffle echoed from below.

"I want you to shelf the Rat Pack remake. I think it's too much. Too much attention. They found her—" The next round of shuffling cards cut off the rest of Mom's sentence.

I tiptoed down the stairs, army-crawled through the entry hall, and peeked around the corner.

"Sass." Dad grabbed Mom's hands, but she yanked them free.

"No." The cards slapped together again. "Julia was a wake-up call. We've gotten too comfortable here. Our guard is down. He could find her again!" Hysteria lit the edges of her voice

"Sara." Dad used his stern voice. Either this was coming to an end, or Mom would spend the next three days locked in her bedroom scrapbooking. "Julia was an accident. No, let me finish. It was an accident. Cassandra . . ." His words trailed off as he leaned into Mom. Dad brushed back a piece of her blonde hair and whispered something that made her pursed lips soften. But holy Skittles, he'd used my real name.

Not Princess.

Not Cassie.

He'd said: Cassandra.

"Okay?" Dad pushed.

Mom shook her head.

"Sara, she's growing up. Unless her father's dead and the Fifth House has given up on a centuries-old quest, you can't hide her forever."

A fifth house?

No way could Dad be talking about the fairytale Mom told me when I was little.

"My God, Sassy, we're talking about four families who've sacrificed *everything* to protect the world from the Shadows. You really think they're just going to give up the search?"

I leaned up against the wall. He *was* talking about the Shadows in the fairytale. The soul-sucking demons King Midas released from Tartarus during his quest to rid himself from the curse of the golden touch.

Could the royal card suits, the Houses of Hearts, Spades, Diamonds, and Clubs, be real?

And what was the fifth house?

Mom shuffled the cards together again and then slapped them down on the table. "I can and will keep that girl hidden until I draw my last breath." Mom pushed away from the table. Determination steeled her spine with each step she took my way. "I promised her I would."

I stood, then ran on tiptoes back the way I'd come, quietly climbing the staircase one carpeted riser to the next until I was safely on the landing and hidden by Mom's dying fern. Yellow light from the garage spilled into the foyer. Mom paused, looked up the stairs before disappearing behind the garage door. The small click of the door closing released a ton of questions.

Who had she promised to keep me hidden?

And why would they be hiding me from my birth father?

ONE

"LOVING SOMEONE SHOULDN'T be this easy," A.J.'s deep-timbered voice whispered next to my ear. Every nerve ending from the top of my head to my toes sprang to life, begging for more.

More lips.

More voice.

More A.J.

"I agree," I sighed.

A.J.'s lips pulled up in a smile along the sensitive patch of skin between my neck and shoulder.

"A.J.," I let out in a soft moan.

His throaty chuckle was the only thing that could make goosebumps spring to life on my arms in 110-degree weather.

I closed my eyes and imagined all the things we could do if we weren't on a boat, with an audience of all our friends, if he'd keep a date—he pulled the lobe of my ear between his lips, cutting off my thought. *Ohmigawd, those delicious lips.* Another kiss slid along my jaw line, assaulting the right side of my body. His breath on my ear made my body spasm in the most delightful ways. He placed another toe-curling kiss on the skin behind my earlobe. I could be devoured by those two amazing—

The wail of A.J.'s cellphone shattered the magical spell he'd conjured.

My eyelids flew wide open. White rays of sun and betrayal blinded me. The soft lapping sounds of Lake Las Vegas thumped up against the side of the boat, drowning out my friends' giggles of freedom. Sadly, no amount of giddy could hide my boyfriend's ringing phone.

A.J.'s gaze locked with mine, widening with guilt. Two inches from my face, I could see every hypocritical line etch into his forehead. He'd been doing that a lot: telling me one thing, and the person who I knew was on the other end another.

I pushed him away, desperately hoping he'd wrap me up in his arms and start showering me with kisses again, but the practical girl in me knew exactly what he was going to do.

A second chorus of "Money, Money, Money" kicked in. A.J. lowered his head, letting his rebellious little curl hang defeated.

He'd promised me.

One day.

That's all I'd asked.

"You brought your phone on the boat?"

I saw Olivia, hands planted firmly on her hips, like she was the girlfriend he'd broken another promise to, over A.J.'s sun-bronzed shoulder. Besides being my cousin and the future Queen of Spades, Olivia had been my social secretary the past three months. She'd received and relayed every canceled date text. She'd witnessed my understanding look transform into hurt. Now, I was plain pissed off when I heard his Pat Benatar, "Heartbreaker" ringtone play on Olivia's phone.

A.J. glanced at Olivia and then back at me. His expression softened with yet another apology, one he fully expected me to accept.

But I couldn't.

This tug of war between his heart and his honor had been going on for too long. A.J.'s eyebrows pinched together, the soft planes of his face growing hard when I didn't accept his apology.

I swore never to draw a line in the sand, but that promise was getting harder and harder to keep.

"Yes," he said to me, then shot a look at Olivia. "Some of us still have to work." A.J. snatched his backpack from beneath my feet, pulled out his phone, and read the screen. Not like we didn't all know who was looking for him.

The man who still wanted me dead.

His grandfather.

Seven weeks ago, I'd cost Midas—yeah, *that* Midas, the one with the golden touch—I'd cost him a centuries-old bet with Dionysus (the god who had a thing for wine and bad wish granting.). About a few centuries before I was born, those two asshats thought it would be a great idea to place a wager on who would find and kill The Balanter. That'd be me, the girl who would end the Shadows.

"I have to pick someone up from the airport," A.J. said, replacing the phone in his hands for the wheel of the boat. I'm fairly certain he'd never responded to one of my texts that fast. The boat motor roared to life— seeming angry at A.J. as well—and a warm breeze floated over my skin. A.J. dropped the throttle to bat-out-of-hell speed, and that gentle breeze turned downright wicked.

Olivia boat/duck-walked toward me. Wind whipped up the edges of her black hair, eyes like emerald daggers zeroed in on A.J. He looked over his shoulder and turned the wheel toward the left. Clean, fresh water sprayed him as we bounced over a swell. Tiny beads of water danced down his broad, tan shoulders, then trickled down the length of his spine. If A.J. wasn't so mouthwatering, it'd be really easy to stay pissed at him. Who was I kidding? My heart would always forgive him. He'd stood up to a god, an immortal king, and a legion of Shadows to keep me safe. That sacrifice deserved a little broken-date wiggle room, didn't it?

The hull skipped over the top of another swell and threw Olivia into the seat next to me.

"You're not gonna say a damn thing, are you?" my cousin pushed.

The warm wind thrashed my hair against my face as the red rocks of Las Vegas Bay sped by. "You of all people should know I'm in as much control of this relationship as you are of this boat."

Her green eyes softened. She knew about out-of-control relationships. The topic of her falling head-over-heels for a Shadow, A.J.'s big brother,

Isaac, had been skirted and evaded since Prom four months ago. The night Isaac tried to save her life.

"You can drop me off and then go back out." A.J.'s voice caught on the wind. My heart dropped. I didn't know what hurt more: the cold tone of his words or how easy it was becoming for A.J. to leave me.

Granted, I was now the heir apparent to the House of Hearts. The Shadows couldn't hurt me now that I was claimed. I was still getting used to the whole underworld of Cards being Royal families, The House of Midas running the gaming commissions around the world, and The Shadows masquerading around as soul-stealing loan sharks. The thought of the catacombs and the quarry of lost souls popped goosebumps on my arms. I rubbed at them, catching Olivia watching me.

"You've gotta let go of that night, Cassie," she cautioned. "You can't do anything for them; you're lucky you got Malory out."

I shook my head. Olivia was wrong. A.J. and I had kept my brilliant blue light show in the Quarry of Souls a secret. I'd freed Malory, my childhood best friend, from her obligation to The Shadows, and if I had a second chance, I knew I could free the whole damned quarry. For now, thousands of souls were left rotting in barely-living bodies lining the walls of Dionysus Quarry. Something turned in my gut knowing I'd left them there.

Water sprayed us as we took a swell too hard. A.J. looked back to make sure I was still in the boat. I knew he cared about me and I was probably being a whiny, clingy girlfriend. Things were tense for him at home. Being the only heir to take over the gaming commission and swearing your life to protect the girl you can never have a future with does that to a guy.

Seven weeks ago, A.J. put a big bullseye on his back when he went against his family and used his power to save my life. I guess that should earn a guy a broken promise freebie. But that's all this summer had been: one broken promise after another. Tomorrow, we move into the University of Las Vegas dorms and . . . and I would be a freshman in college. My heart stammered in my chest. I knew what came next.

Ah, there it was, the familiar pain of loss seeping into my throat that made me either want to curl up and disappear or strap on some kick-ass and raze the Shadows. I may have cost Midas a bet seven weeks ago, but eight months ago, he and Dionysus's bet cost me the two people I loved more than life itself. They cost me the lives of my adoptive parents. And I hadn't forgotten about my promise to make both mythological asshats pay.

"Cassie?" Olivia nudged my leg with her cocoa-brown one. "You want to go back out or you wanna go to your house?"

"Definitely not my house." I snipped. That was another thing I was getting used to. My home, for now, was the penthouse apartment at The Eclectic Hotel. Carina, my biological mother and The Queen of Hearts, owned the entire hotel. And as of two hours ago, my half-sister Cara called it home as well.

"Cass?" Olivia pressed.

"I don't want to ride home with him." I nodded at A.J.

"Lucky?" Olivia hollered to the other boy in the boat. "Can you take us in later?"

Lucky's copper curls bounced his approval. Lucky was from the House of Clubs. He didn't speak much, but that's what made him so charming. When he did speak, you wanted to stop and listen because you knew brilliance would just pour out of his mouth.

A.J. dropped the engine from ear shattering to a low rumble, and a few minutes later, we bumped up against one of the docks in the marina. He slipped a white cotton t-shirt over his chiseled body, grabbed his keys from his backpack before hooking it over his shoulder, and walked to the bow of the boat, not even sparing me a second glance. Either for self-preservation or because he was as pissed at me as I was at him.

Irritation mixed with disappointment as my jaw locked down. Normally, I'd just fold and let him drop me off at home. But I didn't want to go home. I pushed down the warm tingle shooting up my spine, the physical reminder I was tapping into the Balanter's power of persuasion. I needed him to choose me all on my own. No House of Heart/House of Spade special juju mix. A.J. hopped onto the dock, raised his sunglasses, and held onto the bow a few seconds before his gaze met mine. It was there, the way he worked his jaw, the way my body leaned toward him, encouraging him; it really could be this simple. He didn't have to be torn between duty and me. He could have me. I was here, waiting for him to just choose me.

"I'll call you when I'm done tonight," he answered my subliminal plea.

And that was it, seven words that scored another little fissure deep in my heart. I sank back into the boat cushions.

"Don't bother," I said. My heart crawled up in my throat, chasing after the words. By the way A.J.'s brilliant blue eyes dulled, it was too late, they'd hit their mark.

The boat floated away from the dock. Olivia took the wheel and navigated us back toward open water while I watched A.J. climb up the ramp to the parking lot. Not once looking back for me. Not once seeming to care that I was on the verge of shattering.

"Cass, you sure that's the way you want to play this game?" Olivia asked.

"He's not leaving me any choice."

"There's always a choice."

Warm wind picked up as we floated to the no-wake buoy. I could feel my heart holding on to the dock, praying one of us would change our minds.

But I didn't.

And I knew he never would.

I rested my chin on my arms on top of the upholstered engine cover, and watched A.J. leave the parking lot.

Loving someone shouldn't be this hard.

TWO

"I'M HOME," I hollered, tossing my keys into the bowl on the entryway table.

"Nobody cares," a girl's voice chimed back.

"Cara?" Olivia shouted down the hall. "Girl, you best get your Spanish-speaking ass out here and fill me in on the hotties we have to look forward to corrupting us at this year's tournament."

Cara had spent the last six months in Malaga prepping for this year's Royal Poker Tournament. Every year, the Houses came together to *"settle their differences"* in a good old-fashioned five-card stud poker tournament, or whatever version of poker was chosen. This year, the House of Hearts was hosting in our ancestral home of Malaga. Before the otherworld knew I existed, Cara was the heir apparent for the House of Hearts and *"coming of age,"* meaning the poker tournament was her debutant ball. I came into the picture and stole her crown. I didn't like the girl all that much, but I wasn't about to steal my little sister's thunder and poker tournament as well. I also didn't have the first clue how to play poker. Mom had set me up on the Royal Poker Tournament site as a guest to learn, but I didn't see the point until there was a crown firmly latched to my head.

"You're talking to me now, Olivia?" Cara leaned up against the hallway.

We were mirror images of each other. Her hair was more auburn than my chocolate, but her eyes—the color, the shape—they were my eyes.

My mother's eyes.

The white short skirt Cara wore showed off her sun-tanned legs, and her black tank top amplified the other area where we were drastically different.

"Oh, girl." Olivia drawled out the last word like only she could. "You can pull that poor me attitude with Cassie and your mom, but don't even think of pulling that shit with me." Olivia walked into Cara's space, and you could see my sister's body rejoice. Nothing had changed between the two of them.

My body, not so much.

Olivia and I were cousins but with Cara gone, we'd become really good friends. Closer than Malory and I have ever been, not that I'd ever tell Malory. Mal and I had *outcast* and *abandoned* in common, but Olivia and I, we had something more. Olivia risked everything for me—her life. And there were only five other people in this world who had done that for me. Malory wasn't on the list.

"Now kiss and love your sister." Olivia threw her arms around Cara's neck and mine, pulling us in for a group hug.

"Who are you talking to?" Cara and I said at the same time.

"Both of you. You're sisters and that means more than any crown."

"Actually, it did mean my crown," Cara sneered. Her eyes shredded me in the two seconds it took her to pull out of the three-musketeer embrace and walk back to her room.

The door slammed, echoing down the hall and met Mom's, "Stop slamming doors!" holler just about where we stood.

"She'll come around." Olivia squeezed my hand. "And if she doesn't, you can utter those famous words."

My stare never left Cara's door. "What words are those?"

"Off with her head!" Olivia cackled. She turned and walked toward the kitchen.

"You were born to the wrong House." I scoffed. My heart said I should go knock on Cara's door, but my stomach was in control. And Mom was cooking. Plus, I still handled confrontation like a spineless chicken.

"Where's Malory?" Olivia asked, checking her reflection in the entryway mirror.

"Working."

"Can we go watch yet?"

"No." I shot Olivia a look. "And you're not supposed to know."

A few weeks back, Olivia had spun that black bangle on her wrist, tapped into her House of Spades power of influence, and *made* me tell her about Malory's undercover job. Mal's mom, who was gone on business trips more than she was home, landed Malory a job as a magician's assistant's understudy. Most of the time, that meant she stayed behind the scenes, assisting the assistant, but on the rare days, usually summer when there were matinées, Mal was center stage.

I sneaked in twice.

Confronted Mal once.

And was sworn to secrecy for all eternity.

We rounded the corner into the kitchen, taking in every delicious scent of homemade marinara sauce simmering from the stove.

"How was the lake?" Mom asked.

I pulled out the stool and sat down, reliving the massive ditch A.J. pulled.

"Taste this," Mom pushed a wooden spoon full of marinara sauce at my face. I grabbed the wooden handle and brought it closer to my nose.

Sniffed.

Smiled.

And tasted.

The sweet flavor of Roma tomatoes danced across my taste buds; next came the marrying of spices with the sauce.

It was just right.

A hint of merlot and then . . . there it was.

The secret ingredient: brown sugar.

"I think you nailed it," I said after licking the spoon clean. "Oh yeah, you totally nailed it." I met my mother's satisfied gaze.

"It's as good as Sassy's?" she asked. And despite all the time that had passed, the nickname of my adoptive mother being said in the universe killed me, made me want to crumple up and sob.

"You did her proud," I said. The legs of my stool scraped against the white marble floors as I pushed back and went to grab the loaf of Italian bread. Sassy was the nickname of my adoptive mother, Sara Vera. Sara and my mom were best friends from high school. Together, they hid me from Midas, Dionysus, The Royals, and the rest of the gods. My existence not only tipped the balance of power when it came to The Royals (The House of Spades, Diamonds, and Clubs) because I was born from the union of two houses, but if The Shadows got ahold of me and could turn me, I could free the Titans and then all hell would literally break lose.

Mom wrapped her arms around me, pulling me into her before she said, "It's okay to miss her, Cassie."

I swallowed over the lump in my throat. "I know."

"Cass, you have to grieve. You can't keep stuffing this down—"

"I know. I won't." I turned my head and caught the motherly look of concern wash across her face. "I'm working through it." I hushed. Mom had been pushing me to see one of her friends, a psychiatrist, to talk about losing my adoptive parents, talk about my new role in *this* life, talk about being on a couple gods' and an immortal's hit list. I didn't have a thing against a psychiatrist (growing up in Hollywood with celebrity parents, I was used to seeing a "feelings tutor") but here, everything was different and I didn't know who to trust.

After dinner and dishes, I headed back out to the balcony. Warm desert heat mixed with a soft breeze, ruffling the edge of my skirt against my thighs. The night-lights of Las Vegas were blazing bright by the time Olivia left. I still hadn't heard from A.J. and probably wouldn't until tomorrow afternoon when we moved into the dorms at the University of Las Vegas. A few days ago, everything felt so certain. Felt like the pieces were finally creating a picture that was going to be drama free and (dare I dream?) happy.

I pulled the chair over to the edge of the balcony, sat, and leaned my head up against the Plexiglas barrier that protected us from falling. Well, too late, I'd already fallen; just how devastating the crash would be was all that remained. Mom's fragrant scent of Chanel No. 5 caught on another breeze.

"Anything I can help with?" Mom asked.

"Boy problems."

Forty stories up with an unobstructed view of the pools below and all the world around, and nothing seemed clear. I kept my focus on the green and blue club lights pulsing. Mom and I had made huge strides since January. Carina seemed to always know when to talk, when to push, and when to just shut up.

She was my mom, and that word had been a hard one for me to swallow.

Carina pulled over the other chair, sat, and snuggled into the back of her chair. She swirled the white wine around her glass and then pulled a sip through her lips. She was good at sitting still. Letting me figure out if and what I wanted to share. We'd come such a long way, but still . . . there was so far we still had to go. At least we were working on us.

"Can I talk with you about the Jacks?" she asked.

"They're Zeus's way of making sure our lines don't die out. In our house, a Jack would be a descendent from the two of Hearts. They're our protectors. They do the bidding of each suite's King." I raddled off the definition I'd learned from Ms. Maddox flawlessly.

Carina nodded, taking another sip of wine. "But we don't have a king."

"Right."

Mom put her glass on the table, leaned forward in the most un-queenly way, and rested her chin on her knuckles. "Ask the question, Cassandra. I need you to start analyzing every angle of a problem, even if it doesn't look like a problem. Every statement someone utters to you has an agenda."

"Hello, pessimism. Your table for two is ready."

But the royal façade that had slipped over Mom's face didn't budge. She was dead serious. I shook my head, looking at every way her sentence could have an angle. I may have had a crap start in life, but I'd always had a spine fortified in optimism. I didn't think I could look at every question with such skepticism. It didn't fall into my DNA. The skin between Mom's eyes crinkled, proving me wrong.

A few more moments of quiet passed. "I don't see a problem. Right of succession means the rule passes to me."

"Does it?" Mom pushed.

"Yes, why wouldn't it?"

"Sassy had the best saying, I know it wasn't hers, but what she taught me about the rule I wanted to execute from my time on the throne stemmed from: 'Never assume; it makes an ass out of you and me.' Ask the question, Cassie."

The bass from below changed and the crowd screamed, but up here, there was only silence. Mom's eyes squinted tighter, willing me to see something I couldn't. The weight of both my mothers' expectations for me to ask questions . . . then it clicked.

"If the Jacks serve at the Kings' bidding, and the House of Hearts has no king, who does the Jack of Hearts serve?"

A brilliant smile, one she rarely used, shattered the royal tight-lipped façade on my mother's face. "There's my girl."

"So? Who does the Jack of Hearts serve?"

As quickly as it had come, Mom's dazzling smile disappeared.

"That bad?" I asked. I pulled my knees up to my chest, hoping to deflect the only answer that could make Mom pull a smile-to-frown 180 on me. "No, Mom. Really? Midas controls the Jack of Hearts?" I was wrong. My knobby knees did nothing to repel the nastiness. "That's why he was so surprised you and Sara had hidden me as well as you had. He had a high-ranking spy. Cara's dad."

"One of the tradeoffs when Midas agreed to fold our King's line was that he chooses our Jacks, but Cara's dad wasn't a spy. He actually helped me, protected me. It was how he handled your birth that made me fall in love with him." Her voice trailed off in that way that lets you know a girl's gone back to a time when she believed in love, believed there was one person who could be that happily ever after.

"So what happened?"

She closed her honey eyes, but not before I saw the fresh pain well up in them. She really did love him. I never thought it was possible to love two people with every ounce of your heart. I was having a hard enough time loving one person.

"That's for another day." Mom cleared her throat, and I thought for sure the conversation about her love life was closed. "Being the Queen of Hearts is about love and sacrifice. Sometimes it's about sacrificing for those you love."

My heart dropped. I was too chicken to ask what that meant, even though I knew Cara's dad had made the ultimate sacrifice. I guess I always assumed it was for Mom. Actually, I prayed it had nothing to do with me. How could Cara and I ever have a relationship if I was the reason for her father's death?

Old memories and heartache crowded the balcony, making it hard to sit still with Mom. With every wring of her hands, I could tell she was reliving another decision, another regret. The woman had everything and nothing at the same time.

Silence became uncomfortable, like sweat trickling down your cleavage on a hot day.

"A.J. keeps breaking dates, and before you tell me this is a busy time for him, I know. It shouldn't excuse the behavior though," I quickly blurted out. I couldn't handle watching the woman I'd grown to love struggle with years of what-ifs churning in her lap.

Carina's gaze found mine, relief chasing the memories back to the haunted recesses of her mind. "I agree."

I settled into my chair. Even heartbroken, the woman still knew how to throw me for a loop.

"It is a crazy time for A.J., but then again, you've had a crazy year and seemed to have handled it with grace."

I snorted.

"You have, Cassandra." Carina brought the glass to her lips, took another sip of wine, and leveled me with a look before she spoke again. "Life will never be perfect, there will never be a good time, and the sooner you learn to celebrate the stolen moments, the better it'll be for your relationship." Carina put her glass down and sat still. I'd hated her for the stillness when I first moved in. Now I was in awe of the woman's ability to compartmentalize her feelings, push them aside, ask them to take a number in hell, and wait.

"Why do I feel like there's a 'but' in that sentence?"

"No buts. Demand your place in this world and his life. If you don't, then you'll always be the first to be dismissed and the last to be pleased. Those little moments, those little gestures you're holding onto to swing you from disappointment to disappointment will become too little, too late." Carina stood, her fingers dancing across my shoulders before she stopped at the door.

"Cass, also remember to give the guy a break, but only if he deserves it. Once that ache in your heart solidifies"—her eyes went distant and filled with pain—"once it's permanent, there's nothing short of a miracle to break through a hardened heart . . . it might as well be dead."

She slipped into the house, and I turned my focus back to the Las Vegas skyline. The fireworks at the Bellagio went off, showering the sky with gold glittering stars. The water show filled the moments when the sky went dark. Dancing water fountains ripped across the lake, making my heart ache for a time when I was A.J.'s main concern. When he would stand up to his grandfather and defiantly choose me over his house. When his heart didn't seem to be hardening before my eyes. Somewhere deep in me, I knew I wouldn't be his miracle.

The water show ended.

The fireworks died.

And the night air this high up turned cold. I pushed back the chair, and the wine glass Carina left behind on the glass table wobbled. Snagging the glass before it shattered, I found a clear key card under the base of the glass. A heart etched into the front along with the words: Las Vegas. My mind tripped back to the black keycard A.J. had that accessed the hidden passages of the Eclectic Hotel. I tapped the edge of it against my lips and realized I was a lot more like my mom than I'd ever have admitted.

By the time I walked back inside and rinsed out the wine glass, Operation Make Up had already formed. It'd been months since A.J. used his magic key card to visit me. Midas was keeping him busy, but that excuse was wearing thin. I tapped the card against my lips again as I wandered down the hall. And now I had a magic card of my own.

THREE

I PADDED DOWN the rich hallway, toes sinking into the thick runner Mom laid down for me. When I'd asked her why, she'd started by saying the oils from my bare feet were ruining the wood, but then her eyes softened and the façade came crashing down. She'd wrapped me up in her arms, kissed the crown of my head, and said, "Your feet look cold in the morning and you refuse to wear slippers." It was literally the first step in our relationship and one that I'd never forget.

Cara's muted voice mixed with the warm yellow light bleeding out from under her door. Maybe one day the wall she'd built because of me would come tumbling down, too. I wouldn't hold my breath. Being a hidden daughter was one thing. Stealing a girl's crown and birthright was another.

I paused, my hand resting on the ornate doorknob to my room, and listened to the sounds of my home. They weren't the same as the ones I'd had in Malibu with my adoptive parents, but they were becoming just as precious to me. I stole a glance at my birth mom's double doors and the light that illuminated the frame. There was so much about the woman I didn't know. So much she wasn't willing to share. I'd asked her about my father, my birth father. The soft lines of her face had hardened, lips pursed, and her eyes had seemed to stare right through me, focusing on a person in the past.

"Ask me anything but that," had been her answer.

Problem was, ever since the night in the catacombs when Dionysus tempted me with the prospect of who my birth father was, it was the only thing I could focus on. Well, that and a certain boy who'd risked his life to save mine. I gripped the keycard and turned the doorknob.

My room was not like I'd left it an hour ago. Pretty sure I'd picked up all the shirtless men lounging on my bedroom floor. I quickly stepped in and shut the door. The ornate reds and golds of my four-poster bed shimmered under the soft glow of candlelight. The oceanic room shrank down to a picnic blanket sitting on the beach sand-colored carpet, with a box of pizza, a bowl of hot tamale candies, and A.J. and his shirtless body on the floor of my bedroom. Heat flooded every fiber of my being at the grin tipping his lips. A.J.'s eyes swept over me, my body coming to life under his gaze.

"I wanted to say sorry," A.J.'s voice was low, not because he was afraid of my mom hearing, but for all the naughty reasons that made my insides flip.

I leaned up against the closed door, not ready to let him off with a simple sorry and drop-dead sexy grin. Okay, and food. I scanned the carpet picnic, my gaze landing on the pizza box from Fremont Street.

"Is that sausage pizza?"

A.J. flicked a look at the box, then met my eyes. "It is."

"Too bad my stilettos are being re-heeled."

A.J. rose up on his knees, hand extended, and even if I wanted to resist, my body wouldn't let me. I crossed the room on uncertain legs. This was new for us. We never broke the rules. We always stayed in well-lit rooms and had simple kisses.

In one night, all of that changed?

What changed?

The rebellious girl in me drop-kicked the pessimist that Mom had unleashed. My heart gagged and bound my cynical side, locking her up deep inside where she was certain not to escape . . . at least for tonight.

"Pretty sure I told you it was the sausage pizza and the U.L.V hoodie that made me fall head-over-heels for you the first time." A sly smile spread across his face. "And look what you *do* have in your closet." He held up my grey hoodie from the first time we'd met and nothing else.

I bit down on my lip, trying to maintain the coy vixen front, but I was gone. I was his. And by the way his eyes lit up when they met mine, he knew it. I giggled as tension coiled inside me, the kind of tension you wanted to hold on to for as long as possible. The kind of tension that made your heart trip over itself, made your head swim with all the possibilities of what was going to happen, and made the core of what made you a girl want to become a woman.

"I already ate."

"I know. Your mom texted me she was cooking spaghetti and invited me."

"She did?" My heart fluttered.

A.J. nodded. One hand wrapped around my wrist, tugging me down to the blanket, while the other swept my feet out from under me. I landed with a small huff on the blanket and a sea of pillows. In two seconds, I was on my back with A.J. hovering over me.

That was our story: fast and unpredictable.

My breath caught in my lungs as his knuckles grazed my cheek, slipped down my neck, and caressed the side of my breast.

"You agreed loving me was easy, but I saw you take it all back the minute I jumped onto the dock. Let me tell you what loving you is like." A.J. kissed the worried crease between my forehead. "Loving you is like breathing, so natural, so easy, I overlook how vital you are to my existence. I forget. Until I'm drowning with duty and expectations, and all I crave is a breath of fresh air . . . a breath of you." His lips replaced his words next to my ear. Hot breath matched only by the cool flick of his tongue against my earlobe.

My body jerked and rejoiced all at the same time.

"I love you, Cassandra." A.J. pulled back. The edges of his hair fell forward, shielding us from the world outside. I knew he'd let his hair grow out during the summer, but even when we were on the lake, he always kept his hair under such tight reign, it wasn't until he let them loose that I'd realized how wild the black locks had become.

How wild he'd become.

A.J.'s eyes danced across my face, lips not far behind. Months of wondering if we were losing the spark between us exploded and disappeared under every warm, seductive nibble. His lips made their way along my jaw line. With each pass, he erased every doubt I'd had about whether we were a fluke, whether we'd burned too hot, too fast. Any other cliché a girl thinks about a boy who has her heart, he incinerated with his kisses.

I'd been so afraid that he regretted the declaration he'd made to the universes to protect me. Hot breath skimmed along my neck, scattering my thoughts like coins on the pavement. A.J. kissed the hollow of my neck, saying my name like it was the air he'd been talking about.

"Freshman year is going to be hard, but if we can make it past this . . ." He paused, pulling my bottom lip between his and then deepening the kiss when my mouth opened. His tongue swept inside, catching my every moan. Deeper and deeper, he intensified the kiss until I wasn't sure where he stopped and I started. *This* was loving someone. *This* was how we were supposed to be. A.J. pulled back, the tip of his nose butterfly kissing mine while his eyes seduced me silly.

"Cassie, if we can get through all of this year's bullshit, then there won't be anything or anyone who can separate us. You have to trust in us, trust that I will always love you, despite what your eyes see. Listen to your heart." A.J.'s jaw ticked, like there was more he wanted to say, more he wanted to warn me about, but couldn't.

And that, too, was our story: riddles and half-truths that we couldn't share because he was the heir to the House of Midas and I was the heir to the House of Hearts.

"We're never going to be free, are we?" I asked.

A.J. trailed a finger down the side of my cheek, cupping my face like I was the most cherished thing he possessed. "Do you trust me?"

I nodded into the palm of his hand. He smiled, then kissed my cheek. Wet lips singed a path of delightful grazes and nips along the soft skin of my neck.

"And I trust you." The soft tenor of his voice reverberated against my neck. His pleasurable assault picked up along the base of my throat. Warm breath skimmed upward, until A.J.'s eyes were level with mine.

"This year isn't going to be easy, but as long as we trust each other . . ." His lips brushed my cheek. "We have to believe in *our* future." He kissed the other side. "If we do that, then there's nobody, *nothing*, who can come between us."

"Our future?" I asked while white picket fences and blue-eyed little boys ran through my head. It was silly, I know. But when your wildest dream speaks to the hopeless romantic in you, well, a girl can't help but trip and fall into a happily ever after haze.

A.J. nodded as he straddled me. My hands slid down his chest, admiring every chiseled ripple of muscle to his waist. He caged me in with his arms while his blue eyes glinted like the sun dancing on the ocean, admiring me with an appreciation that set my very core burning. Despite the moment, my heart tripped over the memory of my home in Malibu. Like always, A.J. was there to bring me back. His thumb traced my eyebrow. "I trust you, Cassandra. If you trust me, we'll have a future. A future where I'm free to take you home to California. A future where we're free to live our lives the way we see fit."

Tears welled up in my eyes. I knew he believed what he was saying, but I knew what Yayati, the mystical matchmaker, had shown me. I knew this— us—ended with him in a pool of blood and me helpless to do anything to stop it unless I broke his heart.

My hand wrapped around the back of his neck, and before A.J. could ask, I pulled his lips to mine, locking away all the painful visions of the future. His lips brushed against mine. Once, twice, and finally his tongue swept along the seam of my lips. The painful memory of my life in California, my life without A.J., slid back to its proper place in the back of my mind. A.J.'s hands delved into my hair as he slanted his mouth and tugged at my bottom lip. I gripped the denim material of his jeans, pulling him closer to me. I didn't want to think about anything. I didn't want to think about school starting, or him living off campus, or us being tested by him serving two Houses.

I wanted this.

I wrapped my leg around his waist, pulling him in closer to me. Daring him to take us further than we'd ever been. Taunting him with a freedom he could revel in. All he had to do was choose me. Make me his number one priority.

His hips pressed into mine, taking up a slow, sensual rhythm as his hands explored me in ways I'd only dreamed about. Only read about in Rebecca Yarros's novels. My breath stuttered in my chest.

"A.J.," I whispered, hoping he'd hear my need and would finally take our PG pet fest to the next level.

"You will always be my first priority," he whispered like he'd read my mind. Before I could answer, his mouth curved with a tenderness I'd ached for since summer started. His hands skimmed along my top before slipping under my shirt. His hot palms slid along my skin, melting me. His hand skated under the small of my back, pushing my breasts up to the forefront. A.J. ran a finger over my collarbone and down the center of my chest, like he was mapping out all the ways he would touch me when he finally had me naked. I gasped, delight bubbling up from deep within me, from depths I'd never even known existed. When I thought we'd combust from the pent-up heat between us, a guttural growl tore loose from the back of A.J.'s throat as he slipped his hand into my bra, cupped my breast, and freed me from the fabric prison.

Yes! My heart tripled its beat.

A.J.'s hands on me felt like home. Every ounce of tension between us slipped away as his lips followed the path the pad of his finger had just created. My head swam drunk with delight. My hips rolled into him, encouraging him to take the next step. Chase all the insecurities away. But his eyes latched on to mine, and I could see the moment he stopped worshiping me as my boyfriend and slipped back into the role of my protector.

He leaned down, his forehead pressed to mine, "We have to stop," he whispered on ragged breath.

I rolled my hips again, relishing in the fact that everything that made him a man disagreed with his statement. "Your body seems to be conflicted with your mind." I reached between us and cupped him. He jerked, a guttural moan ripping loose from deep inside.

"Cassie," he hissed. "We can't." His fingers wrapped around my wrist, pulling me away from him until he was across the blanket and propped up against the footboard of my bed, chest heaving liked he'd run a marathon trying to get away.

The ache of rejection built in my chest. We'd been together eight months, and this was the furthest we'd ever gone and . . . and he had stopped.

What guy stopped?

I wrapped my arms around my chest, hoping to hold myself together so he didn't watch me shatter a little more in front of him.

"Cass," A.J. nudged my toe with his. "You know we can't."

I bit down on my lip, willing the tears burning the back of my throat to subside. "I know. You don't want to."

"That's not true."

"It's fine." I stood and walked over to the light switch. The harsh light flooded the room, and what once looked like a special interlude lost its luster.

A.J. hung his head, dragging his fingers through his hair. "I wanted to say I'm sorry. I wanted you to know how special you are to me." He leaned forward and blew out the candles. "I didn't mean to hurt you."

"You say you love me, that I'm the air you need but you won't . . . you can't . . . Is standing up for me . . ." The words tripped over the lump in my throat. "You should go."

"I want to, Cassie. I want to be all those things you think I should be. All the things I already am, but can't show you. I just—"

A.J.'s phone vibrated on the table next to me, cutting him off. I snagged it, reading the sender's name.

"Somebody named Zee is looking for you." I tossed the phone at him and left the room. Mom was right; we were wasting our stolen moments. And they weren't going to be enough to sustain us.

FOUR

THE BLAZING DESERT sun beat down on me as we hauled box after box into the penthouse dorm. Heat and rage were the only things I seemed to feel after last night. If I wasn't careful, the fervor I felt with A.J. would do more than burn me; I'd evaporate what little left of me there was. I stepped into the air-conditioned lobby as a warm breeze rustled through the trees outside. The whisper of leaves reminded me that at some point in time, Las Vegas was an oasis. An oasis where a god finished unleashing the Shadows from Tartarus. An oasis that cursed four families and all their offspring to a life of servitude. A life of rules that didn't apply to mortals and a view of riches only gods could attain. An unreal itch to get near water welled up in me as I rode the elevator up; it wasn't an itch to go to the oasis, it was a cellular need to have my feet in an ocean and California wind in my hair.

I stepped out of the elevator into the musty scent of filtered dorm air. Mom waited impatiently in the doorway of my new living quarters, squelching my jonesing for a hit of brine. I picked up my pace, quickly taking in the surroundings. To the right and four doors down, I kicked the itch and the front door open. Olivia and I were the first ones here. I dropped my last box in the living room and waited for the rest of the Queens to arrive before

I picked out a room. I always thought the first roommates who staked a claim to the best room in reality shows were douches.

Carina shut the door and rolled the last suitcase next to me. She chuckled, then walked over to the slider door to the balcony.

"God, it's like a time capsule." She ran a hand through her hair before twisting it into a knot at the base of her skull. That was Mom's tell, she was nervous as all hell and not the normal drop-my-kids-off-at-college nervous. This was something else. She'd taken the day off work, put on a denim skirt and sneakers. Cara and I had about dropped our Cinnabons when she walked into the kitchen this morning and asked us what time we were moving in.

Mom slowly turned in a circle, her eyes scrutinizing every nook and cranny of the dorm room. The front door led into the commons area. A galley kitchen with a granite countertop and four bar stools connected to the living room. Two couches and a chair that looked like torture to sit in stood on industrial grade carpet and faced a fireplace. To the left was a decent-sized balcony that faced east. It looked like an awesome place to have my morning hit of caffeine. Off the common area were two rooms. They were exactly the same: two beds, two desks, and two closets that would only hold a bathing suit maybe.

"You know how the dorm is set up?" Carina asked. "The top floor is royalty and their spares? Cara's just down the hall, along with the common showers. We lobbied for them to add showers to the suite but only got a toilet and a sink." The words flew from her mouth like a royal Uzi gun. "Across the hall are the Kings." She walked to the kitchen and pulled open the fridge. "Good, they've stocked you." Mom grabbed a bottle of water and downed half of it. Part of me wondered if she was hoping it was vodka. "The Kings won't be on campus until your Junior year."

"Really?"

She nodded, polished off the water, and tossed the bottle into the trash. "My room was that one." She pointed to the door closest to the balcony. "Tradition dictates you room with the Heir to the Diamonds." A mischievous grin pulled at Mom's glossed lips. "It was one of the first things we changed. The House of Clubs and I loved getting up early. That room gets beautiful morning light, and in the evening, you can open the window and a wonderful breeze will perfume the air with night blooming jasmine." Mom's eyes went all distant, then watered up; her fingers gripped the edges of the granite countertop like the cool stone was the only link to reality here.

I walked over to her and touched her shoulder, "Mom?" Her head jerked like my voice startled her. "You okay? Something you want to share?"

She turned and ran her hands from the top of my head to my chin, then cupped my cheeks, the movement so familiar, but she'd never touched me like that before. I shook off the déjà vu and wrapped my arms around her waist. I'd never realized how thin and fragile she really was. Mom's defiant chin jut or ice-cold stare always exuded such power, such control. But here, in my arms, in this moment, you could feel all that fear and vulnerability about the future radiating off her.

And that freaked me the frizz out.

I'd already made so many mistakes, cost her so much. My heart stopped as a giggle floated in on a breeze. The melodic tone so reminiscent of my adopted mom, Sara . . . Sassy.

"Look who I found downstairs!" Olivia's voice caught the moment she saw me and my mom.

"Everything okay?" The Queen of Spades, Olivia's mom, asked. Her green eyes darted back and forth between my mom and me.

The thin veil of strength slipped back over my mother as she squeezed me one last time before stepping away.

"I was showing Cassie our old rooms." Mom pointed to the door next to the fireplace. "Memories must have pulled me back to when we were here. What are you doing here, Genevieve? I thought you were overseas."

"I couldn't very well miss a reunion." The Queen of Spades stepped out of the doorway. Olivia was the spitting image of her mother. Classy and refined, The Queen of Spades floated across the mediocre carpet, and I swear the fibers perked up under her toes. Her black hair was folded into an intricate braid that wrapped around her head like a crown. And the eyes—her emerald eyes were just as hard as Olivia's but warmed around the edges. Olivia hadn't perfected that look yet.

"Cassandra, let me introduce you to Her Royal Highness, The Queen of Spades—"

"Carina, are we doing formalities?"

Mom chuckled, shattering the royal and formal feel strangling the room,

"Very well then, Cassie, meet my darling friend, Genevieve."

"Pleasure," I squawked and curtsied like a dork. Yeah, I was going to have to work on this whole Queen in Training thing.

The Queen of Spades, Genevieve, seemed to glide across the room before pulling Mom into her.

"God, I've missed you," Carina whispered. If I hadn't been standing so close, I would have never heard Mom's admittance that not all things were as calm as she portrayed. "How long are you here?"

"Until the girls get settled, acquire what they need from us."

"What do we need?" I asked.

"Ladies," a sultry voice from my past came from the door.

"Mrs. M.!" I squealed, launching across the room. I hadn't seen my adoptive mother's best friend for almost a year. Mrs. M. caught me mid-flight, pulling me into her. All those memories of Malibu, home, my dead parents, came roaring back. The scent of sea-salt and suntan lotion still clung to her skin. I pulled back, wondering what else had stayed the same, what had changed? Her golden blonde hair was pulled up in a ponytail. Blue eyes shimmered with raw emotions.

"You look good, Cassie," The Queen of Clubs said.

"Thank you." I fought back another urge to curtsy, but the need to apologize was overwhelming. "I'm sorry," I whispered.

"She loved you more than life itself. All three of them did." Mrs. M. cupped my face and forced me to look at her.

"We all do," The Queen of Spades said. I'm certain the look that flashed across Olivia's faced mirrored mine.

"You knew, too?" Olivia looked at her mom like she was changing, morphing right before her eyes.

"We all did," a thick Indian accent said from behind me.

"Mafa," The Queen of Spades cooed. "I was hoping you would be able to make the trip."

"Miss seeing the four future Queens' first meeting?" She coughed. "Nothing could keep me away. Helen's downstairs. She's learning how to navigate life deprived of servants." Her shoulders bounced once in what I think was a chuckle, but no sound came out. Not even a peep.

"I see why my mother found this so amusing," she finished, easing herself into the uncomfortable chair. "She and Gia could use some help." Her silver eyes darted between Olivia and myself, and just like that, we were dismissed.

Mom guided us to the door and then shut it in our faces. It was graceful and elegant, but definitely a royal dismissal. I'd have to work on that move, too. We may have been the future queens, but the current queens were most certainly still in command.

"Now that's not something that happens every day." Olivia appreciated the suave move. We stood in the hall on the wrong side of our door. You had to hand it to the four Queens; they had a way of making sure you knew your place.

I turned, more accustomed to being ordered around than Olivia. Our room—that of the future queens—was at the end of the hall. Across the hall were the future kings. Their door was still shut. I leaned up against it, ear pushed tight against the corrugated wood.

"Do you have your breaking and entering kit on you?" I half-heartedly teased, hoping to get Olivia's mind off our diss.

"I'm not in the mood," she huffed, walking down the hall. There were two more sets of doors before we entered the common living area.

"Do you know who these belong to?" I trailed a finger along the "J" placard on the door.

"I think the Jacks."

"Ah, yes. The Jacks. Why weren't they on the final?" I half-heartedly teased. Olivia had helped me study for my pass-or-die final in high school. Few thought I'd make it past Committee Finals, and nobody thought I'd make it to my freshman year as an heir apparent.

We ambled through the common area, which consisted of an L-shaped couch, a flat screen T.V., and a black lacquered console and a hallway that led to the other end of the building. Neither of us were in a hurry to get downstairs and help Gia or Helen.

The elevator hummed to life as I pushed the button down.

"The Kings' first order of business is to protect the Queen. The Jacks are glued to the Queens' side for the four years she's at U.L.V. and usually end up marrying the Queen." Olivia leaned up against the wall.

"That's slightly incestuous isn't it?"

"Ew, no, they're not related. Yayati usually picks them from an old two card's line. Crazy distant relatives, but aren't we all?"

Yayati. That was a name I hadn't heard of in a long time. The Indian Yoda who lived behind the fountain in the Rainforest Café. Midas's key to seeing the future and the man who told me I wasn't suited for this world, along with a handful of disturbing images. A shiver rocked my body at the vision of A.J. lying in a pool of blood.

"You okay, Cass?"

The elevator doors opened, interrupting my chance to answer and stopping my heart.

"Bastian?" I whispered.

The boy looked up. Gold locks peeked out from under his well-used cowboy hat and curled at the edge of his collar. He was over six feet tall and filled with muscles and well, "boy" wasn't the right word, he was all man— *new* man. A worn plaid shirt stretched across his chest and tucked into his jeans. The long sleeves, rolled up to his elbows, revealed tan skin and tiny arm hairs that glinted like individual strands of gold spun silk. A crooked smile pulled at his plump lips, drop-kicking my heart into my throat.

"Close, I'm Beaux. Sebastian's twin brother." The words rolled off his tongue with the most delicious Australian accent. He stuck a foot in elevator door's closing path.

"I didn't know he had a twin," I questioned.

"I didn't know he had any mates in the States, so we're even there, I guess."

A girlish giggle-snort ripped from me.

Olivia's brow furrowed as she shot me a sideways glance. "I'm Olivia and this is Cassie."

"Right, Queen of Spades and Hearts."

The elevator bounced off his foot again, but I didn't care. I could stand here all day and listen to him recite the appendix of a biology book, I was so mesmerized by his voice . . . and green eyes.

"You Sheilas going down or just greeting all the Royals at the elevator?"

I giggled.

Olivia started at my response before answering. "No, we're headed down. More Queens to gather."

"Right, the two Sheilas downstairs. One's doing her best to haul a lifetime of luggage up the stairs, and the other is demanding everyone pick up a bag." He nodded to a Louis Vuitton carryon sitting in the corner of the elevator.

"Helen, I think was her name."

Olivia grabbed me by the arm and pushed me into the elevator. I brushed past Beaux's chest, his scent of soap and man flirted with all my girly parts, and I giggled again.

"Thanks for holding the elevator," Olivia said.

"I'm off to find my pull-out bed." Beaux turned, giving us a view of his back side as we started down the hall.

"Why's that?" I asked, but I didn't get an answer, just a pair of steel doors and a judgmental look from Olivia. "Don't start," I cautioned, feeling another complication slide into the puzzle of A.J., me, and how we fit together.

FIVE

WE FOUND GIA, sour and sweaty, as the doors slid open.

"I thought my mother loved me?" she said, blowing a damp lock of blond hair from her face. "And my relatives . . ."

"We just met your cousin, Beaux," Olivia snarked. "Well, I met Beaux, Cassie just drooled and giggled all over him." Olivia hit the red stop button in the elevator, releasing a loud obnoxious bell. The sound earned us a few glares, but that didn't stop Olivia from doing that Queenly head tilt she'd all but perfected in high school.

"Did you see Helen out there?"

Gia rolled a Louis Vuitton suitcase, not hers, into the elevator. "Yeah, she's gonna be *real* fun to room with."

"Play nice," I said.

"Oh, nice of you to join us." Olivia snapped me a quick look. "You get over your fit of fangirl?"

"I can't help it," I giggled. "It was the accent. I'm a goner for the accent. No effect on you?" I stepped out and grabbed two of Gia's pink suitcases. "Gia, why didn't you tell me your cousin had a twin?"

"Just found out myself. Apparently you weren't the only one this generation of Royals was hiding."

"Why?" Olivia asked, dragging two more Louis Vuitton large suitcases into the elevator. "Shit, how much did Helen bring?"

"At least four more elevators' worth," Gia answered. "And I don't know. All I got from my mom was the 'this is your cousin' introduction and then a 'you're a grown-up, handle your luggage' toss off."

Olivia rolled her eyes. "Gia, you take this upstairs and unload the Louies into the commons. We'll go help Helen. And Gia, don't be afraid to use that new Queen pissed-off-heir attitude. It looks good on you."

"Ooh, see if Beaux'll help you," I giggled again. Even I was getting annoyed at my infatuated flirty self.

The doors slid shut.

"You're playing with fire, Cassie," Olivia said.

"I don't know what you're talking about." I started to the front doors of the lobby. She was right, but so was A.J.

"You're pissed at A.J.; don't go bringing others into your lover's spat."

My jaw fell open. "I . . . I don't know what you mean."

Olivia grabbed my shoulders and leveled her eyes with mine. "That boy loves you. He risked his life to save yours. You shouldn't even be looking."

"Olivia." I felt calm ooze into my voice. "I know you love me, but don't ever tell me what A.J. did for me. I have to live with his choice every night I close my eyes." I took a deep breath, pushing Yayati's vision of him lying in a pool of blood out of my head. "And from the way he's been treating me, I can only assume he's been reliving that choice, too." I stepped out of Olivia's grip and into the Las Vegas afternoon, not waiting to see if she followed.

I found Helen in a fort of Louis Vuitton luggage under the entrance awning. Black bangs were sweat-stuck to her forehead. Silver, almond-shaped eyes stared up at me.

"Will you help me?" she whimpered. Her Indian accent was muddled with a British cadence.

"I'm Cassie—"

Helen's arms wrapped around my neck before I could finish my sentence.

"I knew one of you would come and help me." She stepped back. Helen only came up to my chest, which made her barely five feet, but what she lacked in height, she made up in with hair and moxie. A breeze caught the hem of her sundress, and she reveled in the moment.

"You've gotta be baking out here."

"It's not so bad," Helen said, wrapping up her waist length hair into a bun. "Do you have a pen?"

I shook my head while she grabbed a boy with a clipboard. "Can I have this pen?" she asked, batting her eyes. A smile tipped the boy's lips as he let go of the pen. "Thank you." Helen wove the pen through her bun and then spun around like a little girl. The boy smiled and wandered off.

"Did you just ju-ju that poor boy into giving you his only pen."

"If by ju-ju, you mean utilizing my powers, no. My *ju-ju* only works if the pen was made of gold or some special gemstone. I leave the art of persuasion to the House of Spades . . . and you." Helen took a good long look of me before continuing. "That was the age-old art of female persuasion. I'll teach you before Thanksgiving Break."

I nodded to her fort of luggage. "Only works for writing apparatuses."

"It's a work in progress." She wiggled her fingers dismissively as she walked through the sliding doors into the lobby of the Dayton Residence.

"Where are you going?" I hollered after her.

"I'm going to get a trolley."

"This isn't a hotel." I muttered, grabbing two more bags. "It's a dorm."

A cold shiver slipped down my spine, one I hadn't felt since . . . I spun around and smack into Isaac.

"She's something, isn't she?" Isaac nodded to Helen waiting at the elevator door.

"What are you doing here?"

"Dorm move-in. We're across the quad." Isaac nodded to a small building. From a distance, it looked like normal move-in day. But the closer I looked, the easier it was to see all the students had the same dark hooded uniform, and if I was a betting girl, which I wasn't any more, I'd bet they all had that same give-up-on-life vacant look in their eyes.

"You go to school?" I finally asked.

"We're not completely uncivilized."

"No, you just live in a quarry of lost souls and prey on the desperate. Maslow would have been so proud of how you interpreted his hierarchy of needs."

"Cassie," Isaac's fingers wrapped around my wrist, and for the second time, I noticed they didn't have the frigid feel that most Shadows had. There were no pre-Shadow visions either. Chance and the last two Shadows I'd touched showed me glimpses of their former life. Isaac . . . nothing.

"I've got this. I suggest you head on over to your own dorm. Unless you fancy the Jacks kicking your ass."

"Ooh, somebody's been doing extra credit." He tweaked my nose with his free hand.

"Leave her be, Isaac." Olivia's cold voice made all the play leave Isaac's icy eyes.

"Livi," he said, but didn't turn around. Instead, the light in his eyes struggled to find footing, to find a way to spark something in him, only to be vanquished by the cold frost of disregard that ultimately banished all hope from him. Once he was in control, Isaac turned and faced Olivia.

She stood a step above him, bringing her to Isaac's height.

Eye-to-eye.

It was the subtleties of Olivia that most people missed, that I'd come to count on with my very life, which told me she was terrified. The way she pursed her lips, the way her eyelids tripled in blinks. But I was too curious to see what these two had to say to each other to interrupt. The only time I'd ever seen Olivia and Isaac interact was when Isaac had the tip of a knife threatening to damage more than the side of my prom dress.

"Cass," Olivia wrapped her fingers around my wrist, "leave the luggage. A.J. and Beaux are going to help Helen."

"Really?" I hated the desperate tone in my voice. Just a minute ago, I was telling Olivia that A.J. could go eff himself and now . . . I was pathetic.

"Now, Cass."

I let go of the handle and walked past Isaac. If I didn't know he was the lead Shadow who had tried to condemn my best friend, Malory, to the Quarry of Souls, I'd say he looked like a broken-hearted ex-boyfriend desperate to get his girl to love him again.

And that was wrong on so many different levels.

Nothing but tension and tight lips hung between us as we waited for the elevator and finally made our way up to our dorm and started down the hall toward our dorm room. Olivia only went quiet like this when she was lost in her own thoughts. And she was only ever lost in thoughts after a run-in with Isaac. I knew the feeling; A.J. did the same thing to me. A.J. and Isaac may have been separated by their mother's death, but their ability to get under a girl's skin seemed to be a family trait. A trait both the Vasillios brothers needed to knock the fuck off.

"You remember Prom night, when I told you that one day you were going to tell me what the hell had happened between you and Isaac?"

Olivia snapped her gaze toward me, but her face kept forward. Another Olivia subtlety I'd picked up on. She remembered. And she'd been terrified I would, too.

"Yeah, that day's getting really close," I said, pushing through our front door before she could answer.

The current four Queens sat on our couch sipping . . .

"Are those mimosas?" I asked Gia.

She nodded from the kitchen, putting away the orange juice.

Helen sat on the bar stool at the kitchen counter. "My luggage?"

"It's downstairs, Helen. Don't worry, we'll get it all up here before midterms," Olivia sassed.

"So, no A.J.?" The disappointment in my voice made me want to gag. I should have known Olivia would have used any excuse to get away from Isaac. Even if it was at the expense of my now dejected heart.

Olivia handed me her phone and a text message:

Oli, Tell Cass I'll swing by in the morning to take her to breakfast. I'm moving the Midas candidates into their rooms and have a meeting with my second. She'll understand. Have fun tonight. If you and the other queens-in-training feel up to it, I'm monitoring the Shadow Bar tonight. I'll VIP you.

Thanks,

A.J.

"The Midas's candidates, my ass," I muttered, handing Olivia back her phone.

"Girls," Carina called out as we walked into the room. "Come sit next to us, and we'll fill you in on all the impediments Ms. Maddox won't teach you."

I hadn't seen Ms. Maddox since the day we graduated. I wasn't sure who was more proud, her or Mom.

"Cassandra?" Mom interrupted my thoughts.

"Sorry," I walked over and sat next to Carina, my birth mom, the Queen of Hearts. On my right was Olivia and Genevieve, the Queen of Spades. Across from my mother sat the Queen of Diamonds, Mafa, and her daughter, Helen. To Mom's left was Gia and Mrs. M, the Queen of Clubs.

The air hung heavy with old memories and anticipation. Like the universe knew that these four women, our moms sitting here with us, their daughters, was more than a normal college drop off. This was something that didn't occur every day. And given our ages, I could only imagine wouldn't be happening for another twenty years.

Reigns were being passed.

Tides were changing.

Shit was getting real.

I swallowed hard over the lump in my throat. And Sara, my adoptive mom, wasn't here to watch it.

Mrs. M. started. "You all know about your innate powers. Those are your day-to-day powers that you will fine-tune over the course of your four years here at U.L.V. Today, your designators will activate your pass cards."

Mrs. M. asked Gia for the four-leaf clover pendant she'd worn since the sixth grade and then pulled out an opaque key card, much like the one Mom had left for me last night. She put the pendant into the slot, and a flash of light shot out from the middle of the card, turning the card almost translucent.

"Whoa." Olivia gasped.

"Cassie, do you have your card?" Mom asked.

I nodded, fished it out of my purse sitting on the coffee table, and handed the card to my mom.

"I need your ring." She nodded to my finger. The GPS that A.J. had given me on Valentine's Day released a small pang in my heart. I was starting to question everything the boy had done for me. Nothing was genuinely him— my thoughts cut off as my key card illuminated and then turned translucent. Mom handed me the card and my ring.

Helen had a ring and Olivia had a pendant. We were matched by color, jewelry, suit, and now, we had activated key cards.

"These cards will open any lock in Las Vegas," Genevieve said, handing Olivia back her pendant and her card. "The four of you must find the talisman or clue that will lead you to your elixir. Once you've consumed your elixir, you will have unlocked your battle powers."

"Battle powers?" Olivia asked.

"There has been a war brewing between the gods and the prisoners of Tartarus," Carina answered. "The fates bestowed our ancestors with innate powers. The gods expanded on those powers and enhanced them for battle. To keep the world safe, heir apparents must prove themselves worthy by finding the elixir that activates this power. We can't help you. The memory of the day of our declaration was wiped from our minds."

All four of us, the heir apparents, sank back into the cushions.

"You have no clue, not even a hint?" Gia asked my mom.

"No, nothing," Mrs. M. replied. "There's more."

"Of course there is," Olivia quipped.

"She is your daughter." The Queen of Diamonds smiled at Olivia's mom, then continued, "You have to find and consume the elixir before midterms or the solution expires and a new line is chosen." The Queen of Diamonds winced as she adjusted in her seat. It didn't take a pre-med student to figure out Helen's mom was sick. Really sick. "Find the vial quickly, because you are not protected. The Shadows can hunt you down and take your powers."

"What?" I blew the word out in a surprised breath.

"Mom, seriously?" Gia whispered.

Helen huffed.

But Olivia's response made my blood run cold. She pulled her mom's arm into her lap, snuggling into the side of the Queen of Spades like a child would after a nightmare. Only this wasn't a nightmare, this was reality and Olivia couldn't wake up. I could see Prom night, and the Shadows kidnapping her, play in the dark recesses of her mind. That place we put all our darkest secrets. Olivia wouldn't talk about what happened the hour she was missing. The Shadows had taken so much from me that night. Chance, the Shadow's third in command, had orchestrated the attack on Olivia. Isaac had tried to warn me. I should have listened to him. It's a mistake I wouldn't make twice.

"Oli?" I asked, protection welling up in me from a reservoir of power I never knew existed. "Don't worry, they'll have to get through the three of us before they get to you again." I reached forward and waited for her to grab my hand.

"She's right, Olivia." Gia reached forward and joined my hand.

"I may be small, but I can be right evil when buggers mess with me and mine," Helen nearly spat.

Desert sun glinted off of the tears welling up in Olivia's eyes. Her mother pushed her forward, encouraging her to trust us like she had trusted our mothers years ago. Doubt swirled in the air. Olivia wasn't one to blindly trust. She barely knew Helen, had never met Gia, and trusted me because we shared the same blood. There was no reason to trust us with her life, but that had never stopped Olivia from making decisions with her heart before. Olivia bit down on her lip, hand trembling as she reached out and joined me and the other future queens' hands.

"See, ladies. They're going to be just fine." Mom stood up, triggering the other Queens to also stand. "Work together, there will be enough of those working against you. Well then, enjoy your freshman year."

SIX

WE DIDN'T HEAR our mothers leave. They slipped out of our dorm room as quickly as both my mothers had slipped out of my life. I pushed down the ache in my heart and grabbed my bags. I ended up in Carina's old room with Gia. Helen and Olivia roomed in their mother's old room. It was like the universe had thrown our lives up in the air, and despite our best efforts, we ended up right where our mothers had years before.

We were just like them.

The thought sent a shudder of fear through me. Mom was pregnant with me the last time she spent the night in this room.

Had my father been in here, too?

What did he look like?

Did he know about me?

Those questions seemed to be popping up more and more frequently since the night A.J. and I battled our way out of the catacombs with Malory. And those questions always ended with the one that Dionysus dangled for me to return to the catacombs: Who was my father?

The temptation of the answer was getting harder and harder to ignore.

If my dad was a Spade, that meant he had to have been housed in the

Dayton Residence, too. It was just a matter of which floor he lived on. Given my natural ability to persuade—it almost bordered on mind control—Olivia figured it was someone near, if not actual, royalty.

I smoothed out the black and white damask bedspread and tossed the red accent pillows at the headboard. I hoped the mundane action of settling in would chase the gnawing go-find out taunt away. Quiet enveloped the room. Gia was good at reading me; she knew all of this. Despite my best "it's cool" front, it was overwhelming. I'd owe her big time for helping Helen finish lugging up enough suitcases to clothe half of India.

The sun was setting as I hefted my last duffel bag up onto my bed. Mom was right; the view from our room was amazing. The tips of the hotels on the strip were just glinting to life against the pink and purple swirled sky. Night blooming jasmine perfumed our room from the small crack in the window. It was the perfect blend of both my worlds, my former oceanfront home in Malibu and my penthouse palace in Las Vegas. The peaceful feeling of finally belonging somewhere could lull a person into a false sense of security. I pulled out my summer dresses and hung them in my closet, shorts and tanks going in the drawers, and then found the picture of my adoptive parents and me in the front zipper section of my suitcase. The slipknot of guilt cinched tighter as I pulled out the two letters they had left for me in their will.

I still hadn't read them.

Mom's letter could only tell me Carina was my birth mother, and the heart my dad left me opened her half of the Pithos box (my birth mother's version of a Pandora's box.). My finger trembled as I traced Momma Sara's monogram on the envelope. I swallowed over the guilty lump in my throat, almost missing the small knock on my door. I shoved the letters into my dresser, with my Pithos box and the Shell of Clarity Carina had given me the night Midas almost killed me. I buried the lump back down in my gut.

"Yeah," I answered.

The door opened slightly and Olivia peeked around the edge. "Can I come in?"

I walked over and pulled open the door. "Don't do that courteous knock, okay?"

"Okay." Olivia crossed the room, her gaze scanning every inch of the place. "It's like they purposely designed the place to lack any sort of personality."

"Maybe they're waiting for us to provide the personality."

Olivia threw herself onto my bed and kicked her bare feet up onto the wall. "Helen brought enough 'personality' for all of us, then." She fished out her phone from her back pocket and read the screen. "Catch. It's Prince Charming," she said, tossing me the phone.

I tossed it back at her, the cell landing on my pillow.

"You don't want to read it?" Olivia righted herself. Amusement and confusion swirled in her eyes.

"You'd tell me if it was anything different than his last hundred Midas-has-something-for-me-to-do texts." I unpacked my undies and socks, purposefully placing them in the chest of drawers next to the closet. Olivia was right; the white plastered walls had zero personality. I shut the drawer and pushed the empty wall space in between the drawers and the closet, half expecting a door to pop open and reveal a whole new set of passages.

"No magic doors." Olivia laughed. "I checked in my room."

"How do you think they did it?" I looked over my shoulder, then back at the wall.

"Who?"

"My parents. How do you think Carina and my dad . . .? If he was a Spade, how'd they find the time to . . . you know?"

"Ew, I really don't want to think about how you were conceived, let alone where." She stood up and playfully patted my bed.

"Cassie!" Gia yelled from the front room. "Cassie, get your ass out here."

"Coming." I started toward Gia, casting a disgusted glance at my bed and Olivia. "You're gross. How am I supposed to sleep tonight?"

Olivia giggled and tossed her feet back up on my wall.

I walked into the living room and found Gia holding Malory: stage makeup still on, sweats thrown over her costume, and a look on her face that said she'd seen a ghost—or someone had desecrated her favorite pair of shoes.

"What's wrong?" I hurried across the room. Adrenaline pumped into my blood with every step I took. I grabbed Malory's hands; they were ice cold. I shot a quick, urgent look to Gia before pulling Mal to the couch.

"I found her outside . . . like this," Gia said.

"I—I—You won't believe who I saw," Malory stammered. "Like hell barfed up its very own evil spawn and sat him in front of me, front and center. Which normally wouldn't faze me. Okay, it would faze me, but today . . . today I was on stage. It's matinée Monday."

"Malory." I squeezed her hands, made her focus. "Mal!"

"Cassie, it was *him*," she hissed. Her eyes were as big as dinner plates, fear clawing at the edges.

My mind raced back to the quarry of souls, to the only *him* that could put this kind of terror in Malory.

Dionysus.

I pushed down the terror. "Malory, who?"

She licked her lips, like the name was going to burn her flesh the moment she spoke. "Warren, fucking v-card stealing, Michaels. He was sitting front row center."

"Warren?" Gia asked.

"Where's Helen?" Olivia walked into the living room and pulled up short. "Nice makeup, Malory, you working at Circus Circus as a clown?"

"Stop it, Olivia," I snapped.

Olivia paused enough to see the worried way I was chewing on my lip, Mal's pursed lips, and Gia's scrunched up eyebrows. "What's wrong?" she asked, walking over and taking Malory's hand in hers. Olivia darted her look to mine, then Mal's. Olivia knew the ice-cold touch was one of the signs a person had wagered their soul with a Shadow. "Again?"

"No." Mal ripped her hand out of Olivia's grip and pushed off the couch. "I learned my lesson; I have this beautiful, black, bob-cut hairdo that won't grow out as a reminder of my epic fuck up."

"Grab Helen," I interrupted, ordering Olivia to not follow the fight. "We'll fill you in . . ." My words trailed off as Malory walked past us to the balcony. A hot blast of air ruffled the vertical blinds as she pulled open the door and stepped onto the balcony. I shot Olivia a quick look. She and Malory weren't the best of friends, they were hardly friends at all, but that didn't stop the lines of concern from wrinkling her forehead.

"Let me know if you need anything," Olivia murmured. She started toward the front door, then looked back at me. "And Cass, get her ass off the balcony."

I nodded.

Malory had impulse control issues and bad choice-making skills. She'd proved that a few months ago when she wagered her life for a prom queen tiara.

I padded across the room, Gia behind me, and slipped on the pair of flip-flops I'd already hid on the balcony.

Malory leaned up against the railing, searing hot wind picking up the edges of her bob cut.

"I don't think he recognized me," she said. Her gaze never left the Vegas skyline.

"Why do you say that?" I couldn't imagine the boy I gave my virginity to not recognizing me, not remembering the first time was special.

She turned to look at me; her short black wisps of hair fluttered in the desert wind. "He flirted with me."

Gia choked. "He what?"

"The mother-heffer flirted with me. Same cheesy lines. Same bullshit promise that he was certain God left one of his angels here on earth."

"Did you tell him?" I asked.

"Hell no!" She folded her arms across her chest, anger all but tangibly rolling off her. I couldn't tell if it was because she was pissed he didn't recognize her or if it was because she was wanting to fall for the same lines.

"You're not . . . you're not seriously?" I stumbled back and lowered myself into the patio chair Mom had brought up. "Mal, you're not going to go after him."

Her lips twisted in that challenge-accepted kind of way. The kind of way that made a mother look at her daughter and scream, *"Hell no, here we go again."*

"No." Malory bit down on her lip. "What?" She rolled her eyes. "Good God, you think I want to relive one of the worst memories in my life?"

But there was something in the way she classified her nearly dying because this boy broke her heart as one of the worst memories in her life. And the way she set her jaw said we were far from ending this conversation.

"Please, Mal, let it go," Gia pleaded.

"I just got you back," I whispered. "I can't lose—" The words hitched around the lump in my throat.

"You're being dramatic," Malory said and slipped through the sliding door. "I'll call you later."

My heart pounded against my chest. There were two things I knew about Malory:

One—I knew that look, the way her eyes glinted with the possibility of ramming the past down someone's throat and proving them wrong. And two—I knew I never wanted to be on the receiving end of one of those challenge-accepted looks.

Olivia stepped out onto the balcony. Her look most likely mirrored the one plastered with sweat and fear on mine.

"That was fast." Worry and shock pinched her eyebrows together.

"It's probably nothing."

"You live in Vegas, haven't you learned there's no such thing as probably? Especially when it comes to Malory."

I pulled my knees up to my chin. "We should eat in tonight."

"I'll order pizza," Gia finally spoke before she stepped inside.

Olivia sank down into the chair next to mine. The desert heat rippled off the courtyard below like future problems I knew we were going to have to face.

Growing up sucked.

"Start at the beginning." Olivia nudged my chair. "Why do you and Gia look like Malory saw a ghost?"

"Because Malory did. A ghost from her past that almost cost her her life."

"Yeah, I figured something like that."

It didn't take long to bring Olivia up to speed on Malory's almost successful suicide attempt our sophomore year of high school. Malory had a pretty destructive track record. A small part of me wondered if I wouldn't rain hell on A.J. if I'd given my virginity to him only to have him walk away the next morning like Warren Michaels did to Malory.

"Cass."

"You don't have to warn me, Olivia. I know I'm lucky as all hell to have escaped the catacombs with A.J."

She took a deep breath, and I knew I wasn't going to like the next words. "I know you and Malory are close, but it's time . . ." Her words trailed off, like she wasn't brave enough to say them.

I knew where she was going. Mom had the same conversation with me the night after the Royal Committee had been folded because I sacrificed myself to save Malory.

Thing was, I couldn't walk away from Malory. We were the outcasts. It was us against the world. I was all she had. The weight of our friendship settled in between my shoulder blades.

If the glint of evil doings in Malory's eyes were any indicator of her plans, she wasn't going to leave Warren alone. She was going to take her woman-wronged stick and ram the sucker into the wasps' nest that was Warren Michaels. And God help anyone standing near or in her way.

"I know," I finally admitted.

"You say that, but why do I have the feeling you'd march right back into hell to save her."

"Because you know I'd do that for you, too."

Olivia stood so fast, she made me jump in my seat. "Don't say that."

"Why?"

Her green eyes bore right through me. "Because I'll kill you myself if you ever jeopardize your house again."

SEVEN

AFTER OLIVIA'S "KILL you myself" declaration, I'd spent the rest of the afternoon in my bedroom. I'd pretty much settled in, reorganized, and settled in a second time before the soft knock on my door sounded.

"Cass," Olivia whispered.

I flopped onto my bed and counted the time between knocks like I'd done with my mom, Sara, when she'd get to shuffling cards. Everything could be measured by a Mississippi count.

Everything.

I made it to ten Mississippis before Olivia knocked again.

"Cassie." Her voice was a little more determined.

I stared at the door, a smile pulling at my lips as I tucked my arms behind my head and started my Mississippi counts again. I'd keep counting until my cousin got good and mad and barged her way in.

A few more Mississippis passed before a flurry of curse words filtered through the door, the doorknob turned, and Olivia stuck her head in. "Were you going to answer me, or what?"

"I told you not to knock on my door, didn't I?"

Olivia shoved the door open, the handle clacking against the wall. Long brown legs matched her crossed arms as she leaned in the doorframe. Irritation rolled through her emerald eyes. Now *that* was my cousin, and I seriously hoped she'd bound and gagged the bitch who'd threatened to kill me earlier.

"You're impossible."

"Likewise," I smiled, dodging a few more death dagger looks thrown my way.

"Helen doesn't want to stay in. The walls are virtually closing in on me. And Gia looks like she's planning a forty-course meal she's so damn antsy."

"Okay." Glad to see I wasn't the only one who was feeling the pinch of "freedom" these four walls were supposed to provide.

"Get dressed." Olivia grabbed my purse from behind the door. "We're going out."

"What about pizza?"

"I'm going to buy you a slice of the best damn pizza in Las Vegas."

"Best damn pizza is downtown." I swung my legs off the bed, waiting for the Shadows and our lack of protection to claw their way into Olivia's eyes.

But it never happened.

"I know." Olivia sat down on the foot of my bed, one leg folded up under her the other firmly planted on the ground. She was always firmly rooted in reality, even when the rest of the world was chasing illusions. "I figure I've got two choices. I can either let the Shadows and their threats dictate my life."

"Or?" I pressed.

"Or, I can show them the badass bitch who's about to rule the House of Spades and make them quiver with fear."

I smiled. "You may be pushing it with the badass part, but you definitely nailed the bitch element."

Olivia scoffed, throwing a duster pillow at my head. "Let's show Helen how we roll, Vegas style."

Twenty minutes later, we pulled into The Plaza's underground parking garage. Gia's eyes caught mine in the car's side mirror. It was the first time I'd been in this garage since New Year's Eve. The night the Shadows changed my life and killed my adopted parents. A twang of grief constricted my chest. Olivia parked and we peeled out of her Jeep. I knew where the stairs were. How could I not remember every inch of this hellhole? I slipped my purse over my head, like I was getting ready to run from the Shadows again, and tried to focus on the here and now. Still, the fetid stench of old exhaust and underground air rolled my stomach, making all the memories of New Year's Eve come tumbling back. Gia slipped her arm in mine, and it was only then I noticed Helen and Olivia were two rows of cars ahead of us.

"Old memories?" Gia asked.

I shot her a sideways glance as we started after the others. "Haunted nightmares."

"The last time we were here, I was all but certain you were the lost princess. You stepped across the treaty line and triggered the curse."

"It was an earthquake," I corrected.

We slid sideways between a BMW and Porsche.

"Poseidon always did have a flare for the dramatics," she chuckled.

"You've met him?"

"I've heard stories. The world is black and white with him. No room for gray areas."

"No room for me."

"Even gods can change." Gia pulled open the garage lobby doors. She stopped a moment, her big blue eyes catching mine. "Still, not a god you want to piss off."

"I'll remember that."

Nothing about the lobby had changed in eight months. I could close my eyes and still hear the snap of my borrowed stilettos echo off the walls. Even worse, I could still hear the anger in A.J.'s voice when he told me everyone in Vegas wanted me dead. His decision to save my life still felt like a debt I could never repay. We'd had the conversation several times after A.J. had used his only power to rescue me. He said it was because he loved me. I'd smile and accept it on the outside, but in my heart, I couldn't accept such a sacrifice. I never could muster up the courage to ask the real question . . . why?

Why me?

Before I could chase the question down the black rabbit hole that always made me feel a grade above gum on the street, my stomach grumbled. "Olivia. Best damn pizza is at the other end of Fremont Street."

"Actually, it's in the middle of the Experience." Olivia pushed the already lit arrow up, sparing me a withered look over her shoulder. "Now hush up and let me impress Helen."

"You're impressing her at the expense of my stomach; we both know that's a dangerous thing."

Olivia turned, her eyes examining something on my face before she let out a hardy sigh and pushed the button again. "Your ears aren't red. You'll be fine."

Helen stopped applying a third layer of lip-gloss. "Your ears turn red when you're hungry?"

"No, they turn red when she's lying," Gia offered.

I nudged Gia in the ribs, giving a hush-with-my-secrets-girl look.

"What? She's from the House of Diamonds. She's practically a human lie detector. You think your ears were going to be your tip-off?" Gia folded her arms, and I swear I hated the girl for ten seconds. Ten whole seconds, which was a total record in our lifelong friendship.

We rode the elevator up, and all watched Helen's eyes light up when we stepped out of the very ordinary elevator and into the extraordinary world of Las Vegas.

The music wasn't as loud as it had been New Year's Eve. Instead of a live band on the stage, there was music drifting through the speakers. The yellow bricks still spun in a circle that resembled a conch shell. Looking at the formation now, its resemblance to Poseidon's Shell of Clarity was chilling. The walkway wasn't nearly as full of tourists as it was New Year's Eve, either. But that's where the differences ended. The stench hit my nose about the same time as Helen's.

She wrinkled her nose. "God, what is that smell?"

"Catacombs are at the other end of Fremont Street," I offered up, avoiding a go-go dancer who bounced past me with tasseled stickies on her tatas.

Helen spun around, taking in all the old neon signs. "I heard they smelled. Never took it seriously, though. Are we okay to be here?"

Olivia cleared her throat. "Probably not one of our wiser choices, but isn't that what we're supposed to be doing? Making bad choices and getting it all out of our system so we can be tied to a life of settling."

Gia, Helen, and I stopped walking; our mouths hung open at the pessimism that oozed from Olivia.

"I'm sorry, Debbie Downer? Could you please bring my cousin, Olivia, back?"

Olivia rolled her eyes and turned on her heels. "Not even going to respond, Cass." She pulled the edges of her hair over her shoulder and looped them into a bun at the base of her neck. She was good and pissed, but that was better than depressed or worse, despondent.

It didn't take long for the people and the sounds of Fremont Street to chase away the melancholy. Helen's gaze rarely left the digital canopy over our heads. The Beach Boys' "California Girls" played over the speakers. The canopy changed from advertisements to waves crashing on the shore of a very California beach. It did something to me, made the hole in my heart ache for a place I couldn't call home anymore. The sadness sat in my gut, and there wasn't a damn thing I could do about it except ignore it.

Gia slipped her arm through mine, pulling me close enough that the ends of her ponytail tickled my cheek when they caught on the soft breeze. "Homesick?"

"Home is relative."

We walked a few more steps, side-stepping the old man wearing a loin cloth, angel wings, and sporting a Cupid's bow and arrow. A few months ago, we'd have stopped, stared, pointed, and giggled at the sight. Now, it was just another normal night on Fremont Street.

Crazy had a way of becoming normal, even expected. What used to have us gaping and entranced now became predictable. Which made me worry. How would all of this look in four years? How much would we have changed? And how different would we be when we were our mothers' ages?

In front of us, Helen walked, spinning around every few steps to make sure she took it all in. Mesmerized by the sites and the sounds. She bumped into a girl wearing a G-string and tasseled pasties on her boobs, passing out flyers for a topless bar. Helen's face blushed, and she couldn't get away from the girl fast enough. Olivia kept walking, and Gia next to me barely gave the incident a second thought. The extraordinary had already bled out of those two future queens.

Gia pulled me closer to her. "The morning before I left, I did a shore run. Three miles to your house, three miles back to mine."

"Yeah?" I already knew where this conversation was headed.

"Why didn't you tell me you were putting the beach house on the market?"

"Why? You interested? I can guarantee you it doesn't have any happy memories radiating from the walls. And the people who made it a home are gone." I chewed on the inside of my cheek, willing the emotions to stay away.

"Maybe it's waiting for you to make new ones."

"And maybe you should wake up and smell reality." I pulled in a deep breath, my nose wrinkling at the stench. "This is our future, Gia. This and that." I pointed at a man in a black hood watching us. Even at this distance, the lack of life in his eyes made people walk around him, avoid him. "There is no going home."

"You know I don't believe that. My mom made a new home. She had a career in front and behind the camera. She had friends. She had people who loved her. You don't have to follow in Carina's footsteps, being lonely and sad."

I tried to pull my arm from Gia's, but she clamped down on it, refusing to let me go.

"Gia."

"You know I'm right."

The perky cheerleader from my past life stood toe-to-toe with me, a small muscle undulating along her jaw as she ground her teeth.

"I know everything I thought about Carina was wrong or misinterpreted. I know there are things you want me to acknowledge, emotions I have to feel." I stomped my foot, wanting to take the stupid move back the minute it left my brain. "Carina keeps telling me to grieve, not stuff my emotions. I've done it. They're gone, Sara and Steven, they're dead . . . because of me. I accept that. Keeping a house or talking about what they meant to me isn't going to make my future any better. The best thing I can do is leave the dead as food for the worms." I started to leave, tears thickening in the back of my throat, but Gia wouldn't let go that easy.

"You don't get to steal the best line from *Dead Poets Society* and leave. You have to own your past, or you *will* repeat the mistakes. Here is where you own what happened. Here, where this all started, is where you come to terms with the fact that you're not alone. You have us."

"Ladies." Olivia wrapped an arm around my waist; her eyes searched mine, looking for something. She'd probably had a talk with Carina, as well. They were all waiting for me to lose my shit and go Richter. Helen laced her fingers with mine. The chaos of Fremont Street dulled, the lights didn't shine as bright, the noise muted—even the tourists seemed to slow down. In our own cocoon of silence, the four of us looked at each other, wondering what would happen next.

"Great bonding exercise, Gia," Olivia sassed. "Don't pout, you'll get used to my barbed love bites, but I gotta ask: why right now?"

Gia looked around our little group. "Because you can't build a future on a foundation of lies."

"I never lied," I bit back.

"You did to yourself when you put your parents' house on the market and said it didn't matter," Gia answered. "Helen, Olivia, you two have no reason to trust me. My mom had her reasons for keeping me from interacting with the rest of the courts, but you two need to know that me and my house will stand and support your line and your reign. Sebastian may be the King of Clubs, but until he steps foot on campus, my House and my word are yours."

A smile pulled at Helen's lips. "Same for the House of Diamonds."

"Since we're going all melodramatic, Cassie's my blood. She already knows she has the Spades' support. But you two need to know that once I secure my line, you're family too."

The moment stretched between the four of us. Bound us together in a tangible way that felt unbreakable even though it had yet to be tested.

"Can we eat now?" Olivia quipped, and the moment was gone.

Gia nodded, shooting Olivia a sideways look while stifling a giggle with her palm. "Good, because we're doing that after we eat." Four people, suspended by wire, whizzed over our heads.

"What is that?" A squeal chased after the four bodies, belonging to one of them. "When did they put a zip line over Fremont Street?" I asked. "And Gia, how'd you know about it?"

"It's called SlotZilla!" Gia broke into a skip, glancing over her shoulder when the three of us didn't follow right away. "C'mon, you're going to love it."

"Where was this girl when we were growing up?" I asked Gia.

"Stuck playing hide-and-go seek with her Mother's shadows," Gia yelled back at me. "Catch up!"

I was trying to. That was the problem.

By the time we finished our pizza, Helen was certain she was going to crop dust the people below with puke. I wasn't so sure I wouldn't be following. Sausage pizza mixed with the nerves in my stomach. We crossed the street and headed for the three-story-high slot machine. The pay reel displayed three cherries, lowered, and launched four more people into the air. They flew over our heads, two doing their best Superman poses, one holding onto the harness, screaming for dear life, and the other with her chin buried deep into her chest.

Gia waved for us to hurry up, then slipped into the doorway of SlotZilla.

Before any of us could change our minds or chicken out, we were strapped into body harnesses, taken up four stories in an elevator, and laid face-down on a blue mat behind a beige metal gate. Four future queens, on four blue mats, with four mothers who'd beat us senseless if they knew what we were about to do. My heart thundered in my ears as workers attached my harness to the steel cable.

"This is crazy," Olivia muttered.

One of the workers stepped between us, blocking my view. "Gia, this is your sense of adventure?"

"Yeah!" she squealed.

The worker shook my attachment before he gave someone a thumbs-up, and the mat lowered from my body, leaving me suspended in the air.

"This is how worms on hooks feel," I mumbled.

"No, they haven't a clue that they're bait . . . but we do." Olivia's knuckles paled, she was gripping the harness so tight. Suspended a few feet in the air, we waited centuries for the other techs to finish with Gia and Helen. I couldn't see them, but Helen had gone surprisingly quiet while Gia talked to anyone, anything, not caring if no one was listening. Cool air whistled through the slats of the metal gate, while excited conversations buzzed behind us. A few clicks and the groans of mechanisms catching whined to life as the gate lowered. Dark night and a forty-foot drop filled the enormous space between where we were and the bright lights of Fremont Street.

"This is crazy," I whispered, but it was too late. I was all in. A latch clicked, the cable wiggled, my stomach crawled up my throat, and . . . I was flying! Head first, I slipped into the dark abyss, careening toward a kaleidoscope of colors on digital canopy.

Helen's "Holy shite!" tore through the night. I should've made sure everyone was okay, but I wasn't even sure I was. My cousin and the three other queens soared through the air with me, but in that moment, I was alone. I squeaked at the quick dip in the cable. Soft fingers of wind caressed my cheeks, chasing the fear from me as the whiz of pulley on steel increased. We sped toward the canopy like an out-of-control car heading for a narrow tunnel, completely at the mercy of the fates. I ducked my head, trying not to be decapitated as we slid into the covered section of Fremont Street. The illuminated canopy swallowed us whole, replacing the dark and quiet desert night with the lights and noise of reckless abandon. I clamped my lips shut, refusing to be the one darting above Fremont Street with a terrified scream chasing after me. My grip on the harness loosened. Heat radiated off the bright lights of the digital canopy, while below me the golden bricks formed a pathway—Poseidon's treaty line. The treaty line tied to a curse. A curse I had triggered.

I shooed away the memory and concentrated on the here and now. My heart settled in my chest, as the ribbons of gold arcing along the walkway down below finally spiraled into Poseidon's pools. We slid past the Queen of Hearts hotel, the one where Chance had clamped his hand over my mouth, giving me a brief glimpse of who he'd been. I caught my reflection in the blackened windows, knowing one of them was where I'd first met A.J. My stomach dropped for entirely different reason. We dipped again, picking up speed as we crossed Casino Center Boulevard. Black hooded sweatshirts dotted the walkway by the Golden Nugget. The Shadows were out in force tonight. I stole a quick glance at my friends. None of them seemed concerned.

Helen had yet to pull her chin up from her chest. As terrifying as sliding along a cable was, she was totally missing everything. Olivia's jaw looked like it was locked in place, her eyes firmly attached to the end of the ride not far in front of us. I couldn't see Gia, but I'm sure her arms were carelessly thrust out in the Superman pose.

The Plaza Hotel sign came into my sight, and I couldn't help but search out the thirteenth floor, the council room where I'd almost died. I pulled my gaze and found the swirl where A.J. declared to the gods, to the otherworld, that I was under his protection.

I was his.

My heart fluttered. I'd zip-lined past all the most important events in the last eight months of my life. Events that forever changed the trajectory of my existence. We started to slow down; a blue fluorescent light lit a stage and SlotZilla's end station. The Club 1906 sign caught my attention, but it was the sight of A.J. stepping out from under the canopy that made my breath catch. I craned around in the harness, not caring if it would hold me.

How did he know I was here?

A.J. looked back, his hand reaching for something behind him. The two slices of sausage pizza churned in my stomach. I squinted, hoping I was wrong. Hoping that A.J.'s hand didn't just clasp another . . . another girl's hand.

But I wasn't wrong.

A.J. and a girl, a girl not me, stepped out into the growing sea of bodies. Her hair was dark and full of bouncy ringlets that made me and my limp locks jealous. She was tall and skinny and . . . not me. Long legs spilled out from her lime-green mini dress, the slit of her sleeve caught on a simple breeze, and I was dangling like fish bait from a steel wire above them. A.J. smiled at her, kissed her cheek, but his eyes searched for something over her shoulder. My throat went dry, my vision blurred. Olivia squeaked as the pulleys reeled us in.

The table with the ugly blue mat rose up; the attendant walked over and started unbuckling me. From the way my friends were cackling about the ride, they hadn't caught site of A.J. and the girl. I gripped the mat as heat flooded my body. It was a heat that had nothing to do with my Balanter powers and everything to do with betrayal. A cool hand closed over mine, and I jumped.

"You okay?" Olivia asked. "I thought you were having fun. I haven't seen a smile that big on your face in a while." Concern tipped her lips down.

I plastered on a fake smile. "Think that second piece of pizza wants another chance at the outside world."

Olivia's eyebrows pinched together. She wasn't buying this.

"I get a little motion sick." I pushed up on all fours, wishing that was why my stomach was rolling. Olivia offered me a hand, and the floor really did spin when I touched down.

"We were going to show Helen the Council Room." Olivia's emerald eyes darted across my face. "You feel up for that?"

Gia stopped next to us. "You okay?"

"It's nothing; a little queasy from the dive-bombing Fremont Street. Not even sick. Yeah, let's do the thirteenth floor." The words tumbled from my mouth. If Malory had been here, she'd know I was lying. I wasn't okay. I truly felt like I was going to hurl, and the thirteenth floor was the last place I wanted to visit.

I started for the exit, knowing the girls would follow. Eventually, Olivia wouldn't be able to help herself and she'd take the lead. I pushed through the metal gate and started for the elevator. By the time the elevator doors opened on the first floor, I wasn't quite sure what we'd find. Hoping we'd find A.J. and the girl, so Olivia could be outraged and vocal for me. Gia could hurt him with a betrayed look. And Helen—she examined her nails and then pouted when she found a chip in the red polish— well, I'm sure Helen had something to add, I just hadn't figured out what.

"Cass, you don't look so hot." Genuine concern laced Olivia's voice. She had no idea how "not hot" I really was. She pushed out the glass doors and we stepped back onto Fremont Street. Conversations and music mixed together like a toxic brew, but that wasn't as potent as the empty space where A.J. and the girl stood.

"I think I'm going to catch a cab and head home."

Gia stepped in front of me. The minute she grabbed my hands, she knew something was wrong. She also knew there was no way I would spill my secret. Not here, not with Helen and her perked up ears. I didn't know why I didn't trust her, and I was too freaked out to add it to my list of shitty things to worry about.

"Good times and bad, Cass. We'll do the Council Room another time," Gia finally said, despite Helen's irritated huff.

Helen should be happy I didn't want to share my bad time right now. She wasn't here the last time things went bad.

EIGHT

"YOU AWAKE?" GIA MUMBLED.

"That assumes I went to sleep." I shifted onto my side. Soft purple light filtered into our room from the blinds we hadn't bothered to pull shut last night. "Why can't you sleep?"

Gia folded her pillow under her head. Golden locks supermodels would stuff double-double hamburgers down their throats for cascaded down her pink pillowcase. "Worried about last night. We okay?"

"Yeah, we're fine. I should have told you about the house. It held as many memories for you as it did for me."

Gia edged up on her elbow. "No, I shouldn't have pushed. Not about the house, not about Carina. You'll find your way. I . . . I wasn't the reason you looked like you were going to hurl, was I?"

"No, and before you ask, I'm still sorting it all out." Even in the bruised darkness, I could find her wide, worried eyes. "I promise you'll be the first to know." I smiled, letting tension I didn't know existed seep from my shoulders and disappear. A comfortable silence filled the room, but I knew Gia wasn't done. She was like a light bulb dimmed, waiting for the right moment to blast you with her hundred-watt question.

"Why can't you sleep, Cass?" Gia sat up.

I chuckled. She never could sit still when something was on her mind. Back when Malory and I had started to get close in sixth grade, Gia invited us over for a sleepover and then kept us up until the sky started to lighten, kind of like right now, and she was ready to explode. She'd demanded that she be included in all sleepovers, shopping trips, and excursions to The Grove. Even at eleven, she used big words like excursions. We'd been the three musketeers for the next four years. Unbreakable right up until William showed up, rockin' his knight on a white horse routine.

I rolled over and found Gia, arms wrapped around her knees and a worry line pinching her eyebrows together.

"First day jitters, nothing more." I offered, even though it was only a small portion of the truth. The visual of A.J. and the girl from last night battled with A.J.'s voice asking me if I trusted him. I did, but it didn't mean I was blind either. "It's no different than home."

"Please tell me it will be. Don't you remember everyone staring at us? We were the freak show in high school."

"Gia, you breezed through high school. You've got a few prom and homecoming court sashes to prove you were loved."

"Only thing those proved were that people weren't done with the spectacle of me."

"And here I thought you'd be heading up the reunion committee." I quickly dodged the flying accent pillow. "Don't let this get to you. You've got a boy who loves you. You've got a House willing to go to war to protect you. You've got two parents who adore you . . ." My thoughts trailed off. At one point in time, I had all of those things, too. My heart wrenched sideways in my chest. Gia and her parents had been in my life well before my first words were uttered. She knew what she had by the absence of what I'd lost. The slight tug of her permanent smile said she knew more than my words could ever say.

"You ever think about our moms and how they all fit together?" I asked.

"Not really. Why?"

"Your mom and Carina were roommates, but where did Sara fit in to the picture? If the story she's spun is the true one, Sara left Vegas a week after graduation. Like a bat out of hell, she headed for the coast." The skin around Mom's eyes would always pinch when she recalled her high school years. I never could tell if was out of pain or disgust. "Sara hated this place with a passion I could never understand," I whispered, adjusting the pillow under my head.

"You think Sara knew your birth father?"

"I don't know." I picked at the edge of my comforter, like it was going to uncover some hidden secret. "Carina was pregnant with me around the time she was turning twenty-one. Sara had been gone for years . . . but I keep going back to something that didn't make sense when we were sophomores. Ugh," I harrumphed and fell back into my comforter. The memory was there, sitting on the edge of my brain like the start of a melody that I couldn't place to a song. "Ignore me. I'm speaking in tongues."

Gia chuckled, lying back down. The hum of the air conditioner filled the silence until I was all but certain Gia had fallen back to sleep.

"Did you ever read the letter Sara left you? The one the lawyers gave you at the will reading in the hospital after the accident?" Gia asked suddenly.

My eyes darted toward the top drawer of my dresser: the drawer that housed the unopened lavender letter from my adoptive mother. I still couldn't muster up the courage to open it, to let her go. A heavy breath left my lungs.

"From the sigh, that's a no?"

"I'm changing the subject."

"Thanks for the heads up."

I snickered. "Denial: not just a river in Egypt."

Silence tiptoed back into the room and before long, Gia's head was back on the pillow, soft snores that she'd deny to her dying day fluttering her lips. Our first class was in four hours. My eyes wavered, but I wasn't ready to give in to the sleep that four a.m. was demanding. The car crash and Sara seemed to be back with a vengeance, but it was after the accident that always had me chasing after at my chest. Dreams of a dark room and heavy booted feet standing next to my hospital bed before a nurse chased off the visitor. I swallowed hard and threw back the comforter. It was college. I was supposed to be living on coffee and research papers, right?

Armed with a cup the size of a jug, I slipped out onto the balcony. The lights of the Strip slowly dimmed as morning took over and heat chased away the chill in the air. I had two hours of quiet before we started Ms. Maddox's class. The butterflies in my belly woke and fluttered around for a while before the slider opened.

"Blimey, please tell me you aren't a habitual morning person," Helen yawned. Her black hair was piled high up on her head and a "piss off" sleep mask hung around her neck. She and Olivia were either going to be the best of friends or declare war on each other's Houses by midterms.

"Cute mask."

Helen grabbed the mask and yanked it over her head. "Bought one for Olivia, too: 'The Bitch Is Sleeping.' I'll figure you two out by the end of all of this." She flopped down into the chair next to me. "That hazelnut coffee?"

I didn't have a chance to answer before she swiped my oversized cup from my hand.

Helen's gaze found mine over the rim of the cup.

One sip.

Two sips.

Three sips later, she finally said, "I know I should ask, but trust me, if I go another second without caffeine, we'll all be good and fucked." She handed me back my lightened coffee cup and kicked her feet up on the railing, not caring that her nightgown was showing the world her girly parts. For someone who had been raised with an heir of aristocracy hanging from her every movement, every syllable, Helen was a walking paradox.

"What time is our first class?" she asked, eyes shut, basking in the warm morning sun.

"An hour."

"Bollocks, I'll never be ready." But instead of launching into a frenzy, Helen snuggled into her night gown and seemed to drift off to sleep.

Thirty minutes later, I nudged her knee. "I'm headed in. You going to be okay?"

"Leave," Helen muttered, long lashes lay against her cheeks. She'd gotten the queen dismissal down.

♥

"WELCOME TO YOUR first class of your freshman year," Ms. Maddox held back the parental squeal. Despite her hair pulled back in that unflattering, knotted bun at the base of her neck—and despite the librarian glasses sitting on the edge of her nose—you'd think she was in a Van Halen "Hot for Teacher" music video, waiting to prove good girls could be bad.

"I can't tell you how pleased I am to be part of the transition of power." She hitched a hip onto the corner of her desk, folding her arms over her chest. That was the signal the pleasantries were about to turn sour. "That being said, I heard you had an interesting night on Fremont Street. Nothing like playing in the Devil's front yard."

Helen looked at me. You'd never know that ten minutes ago, the girl was a raving hot mess with half a face of make-up applied and having a sandal vs. stiletto shoe crisis. I shot Olivia a look, which earned me a shrug before my cousin craned a look over her shoulder at Gia.

"Oh, ladies. It's Las Vegas and despite all the attempts to convince everyone what happens here, stays here, nothing is further from the truth. Quite the contrary, Vegas sees everything and they never forget."

"Who's the *they?*" Olivia quipped.

Ms. Maddox pushed farther back onto the top of her desk. Her ankles crossed and despite the heat, the woman was wearing nylons. "Olivia, it doesn't matter who *they* are. Could be House of Midas. Could be another House's security team. Could be the gods checking in on us. Could be the Shadows. In a city that lives on the secrets of the sins, *they* have a hell of a way of knowing everybody's iniquities and then determining when to expose that secret."

"Sounds like a great place to live. Where do I sign up?" Olivia countered.

"Alright." Ms. Maddox clapped her hands. "I won't tell the Kings or your parents about your visit to Downtown. I'm here as your advisor, not theirs."

"Is that sass I'm detecting in your tenor, Ms. Maddox?" I poked.

"Don't ruin the illusion I'm creating for the two Queens who don't know what a pushover I am, Cassandra."

"Got it."

Ms. Maddox shot me a wink. "So what did you find in the Council Room?"

The four of us looked at each other. Were we supposed to tell her we didn't go? Was it a secret? Ms. Maddox *was* our advisor.

"Already proud of you ladies." Ms. Maddox ended our nonverbal game of hot potato. "You don't tell a soul the business of the Court or your House. Anyone lower than you can use it for leverage. Depending on their motives, that leverage can be used two ways: against you or for you. This year is about not only expanding your innate powers, claiming and harnessing your battle powers, but it's also about laying the foundation of what kind of Queen you want to be and how you will reign. With your Kings off campus, this will be the only time you are truly free to rule the way you see fit."

I sank under the intense pressure of the room and the task of determining who I would be for the rest of my life. If I'd thought graduating high school was hard last year, then passing one class of the first year of my college career seemed impossible.

I found my voice. "That's a whole hell of a lot to do in a year. Helen had a hard enough time picking which sandals to wear and now she, all of us . . . you want us to lay a foundation for the rest of our lives?"

Ms. Maddox leaned back on her hands, letting the silence fill the room. "Welcome to Government: 101a. Don't worry. This is a hands-on class. I won't expect papers, save for one. That won't be due until the end of the year. The House of Hearts is hosting this year's tournament. While you are the heir apparents, you won't be required to play in this tournament, but next year, you should be ready for the House of Midas—any House, really—to switch things up. Ladies, you may be building bonds living together, but never forget your duty is to your King and your House. Cassandra, since your House doesn't recognize a King, you bear the weight of your legacy and your House all by yourself."

The mass of her statement hung in the air like a weighted anvil over my head. Ms. Maddox brown eyes met mine, filled with sympathy that said she could only imagine how hard this would all be.

She cleared her throat and continued. "The hands-on portion will be the field games. You will organize, create strategy, and execute a plan that will help you and your subordinates practice their innate abilities until you claim your line. The House of Midas will oversee that the rules are adhered to and then use your wins to create the seating arrangement for the Royal Tournament. So again, no pressure." She smiled, but it didn't reach her eyes.

"The threat of war is always on the precipice. With each transition of power and now the revelation of the Balanter, the threat of conflict becomes more real. I can tell I'm getting ahead of myself. Concentrate on finding your elixir and securing your line. Once you've found and consumed your elixir, your team's battle powers will be activated. First one to activate their powers will have an incredible advantage over the others. Practice is left to your discretion, but Field Games start in two days. I recommend you start those practices sooner than later. The House of Hearts will have Tournament advantage so Cassie, you will be disadvantaged here. You'll run your first game without the luxury of meeting your House. Any questions?"

I had so many questions but no idea where to start. My pulse raced in my ears, only matched by my heart thrashing against my ribs. I didn't even know what a field game was, let alone how to create a strategy. Panicked sweat trickled down my spine.

Gia raised her hand. "Where do I start?" she whispered.

That was my line.

"Um, could you explain more about field games, battle powers, the Royal Tournament?" Gia flipped through her well-organized notes. "I guess I'm asking if you can go over everything as if this is brand new to us?" She popped a pleasing smile.

"No." Ms. Maddox passed out four syllabuses. "Ladies, you're in college now. There's your syllabus, a library, and a world wide web to help answer your questions."

The single-spaced, double-sided syllabus looked as intimidating as the giant three-ring binder Ms. Maddox slid on my desk in February.

"I thought you were our advisor," Helen retorted.

"I am. I advise you to utilize the resources on your syllabus and your Jacks. They're well-versed in art of strategy and tactical warfare."

"Fabulous." Helen's lips pulled into to a well-perfected pout.

"C'mon, Helen." Olivia leaned back in her seat. "Now you and Hondo will have something to bond over."

Helen lobbed a murderous glare at Olivia while Gia raised her hand, and I wondered who the hell Hondo was.

"Gianna?" Ms. Maddox asked.

"Gia. Please, call me Gia. Regarding the elixirs, can we work together?"

"Forming alliances, forming bonds, this is all part of how the Monarchies co-exist. The current Queens signed a pact their freshman year. Since they were the highest ruling figures in their transition team, it was immediately ratified." Ms. Maddox gaze bore into each of us one by one. She'd done that my first day of high school when she was driving home the point that I would survive the Committee Finals.

"What was the pact?" I asked, curious if I was reading her clues right or if my mind had finally overdosed on caffeine.

"I don't know. I'm not a ruling member. I wouldn't have access to the archives in the Council room."

Olivia sat up straight in her chair. Good, I wasn't only the one hearing hidden words in backward comments.

"Can we access the Council Room archives?"

A smile blossomed across Ms. Maddox face. We were getting whatever hints she was giving us. "Once you have"—she smiled like she already knew we'd had plans to tiptoe through the office last night—"you'll find past strategies, alliance agreements, pacts." Ms. Maddox's gaze landed square on me. "It's a wonderful treasure trove of information on the past that might be vital to the present or your Houses' future. So I've been told."

"What about our paper?" Helen looked up from her notepad. She was book smart and street stupid. Hondo was going to have his work cut out protecting her. "What?" Helen glanced around the room. "Did I miss something?"

I shook my head and stifled a chuckle.

"No, Helen. The paper will be at the end of the year. It will be your first, and probably only, decree that won't be influenced by your future King. You will analyze your House's current declarations and protocols. If you see an injustice or a bias, then this is the only time you will be able assert your free will."

Helen was back punishing the paper with her pen.

"Can we pardon anyone?" I asked.

"No, you can only affect the future. You can't amend the past." Ms. Maddox grabbed her satchel and adjusted her watch. Her brown eyes took stock of each of us, as if somewhere between graduation and today, Ms. Maddox developed some keen sense of evaluation. "Get to work, ladies. Elixir first. I really don't want to have a Royal coupe or busted House happen my first year." Ms. Maddox strode back to the front of the class. "Dismissed."

♥

I STARTED OFF toward the north end of campus. Each step carried me further away from the expectations, and as far away from my future as a girl could get on a college campus. I'd pulled my own Queen Diva, demanding I have at least one class a semester with no Jacks, no tens, not even a lowly two in my lecture hall. Mom said I was holding my breath making such a demand, but I'd held my ground. I'd threatened a full-on royal meltdown and won the toe-to-toe stare-down with A.J. to get my way. My first non-royal college course: Computer Science 135.

The auditorium door closed behind me, and a sense of normalcy slipped over me like a comfortable sweatshirt. Warm light flooded the lower half of the stadium seating lecture hall. Beyond the second level split, the theater faded into dark shadows.

I adjusted my backpack and slid into the first row of seats. For the first time in forever, normal air rushed into my lungs. I was just a freshman girl getting ready to geek out on codes and algorithms. There were no Hearts in my class. I'd had Ms. Maddox double-check when we picked up our schedules. I needed one class. One, ninety-minute course where I was just Cassie.

No title.

No expectations except to pass a class and maybe join a study group.

Dr. Misch walked into the class, wearing a black pencil skirt, white silk blouse, and a punch of fuchsia coloring in her Jimmy Choo stilettos that would have made both my moms jealous.

Now, *this* was college.

Dr. Misch went through the syllabus, stated her expectations, and demanded our attendance. The last one wasn't going to be a problem for me. This was my slice of heaven. When class dismissed thirty minutes early, disappointment settled between my shoulders, seeping down my spine and tangling in my gut.

It was time. I had to go back to being *her*. I had to go back to my glass house and be . . . the future.

The hushed murmur of students shuffling out filled the lecture hall, papers rustled, backpacks zipped up. Yeah, ninety minutes two times a week wasn't going to be enough *me* time. The rest of my classes were freshman core classes. Perquisites that meant "students" from the Dayton complex and the Midas Candidates would most certainly be in attendance. Maybe even a few Shadows.

I'd be on show, again.

Ms. Maddox assured us every possible avenue had been taken to keep the Dayton kids and the Shadows separated, but there were budget cuts and only so many classes available. Complete separation would have raised questions and questions lead to investigations and possible exposure of what lies really ran Las Vegas.

"Cassandra Vera?" Dr. Misch called out while I was packing up my bag.

"Here." I raised my hand, feeling the awkward girl I was settle back into my body. I grabbed my stuff and lumbered over to Dr. Misch's podium.

Her smile was pencil thin but still held a warmth to it that would set any C.S. geek at ease.

"I'm a friend of Ms. Maddox."

And just like that, my slice of normalcy came splattering down around me. I felt the forced smile crawl across my face.

"I'm the flip side of the Clubs five."

Each House had a double set of cards. They were usually matched by age and gender. I guess when you're chosen by mythical gods, no form of birth control was effective. When a Card turned twenty-one and if both accepted the honor of serving, the weaker would give up their title and take on the role of spouse. Everything was mapped out, had been for centuries. I chased away the twitchy feeling that my body wasn't my own and focused on the woman in front of me.

"Your husband is the . . ." I searched the lecture hall, double-checking we were alone.

"He is the acting five card. I met Princess Gianna yesterday. She told us you are a lifelong friend to our crown."

I nodded, not sure what to say. Was I supposed to tell my House about the others? Did I only get one ally? Just when I thought I was getting a handle on my crown, it always seemed to slip out of my grasp, leaving me scrambling to save it before it all shattered at my feet.

"I ran a check of the roster. There are no Shadows or Midas candidates in this class. Ms. Maddox said you're looking for a normal college experience."

I nodded.

"Very well. In my classroom, I'll be the one in charge. I'll hold you to the same standards as my other students. No special privileges, your Highness." Her pencil thin smile blossomed, setting loose a twinkle in her blue eyes. "I expect great things from you, Cassandra Vera." She handed me a lab book and a sheet of paper with the computer labs' hours. "Get going. You have Chapter One and the Introduction to Concepts to prepare for."

"Thank you," was all I could muster up. I guess the great things she was expecting would come later.

NINE

I LEFT MY Computer Science class thinking I had this school thing down until I rounded the corner and stumbled into a swarm of black hoodies. Eyes wide with surprise, one of the girls started to make a move on me.

"Not yet," Isaac's voice purred from the middle of the pack. "She's Jessie's girl." My mind tumbled back to the night I first met Isaac in the neon graveyard. But unlike that night, A.J. was nowhere to be found, and I'd already made the mistake of accepting Isaac's card to the quarries.

"You lost, little red riding heart?" The sea of Shadows parted, and Isaac sat on the top of a lunch table. "Where's my little brother? Rush off to do granddad's bidding, again?" he tsked. "If you were mine—"

"I won't be."

Isaac lips split into a full fledge smile. "There's my sassy girl."

I pulled my backpack close to me, thinking it could provide some sort of protection. "I'm not your anything." I spat, quickly turning and making my way back across campus to the Dayton Complex. Ms. Maddox was right. Vegas did have eyes everywhere. I was a fool to think the Shadows couldn't be lurking around every corner, or weren't watching my every move.

My mind raced a mile a minute as I walked back to my dorm. Every where

I went I would be followed by threat after threat. U.L.V. was not just the safest place for me to be, but it was also the most dangerous place for a risk-it-all relative, a neglected girlfriend, and an unclaimed queen. By the time I shut the door to my dorm, I realized there were no lesser evils for me to choose.

"I'll kill you myself if you jeopardize your house again."

"Do you trust me?"

"I know who your father is."

"Cassandra," Helen interrupted my thoughts, collapsing on the couch while I flipped through the TV channels.

"You really want to stay in tonight?" The future Queen of Diamonds batted her almond-shaped eyes at me. "Tomorrow, we're tied to our Jacks forever. All this etiquette and I don't know about you, but I want to go out, shake my booty, and make a whole bunch of bad choices before our duties really get started." Black wisps of hair floated free from the strict confines of her bun. I had a feeling that was kind of the story of her life. Always trying to escape. Hell, if I really thought out about it long and Freudian-like, weren't all four of us trying to escape the inevitable future of royal confines?

Helen was five feet of pure college wild-child logic. And she made perfect sense to me.

"You know, that sounds like a damn good idea." I leaned forward, tossing the remote behind me. "We should go to the Council Chambers."

Gia shuffled into the kitchen, her Green Bay Packer's Cheese slippers firmly planted on her feet. "What sounds like a good idea?" Yellow light from the fridge spilled into the kitchen.

"We're going out," I said.

"Who's going out?" Olivia plopped down on the couch next to me.

"We are. All of us. And Olivia, darling, I hope you brought your special pink make-up bag, because you're going to do some Breaking and Entering." I declared.

Gia walked in, worry hanging from the bunched up skin between her eyebrows. We were best friends in L.A., but here in Vegas, that follow-the-rules-girl she knew died in the car crash on New Year's Eve. "You're kidding, right?"

"Nope. I think we should show Ms. Helen, future Queen of Diamonds, the awesomeness of the Council Chambers, or ASHA, you choose."

"Cass." The fear in Olivia's voice cut me. "You think that's wise? Tempting the Shadows two nights in a row?" Her eyes went serious. "I heard the Shadows cornered you—"

I grabbed her hand, cutting off her imagination and my memory of the event. "It was nothing."

"The Shadows," she whispered, pulling her hand from mine. Her eyes wide with fear made me want to stomp down the alleyway and into the quarry of souls all over again.

"Screw them, Oli." I nudged her leg with mine.

Olivia swallowed hard, her hand knotting the hem of her t-shirt. It should shock me to see her this terrified.

But I wasn't.

The fear they'd instilled into my cousin only pissed me off.

"You tell your boyfriend to fuck off, but The Shadows, the people who can steal everything from you, you say screw them?" She shook her head. "I think we need to work on your cursing prioritization."

Helen scoffed. "Sounds like she's got it pretty right on to me."

"Helen" the tough tone of Olivia started slipping back into place, "what boy went and made you all bitter?"

"I could ask the same about you." A knowing glint of mischief danced in Helen's eyes. She knew something about Olivia. A juicy morsel of my cousin's past that I was suddenly desperate to know. These two had history and I was determined to find out what it was.

Olivia's armor slipped into place. "Alright. ASHA. Should I call lover boy and let him know?"

I shook my head. "One last girl's night out. Just four future Queens ready to take their rule."

Gia giggled. "Cassie, I think I'm really going to like the new you."

An hour later, I stood out on the balcony, waiting for the others to finish getting ready. I kept my outfit sleek and simple. Black, skin-tight leather pants (Malory would have flipped a lid.), silver sequined tank top, and the silver stilettos A.J. gave me for prom helped me kick at the nauseated feeling swirling in my belly. Even at nine o'clock at night, the day school started, kids were still moving into the dorms. Helen was right. We were going to be tied down to a whole lot more than books in the next two days. It was good we were getting out tonight. Even if there was a small slice of pain that A.J. was probably cheating on me.

"I know that look," Helen said, a British lilt danced through her words from her years at boarding school. "Is it A.J.?"

"You know him?"

Helen nodded. "I met him at camp. He had quite a reputation even at fifteen."

I didn't know if she was trying to pick at a sore spot or just being honest with me. We weren't friends yet, and I didn't do the trust thing so easily with girls.

"Camp?"

"Right. You and Gia didn't go to the retreat in Reno. It's where I met Olivia, met my Jack." Helen rolled her eyes. "He's an arse and my parents . . ." Helen stopped herself. More wisps of hair let loose as her gaze landed on me. Sadness etched in the flawless skin around her eyes. "Not all of us are destined to live happily-ever-afters with Prince Charming."

I wanted to tell her I knew exactly how she felt. Some of us weren't meant to live in this world at all. Yayati's image of A.J. in a pool of blood floated to the surface of my subconscious. His jet-black hair caked with debris, eyes wide open, staring right straight through me. Just like my fathers.

"Cassandra." Helen's voice made me jump. "You've got a death grip on the railing, you sure you want to ruin that manicure?"

I pulled in a deep breath, the air lighting my insides on fire; my fingers ached as I let go of the balcony and stepped away. Maybe Olivia should be concerned about my decision-making skills, as well as Mal's.

"I'll . . . I'll wait for you downstairs," I whispered, starting for the front door. "And Helen, call me Cassie." I slipped inside, scurried through the living room, and let the front door shut behind me. So that was the mental cliff my shrink had always said I was in danger of falling from. I closed my eyes and leaned my head back against our dorm room door.

I just needed a break.

A breather.

Space.

That probably had nothing to do with A.J. and Yayati and everything to do with the anxiety of rooming with three girls. Growing up an only child, I'd become comfortable with quiet. Being the only child of celebrity parents, I preferred to be alone. Three roommates, even if two were as close as sisters, was going to be an adjustment.

Who was I kidding? This had everything to do with A.J. and Yayati's visions. "G'day?"

My heart kick-started, eyes springing open, at the thick, delicious Australian accent from the boy across the hall. Beaux swiped back his thick blond hair, giving me a better look at his face. He was an exact copy of Gia's cousin Sebastian. Clearly, they were identical. Sharp cheekbones with a long and angular nose that would look out of place on anyone else was set between two of the most magnificent set of green eyes.

"Beaux, right?" I knew his name, but then again, every girl probably knew his name and fantasized about all the other things she could know about him. Because my girly parts wanted to be one of those girls and go sit next to him, I held onto the doorknob of my dorm room.

His chin tipped up, exposing the length of his neck. His Adam's apple seemed to wave "hi" as he swallowed.

"Are you all settled in?" I asked.

"Right, and you?"

I stepped to the side, slid down the wall, and kicked off my stilettos. The hallway wasn't small by any means, but our toes nearly touched. Beaux looked like I felt: wiped out and overwhelmed.

"Did Bash know about you, or were you a surprise?"

Beaux's eyes flared. "You get right to it, yeah?"

"Sorry, filter is maxed out today."

He didn't answer. I didn't expect him to answer. There was something about the quiet way his gaze fixed on me that said he was most comfortable making everyone else uncomfortable.

Thing was, he didn't know me.

Time stretched between us as we sat in silence. Muted voices leaked out from under my door, begging for attention, but Beaux's eyes never left mine. I met his challenge, never shying away from him. He was raw and dangerous to look at. An angry white scar sliced across the cleft in his chin. The white lines etched around his eyes said he wasn't vain enough about his skin to wear sunglasses. Why would he when those eyes were like a hawk's talons? They latched onto you and never let go. I gave in first and looked down the hall.

"Do you know if the Jacks have moved in?" It was a stupid question, but when I looked back for an answer, my heart stopped. His eyes hadn't moved, still locked on me, taking in every inch of me.

"How do you know Sebastian?" Beaux asked.

An answer for an answer. Momma Sara was an evader. The pain stabbed at my gut again, slicing at my own scars, allowing all those years of awkward, unsure Cassie to seep back in.

"Gia. She's my best friend. Bash came to visit three or four years ago."

Silence crept back into the hallway, testing to see if Beaux would allow its presence. I swallowed hard over the unease. A few more moments of quiet, and I gave up. I wasn't the uncomfortable, jumpy girl anymore. Sweet Skittles, I'd stared down a legend with a golden touch and a Greek god with an obsession for wine and minions.

"Nice talkin' to ya." I stood and started to walk away.

"You want the hottie?"

"Wha?" I choked on the word. "No, I don't want your brother. I have a boyfriend."

A smile cracked Beaux's face. He held up a hand as a chuckle escaped.

"Sorry, the story. You want the whole story? It's a hottie back home."

Indignation crawled up my spine. *Was he laughing at me?*

"No, thanks." I turned and walked toward the elevator. "I don't want your *hottie.* I've got my own to worry about."

Silence filled the hallway. I'd expected noise and parties the first official night of college. Maybe everyone was as unsure about this place, about their future, as I was. I pushed the down button and waited.

"Sorry," Beaux's voice made me jump, he was so close. For someone who was over six feet tall, he moved like a freaking Australian ninja. "I'm not good for company today."

"Next time, lead with that."

He chuckled again. "I like you."

"You don't know me."

"You say what you mean." Beaux inched closer to me. "You're not all rules and etiquette."

I looked up at the indicator light going down instead of up to rescue me. "Yeah, I've heard that about me. I'm sassy."

"That's the word." Amusement danced across his face, replacing the harsh, etched lines with soft, rarely seen laugh lines. He wasn't Bash (Bash never laughed), but he was certainly his twin.

"Can I ask you a question?" I tested his mood.

"Right." Beaux's arms folded across his chest like a breastplate snapping into place. The guy wasn't used to questions. I'd definitely have to ask more.

"The cowboy thing you were rockin' earlier, I've gotta ask: for real or for show?"

He cocked an eyebrow at me. "Are you asking if I'm a jackaroo or if I just play one on TV?

My heart clenched again. *"I just play one on TV,"* was Sara's saying.

"After I left Brisvegas, I worked on a cattle ranch in the Northern Territory."

"There's a Vegas in Australia?"

Beaux leaned against the wall next to the elevator, his foot crossing over his other ankle. A genuine smile filled his face. I was wrong before. He and Bash were nothing alike. When Beaux smiled, he lit the room up. Every cell inside you gravitated toward the warmth. It was the type of smile that made a girl abandon every logical thought and risk everything. I swallowed hard.

"Yeh. Brisbane. The locals are trying to exploit the one casino to bring more tourists . . ." His words trailed off. He ran a thick palm along the side of his face as thoughts raced across his eyes. More scars were on his knuckles, either from fighting or cowboying; both were equally fascinating.

"So if there's a casino, are there gaming commissioners?"

"Yeh, Midas has a protégé there. She's been running the place for the last two years."

"Good to know." I looked back at the indicator light stuck on level one. "Is that why you left? Went to the North?"

"The Northern Territory. Yeh, it's one of the reasons." His green eyes seemed to gloss over. I knew that look. Olivia sported the glossy-eyed-gaze when Isaac's name was brought up. At least Beaux's girl-gaze wasn't the second Shadow in command. Not that a Midas protégé was any more realistic a lover. I knew that one first hand.

"What was so appealing in the Northern Territory?"

"Four million acres of ranch land." He sighed. "Alexandria Station."

"Good place to forget about a girl." I punched the button again, relieved to see the light flicker to the second floor.

"Sounds like you know something about that."

"I have a friend."

"So do I." Beaux's eyes glistened. Gone was the heartbroken longing, in its place was the feral look of a predator. The dude could switch moods so fast, he'd give a girl's heart whiplash. Not that I was volunteering.

"Did I mention I had a boyfriend?"

"You did." Beaux stepped forward into my space. The elevator rang. "Didn't catch the bloke's name."

"My boyfriend's name?" I stammered over the words, the denim covering Beaux's thighs scraped my knuckles.

"A.J. Your boyfriend's name is A.J." The rich voice of my boyfriend was more pissed than pleased. "And you need to step the fuck away from my girlfriend, Beaux."

I jumped away from Beaux, guilt flaming up my face, and looked at A.J. His eyes burned like liquid pools of blue rage.

"I . . . I . . . What are you doing here? I thought you were working," I stammered. Oh god, how did this look?

"This is how you entertain yourself while I'm away?" A.J.'s tone slapped some common sense into me.

"Well, I'm just a girl. Testing out this trust thing." A warm tingle rushed up my spine, the kind that had nothing to do with my innate power of persuasion. This tingle had everything to do with a pissed off girlfriend who'd been ditched all summer long. I'd have to buy Beaux a lager or a vegemite sandwich for helping a lonely girl out.

A.J.'s stare cut right through me. The odd mix of pissed and confused tainted his gorgeous face. "What did you say?"

"This is your boyfriend?" Beaux scoffed before stepping into the elevator. "Sheila, you just made my year." Beaux's chuckle disappeared behind the steel doors of the elevator.

"Answer me, Cass." The confused look on A.J.'s faced dissipated, replaced with pure fury. I bit down on my lip and looked away. He had pizza in his hands, and I needed this anger. All summer long, I'd played second seat. Yesterday, he thought it was okay to dish me off. I get it, he's here now with pizza, but was I the girl who let a smile and an extra-large sausage pie excuse a summer of neglect?

"Cassandra?"

"Why are you here?"

I guess I wasn't just a pretty face with an appetite.

A.J.'s bravado slipped. "I reworked my schedule. I wanted to see you."

"So you can do that? Rework your schedule?" I pushed the elevator button. It was a sweet gesture, but it only pissed me off more. He could rework his schedule? So all summer, he'd *chosen* to leave me? A.J. shouldn't be worried about Beaux, he should be terrified of me.

A.J. shifted the box to one hand. The delicious scent of Italian filled the hallway. "Cassie, I called in a summer's worth of favors. You think I didn't ache all summer to hold you in my arms? See you in that bikini more often?" His gaze traveled up and down my body, eyes burned hot.

My insides rebelled. My heart stammered. I loved this man, but I was so tired of always taking the back seat, so I didn't answer.

"Cassie," A.J.'s voice dipped low. He stepped into my space. The warmth of him lit my soul on fire. "You don't know how hard it was to leave you yesterday." His fingers danced up my arm, brushed back my hair, and exposed my neck. Tingles let lose like traitorous screaming fangirls. "You look so damn hot right now. I should throttle your neck for flirting with Beaux, but instead . . ." His words trailed off as he leaned forward and placed a small kiss where my shoulder and neck met. My weak spot. The rich scent of cologne and A.J. filled my senses, releasing a flurry of shock waves through my body. The boy had skills.

"I thought you were staying in tonight?" He skidded his lips down my shoulder. I think I heard a thump of a pizza box hitting the floor. I couldn't be sure, A.J. was everywhere and my heart and brain craved his attention like I was an addict.

My eyes rebelled, shutting and diving headfirst into the sensation A.J.'s kisses created. "We were." I let out on a breathy sigh.

"So, Cass, why are you dressed like my wildest, wettest dream come true?" He nipped my earlobe.

Warmth blossomed in my belly and spread. I bit down on my lip, hoping to stop the heat from reaching my girly parts. Too late. I didn't want to be cliché, but the man made me wet and reckless. His tongue seared a path along my jaw to the other side before pulling my other earlobe between his lips.

"Plans change." *God, did that throaty whisper of a voice come from me?*

"Change them again. I've missed you, Cassandra." He wrapped his arm around my waist, pulling me in closer to him, closer to physical reaction I had on him.

"I can't."

"Yes, you can. Here"—A.J. put his cellphone in my hand and for a moment, my heart stopped, thinking it was something else—"call Olivia, tell her I'm kidnapping you."

"I can't. Helen wants to go dancing." It was a lie, but I didn't want to deal with A.J.'s

Fremont Street issues, not yet.

A.J. maneuvered his lips up my neck, his breath in my ear. "And I want you." He pulled, pausing a moment before he took me in his arms, dipping me back slightly, and kissing me like my lips really were the air he needed to live.

The whoosh of adrenaline and desire pouring into my system pounded in my ears. The weight of the phone disappeared from my fingers. I didn't care. I didn't care about anything. Not what I saw last night, not what he thought could've happened with Beaux.

I didn't care.

"Olivia. It's A.J. Cassie isn't going to be able to come out and play tonight." His lips seared kisses into my jawline, my head tipped back, wanting more, desperate for more. "No, tell Helen I said you ladies are staying in tonight. There's a pizza by the elevator. And Olivia, don't wait up for Cass."

"They're going to be so mad at me," I whispered.

"Only Helen, but she's used to not getting what she wants." A.J. pulled back. His look devoured me. "Olivia said I owe you some serious woo-time."

"Woo-time?" I hushed.

The elevator doors pulled open, my legs—warm and mushy from the little bit of woo-time I'd already received—happily obliged forward.

A smile pulled at A.J.'s lips, the dimple that seemed to be so scarce these days tempted me. He leaned forward and placed a small kiss on the tip of my nose. Spiced apples and man filled every inch of me that hungered for A.J.

"Yes, woo-time." A.J. pulled back. The normal worry that wrinkled his forehead was gone.

And I'd forgiven him.

I'd hate myself in the morning for giving in so easily. I was totally that cliché girl everyone hated. I hated myself, but his lips. God, they were my weakness. The doors slid shut, and my world dropped from under my feet. A.J. pressed me up against the elevator wall, pushing up the fabric of my top with his hands. His soft fingertips singed a path across my belly and up to my bra. Lips pressed against the column of my throat, finally capturing my lips. His tongue, not waiting for permission, pushed open my mouth, capturing a gasp of delight. Fireworks released behind my eyelids as I let him ravage me with his hands. A guttural roar ripped from somewhere deep inside A.J.

"Cassandra," he said, briefly severing the connection between our lips. "Look at me," A.J. demanded. "Things aren't going to be easy this year, but you have to trust me."

"You said that last time." I leaned forward, skimming my tongue up his neck.

A.J.'s head tipped back slightly, like my tongue or his words were slicing him from the inside. "I need you to trust that when this is all over, after you've chosen to accept the role of the Queen of Hearts, I want you to marry me."

My heart stopped. Time stretched out in front of us. The hum of an elevator, the roaring whoosh of my pulse in my ear, and every bit of my body tingling as I imagined a future with A.J. I could never have.

"You're thinking." A.J. tried to smooth out the crumpled skin in between my eyes with a kiss. "This is where you start trusting me. Trusting that I have this all figured out."

I bit down on my lip, pleading with the words *"I'm not suited for this world"* to disappear. I wanted to run back to Yayati's cave and beg him to look again. Will him into seeing a different future for me in this world.

"I want to marry you."

Did he just propose to me? In an elevator? I'd expected something grand and momentous. But this was exactly how A.J. and I did relationships. Everything was fast, almost rushed, and we'd have to clean up the mess along the way, the mess of him kissing another girl last night. He searched my eyes, looking for the hint that this was what I wanted. Worry lines etched deeper into his forehead. He was right; I was going to have trust him. Trust that what I saw last night could be explained. A smile worked its way across my lips, and like I'd done so many other times before, I dove headfirst into the unknown. My hands wound into the thick locks of his hair, and I pulled him back into me, pouring every ounce of love and trust I had for him into my lips. A.J. wrapped his hand around my leg, pulling it up around his waist and pressing into me. He was hard and ready. I swallowed and watched the light dance in his eyes. We were dancing into all sorts of new territories tonight.

"God, you're beautiful," he whispered. The ding of the elevator destroyed the moment but not the mood.

A.J. released my leg and wrapped me up in his arms. "Are you hungry?"

I nodded, too speechless to say a word.

"I want to take you somewhere special." He kissed my forehead and pushed open the lobby doors. The heat of the night consumed us. My stomach dove when A.J. smiled down at me. There was something about the way the boy could make me mad as hell and then wipe it all away with a single look. This, what we had, was the most intense, volatile relationship I'd ever had. He'd literally risked his life for me and . . . I really couldn't see why. What did he see when he looked at me?

"Hey, Romeo!" Olivia shouted from our balcony. "Catch."

An overnight bag plummeted to the ground, landing with a sickening thud.

"Cassie," Gia leaned over the railing with Olivia, "first class is eight thirty, sharp. Try to make it back before the sun rises!" She giggled, disappearing behind the safety of the balcony and forty-feet of distance.

We walked to A.J.'s car. My overnight bag in one of his hands, me in the other.

"Stop thinking," A.J. tucked me under his arm. The heat radiating from him made the hot summer night seem downright chilly. "Tonight, there's just us. We'll figure the rest of our future out as we go."

TEN

BLUE LIGHTS TWINKLED all around us, the only light the inky cave would allow to coexist. I didn't have a clue where we were going until A.J. turned onto the government service road toward the iolite cave. I still didn't see how my overnight bag played into this, but I had my imagination and the memory of A.J. pressed up against me.

"You know all the best spots," I cooed as A.J. pulled out a blanket from my overnight bag, spreading it out.

Olivia. I ran a hand along the Spade appliques in the quilt as I sat down. The damp soil from the cave floor cooled the blanket but not the heat between us. A.J. moved the overnight bag onto the blanket and settled down next to me. I should've asked him who he was with last night. I should've demanded what he was thinking kissing her.

But I didn't.

I wanted the answer but was too afraid to ask the question. Too afraid to ask the hard question because I was too afraid of the answer. I chased my crazy rationale like a dog after its tail.

"Are you hungry?" A.J. interrupted my thoughts.

I wrung my hands, all sorts of nerves getting the better of me. "I could eat. You?" Heat crawled up my cheeks as Gia's *that's what he said* comeback taunted me without her being here.

A.J.'s smile reached his eyes for the first time in months. I'd forgotten how they lit up when he was happy.

He tucked a strand of hair behind my ear. "You're beautiful when you blush, Cassandra." He leaned in and kissed my cheek. Small smudges of black and blue hung under his eyes. He was exhausted, and I was a bitch for thinking he even had the time to cheat on me.

But I knew what I saw.

"Tell me about your summer, A.J." I ran my hand along the faint stubble on his face. He curled into me. A sigh escaped from his lungs, and it felt like a breath he'd been holding onto for months.

"I'd rather hear about your day."

"I know, but I feel like we're always talking about me." I pressed. "Tell me about the Midas Class. How many are there? Do you like your room? What did you do last night?"

"Cass." A.J. rolled onto his back. "I've been preparing all summer for the next four years. Tonight, I'd just like to lay in a mystical cave with my girlfriend, eat salami and provolone cheese sandwiches, and gorge myself on s'mores and your kisses." A.J. snagged me around my waist and pulled me under him.

"There's chocolate in there?" I giggled. The sensual weight of my boyfriend pressed into me, banishing all thoughts of last night and what I'd seen. "Oli sure knows how to pack a picnic basket, or an overnight bag."

A.J.'s hair hung around his face, curtaining his features from the rest of the world, except for me. Warm caramel scent wafted off his body. I could only hope I was as stunning when he looked at me this way. Heat filled my belly. A.J. lowered his head, nuzzling into the side of my neck. He warmed me from the inside out.

It was the perfect moment, and it was a distraction to get me to stop asking questions. I really needed to stop being the girl who was pacified by stolen kisses and heated moments.

"A.J., please." I pushed him slightly, but it was enough to destroy the magical spell he'd twisted. "I'd just really like to hear about your summer, your day, you. Why won't you share any of that with me?"

He rolled off me, the cool air of the cave rushing in like a slap across the face.

"Cass, there's things I can't tell you. Things you have to figure out on your own. If I start talking about any of it, I'm terrified I'll spill all of it. I'll put you at risk again."

"If you're talking about the Shadows, I know. The four Queens sat us down and activated our cards yesterday afternoon—"

A.J. sat straight up cutting me off. "Cass, this is the shit I'm talking about. I'm not supposed to know any of the conversations you have with the Queens, or Ms. Maddox."

"But you know we're not protected by the council until we claim our powers, right?"

"Cass, I can't tell you what I do and don't know." A.J. stood and walked to the mouth of the cave. "The line I have to walk, it's so damn thin, and if I cross the wrong person, it's not my life that's in jeopardy, it's yours." Frustrated, he raked his hands through his hair before he stalked back to me.

"Then tell me what you did last night?" I pressed.

"I worked."

I bit down on my lip, not sure if I was happy with the answer or ready to let loose on him because he was being so goddamned vague.

This was all we seemed to be doing these days.

Fighting.

Fighting and hiding things from each other and then trying to kiss it all under the carpet like none of it existed.

"What are we doing? If you can't share anything with me, you can't trust me, then why are you with me?" I whispered. Hoping he couldn't hear my question, desperate that he'd answer anyway.

A.J. bent down, his forehead pressed to mine. I could feel the bond between us stretching, whether it was stronger or weaker from the exercise, only time would tell.

He cradled my face. "Because I love you, Cassandra. Despite trouble and fucking catastrophe dooming us at every turn, I fucking love you."

"Then you should better start trusting me, too." The image of him and that other girl settled in my stomach. He wasn't going to tell me about her. He thought his secret was safe and maybe Olivia was right. Maybe this life was us settling. Maybe I was just getting a head start. Sara always said to pick your battles.

Maybe this wasn't one of those battles. Maybe tonight was just about us.

"You have a million things racing across those beautiful eyes."

I banished them all. "None of them seem to matter when I'm with you."

I pushed up, my hands sliding along the planes of his chest, before diving into his hair. If he could kiss me into compliance, then so could I. My mouth found the sweet spot on his neck. The spot that made his body go rigid and compliant all at the same time. I licked at the spot once, twice, and felt him give up all his worries on the third pass. The world spun as A.J. wrapped me up in his arms and laid me down on the blanket. His lips found mine, and for the briefest moment, the world spun right. When we were connected this way, we were invincible. His hands slid up my sides, taking the fabric of my shirt with them. He wasted no time picking up where we'd left off in my bedroom, in the elevator. A.J.'s hips pressed into me, letting me know that every part of him that worshiped me was ready to do so again. A quick flick of his fingers and my bra let loose. My breath caught as he slipped the strap off my shoulder, then the other. I swear my heart was about to break free of its cage. Celebrate the wantonness of what we were doing. Where we were doing it. A.J.'s breath on my breast made me quiver. A gasp ripped loose from deep inside me when he dipped down, his mouth capturing my nipple.

"Oh my god." My body instinctively arched closer to him, to his mouth. "More," I pleaded, threading my fingers into his hair, encouraging him to go farther, faster, slower, all at the same time.

A.J. kept his mouth focused on my nipple while one hand traced a line down my abdomen, making quick work of the button on my jeans before slipping under the band of my—

"A.J." I moaned as his finger circled around the sensitive nub of nerves. He pushed down on the bundle and stars exploded behind my eyes.

He tongued my nipple, sucking it in between his teeth with the most delicious pain I'd ever experienced. "God, you make me want to break every rule, Cassie." He kissed a path down my belly, hot breath so close to the part of me that was burning for more of his attention. "What I would do to you, if no one would know."

"Who would know?" I pushed.

A.J.'s eyes met mine, and I knew it was over. I could feel him settle in between my legs; despite the release he'd just given me, I ached to feel him all over again. Needed to feel him inside me. I knew what everyone said would happen, but I'd be willing to risk it for him.

"We can't, Cass."

"I know, but it doesn't mean I wouldn't be willing to . . ."

"End up just like your mother?"

And that was all the birth control I needed. I couldn't do what she did, so instead, I smiled and reveled in how far we could take things. I would take pleasure in knowing A.J. loved . . . I couldn't finish the thought. Images of the leggy brunette wafted back to the front of my mind, chasing away the momentary bliss I'd just found.

I had to know.

"You know you can tell me anything." I threaded my fingers through A.J.'s hair, basking in the way he curled into my palm. "It doesn't have to be House of Midas stuff. You can tell me . . ." The words died on my lips. I couldn't straight out ask him why was he cheating on me. Who was the girl he wrapped up in his arms? Did he do what he did to me to her? The sickening feeling consumed me.

A.J. sighed, before pushing away from me, both literally and figuratively. He walked to the mouth of the cave slowly, almost stalking. The light from the full moon bathed him in soft silver. I didn't want to fight with him, but if this was the only way we could have serious discussions, if I had to demand to be let into his life, then that's what I'd have to do.

"Can you answer——?"

A.J. held up a finger to silence me. He stepped away from the mouth of the cave, turned, and hurried back to the blanket, signaling for me to wrap it all up.

I quickly reassembled my bra and slipped on my tank top. I grabbed my bag and blanket as A.J. hooked my arm and towed me to the back of the cave. My stomach dropped when he nodded toward the outcropping we'd hid behind the last time we were in the cave. The time when Isaac, A.J.'s older brother and second Shadow in Command, had snipped off the pinky finger of one of my classmates because her father hadn't made good on a wager. A.J. nodded, took the bag from my hand, and pushed me up the first ledge of the cave. Adrenaline surged through my body, turning me into an expert rock climber. My fingers, on autopilot, instinctively found each crevice and pulled me higher and higher to safety.

"Shadows?" I whispered.

He nodded and scaled the wall. Voices started to seep into the cavern as I climbed to the last outcropping. I spun around, searched the mouth of the cave. Three long shadows stretched out like a celestial warning to hurry it up. I grabbed the bag from A.J. and stashed it behind our protective boulder.

Panic clawed at my throat. A.J. was still climbing when Isaac walked into the cave. The Shadows were here, and I wasn't protected by anyone or anything.

ELEVEN

THE OVERWHELMING FEELING of being vulnerable and defenseless became all-consuming: a feeling I'd never experienced in A.J.'s presence.

I followed A.J., ducking behind the boulder when a familiar whiny voice filled the cavern.

Chance? I mouthed.

A.J. really had to stop bringing me to this cave if every time we came, we ran into the asshat of Shadows. Chance was an up-and-coming Shadow who had second in command aspirations despite A.J.'s brother occupying that role. Chance was the one who nearly cost Malory her life.

A.J. nodded.

"Do you think he saw our car?"

A.J. shook his head and mouthed, *They came by boat.*

Isaac's smooth, velvet voice called out, "Did you sweep the cavern?"

My heart dropped. Why would he ask that? He didn't know we were here last time, did he?

"Hello?" Chance shouted. His voice echoed off of the walls above us finally dissipating. "Nobody here."

A sickening smack replaced Chance's smart-ass voice.

"Motherfucker, you're so damn lucky Dionysus still likes having you around. After the stunt you pulled Prom night, you're living under a blessed star." Isaac's tone was cool and calm. There was no anger in his words, no fight. And that made him all the scarier. What he did, the terror he elicited in others, he loved.

"Can we start now, or do you have any more theatrics you'd like to perform?" Isaac asked.

I strained to hear an answer, a peep, but only heard the trickle of the small stream running through the cave.

"We'll have to divide our resources," Isaac began. "The Queens are unprotected until their midterms. We get one shot at this." Wet sand squished underfoot.

"No one has ever captured a future queen's power, Isaac. The Jacks are too strong, too protective." Chance whined. "Kind of why we gave up the tradition."

"Well, none of the other queens were the Balanter, were they?"

Fear slithered up my spine. I was the Balanter. The girl destined to free the world from Midas's curse for greed. Thing was, I wasn't so sure the world wanted to be freed. The more time I spent in Las Vegas, the more of humanity's underbelly I saw, it was painfully obvious that people thrived on the thrill of giving the odds the middle finger. If given the choice, I think humanity would gladly continue their tenuous treaty with the Shadows.

Which left me useless.

I flipped over and inched my way up our protective boulder. There was something about seeing Isaac that seemed to take the frightening tenor out of his voice. How could someone beautiful, so downright handsome, be so utterly vicious. And how could my cousin have fallen for him?

I pulled A.J.'s t-shirt and pointed over the boulder.

Who's the third? I mouthed.

A.J. inched up the boulder, peered over, and shrugged his shoulders.

Isaac paced along the tiny ribbon of water, Chance stared out of the mouth of the cave, but the third person was hidden in the shadows. His outline was unmistakably male. The way the night hung around him, he was clearly comfortable being in dark and dangerous places. He turned and started toward Chance and the glow of the flashlight.

Light cautiously worked its way up the man's form. Flip-flops gave way to muscled legs that strained against the denim of his jeans. His waist was the point of a v-shaped torso, and washboard abs screamed look-at-me behind his black t-shirt. Inch by inch, the light revealed a specimen of a man. Broad shoulders, well-defined pecs, a neck that a girl could spend days nuzzling up to, a well-chiseled jaw, and . . . and . . .

"Holy Skittles," I whispered as the final features of the bastard's face were revealed.

"You know him?"

I nodded and sank down the face of the boulder. A.J. followed.

"Warren effing Michaels," his name rushed out in a hush.

"Who?"

"The bastard who punched Mal's v-card and broke her heart."

A.J.'s fingers balled up into a fist, and I could've forgiven him and fallen in love all over again at that moment. What the hell was Warren Michaels doing here, and why the hell was he here with two of the top ranking shadows?

"Do you two bicker like this all the time?" Warren asked. His voice hadn't changed all that much in three years—a little richer, a little more sinister. His body actually hadn't changed all that much, either. Maybe a little broader, a little more well-defined. Oh hell, who was I kidding? He'd turned from cute and adorable to panty-dropping hot.

No wonder Mal freaked.

"Let's get one thing straight," Isaac hissed. "I get why your daddy hid you away. And we'll keep you and your secret well-protected, but if you think for even the slightest moment that you showing up in Vegas means you're going to be running things, think again."

The smack of flesh on flesh echoed in the cavern, chasing away the question, *Who* was *Warren's dad?* This time, both A.J. and I both flipped over and scurried up the rock to see who hit whom. Waves of fury radiated off Isaac as he massaged his jaw.

"Damn," Chance drawled, echoing my sentiment. "Warren, you may be my new best friend."

Warren stepped forward; gone was his rebellious blond hair from high school and in its place, a high and tight marine cut that brought out the angular planes of his face.

"I like Isaac. You, Chance, are an opportunistic Brutus." Disdain dripped like acid from the syllables leaving Warren's mouth.

"Who?"

Isaac chuckled. "If you weren't the asshole who just clocked me, Warren, I'd shake your hand. But you are, and I don't tolerate that." Isaac let loose a left hook.

Warren's head snapped to the right as he stumbled back to his knees. He stayed down a moment longer than most. You could all but see the fight for control shudder through his body. Warren gripped the sand.

A.J. gripped my hand, a resolve seemed to painfully etch in the planes of his face.

"If he goes after Isaac, I have to help," A.J. whispered.

My heart tripled its beat and then stopped when A.J. pulled back. Determination furrowed his eyebrows.

I knew the answer before I asked, "Why?"

"He's my brother." A.J. didn't wait for my response, turning back to watch the scene below us. There was nothing I could say that was going to change his mind. He'd made his choice, and I would have to live with the consequences.

Isaac slapped his hand into Warren's outstretched hand. A truce. The two men released their grip and then struck matching poses: arms crossed their chest, feet planted shoulder width apart, and a contemptuous look for Chance.

If I were Chance, I'd be worried.

"I'm assuming you have a plan for acquiring the four targets," Warren said. We were targets, not humans. Is that how he felt when he went after Malory?

"I do."

"Care to share?" Chance chimed in.

"Know your place," Warren said. Chance jumped at the minute movement Warren made as he adjusted his stance. "You're a soldier, not a general. You execute commands when they're given. You don't ask the question."

The smile forming despite the split lip on Isaac's face said all we needed to know. He may not trust Warren, he may not like Warren, but they both hated Chance and that was what alliances were made of, hate and distrust.

"I have history with the Balanter's friend. We could use that to get close," Warren said.

"Good to know." Isaac's feet slid shoulder width apart, the stance so familiar to the one A.J. sported when he was leading.

"And you have a romantic past with the Spade's Queen, correct?"

I doubted the other two men on the floor noticed the way Isaac's shoulders tightened when Warren referred to Olivia. "I'll deal with her."

"Is she going to be a problem?" Warren asked.

"Not your place to ask questions, soldier," Isaac threw the words back in Warren's face. A grin flashed across Chance's lips.

Warren adjusted his stance, as if moving his feet softened the blow of disrespect. It was clear to see that Warren would tolerate Isaac's lead, but not for long.

And then it hit me.

I pulled at A.J.'s sleeve. "Is his dad Dionysus?"

"Can't be. Zeus sterilized all the gods after a band of demi-gods tried to overthrow Olympus."

"Percy Jackson, right?" I joked, not wanting to know what mythical shiz went down to make that happen. I stopped laughing when A.J. didn't join. "Serious?"

"Not now, Cass."

"I know I'm a soldier and not supposed to ask questions, but what the fuck are we doing in the iolite cave? This conversation could have easily been had back at the dorms. You interrupted a damn good blowjob to drag me out here to talk about shit that doesn't have anything to do with a fucking cave."

"Chance, we're out here because D wanted us to sweep the cave one last time for the Shell of Clarity. Maybe you should concentrate on the head that houses your brain instead of the tiny head in your—"

"Fuck you, Isaac. I see more action in a week than you do in a year."

"Your nickname is one and done," Warren piped in.

A smirk danced across Chance's face. "That's right."

"That's not a compliment."

Isaac chuckled and started for the backpack near the front of the cave.

"We've already swept the cave for the shell, it's not fucking here," Chance complained.

"My dad thinks it is and so do I," Warren walked over to Chance and slapped him on his back. "Why else wouldn't Cassandra Vera have used it to save her life? She was all but dead; the only thing that would have saved her was Poseidon's shell. And that reprieve would have been a temporary one."

"And if it isn't here?"

"Then Cassandra Vera's a hell of a poker player. If the Shell of Clarity isn't here, then she's got it. And it's going to be as much fun stealing the shell from her as it is her Balanter's powers."

TWELVE

THE TRIO OF terror used the tuning rod that Mr. Bones (the sweet old man from the Neon Graveyard.) had been forced to give up to sweep the cave. They'd come close to the outcropping, but a misplaced foot and slip down the face of the cavern had deterred Chance from making a good show for Warren. We'd waited an hour or so before we left the safety of our bolder. Neither of us dared to speak. Not that I'd had anything to say. I was too floored by Warren's presence and what it all meant. By the time we made it back into downtown Vegas, I was starving, terrified, and completely in denial about every aspect of my life.

We drove through In-N-Out and parked in front of the store, but even a double-double, animal style, couldn't tame the fear in my belly. Warren was a monster.

"He knew who Malory was today," I mused.

"What's that?"

I took a long swig of my chocolate shake, washing down a renegade pickle and my resolve to continue our earlier conversation at the cave. Despite the fear that A.J. was totally two-timing my ass, we had bigger problems than the girl I'd seen him with last night. It was a copout, I knew, but given the Shadow run-in, I'd have to pick my battles. And . . . I was too chicken to know what A.J. was hiding from me.

"Malory said she saw Warren today at her matinee show. Said he didn't recognize her. That he used the same pick-up lines as he had back in high school."

"Is she okay?"

A.J. knew about Mal's suicide attempt after she'd given Warren her virginity and he'd dumped her the next day.

"I'm not going to lose her again, A.J."

"I know, but promise me, if she makes any more hazardous decisions, you won't go following her down the catacombs."

I shoved a fry into my mouth, not willing to make such a promise. Yeah, I heard Olivia's warning to kill me herself if I put my house in jeopardy. I didn't need A.J. making me feel judgment impaired, too.

"Cass."

"I know what you're saying, but I also know the look on Mal's face today when Warren all but challenged her to make him remember."

"That's what I'm talking about." A.J. took a bite of his burger. "This ball's already rolling down a hill toward a cliff of no return. Don't go chasing after it."

"I won't."

A.J. shot me a sideways look.

"I promise. I won't."

A.J. rolled his eyes. "That promise is about as strong as the French fry in your finger."

"Have a little faith in me, A.J."

"I have nothing but faith in you." He shifted in the driver's seat, eyes heating as they devoured me. I knew it was a lie, but there was something in the way he looked at me that always had me taking the bait of believing the illusion. It was easier this way; I wasn't strong enough to do this on my own.

"You know what I realized yesterday when I saw everyone moving in?" A.J. continued.

"How you should have been helping your girlfriend?" I smiled coyly and shoved another fry in my mouth.

A.J. feigned a jab to his heart but recovered quickly enough to dance his fingers up my arm.

"No more curfews."

I smiled.

"No more sneaking around."

Wild butterflies took flight, multiplying as he twined his fingers into my hair.

"Were we?" I asked. "Sneaking around? I hadn't noticed."

"Hidden passageways instead of front doors. Notes on where you were and when you'd be home." I followed the pull of A.J.'s fingers in my hair. Closer and closer to him. The cabin of his white Range Rover heated with each breath. I licked my lips, knowing the act would elicit the small guttural groan of delight from my boyfriend. He was as addicted to my lips as I was to his. And even though I knew there were things between us, things we needed to sort out, I felt my hopeless romantic side beg me to ignore them and concentrate on here and now. There was a reasonable explanation to who she was. He'd given me no reason not to trust him. I rationalized not asking until it was stupid and insignificant. If I couldn't trust him with a girl, then we were in serious trouble.

"I have roommates now," I teased, completely comfortable with my denial stand.

"I don't want them." A.J. bent down and nibbled on the skin of my shoulder. My neck tingled under his praise. The boy was potent and he was mine.

"You want me." It was a declaration, not a question. I knew it every time he chose me over his duty to the House of Midas, and that was enough to completely silence the nagging question for now.

A.J.'s warm breath traveled up the skin of my neck, the heat evoking quivers in parts of me that had never been touched before. Parts of me that until A.J., I thought were hokey lines. The tenor of his voice made my heart quiver. The way his hands slid up and down the skin of my arms made my soul tingle. Even the warmth blossoming in my belly was no longer cliché. A.J. was a force of nature slowly consuming every inch of my soul.

And he loved me.

"Cassandra, I want you so bad, it hurts." His nudged my chin back so his lips could continue their exploration of my neck. I swallowed hard and heard A.J. moan at the movement.

"Why haven't you tried——?"

A.J. pulled the flesh of my bottom lip in between his lips, cutting me off. And there it was. That rush of heat between my legs everyone was talking about. No wonder people spent so much time fixed on this sensation. It was amazing. It was addicting.

"Aww," I gasped. This tip of his tongue skimmed my lips, teasing me, taunting me to ask for more. "A.J.," I protested when he pulled away and kissed the side of my cheek.

"You act like the thought of making love to you has never crossed my mind." His lips skimmed my jaw line. Warm breath with hints of new promises caressed me. "There's not a second that goes by that I don't think about taking you, loving you." His hands slipped under the fabric of my sequined tank top. My stomach trembled under his touch, then flat out fell as he pushed higher up. Cupping my breast. His head dipped lower. Traveled down the column of my neck, across the planes of my exposed chest.

I gasped. If this was what no curfews and dorm life elicited, then I was going to freaking love college.

"You make me want to take all the proper gentleman out of my role and make love to you until you scream with ecstasy."

A.J.'s breath heated the skin of my breast through the fabric of my tank top, the fabric of my bra. My hands twisted into his head, pulling him closer into me. He tugged at the material covering my nipple, taking just enough of a bite to make me squeal—almost mistaking the loud knocking on my window for my labia demanding more.

A.J. buried his head in between my breasts.

"She has the worst timing." A.J. looked up at me, eyes sparkling and heated with desire. His arms tightened around me, pulling me as close as the center console would permit.

"Cassie," Mal's muffled voice taunted through the glass. "You're turning into a full blown hooker, letting him feel you up and suck on your tit in public."

"You better let her in before she gets even more graphic," I said.

A.J. righted himself, gripping the steering wheel like it was Malory's neck he was throttling.

"You may want to adjust there, A.J. I can see your boner all the way from here." Mal tapped on the window, a giggle escaping.

If she wasn't one of my best friends, I know my boyfriend would have told her what she could do with her eyes and his boner. I rolled down the window.

"Whaddaya need, Mal?"

Malory leaned in the open window. She eyed A.J. and then me with a wicked caught-ya smile plastered on her face. "Obviously, I need to teach you how to get a room, so innocent passersby don't watch the porn you two are creating in the front seat of a Range Rover."

I rolled my eyes and unlocked the door.

"I mean, seriously, Cass. Innocent children come to this fine establishment."

"At midnight?" A.J. interjected.

"Well," Malory balked, "stranger things *have* happened."

"Did your show just let out?"

Malory shot me a shut-up look.

"He's my boyfriend and heads up the House of Midas, you really think he doesn't know you're a magician's assistant?"

Malory huffed.

A.J. chuckled. His grip on the steering wheel loosened as the balance of power shifted in his favor.

"You're not going to tell anyone, are you?"

"Anyone in particular?" A.J. asked, knowing Lucky already knew Mal's profession. Hell, everyone already knew. "Maybe the better question is, who doesn't know?"

Malory's weight sank onto her forearms. "Everyone knows?"

"Pretty much, sweetie." I rubbed her shoulder. "Look, nobody's said anything because it really isn't that big a deal."

"It is to me."

"It shouldn't be." I knew that wasn't going to make her feel any better. All her friends were one way or another ranking orders of a world she didn't belong to. To a world she shouldn't know about. She was an outsider looking in, which wasn't new, but what was different was that I *wasn't* standing on the outside with her. I was the future Queen of Hearts *and* the Balanter, to put a cherry on the mythological sundae.

Mal pushed off the car door. "I'll leave you two love birds to get back to steaming up the car windows."

"Let us give you a ride home," A.J. offered. "I've scandalized Cass about as much as I can tonight." He shot me a wicked look.

Heat flamed my cheeks.

"Nah, I'm sleeping at the Eclectic tonight. Maybe order room service and sweet talk Lucky into coming over and letting me practice some of my own magic tricks on his fine ass." She walked backward a few more steps. Warm desert air lifted the edges of her short black hair.

"I love you both, you know that, right?" She waved and turned back toward her car. The black jeep was a graduation present from her never-present mother who had missed her only daughter's graduation. Mom was mortified, especially considering she'd given the woman the day off.

I watched Mal climb into her car, the downcast look on her face reminiscent of the vacant look she'd had in Dionysus's catacombs.

"You want me to call Lucky?" A.J. offered.

"Yeah. She could use some cat and mouse time."

A.J. chuckled while the light from his cell phone illuminated the cab of the car.

"Hey, Luck. I need a favor," A.J. said.

Tonight wasn't exactly how I'd thought I'd be starting my first year of college. A declaration of marriage, a dive and duck in a cliff from Shadows, felt up by my boyfriend, only to be caught by my best friend. And Warren effing Michaels. What the hell did he and Dionysus want with the Shell of Clarity?

THIRTEEN

"CASS, YOU AWAKE?" Gia asked.

"Hmm," I grunted and rolled farther into the darkness of my pillows. A.J. pulled the car into the Dayton Complex around three in the morning, I hadn't made into my room until four. He'd had a few more areas of me to explore. My stomach dropped, thinking of the way his hands had roamed so freely over my skin. At some point, my tank top ended up on the floor of his car, and if it hadn't been for the headlights of another car, I'm pretty sure my panties wouldn't have been too far behind.

I giggled.

"That's the third giggle this morning; spill."

I bit down on the pillow covering my face. It really should be against the law to be this giddy about a boy. But if anyone would get it, it would be Gia. She had to feel the same way about William. I sat up, pulling my knees up under my chin. We'd had sleepovers like this when we were in elementary, but then we grew up. Gia was kidnapped our sophomore year, and everything changed. I pushed the sadness of my past into the corner of my mind. Mom said it wasn't healthy to stuff feelings, but I couldn't fathom dealing with anything but happy thoughts right now.

"A.J. told me he wanted to marry me last night," I bit down on my lip, trying to stop the surely nauseating smile that was stretching them.

"Wha?" Gia sat up in her bed, her hot pink comforter flying through the air. Gia's knees mirrored mine, up and under her chin. "Are you serious?"

I nodded.

"You guys have been dating for, what, eight months?"

"I don't think that was an official date date."

"You don't count New Year's Eve."

And there it was, that pang of the past rattling the part of my gut where I stuffed all my feelings. I smiled, sealing all those *feelings* back up.

"I don't think so. I mean it wasn't really a date, more like a charity case hookup."

"You're not a charity case."

I scoffed. "Thanks for clarifying I was only a hookup."

Gia rolled her eyes and grabbed the edges of her blonde hair, twisting them up into a bun. "You know you weren't a hook up." Her hands stopped. "Wait, you're still a virgin, right?"

My turn to laugh. "Yep. Still wearing pure white and a halo."

"So I need details about last night. Where'd he say it? Knowing A.J., it had to be crazy romantic, right? Ooh, gondola ride at the Venetian?"

I bit down on my lip again, trying not to let the twinge of disappointment I'd felt last night blossom into a full-blown outbreak of disenchantment. It wasn't the place where he said he wanted to marry me, I reminded myself, it was the words.

"He caught Beaux flirting with me at the elevators and . . . it just kind of came out."

Gia sank back onto her bed. The blanket she'd been folding dropped to her lap.

"Daaamn, Cassie." She drawled out like Olivia had been giving her lessons on how to make two words punch someone in the gut.

"I know, I was a little bummed."

"No." Gia stood, grabbed my hands, and plopped down next to me. "That's raw fucking passion right there. And I'll take that over a polished and practiced *Will you marry me* any day of the week."

"Yeah?" I asked. Not sure why I was still disappointed.

"Fuck yeah." The curse coming from Gia's lips sounded strange and foreign. Like all her life, she'd been trying to fit into a mold of how she thought everyone expected to act, and now she was planning on shattering that mold with a giant club of her own.

I squeezed her neck, the scent of coconut shampoo floating all around me.

"So, still a virgin. Good to know that you didn't get too carried away." Gia pushed my hair over my shoulder and tapped at a spot on the side of my neck.

"No!" I gasped. "Did he?" I bolted from my seat and nearly knocked everything off my dresser, trying to get an angle to see the spot Gia tapped. "No. He wouldn't."

But he had; a bright purple mark the perfect shape of A.J.'s lips bruised my neck.

"He. Gave. Me. A. Hickey?" I screeched.

Gia giggled. "Heated love bites—they're heaven going on and hell to pay the next morning."

"You sound like you've got some experience. How do you hide this?"

Our bedroom door swung open.

"Hide what?" Olivia started to ask, and I didn't have to answer. Her cackle and pointing showed my hickey wasn't going to be so easy to dismiss. "Ooh, Ms. Maddox is gonna have a field day with that." She walked over. "Does it hurt?" She poked at the bruised skin on my neck.

"Stop it. This isn't funny, we're supposed to meet our Jacks today and mine's going to think I'm slutty."

"He's not gonna think you're slutty," Gia exhaled, grabbing her shower kit.

"Who's a slut?" Helen asked, toothpaste dangling from the tube as she caught a glance at my neck. "Shite. Who ate your neck, and was he as good downtown as he was up top?"

Olivia hid behind a feigned outraged expression. Trying desperately not to laugh, she said, "She's a virgin, ya stupid Diamond."

"Ew," Gia giggled. "I'm never going to be able to look at A.J. the same again."

"Fuck me, A.J. did that to you?" Helen directed her toothbrush back to my neck. "I knew that boy had skills."

I ignored Helen.

"How do I cover this up? I can't very well wear a turtleneck."

"I'd show it off," Helen interjected.

"Stop it, Helen. The girl's in distress. You've got hooker skills, help her out." Olivia grabbed my hands and sat me down on my bed before whispering,

"Still a virgin, right?"

I rolled my eyes but nodded at the same time. "Why all the interest in my virginity?"

Olivia ran her hand down the back of my head and smiled. "We're pretty damn fertile."

"That's why they invented birth control." I winked.

"Didn't work so well for your mom."

Helen came back with a tackle case full of make-up. She opened up the case, unfolded several layers, pulled out a tray from the bottom and slipped on a pair of librarian spectacles that sat on the edge of her nose. A huff escaped her lips as she pushed my head back and in the opposite direction of my mark.

"You take this serious," Olivia scoffed.

"You like picking locks and hotwiring cars, I like fixing faces. How much time do I have?"

Gia looked at her watch. "Forty minutes."

Helen clucked her tongue, leaned forward and inhaled deeply. "You don't smell like leftover sex."

"She's a vir-gin," Olivia over-enunciated.

"You don't have to have penetration to have the scent, Oli, you of all people should know that."

A hard look fell over Olivia's face before she turned and walked out the door. These two really knew each other. It'd never dawned on me to ask my cousin what the status of her hymen was.

"I'm going to go shower," Gia excused herself, leaving the make-up master and me in silence.

❤

FORTY MINUTES LATER, the three future queens and I booked it across the quad to the library. It was eight-thirty in the morning. The sun was already hot enough for heat waves to ripple off the pavement.

"Here." Olivia handed me a tumbler of iced coffee. "What time did you get to bed last night?"

I pulled in a sip of delicious caffeine and felt my body ease a bit before I answered, "Four."

Helen chuckled.

"What?"

"Nothing. I just didn't know A.J. had it in him," Helen added.

I didn't like the familiar way the future Queen of Diamonds spoke about my boyfriend. It felt . . . icky.

"Helen, for fuck's sake, just tell her already," Olivia spat. "It's not like it was anything serious, and it was over before it started."

My stomach dropped, my pace slowed, and a familiar zing I hadn't felt in a long time shot up my back.

"What's she talking about, Helen?" I asked.

Helen's feet stopped instantly. Reluctantly, her body turned and faced me. She slipped off her sunglasses. Helen's normally full of life and sassy eyes glazed over into a familiar distant look.

"Tell me, now. Helen." Another lightning bolt of heat and electricity zoomed up my back, and I knew I'd not only tapped into my powers of persuasion but I was downright ordering her to obey me.

"It was nothing," Helen started, her tone lacking any expression. "I kissed him when we were in Reno at the retreat three years ago. He didn't kiss me back. He told me he didn't think of me that way and that any relationship I thought we could have only stopped at possibly friendship." She blinked. A tear ran down her face, plopped to the ground and disappeared on the blistering pavement. I wanted to feel sorry for her. I wanted to stop the power coursing up my spine and spilling into my veins, but I needed to know where *this* girl stood with my boyfriend. Helen may have been getting more than her fair share of my wrath, but if I was going to trust her with the future of my house, she needed to respect my boundaries, even if A.J. didn't.

"Do you still have feelings for him?"

Helen tried to move her head, tried to break free from my spell, but another jolt of heat surged up my spine. A ribbon of sweat trickled down the side of my face.

"Answer me, Helen," I commanded.

Helen's forehead crinkled up in obvious pain before she spoke, "No."

My eyes squinted behind my sunglasses.

"Are you sure?" I demanded. Another ribbon of sweat trickled down my face.

Helen gasped, her body bending in half and then just as quickly righting itself back to a soldier-like stance. "I don't want your boyfriend, Cassie. I just wanted to fuck with you a little bit. I was jealous that you're the Balanter. I'm usually the one the spotlight shines brightest on."

"Do you even like me?"

A sob broke free from somewhere deep in Helen's chest. "I'd die for you, Cassie."

And just like that, I turned off the Balanter power. I didn't want anyone else dying for me. I turned and looked at Olivia. She didn't seem surprised, unlike Gia, who had both hands slapped across her mouth.

"Why'd you do that, Livi?" I asked, using Isaac's nickname to show her how vicious a thing she'd done to both Helen and me.

Olivia slipped off her sunglasses. Her pissed-off stare shot holes in my heart. "You two needed to clear the air before her jabs made you do something even worse than what you just did." Olivia put her glasses back on her face, shook out her hands, and walked past me.

I reached for Helen, but she jerked away from my touch. She picked up her sunglasses that had tumbled to the sidewalk, put them back on, and walked away with royal grace I'd yet come close to mastering.

"Gia?" I asked.

Her blonde ponytail swished back and forth, hands still clasped tightly over her mouth a few more seconds before she found her voice. Gia straightened out the white sundress she was wearing.

"How long have you been able to do that?"

I shrugged. Embarrassment, maybe disappointment, now replaced the power surging through my veins.

"Have you ever done that to me?"

"Not that I know of." I kicked at the crack in the cement, wishing I could shrink down and disappear. "Go on ahead, Gia. I'm gonna need a personal moment." I turned and walked toward a bench under a tree. Her exit wasn't hasty, but it wasn't casual, either. What the hell was wrong with me? How could I have done that to someone who was supposed to be my friend? What could I do to someone I hated? I was a monster.

FOURTEEN

My watch said I was officially thirteen minutes late to my first meeting with the Jacks. Hopefully, Olivia had explained what had happened. I wouldn't blame Helen if she never wanted to be in the same room with me.

I'd attacked her.

I may not have laid a hand on her, but I might as well have tackled her and ground her face into the pavement.

I pulled open the door to the learning center. Cool air raced out to greet me as I slipped off my glasses and let my eyes adjust to the darker indoor lighting. A long black table, black like the wood my Pithos box was made out of, sat in the middle of a room with stadium seating.

Ms. Maddox stood at the head of the table. Helen and a dark haired, handsome boy sat next to each other. Next to them were Olivia and another boy. His face was buried behind a book, but his fingers were tattooed with the words Jack and Spade. I could only assume there was an "of" tattooed on his thumb to complete his tattoo—Jack of Spade.

On the opposite side of the table, Gia and William turned. Now their over-protective relationship made all the sense in the world. William was Gia's Jack. He'd probably been activated after Gia's kidnapping when we were sophomores in high school. William already had opinions about me. But the sting of Gia sitting quiet, neither she nor William smiling, led me to believe everyone knew about the Balanter beat-down I'd just executed on Helen. My shoulders slumped under the scrutiny and mortification.

I finally found A.J., an empty chair, and Beaux at the other end of the table. Why either A.J. or Beaux were here was beyond me, but the sinking feeling in my gut said I wouldn't like the answer.

"Come on in, Cassie," Ms. Maddox encouraged. "Welcome to the Breech Ring. This is where we'll meet should there ever be a crisis. If there is need for the ring, then I'll alert your Jacks and they'll escort you here. You'll notice there are four empty seats. Your Houses' Kings complete the ring."

I studied the linoleum floor as I made my way to the rectangular table, pulled out the chair, and sank into my seat. There was nothing royal about me. No pageantry worth bragging about. The weight of the room settled in between my shoulder blades, and I welcomed it.

Deserved it.

I stole a quick glance at A.J. Gone was all the raw passion-filled emotion from last night. He was probably rethinking every word, every promise he'd ever uttered. And truth was, I didn't blame him.

How could he want to be with me?

How could he trust I wouldn't do to him what I did to Helen?

Beaux leaned into me, interrupting my thoughts. "Honeymoon over?"

I shot him a look.

Amusement danced in his eyes, and I couldn't be sure if he was talking about A.J. and me or my Queen counterparts. Given the laughter in his eyes, I was going to go with the Queen counterparts' theory. I couldn't deal with the other. Whichever it was, he acted like it was the most entertaining thing that had happened to him since he'd left Australia. His arms were crossed and that stupid black cowboy hat was back, sitting low on his forehead, blocking everyone's view of him and now me.

"I was concerned I wouldn't know where to start," Ms. Maddox said more to herself than the group. "Let's address what happened outside. Then we'll move on to the introductions of the men around the table."

The hum of fluorescent lights heating up answered Ms. Maddox. Her hair was pulled up in a ponytail, the librarian glasses she rocked like a diva sat on her nose, and she was in full-on teacher mode. She held up a finger, silencing Beaux before he could interject.

"The men around the room are your Jacks. To protect their assigned Queens, they need to know about your power as well, Cassie."

Helen's Jack examined me from head to toe like I was a frog pinned to dissection wax in biology. "How do we protect our Queens from *that?*"

"Watch your tone, mate," Beaux interjected.

My head snapped to look at A.J. Wasn't that his job? To defend me in public, despite all my bad choices?

"Why?" William spoke up. "It's a valid question."

Gia slapped William's arm, but the usual contempt the boy always had for me never left his face. Like he's always known my meltdown was just a matter of time. My eyes burned through him, and under closer scrutiny, I couldn't be certain that he was a little disappointed that Gia wasn't the recipient of my demonstration. He really hated me if he was willing to subject Gia to my power.

"If anyone lays a hand on her, they'll deal with me." A.J. finally spoke up. "For any reason." He looked over my head and nailed Beaux with the comment.

That was it.

I didn't do love triangles.

And I most certainly didn't do threats anymore.

I slapped my hand on the table and everyone jumped. "Can we all just dial back the testosterone and damsel in distress roles we've got going on here?" I surveyed the room. Gia had snapped out of whatever dumb daze she'd been under. Olivia smiled despite her Jack nudging her shoulder. And Helen stared defiantly at me. I'd take defiance over dread.

"I'm sure you boys all have a role to play, but let me clue you in: we're modern women who can take care of ourselves. Compliment us, support us, but for God's sake, don't demean us by thinking we can't walk over a puddle without your jacket or handle a little girl dispute."

"You placed my Queen under your spell. You bruised her ribs, and if you ever—"

"I what?" I cut off Helen's Jack.

He lifted up Helen's shirt despite her protest. Faint purple smudges around her ribs were blossoming behind the angry, red welts on her side. It was the evidence that I'd physically assaulted one of the girls who was supposed to eventually be closer than a sister.

I sank back into my seat. "I didn't mean to," I whispered.

Helen's Jack leaned across the table. His face might as well have been in mine. I deserved it.

"You hurt her again, physically or mentally, I'll be left with no choice but to eliminate—"

Chairs screeched back against the floor. Beaux grabbed Helen's Jack by the collar, dragging him the rest of the way across the table. A.J. snagged William's balled up fist from the air. The Jack of Spades stood and pushed Olivia behind him, I think shielding her from me.

"Enough," Helen whispered. The boys froze, eyes falling to the future Queen of Diamonds. "I don't blame Cassie. I was fucking with her. I poked the tiger and got the claws." She put a hand on her Jack's ankle. His body relaxed instantly under her touch. "She loves you, A.J., and I was letting on that we'd . . ." Her words trailed off.

A.J. let go of William's wrist.

Olivia stepped around her Jack and took back her seat.

But Beaux still held the Jack of Diamonds down by the shirt collar. He leaned in close to the boy's face. The Jack's eyes flared before Beaux hissed, "You and I are going to tangle before Uni lets out. I'm looking forward to the next four years."

The Jack didn't squirm; there wasn't even a hitch in his breath despite the fact that a six-foot giant of a man all but guaranteed they were going to have it out. The Jack of Diamonds pulled in a calm breath and said, "I understand your threat, but receive this one: I don't care who she is or what prophecy she fulfills. My duty is to my Queen and my House. I will destroy anyone who attempts to harm her."

Helen's eyes warmed at the boy's statement. He'd die for her, and I was more envious of that minute gesture than anything she could have done with A.J.

"There it is, mate." Beaux let the boy up and stuck out his hand. Reluctantly, the Jack shook Beaux's hand and both returned to their seats.

"Crisis averted," Ms. Maddox muttered. "Point established: Cassie is the Balanter. As of today, most of the powers she's been prophesized to possess have come to be true. We'll know about the rest when you claim your elixir."

"Will we be notified?" The Jack of Spades finally spoke. A strong French accent laced his words, and if he hadn't just looked at me like I was a deadly white cobra, I'd have found him attractive.

"No, *you* won't," Olivia answered.

"The four future Queens have been advised by their mothers to work together. They've also been informed what I'm about to tell you four gentlemen. Your duty as acting Jacks will not commence until your Queen has found her elixir and your King can officially order her protection."

The three Jacks started objecting, but that left me wondering: where was my Jack? I didn't have one. I didn't have a king. I stole a glance at A.J. on my right and Beaux on my left. Not unless Midas had assigned one of—I cut off the thought of Midas doing anything on my behalf before it could form. He'd never assign A.J. as my Jack, and Beaux was from the House of Spades.

"If your Queen hasn't found her elixir by mid-October, at midterms, then her line will be folded and your King will be assigned a new Queen to protect. You will go about your days like any other suited student. You will participate in House games, and you will maintain constant communication with your Kings. Now, let's get formal introductions out of the way. The House of Spades is represented by Princess Olivia Spathe, her Jack apparent is Francis Du Boix."

"Frank," The Jack of Spades interjected. "Call me Francis and you'll have just as bad a day as Missy Diamond over there."

"Frank," Ms. Maddox said. "I don't think we need any more threats flying around the table."

"C'mon, Francis," A.J. poked. "Could've been worse, you could have been named Sue."

Beaux laughed.

Francis kicked his chair back, ready to launch over the table.

"Sit. Down. Francis," Olivia commanded.

The muscle along Francis jaw ticked as he grabbed his seat and obeyed the command.

"I'm sorry, Ms. Maddox. Please continue." Olivia folded her arms across her chest, shooting a disgusted look at her Jack. She truly did despise the boy, and not the flirtatious I-hate-you-but-secretly-love-you kind of scorn.

"The House of Clubs is represented by Princess Giana Maestrogiacamo. The Jack of Clubs is held by William LaGuardia. Princess Helen Damas represents The House of Diamonds. Helen's Jack is Hondo—"

Beaux masked a laugh with a cough.

"Something you'd like to share?" Ms. Maddox threatening tone quickly silenced Beaux.

"No. Sorry, was watching S.W.A.T. last night and found the Jack of Diamonds' name fitting."

"How so?" Ms. Maddox asked.

"Hondo in Egyptian means War, and given the little demonstration he put on, the bloke sure lives up to his name." The Australian cadence of Beaux's words had all the girls at the table a little mesmerized.

"Then you won't find the irony in my last name: Hasani." Hondo's voice, though quiet, held an ominous quality.

Beaux slapped the table and tipped his cowboy hat up past his eyebrows. "Digger, that's the first thing we've agreed on all day. You sure are one *handsome* motherfucker."

Ms. Maddox pushed on. "That brings us to the House of Hearts. Princess Cassandra Vera and her Jacks, A.J. Vasillios and Beaux Carta di Fiori."

"I have two?" I looked at the two men on either side. "You two?"

"Sounds like a three-way," Helen chortled under her breath.

"After you met with Yayati, he informed Midas the spare Spade, Beaux, was who you were suited with. When you accepted A.J. as your protector, you essentially added another Jack to your House." Ms. Maddox sat down for the first time. "You were aware that you were suited?" Ms. Maddox questioned me. The room hushed, waiting for my answer.

That wasn't what Yayati had said.

He told me I wasn't suited for this world.

He should have seen A.J. would use his power to save me.

Why would he tell Midas something different?

Ms. Maddox searched the room, probably looking for an answer as to why my mother felt I didn't need to know this fact. But then that would assume I'd told her I wasn't suited.

"It really couldn't have worked out better, seeing as A.J. is heading the protection detail to Malaga in two weeks."

"What?" I whispered, turning to A.J. "You're leaving?"

I didn't need him to answer. The cold, hard look in his eyes was answer enough.

Beaux leaned his chin on my shoulder, a move that made A.J. twitch. "What a bloody drongo."

I didn't know what a drongo was, but if it was Australian for asshole, Beaux wasn't far off.

I sat silent the rest of the meeting.

There wasn't much more.

Another binder for the Jacks. Two for my pair. Another warning not to help us until we found our elixir. Something about us having to prove we were able to find and protect our destiny on our own. Olivia mouthed off that it was more or less a girl team-building exercise. Ms. Maddox cracked a smile before dismissing the rest of the Houses. She asked Beaux, A.J., and me to stay.

When the room was cleared, Ms. Maddox moved to the other side of the table.

"I know this is out of the ordinary, Cassie," she started.

God, I hoped this was where the motherly side of her job came in. She'd been wonderful seeing me through The Council Finals in April. I was hoping she could recreate that magic right now, because I had no idea how to handle one protector who was lying to me, let alone another protector who made my insides tingle with the cadence of his voice.

A.J. hadn't moved a muscle after Ms. Maddox had outed his trip. Not even a whisper of *"I can explain."* It kind of put a damper on last night's proposal.

Truth.

I wanted to throw it in his face and shove my *"go to hell"* down his throat.

"How exactly is this going to work?" Beaux finally broke the silence. "I mean, not that I don't like getting freaky with the next guy, but no offense, A.J., I'm not going to be crossing swords with you, mate."

A.J. maintained his composure. In fact, the only indication that he was still listening was the balled up fist sitting on top of his thigh. I reached over, but A.J. moved his hand from my touch and issued a simple dismissive nod.

Ms. Maddox seemed uncomfortable, busying her hands with papers before she answered, "I'm not sure how the consummation ritual will work."

My attention snapped back to Ms. Maddox. "The what?"

"The Jacks, they not only are your protectors, they're your suited matches. Your future," Ms. Maddox stumbled over the words. "They guarantee the future of your line."

What a dignified way of saying they were our baby-daddies.

I wanted to say I wasn't suited, but A.J. grabbed my hand. This time, I yanked away from his touch.

"Cassie, I thought Carina would have explained this." Ms. Maddox steepled her fingers under her chin.

"We didn't think it was necessary once I declared Cassandra under my protection." A.J. draped his arm over the back of my chair. Now he wanted me. His hot and cold emotions were giving me emotional whiplash. How could a person burn so hot for me, profess undying love and devotion in one breath, and then be so cold the next.

"You and my mom had this discussion without me. Like I was a child."

"Yes," A.J. answered dismissively.

"You didn't think I deserved to know that I was expected to *procreate* with you? Do you know how medieval that sounds?" I pushed away from the table. I needed air. I needed room to think. Nothing had changed. Everything was the same. Lies dipped in the candy coating of protection and proposals. "I can't do this now." I turned and stormed out of the learning center.

"Let her go," A.J. said, before the door shut behind me. Yeah, let me go. He was getting great at that maneuver.

FIFTEEN

I RAGED ACROSS the quad, took the stairs to the top floor, and found myself in front of my half-sister's dorm room.

Music shook her door, making me hesitate just a moment before I let loose with a series of rapid-fire knocks. I hadn't met any of the other spares. It struck me that I hadn't even thought to think about them. The door pulled back, taking away any other thoughts on the matter. I lucked out; it was Cara standing there. Her hip struck its pissed-off pose and the rare smile I saw around me fell from her face. She was still in sleep shorts, hair in a messy ponytail like she'd just woken up, and a cup of coffee in her hand.

"What?" she hissed.

"Did you know about procreating?"

She laughed and took a sip of her coffee.

"Did you?" I pressed.

Cara leaned up in the doorway like a cat on a windowsill, bathing in the warmth of my mortification. "No." She clamped down her lips, probably to keep all the questions I'd just asked in the Breech room from tumbling out of her mouth.

"Were you suited?" I leaned up against the opposite side of the doorway.

I had questions to ask, and since the people I trusted, who claimed to love me, weren't giving me any of the answers, I'd go to the one person who loved shoving my face in the truth.

"I am."

"You are . . . still?"

She nodded and took another sip of coffee. Her eyes peered over the rim of her cup, never letting go of me. I couldn't blame her. A tiny knot of guilt uncoiled in my stomach. My being here hurt so many more people than just Cara. "Is he mad at me, too?"

"Yes." She took another sip of coffee. "Why are you here, Cassandra?"

"I have two Jacks." I slid down the doorframe, puddling on her threshold. "And A.J.'s leaving."

Cara shot me a sideways glance. Nothing was behind it, maybe a little shock that melted into an unfazed smirk.

"Of course you do." She matched my crisscrossed sitting position on the inside of her room. I was on the outside looking in, and she was on the other side looking out. It was the perfect representation of our relationship. We weren't friends; she could barely tolerate me, but we were sisters and in this moment, that meant everything.

"I figured the shit would hit the fan when A.J. claimed you." She set her coffee cup in between her legs. "You'd just seen Yayati. So there was the chance he just went with A.J.'s claim and didn't activate your Jack."

"So Yayati would have told Beaux he wasn't suited—"

Cara's laugh cut me off. "Fuck me, your Jack is Beaux from the Outback." She let loose another rich cackle. "That's fucking perfect. Gods be damned, the old man has to be shitting gold bricks."

"Midas?" I asked.

"Of course, Midas. Every bit of the prophecy is coming true." Cara's eyes widened. "He hasn't told you the prophecy? Oh my god, A.J.'s still hiding shit from you." Cara handed me the cup of coffee. "Drink this and let me get dressed. Where's your Pithos box?"

"How do you know I have a Pithos box?"

Cara planted her hands on a hitched hip. "Everyone knows you have a box. Midas made sure your godly contraband was outed. What he didn't tell everyone was what was in your box."

My turn to play coy with Cara's coffee cup. "What was in the box?"

Cara walked back to me, bent down, and whispered in my ear, "The Shell of Clarity." She pulled back, her honey eyes locked with mine.

How did she know I had the shell?

Mom?

"I don't like you, Cassandra, that much is clear, but just like Midas, I hate Dionysus even more. Now, let's grab your box and we'll go see Mr. Bones."

Twenty minutes later, I was in my half-sister's convertible B.M.W. roadster, flying down the 15 freeway. Cara hadn't said another word. Not even when the spare Diamond stopped her at the door and threw me a screw-you glance. My sister waved a dismissive hand and walked right past the girl and me. She'd tossed her bag in the back, eyed the delicate way I was holding my backpack, and told me to hop in the car. Despite the blistering heat, Cara had the top down and the air conditioning running on high. It was just enough cool air to pacify us. Cara turned the car into the parking lot of the Neon Graveyard and cut the engine. Gravel and dust plumed around the car, finally settling before either of us made a move to leave.

"Mr. Bones has a copy of half the curse. He can either tell us about the second half, Zeus's half, or tell us where to find it. Rumor is, there's an addendum in Poseidon's archives." Cara pushed her sunglasses up on top of her head. "And before you ask, A.J. never got into the archives in Fiji. Your trip out west made him stand up Poseidon. But Mr. Bones will be able to tell you the details."

I twisted in my seat. "You're not coming in?"

"Oh, I'm coming in." Cara's grin turned Cheshire cat as she hopped out of the car. "I'm not like Mom or A.J. or the rest of the courts. I won't protect you, Cassandra."

Sweat that had nothing to do with the heat trickled down my spine.

"Good to know." I finally mustered up and followed after my half-sister.

The front door was locked, but after a few moments of banging, an old withered man hobbled to the front door. A radiant smile that filled the room had to be the only thing keeping him on his feet. The electricity from his grin instantly soothed out the knots in my neck. A calming effect swept over me, and I couldn't help but smile back.

"He's good, right?" Cara said reverently.

"He can control moods?"

"No, he's just that pure. There's not a hint of negative energy in the man."
Cara waved, her face fractured into the first real smile I'd ever seen on the
girl. The lopsided grin was downright enduring. "You can't be around that
much positive energy without it changing you." Cara pulled at the hem of her
black tank top. "You can't be mad at the man, not even when he tells you
you'll eventually lose your crown."

My heart stopped. "He told you I was coming? When?"

"Two years ago." Cara kept her eyes on Mr. Bones. "I didn't believe
Yayati, but how can you not trust Mr. Bones? He's got nothing to gain from
lying . . . or telling the truth."

"Yayati knew, too?"

"Yeah. And before you ask, I don't know why he didn't tell Midas. I love
the old fortuneteller too much to out him to Midas." Cara leveled me with a
look. "You will, too, when this is all done."

God, no wonder Cara had looked like she'd seen a ghost when she first
saw me in Midas's penthouse. No wonder she hated me. I took everything
from her. Her spot in court, her crown . . . her mom. Cara's jaw tightened
under my scrutiny, and before I lost whatever sisterly bonding we had going
on, I looked back at the old man. He turned the lock to the door, but his eyes,
his smile, were focused on me. Desert wind mussed the lone, small tuft of
white hair on the top of his head as he opened the door. His olive skin
scrunched up around silver eyes and a frail voice, heavy with an Indian accent,
said, "Cassandra, you've finally come to see me."

Every ounce of fear I'd ever imagined suddenly abandoned its footing in
my soul. Like balloons freed from their tethers, they were gone and in the
fear's place was the warming comfort of hope.

He turned to Cara, the movement slow and fragile. "Are we there yet, Cara?"

She shook her head, shoulders dropping just a bit.

"Ah, but you're making progress. She came to you."

Cara's shoulder straightened, her spine locking back into place.

"I told you," Mr. Bones pointed a gnarled finger to Cara's resting bitch face,
"that does not work with me." He chuckled, the sound tinkling around us.

Mr. Bones waved us in, searching behind us as we stepped over the
threshold.

The lock slipped back into place, and he turned and rested against the plate glass door. A sigh of relief shimmered off him.

"You have questions. Come back to my office, away from prying eyes." He nodded to the empty parking lot behind him.

"It's empty," Cara said.

"There are eyes everywhere." He pointed to the streetlight with a red-light camera, and then to the bank ATM. "And those who want what you have in your backpack will do nothing short of murder to attain it."

Tuesday morning at ten, there was a steady flow of traffic. Not everyone was a college student sleeping away the last days of summer. And not all Shadows abided by a typical Vegas party-till-dawn schedule. We were foolish to think no one was following us. I pulled my backpack closer and followed Mr. Bones. "You know about my box?"

"I should," he chuckled, locking the door behind me. "I made that one."

"How old are you?" Cara asked.

"Old enough, some days." He snickered and shuffled slowly past the welcome desk. "Young enough, the others. The girls, your mothers, came to me when they found *it* in Fiji, not soon after they found out about you, Cassandra." Mr. Bones pushed open the office door, and both Cara and I stopped.

The walls disappeared under shimmering silk. Panels pulled and gathered up into a knot two stories above us. Floral and citrus scents perfumed the air, and the hint of a fountain trickled somewhere deep in the cavernous room. The floor was covered in a thick tapestry that should have been displayed on a museum wall but seemed most comfortable under Mr. Bones' bare feet. In the middle of the room—the tent—was a table, knee height. Mr. Bones' back office reminded me of Yayati's cave. And much like Yayati, Mr. Bones seemed to rejuvenate in the space. Gone was the shuffle of an ancient man, replaced with a fluid moving being.

He reminded me of Yayati.

"Do you know the Pandit?" I asked.

"Yayati?" A smile pulled at the folds of Mr. Bones face. "Good man."

"But he works for Midas."

"He's indebted to Midas." Mr. Bones patted my hand. "There's a difference."

Once fragile legs now purposefully carried the old man to the table. He sat down, poured a glass of tea, and smiled when he saw me place all the random pieces together. He didn't have to confirm my suspicions: the laugh, the hair, the way he moved through time did that for me.

"You're Yayati's brother."

"They're twins," Cara said. "Mr. Bones has followed Yayati all over the world."

"He's my older brother." The man nailed Cara with a look. "It's what family does."

Cara's shoulders took the brunt of the statement. She walked over to the table and sat on the plump cushion.

Without thinking, I fished my Pithos box out of my backpack.

Cara gasped. I'd have laughed, but I wasn't supposed to have a Pithos box (Zeus had outlawed them after Pandora opened hers) and I knew this box may turn out to be even more dangerous than Pandora's.

I carefully sat the box on the table, pushing it slightly toward the man who made it. The black lacquered wood seemed to sparkle and come alive under the lights of Mr. Bones's back room. The vines, with their heart-shaped blossoms, appeared to dance and sway toward the old man. Like they were happy to back in their maker's presence.

His once fragile laugh turned hearty. Hands clasped under his chin, his head danced from side to side as the blossoms followed.

"How are you doing that?" Cara whispered.

Mr. Bones stopped. The vines etched back into the wood. "What you put out in the world is a mere echo of the being you are. Make it good, Cara. When it comes back to visit you, it will be either delightful or destructive."

A moment passed between the two, the question so much more than just a question of dancing vines on magic boxes. Cara bit down on her lip, her eyes glistened, and when she nodded, one of those renegade beads of saline had the audacity to escape.

Cara wiped at the tear. "I got it."

"Not yet, but you're working on it." Mr. Bones covered her hand, then turned his smile toward me. "This box won't tell you why you have two Jacks."

My mouth hit the floor. "How do you know that?" I whispered.

"I can only point you toward the archive that can tell you."

I sank into my cushioned seat. "Poseidon's?"

Mr. Bones nodded his head.

"Looks like my trip out west is going to keep on haunting me."

"No. It won't haunt you. It was good for you to find your place in this world."

Cara held up a hand. "Her place is in Vegas."

Mr. Bones's face folded into an all-knowing smile.

"Yayati told me I'd give up my crown." Cara folded her legs underneath her.

"And you have."

"But—"

"Cara, part of the adventure is in the journey we take to get to a destination. And many times the destination isn't what we thought it would be. Nor is it the ending place of our journey."

My heart hitched, lodging in my throat with so many questions, so many worries, and none of them able to find the words needed to be voiced.

"Then why the two Jacks?" Cara asked before I could. "If I have Jordan, then why does Cassie have Beaux *and* A.J.?"

My breath hitched and I forced my brain to replay what my ears had heard. A smile that probably matched mine blossomed across Mr. Bones face.

Cara's gaze darted between Mr. Bones and me, confusion crinkling the skin of her nose. "What?" she finally asked.

"You called me Cassie."

Cara sank back, arms folding defensively across her body.

"It's not so hard, is it?" Mr. Bones asked my half-sister.

My half-sister searched the back of the tented room. Her eyes darted around, landing on everything but Mr. Bones . . . and me. "Doesn't change anything," she finally professed.

"It's a pebble in a pond. The ripples have started." His eyes lit up and then fogged over. I'd never seen someone go under, but if this is what a trance looked like, Mr. Bones was under deep. He stood and Cara followed. Mr. Bones grabbed both our hands, and without thinking, I finally really looked at my sister. Her skin was soft like rose petals. Her fingers were long and delicate like our mother's.

Like mine.

"You asked for answers. An unseen force will rise up, creating an unlikely alliance. Three Houses will unite while the Fourth mourns and the Fifth is thrown into turmoil. Only the Balanter can restore order. Only the Balanter can seal what has been fractured. The House of Hearts is mighty, and when the two of you unite, it will be a stronghold no one dares to topple." Mr.

Bones bowed his head. "I hope you get there before the storms come."

"What storms?" Cara and I said in unison.

"You are sisters. The blood that binds you will be your tightest bond." Mr. Bones's silver eyes seemed to glow. His gaze focused past us, maybe centuries past us. "Cassandra, one will protect your secret. One will protect your heart. Both will gladly lie down their lives for you. Only one will follow you past the stone. The other will rise and rule." The flame in Mr. Bones's eyes flickered, then quickly extinguished. Mr. Bones's hands trembled as he took a sip of the hot tea. His skin looked more translucent. Like whatever magic he'd just tapped into had taken more than energy from him, it had taken a piece of his soul. "I must rest now." He barely pushed the words past his lips.

I dipped down, catching his teacup before it clamored to the table. "Can we get you anything? Is there anyone here to help you?"

His eyes found mine; they were pale and hauntingly void of life.

"Find your way to Poseidon's archives. I cannot see who dares break the seal. But Cassandra," Mr. Bones' frail hands fished for me, "nothing you find in the archives will unlock the secrets of your heart." He smiled, life rushing back into his eyes. "If you don't mind, fetch me another cup of tea and then some quiet, please. Lock up when you leave?"

I nodded, trying to get rid of the surrealist feeling that I wasn't alone in my thoughts and placed the refilled teacup within his reach. He pulled the amber liquid through his teeth, the slurping sound reminiscent of the days Dad and I would play tea party.

Mr. Bones looked up at me, a smile pulled at the corner of his mouth. "She didn't have that," he finally said, sinking back into the mound of pillows before dismissively waving us off.

I guess he could read minds, too.

Cara found a small afghan and gently placed it over him before we tiptoed out of the back office.

We didn't speak as we locked up the museum, climbed in the car, and started back to school.

"Was that the prophecy?" I finally broke the silence.

"The first half." Cara pulled the car out of the parking lot. "The breaking the seal part's new, though."

"What seal?"

Cara shot me a quick look. "I don't know."

"You don't know or you're not going to tell me?"

We pulled to a stop at the red light. "When I say I don't know, I don't. I won't play word games with you. Given what we both just heard, we can't afford to be questioning each other." She pushed on the accelerator, blowing through the still-red light.

Wind pulled at my hair, lashing the ends into my face as we made the drive back to the dorms. It was too much to talk about. Cara had her secrets with Mr. Bones, and I had mine with Yayati. He knew about me years ago and never told Midas. It was one thing to water down a fact; it was another to completely defy the House of Midas.

Why?

Why would he risk it?

Cara pulled the car into the Dayton Complex parking structure, pressed a button to bring the top up, and killed the engine.

Cara finally broke the silence. "I'm not looking for bonding moments and giggles over hot chocolate."

"I'm not looking for that, either. I'd just like a civil relationship with my sister."

"Half," she corrected me.

"You and Carina are all the family I have in this world." The words caught on the lump in my throat. "You're my sister." My hand covered hers. I didn't miss her flinch at my touch. "I didn't mean to ruin your life, especially when your very presence saves mine."

Finally, her round honey eyes found mine, so much uncertainty churning. I wanted her to trust me. I squashed the warm tingle climbing up my back. I needed this to be because she wanted to be my sister, not because I'd commanded her under my powers.

Cara's eyes broke away. "Thank you for stopping."

"You felt that?"

She nodded.

"What . . .?" My question trailed off. Maybe I didn't want to know what it felt like. Maybe it was painful from the beginning. Gods knew, it could be physically damaging.

"It's like I'm being forced out of my mind. Nothing belongs to me." Cara folded her hands in her lap, studying her polished nails before she spoke up again. "I could hear you."

"You could?" I whispered.

"You want me to want to be your sister." She turned and looked at me, really looked at me. A small bead of sweat dribbled down the side of her face. "Then it got all muddled and I was back. Back in control."

I sank into the leather seat, the need to confess more stifling than the heat.

"I went after Helen this morning."

Cara turned the car on and kicked up the air, then turned in her seat toward me. "I was wondering when that was going to happen. Spill."

Half a dozen "fuck mes" later, Cara and I left the car and headed back to our dorm rooms. Laughter and splashing from the pool sprayed over the bougainvillea-lined rails around the pool and barbeque area of our dorms.

"What are you doing today?" I asked.

"Not sure. I have shit to do." Cara pulled open the lobby doors. She waved to a group of girls coming out. "I'm sure you do, too. A.J. probably needs help before he leaves."

"Found that one out today, too."

Cara punched the up button and leveled me with a look before saying, "I know you want to give this sister thing a try." She held up a hand, stopping me. "So this is my contribution. A.J. may be your Jack, but he's the heir to the House of Midas first. That's why you have two Jacks. Beaux's a spare king. He's been living his life without any rules or repercussions. Now he has you. Both boys have pasts. A.J. will never be totally honest with you. It's not in his nature. And Beaux's never had anything to be responsible for."

The doors to the elevators slid open. Cara smiled at a group of boys coming off the elevator, admiring their chiseled bodies and lack of clothing. I chewed on my lip as we walked into the elevator. The doors shut out the sounds from the lobby.

"Here's my other sister thing: you have two Jacks that together barely make a whole. A.J. loves you, but his House comes first and all the duties and suitings that come along with it. Beaux is easy on the eyes but has a heart that's buried under eighteen years of being told you don't matter. You can change that. I've seen how the world reacts to you. You just have to make them both know you need to be protected. That you're worth protecting."

"I'm not protected, though. None of the Queens are until we find—"

Cara's horrified stare strangled the last of my thoughts.

"None of you are protected?"

"Not until we find and claim the elixir. This sounds so bad. Maybe I shouldn't have told you."

"What happens if you don't find it?"

"I shouldn't be telling you this."

"You want to do this sister thing or what?" Cara grabbed my hands. "Secrets and things you shouldn't tell me are always the things you spill first."

My heart blossomed at her touch, at her words. We were doing this sister thing. I had a sister, someone who shared my blood. But could I trust her with my secrets?

I pulled in a deep breath and spilled. "We have until midterms; if we haven't found our Houses' elixir and claimed our battle powers, then our line is folded."

The elevator doors slid back. Beaux stood there, arms crossed, his cowboy hat sitting low enough to hide any look, any emotion, except the tick of a muscle along his jawline a second before he snagged my arm.

He pulled me up on my tiptoes and into him. "You and I need to talk."

"Easy, Beaux," Cara said. Her fingers wrapped around my wrist. "I was just having some alone time with my sister, and we weren't done."

"Say goodbye," Beaux commanded, but I wasn't sure if he meant it for Cara or me.

"Fine, but the caveman routine is so tired. Do something original for a change." Cara leaned into me. "I'll text you later. We still have things to discuss."

I wanted to say, *wait, don't tell the other spares, thank you*, but all those thoughts were chased away when Beaux tipped his hat back.

"Oh my god," I gasped.

SIXTEEN

THE FRESH BRUISE developing around his left eye made my hand twitch to touch him. A cut at the corner of his mouth did a better job at hiding the purpling flesh.

"What happened?" I gingerly touched his face. "Sorry," I said, when he winced, sucking in air. "Did you get in a fight?"

Beaux wrapped his fingers around my wrist and pulled my hand away. "Where've you been?"

"With my sister."

"Next time, tell me."

"Who hit you?" I dragged my hand across the stubble on his face, tracing the bruise. The subtle rough-man look that so many tried to perfect, Beaux did by just not caring enough to shave in the morning.

His lip quirked into a sideways grin. "That's not the question you should be asking."

"Really?"

Beaux shook his head. A light I didn't know to look for danced in his eyes.

"Don't you want to know who I hit?"

My heart dropped. The light dancing in Beaux's eyes spread to his lips and a full-blown smile.

"Don't worry, Sheila," he pulled me in even closer to him. "I didn't wallop your precious A.J."

"Then who?"

"The other Jacks and I were getting acquainted."

Beaux's grip on me loosened. I slid down the front of him, not realizing he'd picked me up when he'd grabbed my wrist. The sensation of gliding down this man did something to me. Would do something to any normal girl. I felt the heat rush up to my cheeks and take my pulse along for the ride.

"Where's A.J.?" I stepped back, putting some much-needed distance between us.

"He's going to meet us for dinner. In the meantime, you and I have a few things we need to get straight." Beaux reached behind me, pushing the elevator button. He was the only man I knew that could make the crisp scent of soap seductive. And the way the fabric of his black t-shirt pulled and stretched could jump-start a corpse's heart.

I cleared my throat.

"You do the same to me, Sheila," he whispered in my ear. Beaux dipped low, so our eyes were level. It took all of two seconds before I was completely lost in his green eyes.

"I have a boyfriend." I hated the breathy way my words sounded.

"And I'm in love with someone I can't have, either. I guess that leaves us as fuck buddies."

The breathy remains of my voice coughed, then sputtered to find a response. Beaux's arm snaked around my waist, pulling me closer into him.

"Right, like I said, we've got a few things to get straight."

Skillfully, he walked us into the elevator, and once the doors closed, he let me go.

An awkward silence filled the elevator, not that Beaux was aware of it. I was in awe of the way he could balance badass and lazy in one pose, while I searched for anywhere to look but him. Somewhere to put my hands besides the tingling places of skin he'd touched.

One look.

The doors pulled open, and I followed Beaux into the lobby and across the quad to the parking garage. For a girl who was supposed to be enjoying her last days of summer, all I was doing was riding elevators and finding cars.

"Over there," Beaux nodded to the back of the garage. We passed every make and model of luxury car until we stopped at a beat-up white truck. I couldn't even call it a classic. It was just junk.

"Work in progress?" I asked, nodding to the rusted out fender.

"It's a Ford and it hauls my gear." Beaux patted the new utility trunk in the bed of the truck.

"What year is that?" I asked.

Beaux climbed in the driver's side of the door, leaned over, and unlocked my door. I wasn't a prude, but I had grown accustomed to having my door opened.

"Are ya coming or what?"

I rolled my eyes and opened the door. Flecks of rust drizzled to the garage floor. The inside was better but not by much. Despite being old, it was clean. The scent of aged leather and that clean scent of Beaux filled the air. A Mexican blanket stretched across the bench, but there was nothing to hide the cushion oozing out from the slit in the passengers' side seat. I hauled myself up into the cab and shut the door. Then looked for the seat belts.

"No belts." Beaux said. The engine roared to life. Plumes of exhaust filled the garage and seeped into the cab of the truck.

"So where are we going in the deathtrap on wheels?"

Beaux tipped his hat, barely hiding his shit-eating grin.

Gods' love, the cowboy hat was growing on me.

"The only reason to come to Las Vegas—Thomas and Mack Center."

"Bull riding?"

♥

WHERE BEAUX ONCE stood out in all his cowboy get up, now he looked at home with a saddle slung over his shoulder. I carried his helmet, riding vest, and lucky rope.

"What are we doing here?"

"Hey, Beaux." A man with a blood trickling down his face nodded at us. "Heard you were in town."

"Right, mate. Not a bad place to go to Uni. Bushwhacker?" Beaux pointed to the blood-soaked towel the man had pressed up against his eye.

"Yeah. One of these days, we'll join your rank and ride the unrideable. Who's your friend?"

Beaux ignored the question and started down the ramp to the rider's entrance. I hurried to catch up. Questions jumped around, chasing after the answers that were held in tight denim jeans, a black as sin t-shirt, and cowboy boots.

"You ride bulls?" I huffed out once I caught up to Beaux at the check-in table.

"Beauxregard—"

"We know who you are." The blonde girl behind the table cooed.

"We've been waiting for you." A busty brunette surfaced. She held her clipboard under her chest, pushing her boobs up so high you could practically see her nipples waving to get Beaux's attention.

"Ladies," Beaux tipped his hat. "This is my hand, Cassandra Vera."

The girl glared, then focused back on Beaux.

"How long are you here?" The blonde asked, handing Beaux two lanyards with credentials.

"Four years, at least. I'm attending the Uni here." His Australian cadence made the girls sigh. "Here," he slipped the second lanyard over my head. "Ladies, I'll be seeing you."

The girls cooed.

"Man whore," I muttered as we walked away.

Beaux chuckled. "Jealous."

"Not likely. Disillusioned that women still think boobs are the only thing a man's interested in."

"They are great conversation starters."

I huffed. We walked back along the main corridor that had been sectioned off into dressing areas.

"How much farther?"

Beaux turned gracefully, never missing a step, and grabbed the gear I was carrying.

"We're in tent fourteen."

A few moments later, Beaux stepped through the cloth door and into a small makeshift room made up of tarp walls and no ceiling. There was a cot at the back of the room, two chairs, and if you looked up, you could see a closed circuit TV on the wall of the arena.

"What are we doing here?"

Beaux dumped his gear on the cot and then walked back over to me. I came up to his shoulders. I hadn't realized he was so much taller than A.J.

"Getting to know each other."

I craned my neck, wishing away the tingles his proximity produced. "So were you mad because I was making you late to play with your bulls, or were you genuinely concerned about my whereabouts?"

Beaux pushed back his black hat. Thick, corded muscles tightened as he folded his arms across his chest. "First, I don't *play* with bulls, I ride them. Second, I'm your Jack. I may not look like the duty-bound type, but I am."

My feet seemed to shuffle on their own.

"I didn't mean to offend you." I expected the hard line between his eyes to soften, a quirky smile to pull at his lips, but none of that happened. Instead, a vein pulled at the skin along his temple as he worked his jaw. There were things he wanted to say, but either he couldn't trust me to hear or would hurt me if he spewed.

"Yes, you did," Beaux finally said. With one hand, he pulled off his cowboy hat and the other swiped back the blonde locks he kept hidden from the world. "No worries. You lash out when you're hurt. It's in your file."

"There's a file on me?"

Beaux extended his hand to one of the empty chairs. I followed without thinking. How many more surprises could there be in my world?

"This is what I wanted to talk about. Hopefully, you'll agree. Most of the Jacks are of the opinion the less you ladies know, the safer you'll be."

"And you don't?"

"I think knowledge is power. The more you know, the easier my job will be."

I nodded, thoughts racing in my head. If there were files and the Jacks had access, that meant A.J. did, too. Also meant he was siding with the keep-'em-in-the-dark camp.

Beaux tapped my toe with his boot, getting my attention. "Spit it out, Sheila."

"A.J. knew about these files?"

"Right."

"Did you know you were my Jack when I met you?"

Beaux reached behind him, grabbed a bottle of water, and cracked it open. "Right."

"So when I asked you about the Kings?"

"Sheila, the Kings aren't here. They're in Malaga."

"Getting ready for the Royal Poker tournament?"

"Right."

"And despite being my Jack, A.J. is leaving, too. More secrets."

"That sounded more like a statement than a question." Beaux took a long swig of his water, his eyes never wavering from me. "I don't work like that. I think a team is stronger when the weakest link knows as much as the strongest."

"I'd be the weakest link in this scenario?"

Beaux tilted his head. "I want to know more about your powers, what you can do already. It might move you up in my weakest link chart."

I chuckled. "Why should I trust you?"

"Have I given you a reason not to?"

I felt my shoulders pull up. He hadn't given me a reason not to, but that didn't mean he wasn't just as good a heart player as A.J.

"What did you mean you loved someone you couldn't have either?" I changed the subject but stayed far away from the "fuck buddies" comment.

"Fell in love with a girl in Australia."

"The Midas protégé?"

"Right." Beaux polished the bottle of water and crushed the plastic in his hands like it was a paper napkin instead of a bottle. "I told A.J. you were more observant than he gave you credit for."

"You two have had chats about me?"

A sideways grin pulled at his lip, and the mischievous sparkle was back. I'd have to remember that was his fuckin' with you look.

"Just one. It was quickly followed by the keep-your-hands-off warning."

"Hmm." I leaned forward and signaled for the water behind him. Beaux cracked the cap and handed it to me. "You don't look like the adhering-to-warnings type."

That sideways grin danced across his face, giving me all the confirmation I needed. A.J. was leaving for Malaga. He was still keeping secrets from me. Given Beaux's triumphant little smirk and the small pull at my gut, I was in for my own thrill ride.

Nothing had changed.

"Malory," Beaux interrupted my thoughts. "She going to be a problem?"

"Shouldn't be. If I can keep her away from Warren Michaels."

Beaux lifted his eyebrow. "Who's Warren Michaels?"

"An asshole, but . . ." I thought long before finishing my statement. Was I really ready to fully trust the Aussie? "So this is where I start trusting you," I cautioned. "I think he's Dionysus's son. And he's our age."

I didn't know what kind of reaction I expected, but calm and cool wasn't it. Not from Beaux. He leaned forward, grabbed the legs of my chair, and brought me in between his legs. My heart raced despite my brain reminding me I had a boyfriend. He was a lying, no good, secret-keeping boyfriend, but my boyfriend nonetheless.

Beaux's breath trickled down my neck as he whispered in my ear, "Dionysus doesn't have any demigods."

"I'm only telling you what I heard," I whispered back.

"And where did you hear this?"

"In the iolite cave. He and two other Shadows were looking for the Shell of Clarity."

Beaux rested his forehead on mine. Seeing him exposed did something to me. Made me want to grab his hands and reassure him everything was going to be okay.

"You're going to give me a run for my money, aren't you, Cassandra?"

My heart kicked start at the sound of my name on his lips. It had no business being as giddy as it was, but for the first time, there was someone in my life who wanted to be a partner, not just a protector. And that was downright sexy.

"It'll be worth the ride," he muttered before his gaze caught mine. The soft skin of the tip of his nose rubbed up against the side of mine as a devilish grin spread across his face. I didn't need a college degree to know where his thoughts were.

"Get your mind out of my pants," I whispered.

Beaux gripped my hand, pulling it up to his lips and depositing a small kiss. Behind him, the curtain pulled open and the busty brunette from the registration booth deflated.

"You're in staging, Beaux," she purred, but there wasn't as much enthusiasm in her voice as there once was.

"Thanks, Sheila," Beaux said, but his eyes never left mine.

"Amber, actually. My name's Amber."

Beaux turned and leveled her with what had to be an orgasmic smile, because the girl perked right on up.

"Sorry, Amber. Sheila's just a friendly term we use in Australia."

Amber pulled the clipboard tight up under chest. "Maybe you could teach me some more Australian."

"That sounds spiffy." Beaux reached over and grabbed his lucky rope. "Who'm I riding tonight?"

Amber's giggle said she'd hoped it be her.

I rolled my eyes. Really, did he play this way with everyone or just girls that were dumber than toast?

With what little bit of brains she had left not in her vagina, Amber rustled through her papers while she clucked her tongue. "You're riding Revolution tonight." The giddy tone was vacant from Amber's voice. "I'm . . . I'm going to let you get your mind ready." She let the cloth fall back into place, and silence filled the small staging area.

The tick on Beaux's jaw was back. He was working his molars as he tightened up the rope on his saddle. A tenor of mumbles and curse words were barely audible, but they were there nonetheless.

"That sounds bad."

"We've got to redefine your idea of bad and fun, Cassie." Given the hell-yeah look in Beaux's eye, that cut on his lip was about to get company and my heart was in trouble.

SEVENTEEN

I WALKED BEAUX down the dorm's hallway, toward the Jacks' room. I hadn't been wrong about the cut getting some friends. Despite the *you're-a-chicken* taunts, I'd watched Beaux's ride from the staging area on the closed circuit TV. The announcers were just as enamored with Beaux as Amber the busty bimbo was. When the camera zoomed in on Beaux, I had to admit, I could see where the luck and charm came from. Muscles undulated under his skin, and when he smiled at the camera, my heart may have fluttered.

It was ridiculous, but the stupid organ really fluttered.

It fluttered and then filled with guilt. I didn't have too much time to wallow, because the moment the guilt made its way to my gut, the shoot opened and Beaux flew around on the back of a terrifying beast. Revolution bucked to the left, the right, reared up, slammed down, and then lifted its hind legs to send Beaux sailing through the air. I screamed as he crashed down to the floor of the arena. Three clowns rushed in, one stopped to check on Beaux. Nonchalantly, he picked up his black cowboy hat, dusted off his chaps, and waved to the crowd, all as if there wasn't a deadly side of beef wanting to avenge the invention of hamburgers.

"You're sure you don't want to go to the hospital?"

"This is nothing." Beaux smiled down at me, deepening the cut around his eye. "I'll wash it off, and we'll head out for dinner."

"You sure?" I questioned. His muscular arm, draped around my neck, made another attempt to pull me closer to him.

"You could have a concussion." I pressed. We stopped in front of his door, that mischievous smile pulled at the cut from earlier this morning.

"Come to think of it, I could use some help with my sponge bath," his Australian accent mixed with a slight Southern twang.

"Never mind, you're not concussed," I chuckled. "Where are your keys?"

His eyes glittered as he looked down at me.

"Front pocket." He waggled his eyebrows before adding, "Mind the flashlight, once you turn it on, it's hard to contain the light."

I giggled and slipped out from under Beaux's arm, steadying him as I let go. I was getting good at dodging the one-liners. By the end of the semester, I'd have ninja skills to combat his come-ons.

"I think you can handle finding your own keys and *flashlight* from here, cowboy." I turned to walk down the hall, but Beaux snagged the waistband of my skirt and pulled me back into him. The warmth of his body washed through me as he rested his chin on my shoulder, making parts of my body come to life. Parts of me that had no business becoming aware of anybody but A.J.

I shouldn't feel this.

Not for him.

I had a boyfriend, and Beaux was in love with another girl. This had disaster written all over it, which was probably why Midas thought it was such a damned good idea. Beaux spun me around, my hands splayed against his chest, but that didn't stop him from resting his forehead on mine. Every inch of the front of me pressed into every inch of him. I'm certain he could feel my heart pounding against his chest.

"Thanks for coming with me," he finally whispered. The scent of hard alcohol one of the rodeo clowns had given him after he stumbled out of the main arena still clung to his breath.

"I wasn't sure I had a choice." I watched the light in his eyes dull just a fraction and immediately wanted the words back. "You're welcome. I'm glad you got it out of your system."

The glimmer returned; so did the mischievous smile.

"Who says I've gotten you out of my system?"

My pulse kick-started.

"I was talking about the bull riding."

"Sheila, there's no difference between you and the bulls. You're both in my system and you're both deadly as sin. But I will admit, I'm looking forward to kissing you more than I am the bulls."

I stepped away from Beaux and turned so he could see how serious I was when I said, "Flirt with me all you want, but you and I will never happen. I love A.J."

Heat flushed his face a second before Beaux snagged my waistband again, pulling me into him, occupying every breathable space I could find. He towered over me, all the play gone from his eyes, his touch business like.

"We can play this game now, but in three years, the Gaming Commission and The Council are going to expect you to choose to rule or forget. And if you choose to rule, you'll have to take part in the consummation ceremony with your Jack. Midas will never let A.J. fulfill that role, and even if he does, I have it on good authority that The Council won't allow the House of Midas to contaminate the royal line. This is me giving you all the information, not hiding anything from you, because in three years, like me or not, I'm your chosen."

He leaned forward and kissed my forehead. Without pulling back, he spoke softly. "I can court you, make you fall head over heels in love with me, but you need to know that as much as you love A.J. and as much as I love my lady, this is our predestined path and the gods won't let us stray." He let go of me and stepped away. Beaux's glare punched a hole through me as he fished out his keys and then nodded for me to go. The air around me chilled. "A.J. will be here in an hour. We'll come and get you for dinner."

Beaux stood in the hallway until I slipped into my dorm room. He was wise to do so, because every instinct in me told me to get the hell out of Vegas.

I clicked the front door shut and then bolted the lock for good measure. The Pithos box in my bag seemed to grow heavier by the second, confirming the fact I was so screwed. We all were.

"Where've you been?" Gia asked from the kitchen.

"With Beaux." The tone in my voice frightened even me. "We had some things to sort out."

Gia came to my side, her hands felt like fire as she ran them up and down my arms. "You okay? You look like you've seen a ghost."

"Beaux took me to the Thomas and Mack Center. He rode a bull." I plastered on a smile and stepped out of Gia's embrace. "I think the shock of it all is wearing off."

Gia bit down on her lip. The telltale sign that she wasn't buying the poop I was shoveling. "We're thinking about going out tonight. Girls bonding and making bad decisions. You in?"

I nodded. "I have dinner with A.J. and Beaux at six. I'll be home by nine. That work?"

Gia closed the space between us and wrapped me up in her arms. "Something's got you spooked," she whispered.

"It's nothing." I stepped out of her embrace, not really sure if I was ready to share any of this. Not ready to tip my hand. I padded to our room and dropped my bag. I shot Gia a quick reassuring smile.

She didn't buy it.

As much as I hated Beaux's frank way of putting things, I'd learned more about my future from him in two days than I had in eight months with A.J. I wasn't ready to drop my panties and hand him my v-card in a consummation ceremony, but at least I knew what was going to be expected of me. So why did it feel like a noose was still around my neck and with each passing year, the slipknot was only going to get tighter?

I grabbed my shower kit, slipped into my robe, out the door, and padded my way down the hall into the showers. The drip from a showerhead echoed against the walls, the last drops of water trying to dissipate the fruity scent of a Royal's shower gel. White hexagon tiles ran the length of floor, disappearing into eight changing area stalls. I stepped into the third stall, closed the changing curtain, and turned on the water. In no time, steam billowed up from the shower stall. I slipped in and welcomed the warm water sluicing over me. I didn't know what it was about a shower, but I did some of my best thinking in here. And despite the creepy killer lurking in the quiet shower scenarios that seemed to be fighting for my attention, the common showers weren't so bad.

Not nearly as bad as the threat of a consummation ceremony.

I lathered up my hair. One more mythical meet-and-greet, and I was ready to get this semester started. I was inspecting the House of Hearts tomorrow and would probably smell like bull balls and alcohol for another month. Add to that the stench of waiting and anticipation mixed with the uncertainty of elixirs and battle powers. And don't even get me started on the whole consummation ceremony. I rinsed the shampoo out of my hair, grabbed my razor, and slung my leg up on the wall.

"Holy shit," my curse echoed in the shower. God, was the council going to watch us get freaky? I'd watched a documentary when Dad was researching a Mary Queen of Scots TV pilot. I'd been mortified for the girl. People had been allowed to peer in through open slits in the room and watch, like it was all part of the wedding. Here's your cake, toss the bouquet, now everyone follow us to the viewing room where you can watch the newlyweds get it on.

A shiver ran through me.

And if the council wouldn't allow A.J. and me—

What was that noise?

My thoughts trailed off as I strained to listen over the shower. My pulse hammered in my ears, making it even harder to listen for footsteps. I pushed down the fear crawling up my throat. Talked down the paranoia that screamed there was a knife-wielding psychopath on the other side of the curtain.

"Hello?" I called. I stuck my head out of the shower curtain, relieved to find at least no one standing in my changing area. I bit down on my lip, took a deep breath, and quickly finished shaving my other leg and armpits. My pulse picked up as my imagination ran wild. Knowing my luck, if someone was standing on the other side, it wouldn't be a Bella telling me I'm aca-awesome at singing in the shower.

Another noise echoed somewhere in the common bathroom. That was it. I turned the stream of water off and listened. My hand rested on the knob, ready to douse whoever was out there. A few seconds ticked by and I called out again, "Hello?"

Of course, no one answered. I twisted the shower back on, rinsed out the conditioner in my hair, slapped on the shower gel to clean my girly parts, and then quickly dried off. I pulled on my robe, wrapped my hair up in the towel, and pulled back the changing room shower curtain.

And there he was.

The bloodcurdling scream ripped from somewhere primal in me. I threw my shower kit at Isaac, but he smiled and dodged the flying toiletries. His hand clamped down over my mouth, lips close to my ear as he whispered, "Stop screaming, Cassandra. I'm not here to hurt you."

The room swayed, the edges of my vision blurring. This guy had balls that would make Revolution the Bull envious.

"Don't scream. Nod that you understand me."

I nodded.

His grip on the skin around my mouth loosened. My anti-kidnapping instructor had said people think of the most random things when they were in danger. I had to agree. I couldn't help but think again about how when every other Shadow touched me, I had glimpses of their past, but not Isaac. There was nothing with Isaac. No glimpses. Even his touch was surprisingly warmer than the others.

"Good girl," Isaac patted my shoulders, like he was just as nervous to be here as I was.

"What are you doing?" I asked.

"I know you were at the cave with A.J."

I started to object, but Isaac cut me off with a look.

"You know what they're looking for?" he asked.

I nodded.

"Tell me you have it somewhere safe."

"You're a damn fool if you think I'm telling you anything."

"There's my girl." A smile broke across Isaac's face. He and A.J. may not have been twins, but when they smiled, there was no doubting they were family. "Blondie is planning something. He's desperate to get in his dad's good graces."

"And what does that mean for you?" I didn't wait for Isaac's answer; there were more important things I need to confirm. "Warren is Dionysus's son, right?"

Isaac stepped back. "You know Wine Cooler?"

I chuckled despite myself. I pulled the edges of my robe closer. "Yeah, he and Malory had a run-in our sophomore year. He punched her v-card, she has every intention of punching him back."

This time, Isaac chuckled.

"Why are you telling me this? Why are you here?" I asked.

"I'm hoping you learn from your mistakes, Cassie. Warren's going after the four queens' powers."

"I heard that, too."

"Yeah, well, they've already got a piece of Livi, I'm not sure I could hold it together if they got all of her." He ran a hand through his hair. Out of control wasn't a look Isaac wore well. When his eyes locked back on me, he was a man on fire. "Livi's power might be at the top of the Eiffel Tower."

"How do you know that?"

"The Queens' minds are wiped, not the Shadows'. Dionysus has spies everywhere. He's been tracking the places the Queens visit for the last six generations. You all are getting pretty damn repetitive on where you hide your elixirs."

The knowledge that Isaac knew about the elixir was disturbing. The revelation that Dionysus had been tracking the Queens for years was downright unnerving. The fact that Isaac was freely sharing this information stripped away every preconceived notion I'd had of the boy.

"What about the others?"

Ice-cold eyes met mine as he said, "I don't give a fuck about the others. You keep Livi safe, and I'll do my best to keep the others occupied. Who knows? Maybe I'll even drop a line on where your clue is."

The main door to the bathrooms opened. Isaac clamped his hand down over my mouth and pushed me back into the changing room. We both listened to the soft muted footsteps coming farther into the bathroom.

"Cass?" Olivia called out.

Isaac's eyes warmed at the sound of her voice.

"Yeah?"

"You fall in?" Olivia's voice stopped on the other side of the shower curtain.

"Ha! No. Just drying off. Finishing up."

Olivia's toes peeked under the changing room curtain. Isaac stepped into the shower and slowly slid the curtain shut.

I pulled the changing curtain back and put on my best smile. I don't know why I was protecting the Shadow bastard in the shower stall. Maybe I was protecting Olivia. Maybe I was just curious as all hell as to why Isaac would risk certain banishment if he were caught on the royal level of the dorm rooms. Whatever it was, I picked up my spilled toiletries and walked past Olivia. The warm tingle shot up my back and I hoped she wouldn't ask me why I was willing her to come with me.

"Why you so jumpy, Cass?" She asked.

I pulled open the bathroom door and stepped into the hall.

"You're gonna have to give me a few days to get comfortable with the consummation ceremony. I'm still a little grossed out by the whole thing."

"The what?" Olivia asked.

"The consummation ceremony." I repeated.

"What the hell is that?"

I stopped. Letting the moment that I finally knew something my best friend didn't sink in.

"Oh, this is precious." I held onto the bathroom door. "I may need to hold onto this gem of information through dinner."

Olivia rocked back on her heels and assumed her bitch-tell-me-now stance.

"Nope." I pointed to her scrunched up face. "I'm not telling, you're gonna have to buy me at least two drinks tonight."

My friend's stance unwillingly loosened. I guess my amusement was as telling as her posture. Neither of us was going to budge, and since I held all the cards, that meant the draw went to me. I guess some of that poker nonsense had started to pay off.

"You're gonna roll with us tonight after we meet our Houses?" Olivia asked.

"I have dinner with A.J. and Beaux, but after . . ." My pulse skyrocketed when she stepped into the changing stall Isaac was still in. "What are you doing?" I snapped.

Olivia bent down.

Adrenaline dumped into my system. She was going to see Isaac's feet. There was no way I could explain how this looked.

Olivia stood and walked toward me. "You dropped your bra, trust me, with the spares running around, you don't want to leave this out and about."

She tossed it at me.

"Seriously, Cass, you're gonna need to take the drama level down just a tad."

My body slouched up against the bathroom wall. I'd be glad to take the drama down a tad, if there wasn't a Shadow stalking me in the showers.

Isaac leaned his head out of the stall, and mouthed, *Thank you.*

Fabulous. Shadows were thanking me and Jacks were taking odds on who would bed me. No wonder my mother hid me in Hollywood.

EIGHTEEN

AWKWARD, UNCOMFORTABLE, PAINFULLY quiet were only three of the tame words that were floating around my head as A.J., Beaux, and I sat at Serrano's fine Spanish dining in the Monte Carlo hotel.

No one had uttered a word since we left the dorms twenty minutes ago. There was a brief scuffle that ended into a best two-out-of-three roshambo tournament over who would drive. Given Beaux's bench-seat, barely-running truck, I was rooting for A.J.

The odds were not in my favor.

Beaux won.

And for ten minutes, I was sandwiched between the sleek and sophisticated heir to the House of Midas and the kick-ass, pressed-jeans-were-considered-dressy spare from the House of Clubs.

It was a wonder my heart hadn't all out failed.

My two Jacks, my two protectors—I pushed away the consummation ceremony image—were two of the hottest looking men on the planet. And they couldn't have been any more different.

We finished placing our order. Pushed past the small debate about ordering for a woman to be downright demeaning, Beaux's take on women's lib vs. the sign of a sophisticated gentleman, A.J.'s take on chivalry.

"So," I attempted to break the awkward silence, "How do we do this?"

"Seems pretty clear to me." Beaux shifted in his seat, the denim covering his long legs brushed against the skin of my calf, releasing an unwanted flutter in my stomach. "A.J.'s headed off to Malaga in two weeks, I'll be the on-call Jack once you find your elixir."

A.J. squared his shoulders and took a sip of water. His eyes held onto mine over the rim of his glass and stayed fixed as he purposefully placed the stemware back in the appropriate spot at the top of his setting.

Everything in its place.

Everything within his reach and his control.

And the uncomfortable, gut-churning feeling that I was being handled just like the flatware.

"You went to a rodeo today?" A.J. asked, completely ignoring Beaux's statement . . . and my question.

"I did." Steel poured down my spine. I grabbed a piece of the bread, noting the wave of irritation wash over A.J.'s flawlessly composed face. "Watched Beaux fly through the air like a rag doll."

The corner of A.J.'s lip twitched into a faint grin. It was gone as quickly as it came. A.J. fished something out from his pocket. A second later, a new cellphone sat on my dinner napkin.

"I need to know where you are." He tapped the shiny screen.

It was an ongoing debate between us. I refused to replace the cellphone destroyed in the crash that killed my adopted parents on New Year's Eve. The night they were murdered. I waited for the wave of guilt to sweep over me. To pull at the small areas of my heart I'd managed to haphazardly knit back together. But the strings held back the guilt, probably strengthened by the indignation my boyfriend thought he could make a demand, tap a device, and I'd willingly fall in line. This was the first time A.J. had taken the request to a demand with a phone exclamation point. And it piqued a fury in me that nobody should want to see.

A.J. leveled me with a look.

"I don't want a phone." I placed my hand over his and wiggled my fingers. "And you don't need a phone to find me." The restaurant light bounced off the ruby heart ring that housed a secret GPS transmitter. "All you have to do is be interested."

"Clearly, I'm missing something." Beaux rubbed his mile-long leg against mine again.

I felt for the guy. Tough enough to be a spare, but then demoted to a Jack. I crossed my legs, severing the unwanted tingle of excitement rocketing through my rebellious nerves when he touched me. I gave him mad props for attempting to keep up.

A.J and I may have only known each other for eight months, but there was so much history between us.

So many secrets.

It didn't seem fair to keep Beaux in the dark. And I refused to allow Beaux to even think I was this easy to order around. I could tell the moment A.J. knew I was going to air it all out there. His jaw clinched, his eyebrows pinched together, and his once luscious, kissable lips turned pencil thin. The flash of caution in his eye not to do what I was about to only encouraged me.

With a defiant toss of my hair, I turned and smiled at Beaux. "My ring has a GPS locator in it. I found that out when I went to California in the spring. I tend to do things that will drive you crazy. I don't listen to rules. And I don't like being handled." I leaned forward, despite all my etiquette lessons, and rested my elbows on the table. I drew my line in the sand with a quick dismissive glance at the iPhone.

"And you don't like mobiles," Beaux added. His amused grin was only diminished by the shadow his cowboy hat cast. "Anything you want to add, mate?"

A.J. worked his jaw, the muscle running down his neck throbbing like it wanted to leap out and strangle us both.

"I'm not your mate." A.J.'s voice was low and full of anger. He leaned back in his chair, arms crossed on his chest. "You laugh now, Beaux, but you and I know not all things end well because we intend them to. They end well because the hard decisions are made . . . and enforced."

Beaux shifted in his seat. A flash of ire shot across the Australian cowboy's eyes, so hot it could have set off the fire alarm. A.J. always had a way of putting someone in their place. Now that that placement was directed at me, it sucked. The china on the table clattered as Beaux's elbows landed hard. We earned a warning look from the couple next to us, as well as A.J.

"Okay, okay." I placed hands on both boys. "Clearly, A.J. and I aren't the only two with history sitting at this table." I shot A.J. a warning glance that went unacknowledged.

"This is never going to work," A.J. protested.

I squeezed his forearm, hoping to calm him down. "It has to," I whispered. Despite all the pent-up hostility I held toward A.J., I still loved him. I still knew that if this didn't work, Midas would make his life a living hell if he or the gods didn't kill him first. A.J. had linked his life to mine the night he stood on the treaty line and declared me his protected. I had to remember: up until that moment, I had been a dead girl.

"Fine," Beaux resigned. "I'll go first. Yes, A.J. and I have history. I met the bastard . . . fine, I met the boy"—Beaux acknowledged my cautionary nod—"at the Reno retreat."

"Sounds like a ton of *fun* things happened at that retreat," I added, thinking back to Helen's admission about her and A.J. in Reno.

"You don't know the half of it, Sheila."

"Don't call her that," A.J.'s voice was low and full of danger.

Beaux showed his palms. "After Helen shoved her tongue down your man's throat over there, he needed to get the taste gone. He did that with the Midas protégé from Australia."

My head snapped so fast toward A.J., I was surprised I didn't have whiplash. "You kissed his girlfriend?"

"He wishes."

"He wishes what, A.J.?" I questioned.

"He wishes Jezebel was his girlfriend." The thick, unsteady threat leaving my boyfriend's mouth made me shudder. A.J.'s gaze settled on Beaux, narrow slits of pure blue anger with one intent: destroying Beaux. "You're a spare, which means you're brought out by your House to show there's a contingency plan should your brother fail to accept his birthright."

"A.J.," I cautioned.

"The truth is, you have never belonged in this world and you never will," A.J. hissed. "I may have kissed Jezebel, but I at least had the right to." Horror swept across my boyfriend's face the moment the words left his lips. A cold, empty weight settled in my stomach. The world faded away. A.J.'s composed look quickly faltered and turned remorseful, almost apologetic, before disappearing completely from my sight.

"What do you mean you had the right to?" I whispered. Call it sixth sense or girl intuition. Call it that hocus-pocus moment when you know your world is about to turn completely fucked up.

A.J. refused to look at me. Shoulders sagged under the weight of my stare. I knew what he meant. I just needed to hear the words. The words that would shred my heart.

"Answer me," I quietly demanded. A welcome flush of heat raced up my spine. The warm, intoxicating feel of the Balanter power poured into my bloodstream. This time, it was different. This time, I welcomed the surge of heat. Knew exactly what would happen if I didn't reign it in . . . and I didn't care. I didn't care if I hurt him. Part of me hoped there was more than just a mark on him. I hope it scored a long-lasting fissure in his heart.

I was done with his lies.

A.J. raised his head. His bewilderment quickly dissolved into the glazy look of compliance. Beaux shifted in his seat, one elbow on the table, the other playing with the dimple in his chin, suspended somewhere between awe and alarm.

"What did you mean you had the right?" My calm, cruel tone frightened even me. But this was my chance. My chance to know every secret he'd kept from me. Uncover every lie, mistruth. Finally put our relationship on a level field of certainty.

"Jezebel. Is. My. Match." The words ripped from his lips syllable by syllable.

The world spun. Gravity no longer played a factor in my life. I fell helplessly through time and space even though my body sat rigid at the four-star restaurant, held in place only by the weight of betrayal that hung around my heart. I swallowed hard over the lump in my throat.

This was it.

This was the defining moment where I could push forward, break the man, and make him mine or let him go. Instead, his admission and the apprehensive look on Beaux's face were like a violent look into a future where I ruled with fear and demand. And I wanted nothing to do with that life.

I stood—my heart pounded in my ears, its shards tinkling to the floor of my soul—and released A.J.

I walked out of the restaurant as his hand flew out to stop me. Fortunately, it took him longer to find his words. By the time I heard him call out my name, I was already commanding the Shadow valet to find me a cab.

The rush of heat was empowering. I could totally get used to ruling this way.

A thick hand wrapped around my arm, stopping my progress to the cab. The surge of heat was electric, and the thickset fingers quickly released me. I turned on my own accord, on my terms.

"Beaux?"

"You can burn people, too?" He shook out his hand like he'd touched a hot pan or . . . a hot me.

"No," I felt the surge recede, the heat wane. "That was a first."

Beaux stepped into my space. Not afraid, not cautious, but that was him. He rode bulls for fun and poked at A.J.'s sore spots for pleasure. He was the one I should be wary of, but instead, his audacity encouraged me to be bolder, tougher. He made me want to demand more for myself.

Beaux shoved the iPhone into my hand. "I know you have a locator ring, which is bloody awesome, but I need to be able to find you. So carry this." He held up a finger, cutting me off. "I'll text you my number so you can answer only my calls." He crossed his arms across the widest part of his chest and broadened his stance like he was preparing for the physical assault of my protests.

"Fine"—I slipped the phone into my purse—"but you're not coming with me."

Beaux held open the door and helped me climb in. He told the driver the address to the Dayton complex and hesitated a moment.

"I know this was a rough day for you." He searched for something over the roof of the cab. "If you're going out tonight, go to ASHA. At least I'll know you and the others will be looked after." He spoke in code, which meant the cab driver was a mortal, but that's not what threw me. He was giving me permission to go out.

"You're a Royal, Cassandra, not a child. Although I can see how the two could be confused." A rich chuckle rippled the muscles through his black t-shirt. His green eyes caught mine. "I'll give you as much freedom as possible. But that means you treat it with respect. Don't lose your temper. The four of you together are going to draw attention. You're all too fucking beautiful not to, and that's before you throw in the mysterious."

I knew he wanted to say mythological but couldn't. The cab driver was already watching us too intently by way of the rearview mirror. Probably trying to figure out what royal family I came from or which tabloid he could tip off.

I folded my hands in my lap, controlling the urge to *encourage* the cabby to mind his own business. "Understood," I answered.

He smiled, the skin pulling at the cut on his lip. "We'll try this come-to-god moment tomorrow at brunch." Beaux shut the door on my protest and slapped the back of the cab as it pulled out.

I grabbed the phone out of my purse, the taste of rebellion sweet on my lips, and dialed Gia's number.

"Hey, it's me. Get the girls ready. We're going out tonight."

NINETEEN

THREE GIRLS SAT primped and ready to paint Las Vegas red by the time I walked in our dorm room. Helen was in black leather pants with a freshly painted-on sheen to them. A black see-through blouse covered a silver-sequined bra. Gia was in a red mini dress that barely covered her girly parts and devil-red stilettos. A welcome rush of warmth that had nothing to do with my powers as the Balanter washed through me.

I fought back the tears, fought back the urge to be that girl who curls up and rocks herself into oblivion hoping something will change without being willing to change it herself.

Olivia stood, pulling down her animal print, form-fitting dress. Concern hung between the crinkled skin of her eyebrows. "I texted Malory. She'll be here in five."

My eyes welled up.

"Don't get weepy on me. Whatever it is, we're going to need all that pissed off estrogen flowing freely tonight."

"Hell yeah we are. None of us knew about a consummation ceremony." Helen crossed her legs, her silver stilettos bouncing rays of light at the window like a warning beacon to the world to prepare. "Although I have a feeling this has nothing to do with ceremonies and everything to do with boys who act like little dictator shites."

I strangled a giggle, afraid to trust my voice, and headed to my bedroom. On my bed were a pair of black leather pants, a copper tube top, and matching copper stilettos. None of them was mine, but I knew who each piece belonged to. I could see why these next four years were going to be so damn important. I'd known some of these girls a day, a few months, but they all acted like they'd known about me our whole lives. In some way, they had. I was a face to an entity they knew they would love like a sister. Being virtually alone my entire life, I didn't know how to process that blind friendship.

I slipped off my dress and started getting ready.

I could see why Cara had been so mad at being demoted to a spare. With each passing day, each passing challenge, the opportunity for me to deny my birthright was becoming less likely. And Cara's chance to rule was fading. Even if I did opt to forget this world on my twenty-first birthday, my little sister would have missed out on all of this. I slipped into the leather pants. She would have forfeited all these moments that would bond me and the other three queens for life.

A small knock on the door shook me from my train of thought.

"If that's you, Olivia, I'm going to throttle your neck."

The door opened and Helen poked her head in.

"It's me. Just checking to see if the pants fit."

I slipped on the tube top and fished out a bra that would never go with the outfit. "Do me a favor?" I asked. "Don't knock. Just walk in, okay?"

Helen nodded and started to close the door.

"Helen," I called out. "Could you help me do my makeup?"

A smile blossomed across her face and reached her eyes, silver irises gleaming with delight.

"You sure?" she asked.

"Yeah, I tend to need all the help I can get in the fancy girl area." I sat down on the bed and fastened on a borrowed stiletto. "Whose are these?"

"Gia's. I'm going to get my kit," Helen said, quickly leaving the room before I changed my mind.

"Gia," I called out.

My best friend and roommate sauntered into the room. "Yeah?"

"You know what happened to the last pair of stilettos I borrowed, right?"

"Yep, but those were Manolo Blahniks. *These* are Jimmy Choo. There's a difference." She crossed her arms, daring me to say there wasn't. It was an ongoing debate between her and Malory.

"Don't forget your bracelet," Gia shook her wrist. The tweed bracelet with the V and the New Year's Eve that changed my life jingled.

By the time Helen was done with my makeup, Malory was in the front room with shots of Fireball poured. Helen handed me a shot glass as Olivia said, "Here's to starting fires and breaking hearts." Olivia didn't wait for approval or rebuttal; she tipped her head back and emptied the shot of amber liquid into her mouth.

"Hear, hear." Gia raised her own glass, then tossed back the amber liquid.

Helen threw back her glass, eyes pinched tight for a second, but her smiled deepened. "Bugger, that's good."

Malory clinked her glass to mine. "To breaking hearts."

"Long live the heartbreakers." I smiled and swallowed the amber liquid. Cinnamon exploded on my taste buds, the cool sensation of alcohol warmed the path it made down my throat, picking up heat. The cinnamon flavor intensified, chasing after the alcohol until they collided in my stomach, warming me from the inside out in the most delicious way.

"It's like a melted hot tamale!" I squealed.

"First shot?" Helen questioned, pouring another round.

"I'm not twenty-one," I answered.

"No . . ." Olivia took the shot glass from Helen and handed it to me. "But we're Royals, the rules don't apply." The spark in her eye told me she believed every word she was saying. An uncomfortable silence fell across the room. I knew they were all wondering what happened at dinner. I just . . . I just couldn't admit it yet. All of the lies A.J. told weren't because he was protecting me. They were because I was the other woman. My throat thickened. I was his dirty secret.

♥

THE CAB DROPPED us off in front of The Plaza Hotel on Fremont Street. We walked past the line to get into ASHA. A small man dressed in a safari jacket with a red sash and khaki tweed pants emptied the elevator and allowed us to enter.

I knew him.

"Hi, Jay," I quickly waved.

"Your Highnesses. Here are your VIP charms. I've alerted Omar to your arrival. You met him last time, Princess Cassandra."

"Princess," Malory giggled under her breath.

"You're here as a guest." Jay leveled Malory with a cautionary glare. "Any disrespect to the crowns will not be allowed."

"Whatever," Malory muttered.

Jay grabbed Malory's wrist, his grip so tight, you could see the lack of blood flow immediately turn Mal's hand pale.

"The Royals may allow you in their presence, but disrespect by a mortal will not be tolerated. The harshest of repercussions will be administered."

I stepped forward, my fingers carefully covering his wrist. "Jay." His eyes went glossy, and I searched for the warm sensation that usually accompanied my power of persuasion. The sensual current trickled through my body. "She's my friend. She meant nothing of it."

Jay's grip loosened but didn't let go. The boy was loyal to the last breath.

"She won't disrespect us again, will you, Malory?'

Mal shook her head, fear widening her eyes to the point where they looked like they were going to pop out of her head.

Jay finally released his grip, clarity rushing back into his brown eyes. He pulled at his jacket, hit the top floor button, and bowed before the elevator shut.

"Is that what I bloody looked like?" Helen whispered to Gia.

"Worse," Olivia answered. "A whole hell of a lot worse."

I couldn't turn around to face them. Either I was a freak who couldn't control her powers or I was a secret who couldn't see the light of day. Either way, it was clear—I didn't belong here. I never would.

I jumped as warm arms wrapped around my shoulders.

"You've been practicing?" Olivia whispered.

I shook my head.

I hadn't.

All of this was coming naturally to me. Who knew what kind of monster I would be when I claimed my House's elixir? What monster would I become when I graduated? Maybe Midas and Dionysus were right; maybe it would be better—

"I know where your head is wandering off to, Cass." Olivia interrupted my thoughts. "You belong here. You belong with us."

I swallowed hard over the lump in my throat. It was one thing to wish you belonged somewhere; it was an entirely different thing to know you never would. I caught Mal's reflection in the stainless steel doors. That's what the Queens would never understand. They were all expected and welcomed. I was merely the genetic freak who happened to trigger Poseidon's curse. Everyone else would always suffer the consequences of my existence.

The doors pulled back and we were quickly ushered into ASHA. The tempting floral scent of the club rushed out to greet us, along with the Punjabi warrior I'd met the last time I'd been here. Light glinted off his scimitar as he hurried toward us. I didn't think it was possible, but the dude was even bigger, taller, and scarier than before. He said nothing, just clicked his heels and bowed ever so slightly before turning and carving out a path through the sea of people.

"Holy shite," Helen remarked over the music.

No one answered.

My heart bounced off my rib cage, quickly picking up the beat of the music.

We followed in the wake of the giant as people stopped to see who we were. Bright blue lights shot straight to the ceiling, but where there had been levels of seating before, now cages hung from the ceiling, rotating above the dance floor. A massive LED screen crawled up the length of one wall, forty feet tall and spotlighting everyone on the dance floor.

The Punjabi warrior stopped at the center of the floor as the middle cage dropped to the ground.

"I'm not going in that," Helen smarted off.

"Still afraid of heights?" Olivia asked.

"Among other things," Helen said, but I noticed the subtle look my way. I'd screwed up so bad. We were supposed to be bonding, giving facials, sneaking sweets, and having late night swoon sessions over boys we weren't allowed to be with.

The Punjabi clapped his hands, and somehow over music that already had us swaying to the beat, four men with red ropes and posts came and sectioned off the area surrounding the cage. The warrior stepped forward and opened the cage, allowing us to step in.

The music dulled as we stepped through the glass door. Plush purple seats circled the sphere that could easily hold twelve people. A small see-through table sat in the middle.

"Is this more suitable, Princess Helen?" The warrior asked with a thick Arabic accent.

Helen, speechless for the first time since I met her, nodded.

"The glass is tempered for sound. The phone will connect you with your personal attendant. The guards will make sure your privacy is maintained."

I looked over my shoulder; people already gawked, pointed. It was everything my parents had tried to avoid. "Our own glass house," I murmured.

"I can make other arrangements, Princess Cassandra," The warrior remarked.

Heat flushed my face. All eyes, inside and out, were now on me. I shook my head. "No, we're fine."

The warrior bowed again and held open the glass and iron door.

"You alright, Cass?" Gia asked.

The itch to run and hide, to sneak into the shadows of anonymity, begged me to say no, but I was here and the excitement that lit up my friend's faces— the newness of it all—made me sink back into the seat. Whatever issues I had tonight about my love life were going to have to be solved another time. The Queens had bigger problems. We were in a gilded cage and my friends were all so willing to be locked up.

TWENTY

MOM WAS RIGHT about one thing: mornings on this balcony were going to be amazing. A cool desert wind snuck down the collar of my sweatshirt. Rich hazelnut coffee filled my nose. It wouldn't surprise me if my roommates slept well into the afternoon. We'd stumbled into bed around four in the morning. Gia had started snoring before her golden halo of hair hit the pillow. With the aid of blackout curtains, our room was still pitch black when I'd finally given up on sleep at six. Too many things swirled in my mind. Mom, my sister, finding the elixir, Beaux, and . . . A.J. With all these people around claiming to love me, even my sister in her own way, I still had never felt so alone.

"Mind if I join?" Olivia asked. Her black hair was piled up on her head in a messy bun. Emerald eyes searching for an answer as she leaned in the doorjamb, steam billowed from her coffee cup.

"Did I wake you?"

"Never went to sleep." Olivia nodded to the seat next to me.

I nodded.

"I kept waiting for you to spill."

"Spill?" I pulled a sip of coffee through my teeth. I knew what she was talking about.

"Our impromptu girl bonding night. 'Starting fires and breaking hearts?'"

So why do I get the feeling the only broken heart that happened last night was yours?" Olivia folded her tan legs up under her and snuggled into the chair. It wasn't cold, but when the wind hit just right, it seemed to go right through you, chill you to your core, until the sun warmed you up.

"It doesn't matter."

"Cass, we may not have grown up together. Lord knows we don't do the bonding over makeup or clothes thing, but we're family. You're my cousin. You're my blood. What the fuck's going on?"

I swallowed the answer. It hurt too much to think about anything, even the good things in my life. Olivia nudged my slipper with hers.

"It'll only fester and grow, Cass."

"I know. I'm just not ready to . . ."

"Did Beaux do something? Did he try?"

This time, I did laugh. "Nah, Beaux's been great. The only one to be upfront with me."

The soft lines of my cousin's face hardened. "You saying I haven't been?"

"No," I set my cup on the table and tried to zip my sweatshirt up over my head and transport myself to a simpler time. "What do you know about a girl named Jezebel, the Midas protégé from Australia?"

The blank look on Olivia's face said she didn't know who I was talking about. She could play poker with anyone, just not me. I leaned forward, cradling my chin in my hands. "A.J. is suited."

Olivia's face pinched up, then lost all expression, only to pinch up again.

"Nah, House of Midas is *never* suited."

I snorted. "A.J. is."

"To you," Olivia added.

I shook my head. The reality setting in that my boyfriend (could I still call him that?) was already promised to someone else.

The morning sounds of wind whistling through trees and the quad filled up the silence.

Olivia pulled in a big breath, one that spoke to the level of crapness I'd just dumped in her lap. "Cass, you still have A.J. I see how he looks at you. He loves you. Despite fate, you have his heart. So, what girl are you going to be?"

I shrugged my shoulders.

"You've got two choices: You can be the girl who begs Jolene to not take her man, or you can be the girl in the song 'Jezebel' and tell the Australian protégé that you're going to fight for love. It's up to you."

"Did you just use old country songs to sum up my love life choices?"

"Don't knock the cowboys. They know their shit when it comes to love." Olivia grabbed her cup of coffee. "Clearly we should be piping those twangy tunes into Yayati's cave; he's seven ways of screwed up when it comes to sorting."

"You can say that again." Helen's voice drifted out onto the balcony. "He's bloody mad."

"Why, don't you like Hondo?" Olivia asked.

Helen's face contorted like she was sucking on a three-day-old lemon. "Hell no." She slipped out onto the balcony, sank down to the floor, and leaned against the metal railing. My heart flopped at the blind trust she had that those rails weren't going to give way. "Can you keep a secret?"

Olivia and I nodded.

"I lied. I told my mother what she wanted to hear." She looked away, searching for something. "When I was sixteen, I crushed hard for Hondo. He wasn't ranked very high, but he was cute . . . from a distance. When Yayati said I wasn't suited, I figured it was his way of saying 'you pick.'" A crooked smile pulled at her lips, but there was something else there.

Pain.

"What?" Olivia asked.

"I'm not suited."

I wanted to pick her up and squeeze the lemon curry out of her, but something inside me told me not being suited was not only out of the ordinary, it was downright damning.

Olivia leaned forward, her hand rested on Helen's knee. "You have to tell someone."

"Why?" I bit back for Helen. "Why's it anybody's business?"

"Cass," Olivia cautioned.

"Hear me out. What if Yayati is trying to give us the freedom to choose our partners? What if, after all these years, he's figured out that the Queens aren't just cattle to be mated?"

"That'd be fine," Olivia leveled me with a look. "If you and Gia and I hadn't been suited."

Helen's shoulders slipped.

"It doesn't have to be this way." I could hear the plea in my voice.

So could Olivia.

"Before the Kings come on campus, we can change things," I continued. "'We're royals, the rules don't apply to us.' Or was that all BS?"

Olivia sank into her chair. Coffee cup up to her mouth and then back onto the table. "There are some rules you can change, some rules you can bend, and then there are the rules you don't dare break." She grabbed my hands, urgency coursed through her veins and into mine. "Cass, I'm all for change, but there are serious consequences for the actions you're proposing."

"From whom?"

"From the gods themselves," Olivia's voice was firm. "We're royals, but we rank very low on the mythical pecking chart. We're here to protect the humans from the Shadows. No more, no less. But more importantly, we're here to do the gods' bidding."

"Then where does that leave me?" Helen asked.

It was a good question. One I wanted to know the answer to as well. Because just like Helen, I wasn't suited for this world, either.

♥

AFTER BREAKFAST, GIA was in the kitchen cleaning up Olivia's cooking mess. Helen was in the shower and Olivia was scowling at her computer. I hung my feet off the back of the couch and let my head hang from the seat cushion.

"What are you doing?" Olivia peered over the lid of her computer.

"This is my optimum thinking position."

"Who's got you optimizing your position?"

"Not who, what." I started twirling a small piece of hair around my forefinger. "I have no idea how I'm going to balance everything and Queen Training for Dummies."

"That's not the name of our course," Olivia chuckled.

"I may have altered it to fit my skillset. But seriously, there's QTD, my general education courses, hunting down elixirs, and the boyfriend/Jack balancing act, which let's be honest, I'm already failing. I guess I'm feeling a little . . ."

"Overwhelmed?" Gia offered.

"Yeah." Truth was, I may not have known how I was going to balance everything, but I sure knew where I was going to start. Thanks to Gia, I had the perfect opening to track down Olivia's elixir. "Why are you banging away on the computer? Are ya hunting down elixir clues? Ooh!"—I kicked my feet—"Tell me what happened last night at the Council Chambers."

Olivia shut the lid to her laptop, but I didn't miss the way her gaze darted to Gia's. Or how Gia quickly focused her cleaning on an already polished piece of granite.

"I was practicing," Olivia offered.

"Is there a Queen app you're not sharing?"

"No. I was playing poker."

"High roller alert," I chided.

"No." Olivia rolled her eyes. "But you should probably kick your practice sessions up. As heirs, we have to be able to step in for the Royal Tournament."

"Ahh, the Royal Poker Tournament." Mom had started an account for me on the R.P.T. site. There were almost a hundred thousand users already on. The House of Midas regulated the site, and the Four Houses delegated the money to charity. Mom said my grandmother was the one who'd come up with the idea. It was one of the current queens' first contributions to society. The gods signed off, and thus the Royal Poker Tournament site was born.

Olivia heard the sarcasm in my voice and tossed a pillow at me. "You've been practicing, yes?"

Helen walked in the front door in a robe and towel drying her hair. "Practicing Poker? Every chance I get."

"I was asking Cassie." Olivia nodded my direction.

"Sort of. I don't really like poker. I don't get it."

The room fell silent.

"What?" I asked, spinning myself right side up. Olivia glanced over my shoulder, and I felt two pairs of eyes heating the back of my neck.

"Cass, don't let that out, okay?" Gia's tone was different from her normally light and airy voice and knotted my stomach.

I shifted in my seat. "Why?"

Gia let loose a big sigh, which could've been how Helen treated this place like her own castle, but it was likely directed at me. "Cass, we love you, and we will always be like sisters, but we represent different Houses; we're your opponents."

"And you'd let a stupid game come between our friendship?"

"It's not a stupid game, Cassie." Gia leaned on the granite kitchen countertop, her washrag flung over her shoulder. "When you win the tournament, you control the fate of another House. Most of the time, it's just for material things, hotels, holdings, etc., but it's not unheard of for one House to demand more."

I didn't want to think about the "more" part of that warning.

Helen spoke up. "Cassie, just keep those things to yourself. I don't even tell my spare my faults."

"That's a lonely place, Helen." I scanned the room, looking for backup, but only found the others agreeing with Helen.

"I'm totally changing the subject. I don't want us to worry about things that are four years in the future." Gia slapped the counter. "I'm going to finish the kitchen, and Olivia, tell her what we found in the chambers. We need something fun to do today."

Olivia took Gia's cue; her eyes shimmered like she'd finally broken into a lock that had perplexed her for years. A rush of excitement let a smile loose.

"Oh, God. You didn't give her the normal chamber tour, did you?"

Olivia shook her head.

Helen scooted past Olivia before collapsing next to me on the couch. "You were right, Gia." Helen flipped over, hanging to the back of the cushions. "The girl knows her cousin. I do believe that's an evening at Club ASHA, your treat."

I ignored the side bet at my expense and kept my focus on Olivia. Whatever she'd found had to be really good not to be chiming in.

"What did you do, Olivia?" I whispered.

"I found something."

My heart flopped in my chest. We'd been looking for a few things this summer that would make my cousin sport a Cheshire cat grin, but I was banking on the one nearest to my heart.

I stole a quick peek at the two other queens arguing the terms of their wager before looking back at my cousin. "My dad?"

Olivia nodded, inching closer toward me. Double-checking we were still having a private discussion, she fished out a folded up piece of paper. "He's still alive, Cass. This was in Midas's private study."

"How do you know it was a private study?"

She smiled. "The lock I picked screamed stay out, but it was the name plate and the safe I found this in that confirmed it. Cass, he's got individual lock boxes inside a floor safe, tucked away behind a near impenetrable locked door in the council's chambers. Whatever else is in there, it's huge."

"Then won't he miss this?" I held up the paper.

"He also had a photocopier." She smiled.

All of a sudden the paper she'd handed me seemed heavier, more important. I carefully unfolded it. At the top of the page were dates, but it was the grainy black and white picture that caught my attention. His hair was buzzed short, in a military cut. In a sea of people, he stood out like an island. He wore black pants and a black coat, and despite the bulk of the coat, I could tell he was a muscular man . . . or had been. I focused on the people behind him. One girl was clear enough that I could see her crying. The sign she held. I pulled the picture in closer.

"Rest in Peace, Julia?" My heart dropped.

"We don't know who Julia is?"

"I do." My gawk met Olivia's. "I was at her funeral."

Olivia's green eyes went wild before searching past me. She pushed the paper in my hands closed before I could process, reel, or react to the fact that my father had been at Julia's funeral. The day came crashing back. Mom had wanted to move to Fiji.

Poseidon.

She'd wanted Dad to scrap the Rat Pack movie he was making.

Las Vegas.

She'd vowed to keep me safe from the Fifth House and my father until she drew her last breath.

Midas.

She'd done just that . . . but why?

Olivia nudged my knee, bringing me back to a new conversation. My questions would have to wait. Olivia obviously didn't want Helen to know my Dad was still in play.

"Yeah, I'm thinking my elixir's got to be somewhere we wouldn't think of. I mean it's not like it's going to be at The Paris or Helen's is somewhere in the Luxor."

"Why can't mine be at the Luxor?" Helen asked.

Olivia rolled her eyes, and I couldn't help but giggle at the two of them. They were an Abbot and Costello act.

"Why can't it be that simple?" I asked. "Why wouldn't the elixirs be in the most obvious places? Think about it. It's going to have to be somewhere that's sure to last. Hotels last here."

Helen contemplated my thought as she hitched a hip on the back of the couch. Olivia shot her another look that went completely ignored.

"Yeah, but some are lost in the yearly tournament," Helen said.

"I think we should rule out the obvious before we go hunting the obscure." I reached for Olivia's computer and pulled up a map of the hotels in Las Vegas.

"Cassie might be right." Gia joined me on the couch. "I mean what can it hurt to look?"

"So we're going to the Luxor?" Helen hopped off the couch.

"The Paris is closer." Gia pointed to the map on the screen. Our looks collided, and I wondered if Isaac had gotten to her as well. Gia and I were friends in California, but here in Vegas, I think the girl had more secrets hidden than even I did.

"Alright," Olivia chimed in. "I say after class, we take Cass's car, hit The Paris, and hopefully find us something to drink. Okay, find *me* something to drink. Who's telling the Jacks?"

No one volunteered as tribute to tell the Jacks where we were headed. Not that we needed to. They were ordered to stand down, but for some reason, eluding them made our treasure hunt more appealing. It was silly, childish even, but I'd take what I could get. Once Olivia was safe, then I could focus on my pair of Jacks and tattered love life.

We pulled into the self-parking at The Paris, an uncomfortable lump lodged itself in my throat. The four of us together were hard to miss; security would have eyes on us the minute we stepped out of the car. That's how we'd rationed the ditching of the Jacks. Helen, however, led a sheltered life and decided that Audrey Hepburn glasses and a red silk wrap around her head was the perfect disguise. The rest of us were in our normal hot as hell Las Vegas summer clothes: flip-flops, shorts, and tank tops. The cold casino air rushed out to greet us, and we quickly found the escalators to the main floor.

"Where should we start?" Helen asked, scurrying up next to me.

"I'm thinking the obvious. The Eiffel tower."

"Promise I'm not a rain cloud, but that's a really public place." Gia pointed to the sign directing us to the base of the tower.

"This is so obvious, it just might work. I mean how bad could we cock up?"

Olivia snorted at Helen. "What did you say?"

"What?" Helen's well-threaded eyebrows climbed up her forehead. "Cock up?" She searched the sky blue ceiling of the casino a moment. "Botch up? Mess up?"

"I'm going to need a British urban dictionary to keep up with you," Olivia snarked, pointing to another sign toward the Eiffel Tower.

A few more labyrinthine turns, and we found the line for the elevator ride up to the top.

"Livi," I drawled, dodging the heated look Olivia sent my way. "You've been here the longest. Is there another way to the top?

Olivia shook her head.

"What's that?" I pointed to the wonky look crawling across her face.

"I've never been to the top. Ever. I wanted to come here when the hotel opened. Mom told me the time wasn't right." Olivia's lips thinned out as she bypassed the roped off line and headed to the attendant manning the elevator door.

"Olivia, you think this is the best idea?" I asked, eyeing a mom with whiny kids who looked like she was about to let loose on us and all the reasons we couldn't cut to the front of the line. Given the eight-year-old princess with a tantrum she was trying to calm, I didn't blame her.

Gia slipped her arm through mine and pulled me close. "Let her be. Something's clicked."

"Speaking of clicked, why the sudden rush to get Olivia's elixir?" I turned around and looked for Helen. She trailed behind, taking everything in. I didn't know how to read her, and I knew I couldn't trust her.

"Mom told me about prom," Gia whispered. "She also showed me the video footage."

My focus snapped back to Gia. "I was told there wasn't anything to see."

"That doesn't surprise me. Your mom is pretty protective. I'm not sure all the sheltering she's done has helped or hurt your cause."

"You'd tell me if it was because of something else, or someone else."

"Just like you would, I'm sure."

I didn't get a moment to ask what she meant. Olivia waved at us, and we picked up the pace to the front of the line.

"This is Randy," Olivia patted the red and gold bellhop's coat. "He's the supervisor of the tower. Randy wants to know why we're here so early?"

"I was told to expect you, but you aren't allowed up until after sunset." His muddy brown eyes darted between the four of us. "Closer to the start of the Bellagio's water show." Poor guy looked like he was about to pass out. Then again if I'd had Olivia's glare trained on me, I'd probably look the same.

"Who told you to expect us?" Olivia angled her body so the family at the front of the line can't hear.

"Um, Mr. Baudin, the hotel manager. I'm supposed to let him know you're here."

"I know that guy," Olivia hissed. "He's always kissing my mom's ass. Get him on the phone. Let him know we're here."

Ten minutes and a few tourist stare-downs later, Mr. Baudin strode around one of the iron girders. He was handsome, well-polished, and barely in his thirties, which told me he was a ladder climber. If we pushed hard enough, he'd probably take us to Olivia's elixir, thinking it would earn him extra points with both the current Queen and her heir.

"Ladies, your arrival wasn't expected for quite some time and most certainly not in the afternoon." Mr. Baudin's voice was like a French latte on a cold day. There was something so tempting, seductive. It knocked all your defenses to their knees.

Except for Olivia.

Olivia bristled under the proper scolding. "Mr. Baudin, I think you'll come to find I rarely do things on other people's schedules." She leaned into him and Mr. Baudin's eyes flared. "You know who we are, and I'd like you to take us to where we need to go."

Mr. Baudin's spine stiffened. He didn't pull away. Just the opposite, he matched Olivia's gesture and invaded her space farther. "You're correct; I do know who you are. I also know who your mother is, as well as her decree that you not be allowed up the tower until nine p.m. or thereafter. Until you wear the crown and not the tiara, her rules will be followed. Yours will be evaluated. I'm surprised you figured out your clue so quickly."

Mr. Baudin pulled back at the same slow, authoritative pace he entered, completely unfazed by the encounter. Olivia, on the other hand, was not. Her sun-kissed coco skin was pale, her mouth hung open in a small little "o" that kind of freaked me out. She was calm on the outside, but if the slight tremor in her balled up fists gave any indication, she was far from unaffected by the encounter.

"Ladies," Mr. Baudin's voice held a hint of amusement. Olivia wasn't the only one left speechless. Gia's head tilted with a star-struck expression. Helen watched with wide eyes and open palms, like the guy's presence had stunned her, but his words had made it all okay and she was ready for another comeuppance.

"Thank you, Mr. Baudin." I stepped forward, extending my hand. This time, his eyes flared.

"I've heard about you, Ms. Vera."

Was that disdain I heard in his voice?

Mr. Baudin ignored my hand and turned back to Olivia. "Nine p.m., not a moment sooner." He turned on his long legs and strode away.

"What did he mean, he'd heard about you?" Olivia's voice still held some edge. "And not shake your hand? What a prick."

"Where was that silver tongue ten seconds ago?" Helen asked. "More importantly, how does sex on a stick look so good and sound so bitter? Isn't he quite the dogsbody?"

Whatever spell Mr. Baudin seemed to have cast over my friends seemed to dissipate.

"What the fuck is a dogsbody?" Olivia craned her neck around the corner Mr. Baudin had disappeared beyond.

"An errand boy." Helen abandoned our British slang education and dug in her purse about the same time my cellphone went off. "Ladies, I'm going to have to put Operation Elixir on hold. My Jack is threatening to hunt me down if I don't get back to the dorms in the next ten minutes. He's even using our danger word."

My cell pinged again with another message. "You have a danger word, Helen?"

If she answered, I didn't know. The second message was from Beaux, asking me to get my hot arse back to the dorms and then a single word that would always dump ice into my veins: Shadows. I leveled a look at Olivia and Gia as their phones joined the symphony of Jacks gone mad. "Looks like all our boys are up in arms."

"When did that start?" Olivia nodded at my phone.

"It's a courtesy to Beaux." Judgment rushed through my cousin's face. "Relax the glare. A.J. bought the phone, Beaux convinced me I should carry it."

The hard lines around her eyes softened and a sly bow-chicka-wow-wow smile pulled at her lips. "Uh huh." Olivia bumped my shoulder as we started back to the parking lot. "I bet he did."

TWENTY-ONE

FOUR GUYS WITH anger etched into the planes of their faces stood like sentinels at the entrance to the parking garage. The twang of disappointment from my heart hurt. Four boys—not five—looked like their next breath depended on us climbing out of the car safely. I caught Olivia's glance when she noticed A.J. missing from the lineup. I winked and pushed the gnawing feeling of abandonment away. How could a boy claim to want to marry me, but be promised to someone else? He begged me to trust him, but when the world seemed to be on fire, he was nowhere to be found. I swallowed over the lump of disappointment lodged in my throat. A.J. may have physically been leaving for Spain in two weeks, but he'd mentally checked out of our relationship the minute our high school graduation caps hit the ground. I turned off the engine and didn't jump when all four doors of the Mustang flew open by the four boys who didn't care that they had been ordered down.

Four boys were still going to protect us . . . not five.

Beaux bent down, wedging his fine-ass body between the car and the door.

"Look at me." His Australian lilt seemed to only stir up the emotions building behind the lump in my throat. "He's not here because he's briefing the candidates. Don't shake your head, I'll be the first to call the wanker out, but now's not one of those times. The Breech Ring's been activated; we're taking you the library now." Beaux raked his hand down his face and I knew there was more.

"The Shadows have bounties on all your beautiful heads." His hand hesitated a moment before tenderly gliding down the side of my face and cupping my chin. "Cass, you were right. Dionysus has a son. He's the one leading the charge. Dionysus agreed to dissolve the debt of any Shadow who can capture you or your power. Freedom from their sins in exchange for each heir apparent delivered to the catacombs." The skin around his blue eyes crinkled as he searched my eyes for some kind of understanding. Thing was, I understood all too well what was happening. I had a Shadow who'd told me.

This was what Isaac was talking about when he stalked me in the shower. I stole a glance over my shoulder at Olivia. Francis had her pinned in the same way Beaux had me pinned. Given the tight pull of her shoulders, the ram-rod way she was sitting in the passenger's seat, Francis was delivering the same news.

Beaux squeezed my thigh, earning him more than my attention. "Cassie, why do I have this kick-in-the-balls feeling you already knew this?"

"Not here." I turned in my seat and touched Olivia's shoulder. She jumped at the contact, and when she turned toward me, the pallor of her complexion, the worried lines I never knew existed, set off my own protective hackles. Her eyes shimmered, but she was too strong to let a tear drop. She pursed her lips together, but even I could see the small tremor of her chin. She frantically reached her hand for mine, and all I could think was, *Damn Mr. Baudin for not letting us find Oli's elixir.* All of this fear could have been avoided.

"They'll have to get through me before they lay another hand on you." I squeezed her fingers. Olivia inclined her head like I'd seen my mother do when she was terrified but still had to maintain a royal decorum. "Lock up the car when you're done. I'll see you inside."

Beaux tucked me into his side as we stepped out of the parking garage. I slipped on my sunglasses and matched his urgent pace. Sweat trickled down my back by the time we rounded the quad and found a bench under a tree not far from the room we'd been in yesterday.

"Spill it," Beaux said as he sat down on the bench. He rested his elbows on his knees, and part of me was fascinated with how he was wearing pants and a black t-shirt in 100-degree weather. I searched the horizon, trying to figure out a way to tell him how I knew the Shadows were coming without compromising Isaac. I knew what A.J. would do if he knew Isaac had cornered me in the shower. I could safely assume Beaux's reaction would be along the same lines.

"You said we were a team, right?"

Beaux nodded.

"And I'm the weakest link, right?"

Beaux nodded again.

"Okay." I wrung the hem of my tank top. "Okay. If I tell you, then you promise you can't share this with anyone?"

"That's not how I work, Cassie."

"Neither do I, not normally, but in this case, you can't tell anyone, especially not A.J."

Beaux leaned back, his arm resting on the back of the bench, close enough to me that I could smell all that delicious man soap he'd showered with this morning.

"Beaux, swear it. I don't want to keep secrets from you, but if I don't have your word, then how will I know what stays just that, my secrets?"

"You're going to spill a tale and you don't want A.J. to know. This has to be a doozy. One that sounds like I'm going to be siding with A.J. on."

"That's the deal." I leaned into the bench, closer to Beaux's side. Isaac in my shower stall altered between mortification and downright anger with a vein of understanding. Isaac clearly loved Olivia. If I read my cousin correctly, Isaac still did it for her. They were as star-crossed as A.J. and I apparently were.

"Fine," Beaux let out on a breath. "Spill and I'll keep it between us."

"I have your word?"

His green eyes sparkled as his look met mine something passing between us: a mutual respect, a trust, that nearly floored me. I'd been taken care of all my life, but this was the first time I'd been trusted to know what was best for me.

"Isaac paid me a visit." I left out the where. New respect didn't mean Beaux needed to know all the skin involved in the discovery of The Shadows' plans. "He and Oli had something a few years back and . . . and he still loves her."

"You trust him?"

"No, not as far as I can throw him, but when it comes to Olivia . . . yeah, I trust him with her life."

"But not yours?"

I thought about it for a second. Isaac had been willing to sacrifice me to keep Olivia safe once before. Who's to say he wouldn't do it again? When it came to Isaac, the ends always would justify the means, even if it meant sacrificing me. He'd be okay with Olivia mad as hell with him as long it meant she was protected.

"No, I don't trust him past Olivia."

"Damn it, Cassie." Beaux leaned forward, taking all that understanding and protection along with him. "You should have told me. When did this happen? Where?"

"The night I went to ASHA with the girls. The where doesn't really matter."

"Fuck me 'the where doesn't matter.' You're telling me the top ranking Shadow was in your presence, and it's not my business to know where? Cassandra, I told you before, I may not look the duty-bound type, but I am. You're my—"

"You've been ordered to stand down." I cut Beaux off before he could finish. I knew I was just a job. I was everyone's duty and no one's purpose in life. It was a fact that constantly stung, and I didn't need it thrown in my face.

Not now.

Not when everything was falling apart, and there wasn't a soul on earth who wasn't playing a game where I was a pawn. I leaned forward, matching Beaux's pose. "I get your loyalty. I really do. I appreciate it, but let's not lose sight of the fact that at some point in time, your loyalty to your House is going to be in direct conflict with your loyalty to me. I think the sooner we acknowledge that I'm just a job, the easier this will be." I held up a finger to stop his objection. "I know about the consummation ceremony. Let's just agree to cross that bridge if and when it comes."

"There's no if, Cassie. When you choose to take your place at the head of your House, when you choose to wear the crown, then . . ." His words trailed off as he ran a hand down his face and let all those gold locks curtain his expression. "You're thinking about forgetting." The pain in his words sliced me.

"Where's your hat?"

"What?"

"Your cowboy hat, I've never seen you without it."

Beaux shot me a sideways glance. "You just told me you're not sure you want to rule your House, and you're worried about my hat?"

"It's the mundane that keeps me grounded."

Beaux fished out his phone from his back pocket and swiped the screen.

"I've got to get you into the Breech Ring. They're ready to start. Cassandra, my hat is the least of my worries and should always be the least of yours."

There was so much we had to learn about each other. Why did he care if I chose to rule or forget? There was no life for him as my Jack. I couldn't have a king. And Beaux needed to learn I didn't do confrontation. These days, I made my decisions without anyone's help. The only people who I could trust were killed in a fiery crash eight months ago. I'd die before I let anyone fall on another sword meant for me.

♥

PEOPLE WERE STILL leaving through the upper level exits when Beaux and I walked into the Breech Ring.

"The Midas Candidates," Beaux said, noticing the way I reacted to him holding open the door for me.

"I didn't realize there were so many."

"These are the candidates who have been activated. There are thousands more students on campus who attend the International Gaming Institute. Almost a hundred thousand worldwide."

"I didn't realize."

"That you were part of something much bigger than the four houses and a deck of cards? Cassie, our four families made the ultimate sacrifice for humanity. They were asked to serve and protect civilization as we know it. Before you start making decisions on your future, you may want to know your past."

Beaux slipped his calloused hand in mine. Two days and he felt that comfortable with me? Worse, I felt that comfortable with *him*. And where was that gnawing feeling of guilt I was supposed to have for holding another boy's hand who wasn't my boyfriend?

I felt A.J.'s heated stare fall on our linked hands long before I found his blue eyes bearing into me. All sorts of accusations rolled off his tense shoulders, but none of them fazed me. This was me fending for myself.

My gut recognized the leggy brunette in a white sundress long before my mind did. She sauntered up to A.J., stopping a moment before she followed his glare. Her eyes widened when she found me. A small little "o" formed on her lips when she saw Beaux and me holding hands.

"Who is that?" I asked, though I didn't need too many guesses. I may not have known Beaux more than two days, but the look he threw across the room was the same one he was sporting last night at dinner.

"That's Jezebel?" Beaux flinched at the sound of her name. "I thought she was in Australia."

"So did I." Beaux pulled his hand from mine, placing it on the small of my back; the heat of his palm spread up my spine as he directed me to the seats we'd occupied yesterday. I guess Jezebel's heated look burned a lot hotter than A.J.'s.

"Come on in." Ms. Maddox pointed to the seats around the table. "We've just briefed the candidates on the situation your Jacks updated you on. We expected some heightened interest on the acquisition of the future queens' powers. However, this . . . this is not what we expected." Ms. Maddox nodded to A.J. and Jezebel, the girl next to him.

She was beautiful. Brunette hair that looked like fresh spun silk hung down to her elbows. Her skin was flawless and touched with just enough sun to make her alabaster skin shimmer. When she spoke, she shocked me even further when there wasn't even a hint of an Australian lilt. She was American as apple pie and the Fourth of July, and I could see why both the boys in my life would fight for her.

"Zee," Ms. Maddox signaled Jezebel to start.

How I was still seated in my chair was beyond me. Maybe it was the stares of disgust and disbelief that whizzed past me from Olivia. Could have been the tight grip Beaux had on my thigh, although I'm not entirely sure he knew that the girl he loved had been picked up at the airport by my boyfriend. He ditched me on the lake for her. Really though, I think the only thing that held me in my seat while Jezebel stepped forward was the mortification of being made to look like a fool.

"We've been working our contacts all night long." Jezebel directed our attention to the white board behind us, but my glare stayed with A.J. He didn't even have the decency to look at me. The room shimmered behind the tears I refused to let fall. I bit down on my lip, willing them back.

"Over the summer, we knew Dionysus was planning something big."

Jezebel clicked her pointer, and a picture of the Brad Pitt Greek god lookalike popped up on the screen. "What we didn't know was that he had a son." Another picture replaced Dionysus.

"Warren?" Gia whispered. Questions swirled in her eyes. Questions I didn't have the answers to, not now. There was nothing left in me, nothing that hadn't already been hollowed out by A.J.'s lies.

"We're not sure how this girl plays in." A picture of Malory from last night flashed on the screen. "This was taken a few nights ago at ASHA near the emergency exit. She's not from the underworld and she's not a card."

I nailed A.J. with a look. We could play this game all he wanted, but Malory was his friend. She was the reason I was even—I cut that thought off before it formed. His blue eyes hardened, and I knew he wasn't going defend Malory.

"That's Malory, she doesn't play into any of this."

"Princess—"

"Cassandra," I quickly corrected. A.J.'s eyes narrowed in on me and the demand of my formal name.

"Cassandra," Jezebel continued. "I beg your pardon, but if she's talking with the son of Dionysus, then she does play into this. I know the history. Atticus filled me in."

The room constricted, all eyes on me and the next move I would play. I was wrecked when I told him Malory and Warren's history. How the slime slept with Malory and left her to handle her shredded v-card. Malory had almost died because of Warren, and now A.J. was using it like a play in a game plan? A.J.'s full name and the fact that Jezebel knew it too wasn't lost on me, either. They had history, and as of last night, they apparently had a future, too.

"I'm glad he's trusting someone with all his secrets." I turned in my chair and focused on the white board. Fingers of adrenaline crawled across my skin. He was a lying, cheating bastard, and I'd be damned if I played the victim in this role. I may not have known about Jezebel, but that didn't mean she wouldn't know about me.

Beaux leaned his chin on my shoulder. "They hurt, don't they? The lies. They all rear their ugly little heads at some point in time."

"Shut up."

"Remember when I asked if Malory was going to be a problem and you assured me she wouldn't be? Not the case."

I ignored him and focused on the melodic tone of Jezebel's voice and wondered what it would sound like when I choked the life out of her. I quickly stomped out the warm twinge that raced up my spine.

"Midas spoke to Dionysus this morning. The god of wine agreed to honor the campus as a hands-off zone. Despite his assurances, Midas Candidates have been advised to start their patrols of the Dayton Complex. Our spies assure us something's brewing in the Shadow's Catacombs. Your future kings have been advised of the situation, and the Council agrees with their decision to keep with protocol. Your Highnesses will remain unprotected until you find your elixirs."

Frank rammed his fist into the table. "First, we're ordered to deal with her." I didn't have to look where his finger was pointed. He loved me about as much as Gia's protector, William, did. "Now my Queen is left defenseless?"

"Francis," A.J.'s tone was cold and condescending. "Your Queen isn't defenseless. Olivia knows how to handle herself, and she has her innate power. Please remember we didn't make the decision not to activate you."

"No, you're just doing what you're told." I cut A.J. off.

He snapped his glaring eyes at me, and I met him blink for blink. That's been his mantra since the beginning of summer. He was just doing what he was told. Thing was, if he'd done what he was told, I wouldn't be sitting here. Somewhere in all the half lies and partial truths of the past three months in doing what he was told, he'd lost his purpose, and he was losing me.

A.J. didn't dignify my outburst with a response. He moved on about curfews and protocol. I'm sure word would get back, and Midas would be proud of his grandson. At the end of the meeting, we were left with little more protection than what we'd walked in with. It was a giant waste of time and a show of procedure. Something I was all too familiar with when it came to this world. Chairs scraped against the floor as Ms. Maddox tried to further calm down Olivia's Jack, Francis. The girls and I needed to get back to the dorm. Operation Elixir had just been kicked into overdrive.

"Cass, stay," A.J. called out but didn't look up from the papers he was reviewing. He nodded to Jezebel, handed her the stack, and leaned against the railings separating the stadium seats from the floor. His face was smooth, unreadable, and sent my heart thrashing against my chest, wondering what emotions he wasn't letting me see.

Beaux gave me a quick look as he picked up his keys. A look that said he'd beat A.J. to the dark tan color of his saddle if I wanted him.

Call you later, I mouthed instead.

He shook his head. I'm pretty sure he was laughing at me and all the girlish daydreams I was certain he knew about. I hitched a hip on the black table and stared at my watch, listening to Beaux's cowboy boots clank along the tile floors. The door clicked behind him, launching an ominous sound into the Breech Room. It rattled off every empty seat, every broken promise, and finally faded into nothing. A girl like me could get lost in the quiet of a room this big. Lost in the hope that the promises would mend themselves. Thing was, it hadn't been that long ago I could feel a room fade away when A.J. was in it. Everything had happened so fast at the beginning of the year. Maybe we'd flamed out. Run our course. Maybe all we'd really had was a mutual attraction, a summer fling, and now that was gone. How could one moment stretch into eternity and seven months of passion fizzle in an instant?

I checked my watch again. Five minutes. He'd kept me sitting and waiting for five minutes. A.J. would always be in control of our relationship. I'd gladly given up a say, and making me sit here was proof. I was merely a moment in time he'd get around to when it or I was convenient.

"Right, good talk. We should do this more often, really clears the air," I finally whispered.

"Don't be a smartass."

It's something he'd said a million times in the past, but this time it took all my insides and crushed them. I looked away, afraid the hurt would show in my eyes. All the betrayal would leak out in the form of stupid tears. The last thing I needed from him was his pity. I'd had that for the last eight months, and all it was doing was devastating me.

"You're not going to say a word?" A.J. folded his arms over his chest.

"What do you want me to say? 'Oh, look, Jezebel, the girl you're suited with is here.' How about this one: 'Hey, A.J. can you clue me in on what towels I should order: His and Hers or His and The Mistress's?'" My chest constricted, making it harder to get out the next jab. "You should have told me." His perfect form started to blur behind the tears. "I don't play the fool very graciously."

"I didn't know she was coming."

"You knew when you left me on a boat to go pick her up from the airport. You knew when you came over to my house to *apologize* for leaving me. And you damn well knew Jezebel was here when you and Beaux nearly went to blows over her last night at dinner. What the fuck is wrong with you? You didn't think this moment was going to come? You didn't think the entire world wouldn't laugh at me? You made me a joke, A.J." His name hitched on the tangible hurt my body ached from. "Or maybe this summer was just your way of letting me down nice and easy. You were almost there until you told me you wanted to marry me," I choked out. Humiliation mixed with the slick tears forming in the back of my throat.

Before I could even think to leave, A.J. crossed the room, sandwiching his body between my legs, the warmth of his arms caging me in, and his face, his beautiful face, inches from mine. Electricity arced between us, but then again, heat and passion was never an area where we lacked. What this boy did to my heart shouldn't be legal. Every fiber of my being needed him. I swallowed hard, tracking every grout line in the tile flooring and cursing the pull one human being could have for another.

"I told you things were going to be hard and that you were going to have to trust me." A.J. dipped his head, trying to capture my gaze. "Cassandra, look at me."

My mind didn't want to listen, but I knew my heart, no matter how broken and battered it was, the stupid organ would give in. I knew what a fool I looked like. I knew how this would end: with me shattered. But my heart wouldn't let go of the ride. Wouldn't let go of the thought of A.J. and the man he promised me he'd be.

"Cass," A.J. slipped his finger under my chin. I must have looked destroyed, what else could have etched such worry in his beautiful face? The blue glaciers that crushed me with a single glance during the meeting were gone; in their place were warm pools of calm that begged me to listen. "I tried telling you at the cave, but we fought and then . . ." A wild smirk pulled at his lips. Heat flooded my traitorous body, remembering every moment after the cave. Every place his lips had explored, everywhere his hand had skidded . . . his fingers had touched. My heart caught on the memory, sending flames licking up my cheeks.

"There's my girl." A.J. pushed back my wild hair, tucking it behind my ear. "When I went to find you the next morning, you were already headed here. Then you took off like a bat out of hell, and when I did find you, you'd spent the day with Beaux." His lips thinned and whitened. A.J. pulled in a deep breath, the fabric of his white polo shirt pulled against his chest. It was wrong to want him after the shit he'd pulled. But the excuses he gave made so much sense.

"And after that?" I pushed. He may have made my body rocket under his touch, but he wasn't getting out of this that easily.

Warmth shot through me as A.J. pushed farther in between my legs, brushing his stubbled cheek against me. "You wouldn't answer my calls all night long. I was going to go to ASHA, but Beaux thought a girl's night would cool you down." A.J. brushed his lips along the side of my jaw, igniting tiny jolts of electricity in places that had no business arcing such force. "At dinner, I'd never seen you with that kind of fire in your eyes, Cassandra . . . so hot."

I smiled despite myself, despite the situation, and because of our history.

"I thought it could wait until this morning." A.J. tickled my earlobe with his nose, and I curled into him before pushing him back. "I thought cooler heads would prevail and I could explain who Zee was. When I went to your dorm this morning, you and the girls were already gone."

"Operation Elixir." My hand splayed on his chest, keeping A.J. and his pursuit of forgiveness at bay.

A chuckle leaked out. "I should have figured you'd be leading the charge." A.J. held a finger up, silencing me. "Don't tell me anything. It's that fine line I was telling you about."

"You promised no more lies."

"I also told you that you were going to have to trust me." His fingers wrapped around my wrist, and we both noticed my pulse bounding through my skin.

"Then give me a reason to."

"I thought I had the night I saved your life."

And there it was, the sacrifice he'd made that I could never repay hanging around the one-word question I never had the courage to form . . . until now.

"Why? Why did you save my life if you were already suited?"

"She doesn't want to be suited with me anymore than I do with her."

"That's not an answer to my question."

A.J.'s Adam's apple bobbed with the hard, forced swallow. Another telltale sign that he wasn't ready to tell me the complete truth. My ears turned red when I lied, A.J.'s Adam's apple did the mambo when he lied.

"You're getting good at this game, aren't you?"

"I told you one day a kiss and a smile wouldn't be enough of an answer. Today's that day, Atticus."

A.J.'s eyes darted across my face. I'm not sure if it was admiration or irritation that made the blue glint like the sun on the ocean. When he pushed away from the table, from me, sending his chair clattering to the floor, I knew it was irritation. He stormed across the room, stopping in front of the window with his hands resting on his hips. The midday sun filtered through the windows at the top of the room, hitting A.J. in such a way that he looked more god than human.

"Cass, I don't know how many ways to tell you I saved you because I love you."

"Then stop telling me and start showing me."

He tossed me a look over his shoulder, but I kept going. I didn't want the secrets between us. If there even was an us.

"Don't keep secrets like leaving in two weeks or being betrothed to another girl from me. Don't leave surprises like the consummation ceremony lying around for me to discover." I held up a finger and silenced him when he tried speaking. "If you want to know what Beaux's told me, start unpacking your secrets. If it takes all day, all night, lay them out and I promise I'll listen. But don't keep us on this path. You leave in two weeks." My heart lurched at the thought. "And I can only guess you're leaving with Jezebel. God, her name is perfect." I shook off the Chely Wright song. "You want me to trust you, then start showing me why I should."

"And Beaux?" A.J. spat out the name.

"What about Beaux?"

"You walk in here hand in hand, you take his phone calls, you ride bulls with him, what are you showing me?" A.J. air quoted the 'showing me.'

"I didn't ride bulls with him." I hopped off the table and crossed the room. My hand hesitated a moment before I touched him. The muscles in his back tensed and I swore the man would be my downfall. "I took his phone because you have my ring, and I took his hand because you already have my heart."

A.J. turned, his arms sweeping me up and into him. His eyes blazed with a heat I'd only seen one other time. I'd been too far away to realize how much power radiated from A.J., but now I was up close and personal. The passion storming just beneath the surface of A.J. was terrifying and addicting all at the same time.

"I love you, Cass. You have to know that. I love you so much I can't breathe." His words beat into me like fists. "I don't want to go to Malaga. I don't want to think about all the odds stacked against us. I don't want to do anything but love you."

A.J.'s raw and heated statements slammed into me, shredding all the resolve I'd mustered to be strong. It all melted under his familiar forgive-me. The room spun. He cupped my backside as he lifted me, my legs wrapping around his waist like it was second nature. The familiar feeling of weightlessness that came when I was with A.J. came rushing back, and I had fallen. Fallen like no girl in history had a right to. His lips found mine. His first kiss was far from subtle and nowhere near apologetic, filled with a rawness that many would misinterpret as dangerous or forceful, but it wasn't.

Quite the opposite.

I could taste the fear on his breath. Fear of the unknown. Fear that he wouldn't be able to control what happened in our future, let alone the next few minutes. A primal growl ripped from his throat. The stubble from a rough night raked against my cheeks. Lower and lower, he dragged his head. My common sense fried, I curled into him. His tongue skidded along my jaw and up to my ear.

"Oh, god," I whispered when he pulled my earlobe into his mouth. Heavy breaths and hot air shot through me like lightning bolts, each one fastening my very being to A.J. His hips pressed against me, driving into me as if I was the last thing between him and paradise. And his mouth, oh god, his mouth. He turned his focus back onto my lips. Raw, carnal claiming kisses, one after another, pushed every ounce of concern from my head.

"Cassie," he growled, his lips sliding up my jaw line. "Don't ever let me catch you holding his hand again."

"Then don't lie to me. I'm running out of reasons to forgive you."

TWENTY-TWO

AFTER THIS MORNING'S Breech Room briefing and not too far after Beaux and A.J. walked me back to the dorm rooms (Beaux evaluated every whisker burn A.J. had left and the second fresh bruise on the side of my neck), the Jacks decided they wouldn't follow protocol; they were activating themselves. We didn't quite know what the full meaning of their "activation" meant until Gia went to shower. Almost two hours later, Gia marched into our living room, done up with attitude and a face full of makeup to match.

"Girls, we got a problem. William wouldn't let me out of his sight. He totally would've walked into the bathroom if Cara hadn't screeched and threatened to tell the Council." She flopped onto the couch with a huff and all her shower stuff. "I really think he was going to sit and listen to me shower."

"That's so twisted," Helen chimed in from the kitchen.

I muted the TV and shifted in the couch. "Sweetie, William's always been a little wonky when it comes to your safety."

Gia rolled her eyes, launched herself out of the couch, and continued her march to our bedroom. "This is different, Cass," she hollered over the sound of things hitting the floor and the ribboning of curses that had no business coming from Gia's mouth. One last f-bomb from her had us all giggling when she reappeared in the doorframe. "You all laugh. Stick your head out there. Francis is by the elevator, Beaux's by the emergency staircase. Who knows where Hondo is?"

"Probably scaling a wall or marching on the roof," Helen quipped. She threw her body into the seat next to me.

"He's that bad?" I asked, as she leaned her head on my shoulder.

"He's worse. He actually thinks being a Jack is an honor."

"It's not?" I brushed back the thick black locks from her forehead. "I mean he gets to have and hold you."

Helen's eyebrows furrowed together at my sarcasm, but when she turned her big silver gaze on me, I could see all the hurt hidden behind them. "They're glorified babysitters and sperm donors."

"You don't really believe that." Gia picked up Helen's feet from the couch and put them in her lap when she sat down. She caught my wistful gaze and smiled. Gia knew I didn't have this growing up. I missed out on the slumber parties and late night ice cream sessions.

And boys?

Only Justin, my ex, had braved my dad's six-foot-high/six-foot-wide stare-down. I was being protected, I thought from the paparazzi, but it was from this life and all the glorious nightmares that came along with it.

"Not all of us have knights in shining convertibles waiting to rescue us, Princess Gia," Olivia playfully tossed her thoughts into the conversation.

I snorted. "William's had it bad for Gia since the sixth grade. He showed up mid-school year with nothing but Gia in his eyes. Malory and I would sit in the back of Mrs. Perry's class and count the number of times he'd glance over at Gia."

"You would not," Gia gasped.

"We did. Seventeen looks in a fifty-minute class."

Olivia chuckled.

"That's almost pathetic," Helen snorted. "Almost. I think I own the medal in pitiful. There wasn't much opportunity in India, none at the all-girl's boarding school in Berkshire, England. I wasn't expecting much the summer I met Hondo. When I saw him in the marketplace, my heart stopped. Seriously, stopped! We were both fifteen. I thought my Disney Princess scenario was unfolding right before my eyes when Hondo started delivering groceries to the house. For a month straight, we'd talk about my upcoming trip to the States, the boarding school in England." Helen adjusted, sitting up right. "I thought he was interested in me, but really he was only interested in what I could give him.

I wish I would have known before I named him as my suited."

I nudge Helen out of the past. It didn't do anyone any good to linger there for too long. "I don't get that from him."

"Wait around. You don't see him guarding an entrance, do you? The lazy cow is probably sleeping."

Olivia unfolded her legs and sauntered off to the kitchen. "Not that lazy cows remind me of Malory, but what the fuck was she doing talking to the spawn of Dionysus?"

"Nice, Olivia," I scold her. "Bring me back a yogurt, would ya?"

"Cass, did you know about Warren's mythical side?" Gia asked.

I plucked the yogurt Olivia tossed me out of the air and peeled back the tin foil lid. "Yeah, I knew about Warren, but only recently. Two nights ago, A.J. took me to the iolite cave. Warren, Chance, and Isaac crashed our picnic."

Olivia's shoulders reacted at the mention of Isaac's name. Funny, his body had the same involuntary reaction to *her* name.

"Do you think it's a coincidence that the god cursed to oversee the Shadows has a son who happened to deflower our best friend?" Gia folded her legs up under her.

"No, I don't think it's a coincidence. I also don't think it's much of a coincidence that you went missing not long after Warren broke things off with Malory."

"Here's the million-dollar question: How bad is Malory going to fuck all this up?" Olivia leaned up against the breakfast bar in the kitchen.

"I told Beaux she wasn't going to be an issue."

Helen laughed.

"What?" I shot Helen an inquisitive glare.

"Malory is the Achilles' heel."

"Malory is my best friend. She's been there when everyone else walked away." Heat rose up my spine. I don't know which terrified me more: the feeling of my powers radiating up my spine, begging to be unleashed, or the look in my friends' eyes when they knew I was battling for control.

"Cass." Gia's cool fingers on my hand jerked back the power. "Sweetie, nobody's arguing how much Malory means to you. I think all we're saying is Malory's a little reckless. Just be careful." Gia absentmindedly rubbed her hand on her leg.

"Cassie," Olivia called out. "Put the fierce eyes away."

I shut my eyes and embraced the cool icy trickle down my spine, the flow of it out to my fingertips; my heart slowed and a calm washed over me.

"Fierce eyes?" I asked, cautiously opening my eyes.

"Your eyes glow like amber when you tap into your power," Gia offered.

"Did they before?"

Olivia shook her head. "It just started." She glanced at Gia.

"Did I burn you, Gia?"

She nodded.

"I'm sorry."

"It wasn't anything serious, just a zing."

Silence invaded the room. The muted TV screen washed out by the setting sun bounced back shadows of the future Queens and me.

"Okay, vote time." Gia jumped off the couch and closed the curtains.

"I love vote times," I muttered.

"I say we take showers one by one and wear the Jacks down. Make them think we're staying in for the night. We'll even order a pizza. Then when the time's right, we'll slip out the door and go find Olivia's elixir."

"Are you reactivating Operation Elixir?" I chuckled.

"I am."

"I'm in." Helen boldly raised her hand. "I even found a hidden passage."

"Where?" I asked, but something already told me it was in the girl's bathroom. How else could Isaac have snuck in while I was shaving my legs?

"Hell, count me in, too. Lord knows I haven't done anything covert since I drove Cassie to California."

I jumped at Olivia's touch on my arm. I didn't deserve her. I didn't deserve any of them. "That didn't end up too well."

"A lot better than your failed New Year's Eve attempt," Olivia countered

"I vote yes," Helen cut in before any real memories could surface.

"You already voted, Helen." Olivia sauntered off to the bedroom. "I'll go shower."

Two hours and a pizza later, we slipped out our door and tip-toed to the girls' bathroom.

"I'm pretty sure the Jacks wouldn't like this," Helen whispered. The hidden staircase door clicked shut and we all held our breaths. The fluorescent motion lights flickered to life, reminding me of the passageway that ran underneath the city.

"Yeah, well, the Jacks aren't going to like a lot of things we do," Gia sniggered.

"Who is this badass, and where have you been keeping her all these years?" I slipped past Gia, nudging her shoulder to follow.

"How are we getting there?" Helen asked

"Dude, could you stop worrying and enjoy Operation Elixir?" A two painted on the wall sent a jolt of excitement through me. We were totally ditching the Jacks and they had no clue.

"I would if it was my elixir we were hunting down."

"I called Malory, and before anyone says anything, she thinks we're going to the Paris for the tower ride."

"Right, you think she's going to buy that?" Olivia bolted past me and slapped the painted one on the wall.

"I may have said we'd go to ASHA, too."

"I'm not going to ASHA," Helen mumbled. "It's a school night. My parents don't care much about the General Ed stuff but definitely the training. I'm certain I'll have a call from them tomorrow night."

We pushed open the exit door, holding it so it didn't slam shut.

Mal honked her horn from the parking lot. Three sets of hands shot up in the air, waving off Malory.

"What up, bitches?" she hollered from the open-air top of her Jeep.

"Jesus, Mal," Olivia scolded as she climbed up and into the back seat. "Could you make any more noise?"

"We're kind of ditching the boys," Gia said, joining Olivia in the back seat.

Malory's eyebrows crawled up her face. "Any sass from you, Highness Helen?"

"No, I'm still waiting for Hondo to repel down the wall and carry my ass upstairs."

"Nice," Malory cooed.

I flipped the seat back, climbing in the front, and added, "Not nice, he tends to take his protection detail a little too seriously."

"Still, must be nice to have a guy concerned about you." Malory slipped the car into reverse, leaving her comment on the curb for us to contemplate later.

Warm desert air whipped through the open cab as we headed off campus. The dry acrid air filled the silence we had all slipped into. I caught Gia's gaze in the sideview mirror. She was gnawing on her bottom lip, her tell that she was worried. If I had any doubts about Isaac having gotten to her, they were immediately put to rest. The question was: *why?* Not why was Gia willing to help Olivia, but what fate was Isaac so desperate to protect Olivia from? And would he be willing to sacrifice us if it meant keeping Olivia safe?

We pulled into the Paris self-park and retraced our steps to the Tower's entrance.

"What time is it?" Olivia asked. Mr. Baudin had rattled the poor girl today. I had half expected her to march up and demand a first class ride. Instead, she was bringing up the rear, eyes darting around like she was expecting an ambush. Given the info we received this afternoon, I couldn't blame her.

Isaac was right.

The Shadows had already taken too much from her. They'd taken her security.

"Nine thirty-seven," Gia offered, rounding the corner.

Mr. Baudin stood at the front of the line, next to a girded leg. We'd gone from a novelty to predictable. My heart lurched. Who else could follow us like a playbook?

"Ladies," Mr. Baudin inclined his head. He held the line and ushered us into the next elevator up. He stopped Malory at the door. "I'm sorry, this car is only for . . ."

"She's with us," I corrected him.

"This car is for the four of you. She is not of this world."

"She's with us." Olivia reached around Mr. Baudin and pulled Malory into the car. "You can make me wait until my mother's designated time, but I draw the line at telling me who can and can't come with me."

Mr. Baudin's eyes seemed to leap out of his face and attack Olivia, almost demanding she stand down, give in, or at least show a little respect.

I disguised a chuckle with a cough. Mr. Baudin had no idea how stubborn Olivia could be. Even when it came to Malory.

"Very well. Your card, Princess Olivia." Mr. Baudin extended his open palm and waited. "Your mother will have activated it with your suit identifier."

Olivia pulled out the translucent key card from her back pocket.

"That's the one." Mr. Baudin examined the card before opening the elevator's emergency phone case and swiping it along the card reader at the top.

"Where does this take us?" I whispered.

"To the observation tower."

"Then why the cloak and dagger card?" Olivia asked.

The glass doors closed. A hum filled the elevator before it lurched up, soaring through the steel girders. Crisscrossing beams of steel and rivets seemed to race us to the top. We popped through the roof of the casino, and the 180-degree view of the Las Vegas Strip was easily visible from the glass-encased car.

"Your card alerts the keepers that an heir is close. Princess Gia, do you have your card?"

"Yes." Gia whipped her backpack around to her front. "Why?"

"I can notify your keeper as well."

"Our elixirs are at the same place?"

Mr. Baudin exhaled so loudly I thought for sure the elevator would change its mind and take us back down.

"I thought you ladies had solved your riddles?"

"What riddles?" we asked in unison.

"Fall term has started, correct?" Mr. Baudin folded his arms over his chest.

"Yesterday," Olivia answered this time. "What riddle?"

Mr. Baudin shifted on his heels before running a hand over his jaw. "You ladies are very skilled. Your mother was right about that."

"Riddles?" Olivia pressed.

"Hints the gods have left to help aid your pursuit. They're not completely without gratitude for your sacrifice."

"What's the riddle?" Olivia asked again.

"I don't know the riddle. I was only informed that should the four of you come together and once the Spade's key was activated, the Club could notify her own keeper if she wanted. Is that your wish?" Mr. Baudin extended his hand toward Gia.

Gia nodded and handed Mr. Baudin her key card.

"I don't see why everyone was so worried." Mr. Baudin swiped Gia's key card as the elevator slowed to a crawl. "You seem to be outsmarting the Shadows already." The elevator stopped, but that wasn't why my stomach lurched.

The elevator doors pulled back as a large pillar of water launched into the air. Malory and Helen stepped out, captivated by the water show.

Mr. Baudin stopped Olivia. "Watch the Bellagio's water show for your clues. But be careful. Your keycard notifies the keepers of your presence, but not all of them are loyal to the crowns."

"What does that mean?" Olivia asked.

"The lines of loyalty are murky at best during the transition. Claim your birthright and secure your line." Mr. Baudin spared me a quick glance. "House and honor above heart."

Olivia nodded before grabbing my hand and slipping out of the elevator.

The air was cooler up on the observation deck. The lights seemed to shine a little clearer. Several more columns of water rocketed into the air as we made our way through the bodies pressed against the edges of the Eiffel Tower.

"What did he mean, 'House and honor above heart?'" I asked.

Olivia glanced at me before wrapping her fingers around my wrist. "My duty is to my house. Mr. Baudin was reminding me that as much as we're family, my duty will always outweigh my heart, even my blood."

"He was warning you against me? I'm the murky line of loyalty?"

"Yes." Olivia's emerald eyes tore through me before she excused herself past another tourist and stepped up to Gia and Malory.

I didn't know what hurt more: the one-word answer or the fact that Olivia seemed to be buying into the warning against me. Either way, we'd find her elixir and Gia's too, and my best friends would be safe. She may have had her priorities set on House first, but mine would always be to my heart and those I loved.

"This is amazing," Malory cooed as lights and water sprays ripped across the Bellagio Lake. Up this high, you couldn't tell a major boulevard separated us. You couldn't hear the drunken catcalls; you couldn't make out the ground littered with papers advertising local burlesque shows or the latest "it" spot. Up here, there were only the lights and the magic of Las Vegas.

"What are we looking for?" Helen asked.

"Some sort of clue." Olivia answered, her jet-black hair fluttering on the breeze.

"Where's the music coming from?" Malory asked.

"Must be piped in from the water show." I looked up and around for the speakers.

"I'm not complaining; *Luck Be a Lady* has a soft spot in my heart." Malory bumped my hip with hers.

"How is my favorite Leprechaun these days?"

"He's good." A blush stained Malory's cheeks.

"Maybe you should bring him back here. Date night and all."

"He's been busy getting ready for school."

"Seems to be a lot of the getting readies going around these days."

Gia pulled me back into her. "He loves you, Cass. I know there's a ton of shit A.J.'s hid from you, but you have to believe love never fails."

"Says the girl who's never had her heart broken," Olivia quipped.

"Bitter doesn't suit you, Olivia," Malory answered before I could.

"Aren't we supposed to be looking for a clue?" Olivia folded her arms on the metal bar and huffed.

A silver circle of water shot high into the air before the music ended, and the lights from deep within the lake shut off. The soft tinkle of water drops hitting the lake echoed up the tower. A second later, the unmistakable melody of Andrea Bocelli and the Bellagio's theme song softened the dark night. The fountains sprang to life a moment before the lights from the lake clicked on, illuminating a heart on the far side of the lake. At the opposite side, the fountains illuminated a diamond. As Sarah Brightman's angelic voice joined in, a club and a spade came to life in the middle of the lake.

"Ladies?" I questioned. "You all are seeing this, yes?" I spared a quick glance and found four faces pressed up against the chain linked fence.

"What song is this?" Helen asked.

"*Con Te Partiro*," Olivia whispered.

"And in English?"

"*Time to Say Goodbye*," Gia answered. "This is it."

Our house symbols fell into darkness, but the song climbed. Octave by octave, the two angelic voices ramped up my heartbeat with the Italian verses. I had no clue what they were singing, but every fiber of me knew this was what we'd been looking for. This was the clue. We were totally going to kick some Shadows' asses.

"What's it saying, Gia?" I asked.

"It's time to say goodbye . . .
When you are far away
I dream on the horizon
And words fail,
And, Yes, I know
That you are with me;
You, my moon, are here with me,
My sun, you are here with me,
With me, with me, with me."

A silver stream of water flew across the lake, culminating in an arrow pointing at us. Behind it, a wall of water erupted, forming a spade.

"That's it," I squealed. "Where's it pointing?"

Olivia, on tiptoes, strained to see. "I can't tell."

"It's the archy thing," Malory said.

"You sure?" Olivia's fingers tightened their grip on the fence, pulling her farther up. "Make sure, I don't know how long the water's going to hold."

The lights cut off, and the water fell back into the lake.

"You're sure it was the Arc de Triomphe?"

Malory nodded.

Another line of the music cut into the darkness.

"What's it saying, Gia?" I asked, straining to make out the next clue. There has to be one for Gia. Her keeper was notified. If I could protect them both . . . My heart crawled up my throat as Gia started translating again.

"On ships across seas
Which, I know,
No, no, exist no longer,
With you I shall experience them again.
I'll go with you
On ships across seas
Which, I know,
No, no, exist no longer;
With you I shall experience them again.
I'll go with you,
I'll go with you."

Another silver line of fountains split the black lake in half. The tip formed an arrow and behind the explosion of water, the House of Clubs symbol.

"Where's it pointing, ladies?" I asked again calmly, a façade that masked the creepy "you're being watched" feeling climbing up my spine. A quick peek behind me saw the elevator doors close. "Quickly, girls. I get the feeling we're not alone up here."

"You're just now getting that feeling?" Malory quipped. "Do you mind?" She pushed back an overzealous tourist with a camera.

"Gia, you see it?"

Her big blue eyes found mine. As if she could sense the danger lurking on the observation deck with us, Gia nodded. "I got it. Let's go."

"Where is yours?" Olivia asked.

"I'll tell you later. Let's go."

"We should wait." Helen's fingers tightened around the fencing. "Maybe Cassie and my clue—"

"Time to go, Helen." Gia stepped into her space.

Helen's shoulders squared and fell at the same time. I peeked over my shoulder as a boy slipped his hood over his head. "Stairs, Oli?"

Olivia's body shuddered under my touch. I hated the Shadows. I hated Isaac that he couldn't rein in his rabid dogs. "Olivia, we need to move, now."

"Right. Stairs are on the other side of the structure." Olivia started pushing her way through the crowd.

"Got your key card ready? I have a feeling we're about to mad dash this sucker." I peeked over my shoulder to make sure the others were following.

We slipped into the sea of bodies all pushing to catch a glimpse of the water show. I spared one last look to the elevator and felt my heart sink further when the doors opened and another set of hooded heads stepped onto the observation deck.

"Gia, you guys go in front of me. I'll bring up the rear."

We pushed past a family with three boys earning a sideways glare from the mother. The odd sense of déjà vu settled in the pit of my stomach. Just another night where I'm running from the merry Shadowed monsters. The crowd of people thinned the farther we pushed away from the Bellagio side of the deck until we found the emergency stairs.

"If the alarm goes off, they're gonna know." Malory's fingers knotted.

"Use the key, Oli. The alarm won't go off. And ladies, let's grow some balls. They may be able to pick us off one-by-one, but together, we're a fucking force to be reckoned with." I welcomed the rush of heat up my spine. If they weren't going to be the badass bitches I knew they could be, then I'd be enough for all of us.

Olivia slipped her card into the reader as we all held our breath, hoping the alarm wouldn't sound. The red lights turned green and the lock clicked free.

We stepped into the stairway and slowly started making our way down the steel giant's insides. Round and round, we went, the elevator marking our descent by the number of times it flew past us. We made work of the staircase in silence, none of us willing to voice our concerns about what or who would be waiting for us at the bottom of the girders. We were half way down when an ear-piercing wail shattered our rhythmic huffing.

"There they are," a male voice growled.

And just like that, our slow and methodical descent ended.

Olivia led the breakneck race down the rest of the stairs. Converse and flip-flops slapped against the risers. Helen stumbled and I swept her up in my arms.

"Keep going."

She winced at the next few steps.

"I think it's sprained."

"If it isn't broken, then push through, girl," Malory hissed.

"Easy for you to say, they're not chasing after you, Malory."

I let the two continue to bicker; as long as they were moving and Helen wasn't whining, then life was good. We came to a stop at another door, this one at the roof level. Olivia fumbled for her key, cursing as she saved it before it fell through the strut, and shoved it into the reader.

"Breathe, Oli. They're still way behind us." I leaned over the edge and looked up at the middle of the Eiffel Tower replica. The stairway oozed with black hoods snaking their way closer and closer toward us. The door gave way and we pushed through.

"Does it lock?"

"Does it matter?" Olivia answered. "We can lose them on the floor. They're not allowed in the gambling pits."

"Yeah, well, neither are we," Gia pulled Helen into her arms, and we picked up the pace of making our way down the steel staircase. "Your Mr. Baudin should be waiting for us."

"Don't count on it. If the Jacks were ordered down, I'm pretty sure that means everyone has been put on notice to let us fend for ourselves."

"Right barbaric of the lot, don't you think?" Helen winced as she took a bad riser.

"You're going to be alright." Malory slipped Helen's other arm around her neck, helping Gia shoulder the weight.

"Bloody fine, but Malory, I'm not going to ASHA tonight."

"Yeah, I'll take a raincheck myself," Malory scoffed. "I've had enough thrills for one night."

"So here's the plan: we'll come out the leg by the casino cashier's cage and cut across the gaming floor. The Paris Theater let's out at nine-thirty; time it right and we'll blend in to the cab line." Olivia slipped the key into the last lock. Hopefully, these would slow down the Shadows. Then again, they probably had keys of their own.

"Why are we taking a cab if my car's here?"

"Leave the Jeep, Mal. I'll drive you back tomorrow. Right now, we just need to get back to campus."

"What about the elixirs?" Helen asked.

I looked up the Eiffel Tower's inside, hoping to catch a glimpse of our lead. "We can't search for them with a brigade of Shadows on our asses. We'll come back tomorrow after our classes and find them both."

"And if they find the elixir?" Malory asked.

"They don't want the elixir."

The sounds of the casino wormed their way into the almost melodic pace of our feet smacking on the risers. We came down through the roofing, giving us a good look of the casino floor. The sky-painted ceiling finished the illusion of a Parisian city. I stole another look; the Shadows were far enough behind that our ditch plan might work.

We spilled out of the leg of the Eiffel Tower and quickly cut across the cobblestone walkway toward the slot machines. The casino floor welcomed us in as we padded across the blue floors. Like a band of rattled misfits, we made it to the Paris Theater as it let out. I scanned the new bodies, looking for hoods but finding none.

"It's about time something goes our way," Olivia huffed.

We made it back to the dorms without an all-out Shadow smack-down.

Not that the Shadows weren't a mere courtyard away or anything. We were as much open game here as we were anywhere else in Las Vegas. Maybe it was the high of outsmarting the bastards. Maybe it was sneaking back in and leaving the Jacks clueless. Whatever it was, it felt good to be in control of our lives. Even if it was only an illusion.

We tiptoed past the light from the Jacks' room bleeding out from under their doorway. Two more seconds and we'd be home free. Gia opened our door and dove into to the darkness of our dorm room, not trusting the light until the door was locked.

"Hit the switch," Helen muttered.

I half expected Beaux or A.J. to wrap their hands around my wrist and shake me stupid. But the light flipped on and our dorm room was empty. We'd either pulled off our fieldtrip without a hitch, or they were letting us have a small controlled victory. Either way, the thought didn't sit well in my stomach.

Gia settled Helen on the couch and headed off to the kitchen. "You need ice, Helen. Mal, grab my laptop from my bed. Olivia, pull out the pizza, we need to decode the arrow and the lyrics."

"I thought you said you knew where your elixir was?" Olivia slapped Gia's butt as she passed her in the small kitchen.

"The arrows were a hint in the right direction. I've got a feeling the words are the locations they're hidden."

"Why?" I asked, pouring a round of fireball shots. "What?" I chuckled at all the inquisitive looks. "You can't tell me you're all not a tad bit freaked out?"

"Freaked, yes. Driven to the bottle?" Olivia ripped the fireball whiskey bottle from my fingers. "Not a chance."

"Yeah, well, I don't have your nerves of steel Superwoman." I fished back the bottle and finished pouring the shots into the red solo cups. "So, all mighty Riddler—" I tossed back the amber liquid and poured a second shot for myself. "Olivia's elixir's got to be in the Arc De Triomphe, which is totally fitting, by the way."

"Right?" A lopsided grin distorted Olivia's face.

I slammed back the second shot and stepped away from the bottle. "Have you seen the size of the Arc de Triomphe? Even a mock up at two-thirds the size, there's a whole lot of place to hide a vial of elixir. We've got to be smart about this. We have to assume the Shadows saw the same clues; that means they'll have people watching for us."

"I could go get it," Malory offered.

Gia wrapped her arms around Mal's neck and pulled her in for a hug. "Sweetie, that's kind of you, but I have a feeling it's gotta be claimed by the heirs."

"Why do you say that?" I asked, sinking into the couch. "Here, Helen." I handed her a red solo cup of her own.

"We've got key cards. We've got keepers and we've got hidden lyrics." Gia booted up her ancient laptop.

"We've also got Jacks and Shadows, but that's neither here nor there," I quipped.

"Mr. Baudin asked how we'd figured out the riddle so quickly. The riddle has to be in the lyrics. *Con Te Partiro* is the only song always played during the fountain show. Learn to read between the lines, ladies." The blue light of Gia's computer flickered off the glint of mischief in her eyes.

She was right; it was between the lines and staring us right in the face. "If we're the only ones who have the riddle, then the Shadows aren't hunting the elixir, they're hunting us." I scanned the room. "The question is: why?"

TWENTY-THREE

THREE DAYS LATER, butterflies still swarmed my stomach. The hands of time ticked by slowly. Each click marked how we were total failures in securing our lines. Every day Olivia was left unprotected threatened a visit from Isaac or worse, her capture by the Shadows.

I tossed in my bed, careful not to disturb Gia. A soft snore fluttered from her lips. I stifled a laugh. My roommate was quite a sight with her Diva sleep mask. She was far from the Diva and every bit the Martha Stewart.

We'd spent every waking moment chained to schoolbooks or hunting down clues. We'd narrowed down the search to either a moon or a sun. I'd Google Earthed the shit out of the Arc De Triomphe, comparing the one in Paris, France to the hotel in Las Vegas. I knew every square inch of the marble tribute. If we'd been in Paris, I had a pretty damn good idea where the elixir would be kept.

But we weren't.

And the tiny discrepancies in the two Arcs made all the difference in the world. Olivia's elixir wasn't in the Arc, which meant we were back to square one. The Eiffel Tower Clue was a bust, or we were stupid and couldn't figure it out. I threaded my fingers through my hair, staring at the ceiling tiles.

Last night, we'd made another dorm break but were thwarted by the swarm of black hoodies casing the Paris Hotel. I'd tried to blend in with a tour group, only to find myself face to face with a girl from high school who now resided in the catacombs. Her ear-piercing scream alerting the other Shadows that I was there still raised goosebumps on my arms. Some quick sprints through oncoming traffic and a killer job of get-away-car driving by Malory, we'd made it back to the dorms. We did solve one thing: the Shadows knew we were focused on Olivia's elixir, which meant they were, too.

Gia figured her elixir was hidden on a ship, but given the fact that there were no ships in the Bellagio and Midas owned the hotel with the big pirate ship, we were left with nothing for her, too. By the time we'd finally crawled into bed at three in the morning, we were no closer to deciphering the lyrics of the fountain song and slightly intoxicated.

My bad on the intoxication.

Fireballs seemed like the perfect "find the hidden riddle cocktail." It didn't work. My chest tightened around the thought of the Shadow from high school; she could've been Malory. She could've been me if A.J. and I hadn't been lucky and strong enough to break Dionysus's spell.

I kicked back the covers and snagged my robe from the foot of my bed and my laptop from my backpack. There was no sense trying to pretend I was going to get any sleep.

The living room was just as quiet as the rest of the dorm. I tiptoed to the kitchen and flipped on the Keurig. I was going to need black tar to get me through today.

A few minutes later, I settled into the couch and pulled up the Bellagio's website. If the Shadows were focused on Olivia, then we should focus on Gia's clue. A shudder ripped through me. That wasn't going to make Isaac happy, but even one of us being claimed by the dark side wouldn't go over too well with our mothers.

I clicked through the Bellagio's website, confirming my suspicions that there were no hidden ships or ship exhibits. My fingers rapped on the edge of my computer, marking the time between my current failed thought and the next. I polished off my first cup of coffee and decided I was an utter failure when it came to riddle cracking. Another cup into my quest, I pulled up the ownership chart of every hotel in Las Vegas. One of the hotels under the House of Club's rule had to have a ship in it; it also had to be North of the Bellagio. The water show's arrow made that pretty clear. Another hour later, I was no closer to an answer and my veins felt like they were trying to extricate themselves from my body in retaliation for all the caffeine pumping through them.

"What are you working on?"

"Sweet Jesus, woman." I jumped at Olivia's voice, sloshing cold coffee onto my lap. "What are you doing up?" I did a quick double-take. "Are you seriously going for a run this early?"

She nodded, sunk down next to me, and started tying her shoe. "If I'm going to get a run in—a real run, not a hamster on a treadmill run before the heat takes over—then five in the morning it is."

"Treadmills are that bad?"

"Humanity is one treadmill away from a gerbil's cage."

I snorted.

"And before you ask, Francis is going to run with me." Olivia fished out her phone and sent off a message. "What are you doing up so early?" She grabbed the edge of my laptop. The way her nose crinkled said she wasn't too surprised to see me working on Operation Elixir. "You need to be working on battle plans for this morning. Your House is up first and that's the toughest place to be."

"I haven't even met my House yet. I know they should all be focused on me, but my gut says they'll be answering to Cara. I'm just going to be the spectacle trying to stay upright on roller skates." I nodded to my duffel bag next to me. "Do you know how long it's been since I've been on roller skates?"

"Cara was a great leader. She commanded their respect." Olivia sat down next to me, completely ignoring my roller skate comment. "They may not know you, Cass, but they're terrified of you."

"They're terrified of my powers," I corrected. "My little meltdown with Helen has probably already made the rounds."

Olivia nodded her head. "Terrifying isn't a bad rep to have when you've got none at all."

"Thanks. Great pep talk, cuz." I sank under the weight of everything, letting the quiet that only early morning could bring ease the tension in the room.

Olivia's phone vibrated.

"Francis said Beaux was up all night, pacing the floor. He wouldn't say it, but my money's on you being the reason. Given the awesome whisker burns you were sporting a few days ago after the Breech Room . . ."

"Burns were from A.J."

Olivia's mouth formed a small "o," and she asked, "So all is forgiven?"

"Far from it." I snorted. "He gave excuses."

"And you sucked his face?"

I snorted. "No. Yes. It's complicated."

"No, it's not. You love him and that means you're willing to hold onto the illusion instead of walk the plank of reality. I get it. God, I get it."

"And somehow I thought we were talking about me and A.J., not you and Isaac."

Olivia straightened her shoulders, stood, and headed for the door. The girl had it bad for the worst kind of human. Me, I was just a mistress. I couldn't imagine loving someone who fed on the souls of the innocent.

Olivia opened the door, pausing a moment while she searched the back of our dorm's living room. "Cass, I get loving someone you can't have. Doesn't make it right, just makes you a fool like the rest of us who've chased our hearts down a rabbit hole and wound up in a bad Tim Burton nightmare." Her fingers rapped on the door like she wanted to say something else but wasn't sure this was the right time. "If I'm not back before you leave for the field, good luck." The door clicked behind her. Apparently, complicated was an understatement when it came to my cousin's love life.

I stared at the door for lord knows how long, only giving up when my computer dinged with a message from my half-sister:

Please tell me you're up.

I want to head to the Menden Center with you.

You need to know the formations the House is going to use today.

Curiosity replaced frustration and I messaged her back:

Thanks? Meet you by the elevator in ten minutes.

♥

CARA MARCHED INTO the Menden Center with her tablet under her arm, a duffel bag slung over her shoulder, and an authority like every inch of this place was hers. We walked up a flight of stairs and into a darkened room. The lights flickered to life as Cara headed to the front podium. The room was nothing like I expected. Thick red carpet was where stained linoleum should have been and executive leather chairs that looked softer than butter took the place of aluminum folding chairs. A state-of-the-art film setup that Cara was already connecting to obliterated my vision of a green chalkboard and dust hanging in the air. Despite all the opulence, the hint of sweaty basketball players still hung in the air. Four rows of tables, five seats at each table, finished off the room.

"Here, pass those out," Cara called. She nodded to the duffel bag sitting on the first table. "They're jerseys and shorts. Twos go in the back and work your way to the front. I already gave Beaux his jersey and shorts." Cara pulled an electrical cord out from a zipper in her bag and headed to another switch. A moment later, a smart board flickered to life.

Thoughts of Beaux in shorts and sweaty clouded my mind. "Beaux's playing?"

"He *is* your Jack."

"So's A.J."

Cara paused. Her shoulders hung just a little bit lower and I knew the answer before I even asked the question. Ms. Maddox's warning gaze made sense now. A.J. wasn't going to be on the field with the rest of the Hearts, he'd be representing the House of Midas during the Field Games.

Second pick again.

"Right, House before Heart." I swiped the bag off the table and headed to the back of the room. "Good thing I have a Beaux." I yanked the first jersey out of the bag, my mouth gaping open. I held up the black matte shirt, mesmerized by a flaming heart over the left breast. On the back was the number two and the last name Payan. Given the extra-large black shorts, the first two was a beast. I could only hope the rest of the numbers were the same size. "When did you do this?"

"It's no big deal."

"Cara," I pressed.

"I ordered them when I was in Malaga." Her hands stilled, eyes so similar to mine boring into me. "I was certain you wouldn't be passing Committee Finals. I had to be prepared."

"And if I did, what was your plan then?"

"I still had to be prepared, because you wouldn't be." She tried to be a badass, but her voice didn't carry the same caustic tone. Her eyes didn't sharpen into ice picks tracking my vital organs.

I worried the fabric between my fingers. "Thank you."

"No big deal."

"It is to me," I sighed.

Cara turned her back and continued syncing her tablet, but I saw the small grin dimple her cheek before she shut me out. That must have come from her dad.

I placed the next matching number two jersey belonging to Bustillos on the next seat. It was extra-small, and the shorts would probably fit a six-year-old instead of someone in college. Bustillos was the girl. Payan had to be the boy. I guess everyone had their life dictated to them in some way or another.

Maybe that was the reality and the ability to choose was the illusion. None of us really had free will. There were parents to please. Houses to appease. Friends to compromise. Boyfriends to question. I kicked the last thought in the junk. I couldn't afford to have my mind clouded with the drama of my love life.

We worked in silence. I placed jerseys on the tables and tried to commit their last names and ranks to memory. Tried being the optimum word. Cara dimmed the lights and quickly ran through a series of field photos. When I was done, I hiked my hiney up on the table next to her.

"These the formations?" I asked.

Cara settled in next to me. "Yep. Your male Eight is crazy gifted with coding and gaming. The summer of our sophomore year in high school, I had him create a game that simulated FG, field games. Your numbers have been playing these formations and any new ones from Jordan, my . . . match." She stumbled over the new word. She'd been calling him her Jack for so long. I'd not only stolen my sister's title, I'd hijacked his as well. "You listening?"

"Yeah, sorry."

"Cassie, you've got to pay attention. The cards will be here in thirty minutes. If we're going to have any chance at winning this year's tournament, then Mom has to have optimum seating."

"Why?"

Cara pursed her lips together, weighing the option of not telling me or passing off a version of the truth. My half-sister may have only been physically in my life a total of two months, but the girl was easier to read than a Dr. Seuss book and almost as much fun to figure out.

"We don't have a second chair." She huffed at my blank expression.

"You're killing me, you know that, right? Each house has a King and Queen."

"I know this. The Hearts retired their King."

"Very good. It can be taught." Cara's tone softened as she nudged my shoulder. "Before, the tournament seating was based on each House's annual generated revenue. Now that the power shift generation has come of age, field games will determine the seating."

"Then I better get my shit together."

"Yes, you better." She clicked the first slide. U.L.V.'s basketball team's practice arena sliced across the screen. It wasn't nearly as big as the Thomas and Mack Center, but there was enough space to either screw you into a loss or ride triumphantly to the W column. The picture showed the arena darkened and ramps cutting the court into fours.

"I know you already know this, Cassie, but bear with me. My stomach's about to crawl out of my mouth, I'm so damn nervous. Field Games is a cross between laser tag, chess, capture the flag, roller derby, and crack the whip. The only sources of lighting are the illuminated scoreboard, the under-lighting of each House's 'castle' or platform, and the wheels on each player's skates. The two Houses' flags hang from the center scoreboard. No space is out of bounds, and only the capture of an Eight or higher can activate the whipping station."

Yeah, I knew about the crack the whip station. The perimeter of the basketball court would light up, and the gates to the lower four ramps would lower. Your team would whip either their strongest player or their lightest player up a ramp that lead directly to the two flags in the center of the stadium. When the whipping stations were in play, anyone could link up and sacrifice the lowest numbered player by hurtling them at an opposing team's protective formation. Human bowling would have been a better term.

Cara clicked the next slide. "Formations one through nine are offensive maneuvers. Ten through thirty are defensive."

"Why double the defensive maneuvers? Isn't the best defense a good offense?"

Cara shot me a sideways glance, eyebrows crawling up into her hair from the glare of indignation.

"Sorry," I offered.

"You're lucky I'm even sharing this much. If we don't keep our eyes on—" Cara stopped herself. A few calming breaths later, she continued. "Protect the Queen. That's the name of the game. You or your castle fall—"she pointed to a raised wooden platform with three small ramps as access points—"and the House is lost. Game over. It's happened in as little as eight minutes, and our grandmother never lived down the shame."

"Got it. Protect the Queen."

"I'm your Rook, your second, so I'll be close enough to help you call the plays." Cara reached behind her and pulled out a black helmet. The same flaming heart was on one side and a number on the other side. "There's a speaker in the earpiece and a microphone in the chin strap." She handed me the helmet.

My worried reflection bounced back at me in the high gloss covering. "Standard issue or did you design this?"

A blush stained Cara's cheeks. "Your male Ten came up with the idea after his father cost Carina a win because he couldn't hear her call. Anyway, I'll mute my speaker and . . ." Her words trailed off under my intense evaluation. "What?"

"Why are you doing this, Cara? Why are you helping me?"

"Psh, I'm not doing this for you. I'm doing it for the House. For Mom."

"No, you know I'm vulnerable. I don't even know the team's ranks, let alone their names. You could've made a statement, taken over on the field, and proven me ineffective. But you didn't."

"I think you're giving me too much credit."

A giggle floated in with the opening door. A petite girl with long, black, curly hair and bright blue eyes looked startled. "I'm sorry," she whispered, starting to back out of the door she'd come through. "I can wait outside." She started to turn, her feet already searching for traction to hightail it out of our presence.

"No, not necessary, Bustillos. Come on in." I waved her in and pointed to the back of the room. "Your uniform is in your seat."

The girl's eyes flared at her last name. It wasn't rocket science; she had to be the tiniest person on campus and the House of Hearts' number two.

I excused myself and changed into our uniform. By the time I'd come out of the back bathroom, my nerves were exploding like fireworks. The rest of the House of Hearts' numbers filtered into the film room. I joined Cara at the front, greeting each numbered pair from the mismatched Twos to the bickering Tens. Beaux was the last to arrive at the film room. The minute he stepped through the door, the room shrank to fit him. Whispers peppered the room. My Numbers didn't know what to make of him.

He'd been hidden like me.

He was from another House who had been asked to represent this one, like me.

And given the locked jaws of all the male Numbers in this room, Beaux's presence was about as welcome as mine.

We really were two peas in the same fucked-up pod.

Beaux's eyes locked onto mine as he skirted an obvious macho territory marking from the male Seven. The way Beaux's jaw ticked said the Seven was lucky he was on his best behavior. He'd traded out the cowboy hat for a black baseball cap with the flaming heart insignia. Like always, Beaux had to be different; the cap sat backward, allowing strands of blonde hair to peek out. Black jersey shorts showed off his tan legs. I'd have bet money they'd never seen the light of day, but the golden hue said he was full of secrets. And a defiant part of me wanted to explore every single dark one of them. I hadn't noticed the room quiet or the tangible tension building between Beaux and me.

Cara's Chanel No. 5 scent invaded my space. "This 'make 'em jealous' maneuver only works when the person you're trying to make jealous— A.J.—is in the room."

Heat crawled up my spine and puddled in my palms.

"I'm Cassandra Vera." I quickly changed the subject, turning to greet my future house. "I know we haven't formally met. I know you have lots of questions about me and what my being here means, but not now." I ushered everyone to their seats with a wave of my hand. "I can imagine you've heard rumors there's tension between Cara and me. There's nothing further from the truth." Cara stiffened under my arm around her shoulder. "Our formal meeting is tomorrow; today, I need you to do your duty to your House and your Queen."

A girl with an auburn braid hanging over her shoulder smiled, stealing a quick look at the boy next to her. He bristled under her inspection.

"Cara, you want to discuss the game plan?" I gave up the floor despite Beaux's disapproving look.

I hadn't expected my first pep talk speech to go down as a motivational hall of fame moment, but the quiet spoke volumes. They didn't trust me and I couldn't blame them. The lights dimmed and Cara brought up the first formations.

Cara ran down the plays, calling on each House member and quizzing them on their function for the play. Each play was well-organized, thought-out, and didn't include me. I was merely a cake topper they had to keep from falling. Cara finished up the last play, and without a cue, the House of Hearts hollered in unison, "Protect the Queen."

"Finish getting ready," I ordered.

A low hush filled the room as everyone took turns slipping into the bathroom as an individual and emerging as a member of the House of Hearts. The lower Numbers chatted on whipping techniques, while the higher Numbers went over offensive strategy. A.J. was the highest-ranking target. Zee was his Queen. A small twang sprung loose in me. She was his Queen in more ways than just this game.

Beaux stepped in front of me, his thumb freeing my lip from the worried working I was giving it.

"Stop it." He folded his arms in the protective way that left him cold and unapproachable. "They think you're worrying over the games. They don't know it's over A.J."

I cocked my head back, not sure whether to thank him for his concern or to mind his own business. After the Breeching Room, we were running hot and cold when it came to civility. Helen said we should just shag and be done with it. Gia quickly reminded her that we were of age and shagging had consequences.

Today, we were running hot.

His knuckles tenderly slid down my cheek, freeing some of the worry about the games but bundling up a new set of nerves that had no business being in my belly.

"Don't do that." I pushed away his hand. A smirk pulled at his lips, but Beaux did as I asked, letting me storm past him without a fight. He and A.J. couldn't have been more different. His hot temper and calloused knuckles were the opposite of A.J.'s cool demeanor and soft hands. Beaux's "hide nothing and let me sort it all out" was the antithesis of A.J.'s "handle her with kid gloves" approach. But the biggest difference was that A.J., the boy sworn to protect me, was now the person I had to not just defeat but destroy.

TWENTY-FOUR

MOST OF MY fight left a few rolls in on my skates. Unruly hisses and wails echoed down the darkened tunnel connecting the film room to the arena. A bright white light lit up the entrance, shining a spotlight on all the reasons why I wasn't qualified to lead the House of Hearts. I worried my lip. Beaux was right, my talk was shite and I was a fraud with a stolen crown. My heart tripped over itself as I heard a guttural roar echo down the tunnel. The Midas Candidates were born to protect and battle. I had no idea what my House was born to do: make love, not war? Beaux working the hippie look pulled a painful giggle to my lips.

The walls bleached around me as I teetered on skates toward the mouth of the tunnel. With each roll, I pushed closer. My heart pounded against my rib cage. Despite every instinct in me pleading for me to turn and roll my sorry ass away, I headed toward the light at the end of the tunnel. Which admittedly never really worked out well for anyone. Finally, there was nowhere else for me to go but forward. No matter how unsure of myself I was, I stepped into the light of my future and felt my blood run cold.

Cara's slides had no way of accurately conveying the scale of our arena. The court's floor was covered with a polished mahogany wood. On the floor outside our tunnel was Cara's flaming heart. The symbol was repeated in the middle of the floor, along with a gold dollar sign that seemed to be dripping liquid gold. Both marks were under black flags suspended from the scoreboard.

I jumped at the hiss of skates on wood above my head. Lights from the skates tracked the path of the ramps up into the darkness of the rafters above the arena. Like an outline of a rollercoaster, I saw the lights attached to a series of ramps circling the arena and emptying onto the game floor.

Another sizzle of the skates above our entrance warned I was in for a serious ass whipping. I flinched under the set of hands touching my shoulder. I knew it was Beaux by his unique scent of soap and man.

"Crikey," Beaux's Australian lilt tickled my ear. "Remember, everyone behind you is seeing the arena for the first time, too. Turn around and show them it doesn't bother you. Lead by lying. It's worked for all the greats before you." He worked the inside of his cheek and I could tell he was far from done. Beaux leaned into me; his lips inches from mine seemed to make the air crackle between us. Bright green eyes softened before he licked his bottom lip one last time and pulled on the hem of my jersey. "On the side, you storming out of the film room—sexiest thing I've ever witnessed."

My rebellious heart fluttered. It should have been because of Beaux's unwavering belief in me, but I was certain it had to do a lot more with the close contact and the thrill his thumb touching my belly created.

I pulled in a deep breath, chasing away all the bad-girlfriend thoughts.

I could do this. The whole fake it 'til you make it thing. I'd lived with an actress for eighteen years of my life. Unfamiliar warmth raced up my spine, seeping into my bloodstream; it wasn't the Balanter power, it was something else. Something I'd never felt before. I turned around and found twenty-three sets of eyes wide and focused on me.

"Crazy, right?" I proclaimed to my team. Yeah, I totally stole a page out of Beaux's book of calm and crossed my arms. "It's bigger, brighter, louder than anything I could have imagined. Here's the thing, the Midas Candidates said the same thing because this was the first time they saw the arena. They had no way to prepare, but you did. You've played this game for two years. I've seen the way you work together online, now it's time to show the House of Midas just how badass we are in person. All I ask is that you run the routes called. Play with the passion I know flows in your veins. Make the House of Midas pay for the privilege of playing against us and make them wary to ever dare to take *our* field again!"

The tunnel erupted with a roar, shaking the caps on my teeth. Even little Bustillos had climbed up Payan's back and was hanging off his shoulders. She looked like she was ready to behead Goliath himself.

"You heard our future Queen, take the field," Beaux roared. Black clad warriors streamed past us, determination perfumed the air with the aroma of victory.

Cara rolled up next to me, hands on her hips like I'd seen our mother do countless times. "Sounded a little reminiscent of *Hoosiers*."

"I did grow up in Hollywood."

Beaux chuckled behind us. "Shall we take the field?" He skated past us, slapping my ass. He let loose an eardrum-shattering holler that clarified he was now a member of the House of Hearts.

Cara grabbed my hands, her forehead pressed against mine, our mother's eyes staring back at each other. "Run the formations. Defend the Queen. Got it?"

"Yeah, I got it."

We skated into the arena, Cara showing me to the platform nearest the tunnel we'd left. Around us the Houses of Midas and Hearts sailed past us on wood ramps that disappeared into the darkness of the gym. Skates hissed high behind me. I couldn't see them, but they could see me, and across the modified gym floor stood A.J. His blue eyes cut into me with a white-hot anger. He'd witnessed our pow-wow, Beaux's ass-slap, and he was going to try to make my House pay.

I skated up onto the Heart's platform, sweat pooling in the creases of my palms, and fastened my helmet. The cadence of Beaux's voice bellowed in my ears, calming my racing pulse.

"Give 'em bloody hell. Eights, you know your plan, prepare for the whip. Bustillos, when the gates go down, you're flying to victory. Have you seen the size of their flyer? She won't be able to make it up the ramp with the lot of 'em swinging her fat arse."

I giggled.

"Right, they're primed and ready for you, captain my captain." Somewhere in the arena, Beaux was skating with my House emblem affixed to his body. In a week, his consistent acts of being there proved more valuable than A.J.'s one overt act of protection. I scanned the arena, wondering where the spare enigma was. How many other ways would he prove to be of value to me? How many other ways could A.J. disappoint me?

I tapped my ear twice, leaving the microphone open but still ready to receive. "Let's hope I fair better than Whitman's Captain."

"Clearly, I was referring to the first few stanzas of the poem. Don't want that precious face of yours dripping blood anywhere on a deck."

"Fantastic," Cara interjected. "You two done playing footsies over the mics? We've got a game to win here." A few seconds later, she rolled up to the platform's edge, signaling me over with a nod of her head.

I rolled toward her, muting my microphone. The hiss from skates swelled behind us. "What's up?"

"Viewing gallery has all the royals this morning, Mom and Midas included."

I stole a quick glance at the space she nodded to over her shoulder. A bright light sliced through the darkness of the upper arena. Carina stood at the window, arms crossed in that confident way that only Cara and I knew meant she was nervous enough to spit. Next to her was Midas, his eyes firmly fixed on the other end of the arena. Dionysus stood next to him, egging Midas on with a nudge. Probably coaxing the foolish king into another bet that included me, my life, or my offspring. But it was Warren standing off to the side, with his gaze set on me and a smirk miring his lips, that made my ribs collapse. The swarm of butterflies I'd held at bay released into my belly.

"A.J. will try to show his House's brute force." Cara's voice fought for my attention. "Run the first defense play, and we'll take out enough of his team to lower the gates."

"He's going to do more than show his House's force. He's going to ram it down my throat. We should run Offense Seven."

Cara shook her head. "You wanna storm his castle?"

"Hell yeah, I want to storm his castle. I want to obliterate the castle and send a fucking message to everyone in the viewing gallery. Don't you?" My vision honed in on A.J. and his Second, Zee.

Zee hollered orders at the Midas Skaters as they sailed past. But A.J.—he stalked his platform. Eyes trained on me like I'd morphed into his enemy and not his girlfriend.

That's how it was?

Honor and House before Heart.

I'd show him exactly what that felt like. I'd show him how every cancelled date, every postponed moment burned away a piece of your soul until you questioned every breath.

Cara slapped the platform, pulling me out of my revenge-fueled moment.

"Protect the Queen. The only way to play this is to protect you. Defense One." Her eyebrows crawled up into her helmet. "Cass, you hear me? Defense One. Say it!"

I pulled a quick look at A.J. He knew exactly what we were going to do. Defend the Queen. We were skating into a trap.

"Defense One," I conceded.

Cara pushed off the platform, rolling to her position as my second, jaw firmly clamped down.

A hush fell over the arena. Skates calmed and the world stilled, until there was only A.J. staring at me.

Defense one.

Defense one, I chanted.

A microphone crackled to life. "Welcome to the first Field Games of the year," Midas's voice echoed off the rafters. "The House of Midas against the House of Hearts. The games will commence at the sound of the buzzer. Remember, Cassandra"—my skin crawled at my name on Midas's lips— "seating at the Royal Poker Tournament is decided by your victory . . . or failure." The microphone clicked off and silence bled into the arena.

My pulse sloshed in my ears, matching its cadence with the rattling of my heart against my rib cage. Adrenaline poured into my body until I could hardly stand to be still. But I did; we all stood motionless, waiting for the signal.

The arena jumped at the wail of the buzzer. Skates pounded on polished wood, searching for traction. The hiss returned and my nerves seemed to settle. Up in the rafters, red lights from my House's skates circled the arena, battling with the gold lights of the House of Midas. A grunt echoed behind me. I didn't dare turn around. My eyes focused on A.J.'s lips, waiting for him to make the first move. Waiting for him to confirm this was his first priority and I only factored in when it was convenient.

"They're setting up, Cassie," Beaux's voice crackled in my headphone, followed by a grunt and deluge of Australian curse words. "Cassie, call a route."

I scanned the arena. The buildup of gold lights now moved like a synchronized pod of fish. Piranhas wanting to take me out. It wasn't hard to see the force of the Midas's house swarming above. They circled over A.J.'s head, dipped down one ramp, and then flew up another, picking up more gold lights, more Midas candidates with each pass.

My look fell on A.J. He'd do this to me? Humiliate me by destroying any chance of my ability to rule in a matter of minutes—because of Beaux. I couldn't let him take this from me. If this was how we were going to play this game, then I'd play just as dirty as he was.

A.J. circled his finger in the air, bringing it and my heart down with a sickening swipe. The swarm of gold lights split into two. The next round, they'd take me and my castle's platform. We'd lose in less than three minutes.

"Offense Seven." The words left a sour taste in my mouth.

"Cassie, no! We're not set up! You'll be completely unprotected." Cara screamed, but no one else heard her. She wasn't the future queen. I was and this was how I planned on ruling. Brutal force would be matched with savage strength. There would be no mercy. If A.J. planned on sending his entire house after me, then I'd send all that I had after him.

"Offense Seven, now," I hollered. Cara pushed off from her station as my second. She bolted across the arena floor as red lights descended the ramps closest to the House of Midas platform. My House hit the arena floor simultaneously. Synchronized skating that looked as deadly as it did beautiful.

They reached A.J.'s platform as Beaux cried out, "Cassie!"

Arms wrapped around my waist. The air in my lungs rushed out as the arena tipped sideways and I landed with a sickening thud. My ribs crashed in on each other, wringing out what little breath they still had in them and my head cracked against the platform.

The world blackened around the edges. A tilted Beaux skated toward me. Anger radiated off his body and in the distance, A.J. stood still. Another fissure split my heart. This was how it was going to be . . . so be it.

My world slipped into darkness.

TWENTY-FIVE

I WOKE UP in my bed, surrounded by darkness and defeat. I stirred under the weight of a hand on my foot and pushed up to my elbows, but the silver ray of moonlight lit up a strand of blond hair. A small piece of me allowed the disappointment that the tuft of hair wasn't black. It wasn't A.J. at the foot of my bed. It was Beaux.

"You okay?" His voice was heavy with sleep.

"Yeah. What was the time?" I gingerly touched the painful spot over my eyebrow.

"Don't touch that, you were lucky you didn't need stitches."

"Time?" I asked again.

Beaux's eyes found mine in the muted darkness. The muscles along his jaw worked over time, and I knew it was bad.

"Three thirty-seven."

"No, how long before I lost—"

"I know. Your castle fell in three minutes and thirty-seven seconds. It's just after two in the morning, Cass. Go to sleep. You're going to need your rest when you meet your ranks tomorrow."

"Three thirty-seven," I mumbled. The crushing blow of defeat and not the pain radiating from my eyebrow pushed me back into my pillow. I'd let them down. I'd let my House down. And worse, I'd let my mother down. At least my grandmother was in the clear. I'd taken her world's worst title.

A few hours later, I woke up in an empty room. Looked like loser status had cleared not only my bedroom but also the future Queens from their living quarters. Humiliation kept me from the showers. The memory of whispers always chasing after me at home in Hollywood came rushing back. Three minutes and thirty-seven seconds was hardly enough time to work up a sweat. The stench hanging from me had nothing to do with my body and everything to do with failure. I padded to the bathroom and washed the important parts. I'd missed my first class with Ms. Maddox but had ten minutes to get to the House of Hearts meet and greet.

I grabbed my backpack, what was left of my ego, and slipped down the staircase, not wanting to risk seeing anyone in the elevator.

I crossed the campus and made my way to the Student Union. It was time to meet the rest of the House. Time to face the firing squad. From the tens down each rank to the almost free-from-this-life twos and all the cousins standing in the wings should their representative fail, each member of my House would be present for suit inspection.

Depending on which future Queen's take you took, suit inspection was either a shining moment of validation or the most awkward and torturous moment one could experience. I was hoping for Gia's meet and greet, but history had me prepared for Olivia's kiss-ass, torture comment. But none of them had to factor in a pre-meet ass whooping.

"G'day," Beaux's Australian lilt made me jump higher than the Stratosphere Casino. "Sorry, didn't mean to scare you." Beaux chuckled. "How's the head?"

I resisted the urge to touch the gash over my eye. "What are you doing?"

Beaux fell into step with me. He seemed to do that with an ease that left me impressed, uncomfortable, and furious at A.J.

"Heading to the Student Union." His fingers tightened around the strap of his backpack as a brief wind picked up the ends of his hair.

"I know you can't tell me, but the House of Clubs are meeting there, too?"

Beaux shot me a sideways look. "No, I'm headed to our meeting place." He pulled his backpack around to his chest. The action pulled his black tee shirt taut against his back. I swallowed hard, jumping again when he handed me his schedule.

"The Cohen Theater? But you're a Club." I handed Beaux back his schedule.

"I was a Club by birth, but I'm your Jack until Bash carks it, chooses to forget, or produces an heir. Since I don't see any of those happening, I'm your Jack of Hearts. I thought me skating with your emblem on my chest cleared that up for you yesterday. Or did your castle falling give you amnesia, too? I'm all yours . . ." Beaux bowed like you'd see a prince do in a Disney movie. He lifted his gaze, making my cheeks flush with heat. "If the future Queen will still have me."

A group of girls passing swooned.

"Get up." I pulled at his arm. "Truth?"

"Give it to me."

"I'm glad you're here. I thought I was going to have to meet the ranks by myself. At least with you by my side, they'll be terrified into staving off the revolution."

"Ahh, *the scare them into respect* approach. I'd taken you for a *kill 'em with kindness* kind of ruler. Go in barrels blazing, like yesterday."

He was joking with me. I shook off the indignation and focused on the fact that at least someone still wanted to stand beside me.

"You were gone this morning."

Beaux nodded. "Perception is everything. Couldn't have the *perception* of you losing all control and letting me stamp your v-card—that's what you call it, right?—hanging around us. What would the boyfriend say?"

"The boyfriend can kiss my ass right now." I huffed. "And thanks."

We walked in silence until we saw people filing into the Student Union.

"Maybe I'll try on a few hats and see which one fits the best? The *strike first* leader hat certainly didn't work."

Beaux pulled open the door to the Student Union letting me pass by. "I could help," he said, his rock-hard body filling in the personal space behind me. Warm breath danced down the back of my neck, stopping me cold. "I'd love to see what you look like in hats . . . only hats." I caught the wicked wink out of the corner of my eye.

Heat flushed my face again as I stepped out of his magnetic pull. "And A.J.?"

"A.J. had no problem decimating you yesterday. He's not quite as torn between his heart and his House as you'd like. With A.J., you have a fuck buddy. Nothing more."

I spun on my heels and smacked into his solid granite chest. Beaux's arms snaked around me, the heat of his body scorching me as he saved me from falling to the floor.

"He's not my fuck buddy," I whispered. "I'm still a virgin."

Beaux's blue eyes darted across my face. His lips tightened, pulling at the scab over the corner of his eye. "Sorry. Right dickish move. Forgive me?"

"Only if you promise A.J.'s off-limits." I pushed a finger to his lips before he could answer. "I know you don't understand. I know you don't approve. Yes, I'm mad as hell at him. And yes, yesterday factors in, of course, but I love him . . . and I have to trust love always finds a way."

"He hasn't come to see you yet, has he?"

I shook my head. A.J. had kicked my ass in battle and didn't have the decency to face me in person.

"That's why you left this morning?"

Beaux licked at the answer sitting on the edge of his lips; his tongue sliding along the edge of my finger did something to me. Something I liked and despised at the same time. That was Beaux, a walking contradiction to every emotion or thought I could form. The buzz of students walking around us, wondering if we were going to kiss or move, faded away. For a moment, it was just the Australian cowboy who happened to be a spare, and me, the girl who was either going to free Midas from his curse or unleash the Titans on humanity.

"You deserve someone who'd walk away from everything to be with you." The husky tenor of his voice burrowed its way into my heart.

He was right.

I did deserve that, but then, I came to Las Vegas and annihilated anyone who was close to me. My parents, Cara, Carina, A.J., even Malory—their lives were irrevocably changed and altered because of my choice, my existence. I didn't deserve that kind of love. I barely deserved to draw the next breath.

"You've known me a week," I whispered. "I doubt you'll feel the same in three years."

Wind rushed past my face as Beaux righted me, fury burning in his eyes, and there was a barrage of accusations I could feel his ropy muscles holding back. Had I not been a future queen and had he not been tasked with my protection, I couldn't be sure he wouldn't haul me over his shoulder and take me somewhere until I saw things his way. Brute force and unwavering determination was how Beaux operated, but I wasn't one of his bulls. I was in charge and he bowed to *my* will.

"How I feel has very little to do with time and everything to do with reality. You are my future. I've accepted the fact that whom I wanted and the duty I'm demanded to execute are not the same. The sooner you give up the fantasy of happily ever after, the better." Beaux yanked on the edges of his backpack and stormed past me, blazing a path to the theater.

"You've already said that to me," I threw after him.

"Then I suggest you start listening."

As I rounded the hallway to the Cohen Theater, the people hanging outside scurried through the doors. I pulled in a deep breath and opened the heavy theater doors. Whispers raced in front of me, announcing my arrival, only to be met with a hush that hung on my body like a heavy brocade cape. Each step I took down the aisle, people would peek and then quickly avert their eyes. What were they told? Did they know I was more than a Queen? After A.J.'s declaration on the treaty line, all the worlds knew he protected me, but did they know why? Each question locked another piece of my spine into place. The weight of the crown was never heavier than when it hung over my head.

I climbed the stairs and thanked the gods the house lights were off. The sea of inky black was a welcome gift. I was used to being watched by people I couldn't see. I crossed the stage, nodding to a couple sitting next to Beaux and the empty seat A.J. was supposed to occupy. Dropping my backpack in my chair, I took a steady breath and channeled the actress my adopted mother had been. I could play the part until I found which role fit.

"Good morning," I started. I didn't give my House a chance to answer. "I'm sure you all have questions and have been hounding your ranking representatives for answers. Yesterday, I told them we'd do formal introduction today, so I'm Cassandra Vera. Given your silence, I'm going to assume you know my formal title, heir apparent to the House of Hearts. But I won't make that assumption when it comes to my other title." My mouth turned to cotton balls. I'd have given Malory's left kidney for a bottle of water. Heat snaked its way up my spine, and I quickly stamped it down. I didn't need to scare my subjects before I'd confirmed the gossip. "I am the Balanter."

A collective gasp scurried up the risers and back down.

"I'm certain you all have questions and rather than spend our first official meeting on what I am, I'd like to share my vision with what our House can be. Rest assured, my vision does not include ass-whoopings like yesterday. I tried something . . ." I stole a quick peek at Beaux. My heart jumped when his eyes connected with mine.

". . . I know my presence here elicits some fear in you—most of you. The myth is flesh and blood, standing in front of you. Our ancestors were tapped by the gods to protect humanity's hearts. I see no reason why this should alter because of me. The bedtime stories you were told are true. The Shadows exist with one purpose in life: to free the Titans from their prison in Tartarus. They've never come close to overthrowing Dionysus before, and with my last dying breath if need be, they won't succeed during my rein.

"Now, as to the Field Games . . . I know yesterday was a disappointment. I know you're all wondering if I have a clue what I'm doing. Here's the thing, that's not for you to ask or evaluate. I am your future queen. You will obey my orders. And one day, I hope you'll have as much trust in my ability to lead as I already do in your ability to execute. Yesterday wasn't your fault. It was mine.

"That said, if you have not practiced your innate powers, I order you to level up and learn. Whether you are a Two looking to free your children from service, or a Jack committed to my protection, I expect—demand—the same level of dedication. We are the House of Hearts. We will not be the weak link in the collective Houses' line of defense. Questions?" I listened, hoping I hadn't just delivered a speech to an empty room.

"Your Highness?" a female voice called out from the back of the auditorium.

"Cassandra. Until the crown is on my head, you can call me Cassandra." Out of the corner of my eye, I saw Beaux flinch. My stomach nose-dived, hoping I hadn't shown a weakness.

"Your Highness," the voice reiterated. "Is it true you have to claim your line by midterms?"

I shifted from one converse-clad foot to the other. "It is."

"Have you? I mean, are you close . . ." Her question trailed off as bodies rustled in their seats.

"It's a fair question. The other future Queens and I have made steps toward solving the . . ." Beaux flinched again and my words trailed off. "No, the line has not been claimed yet. When it is, your battle powers will activate. I expect you to be ready to use these powers like an expert. Any more questions?"

"Is it true you have two Jacks?"

"It is."

"What does this mean?" another, more timid voice closer toward the front of the room asked.

"It means I am no ordinary queen. It means our house will be under greater scrutiny and I expect you to measure up. I will give you until Friday to settle in, but come Saturday morning, I will expect you to be at the practice field ready to show me you are prepared to serve your House and honor your Queen. Dismissed."

I turned my back, fully expecting holy water to be thrown at me, the abomination. The couple I'd breezed past sat still, their head and body cemented forward, but their eyes appraised every move I made.

"I know you're my Tens, but who are you and how can you better my reign?" The words tumbled out harder than I'd expected. Screw the talk of the Balanter; I needed to be more concerned about my future Queen bitch persona. "I'm sorry."

Beaux flinched again.

"Damnit, Beaux, stop flinching or leave. Sorry," I said to the couple. "I'm Cassie. Cassandra. Don't call me Your Highness. I'm not. Not yet. Obviously, I'm very new at this." I flinched. What was I doing? Way to diminish your role as ruling leader and terrifying Balanter. I sat down in the empty chair next to the couple. The boy had fire engine-red hair and alabaster skin that looked like it would blister at the thought of being in the sun. There was no way this dude was leaving Las Vegas without skin cancer. His green eyes darted from my face to the floor, warring as to which place was appropriate to hold his gaze while his new queen had a mental breakdown.

The girl was beautiful.

She had long auburn hair that reached the small of her back. Her alabaster skin held a hint of olive and didn't look as likely to burn as her counterpart. Her copper eyes were much more sure of where they looked.

Straight at me.

She was either going to be my strongest ally or my fiercest foe. I'd decided all of this before I knew either of their names.

"I know you're my Tens. What I don't know are your first names."

The boy shifted uncomfortably in his seat, looking for the girl to take the lead. Finally exasperated at the boy, the girl rolled her eyes and looked me square in mine.

"I'm Kate. The bumbling idiot who should be downgraded to court fool is Leopold. He's new, too." Her head tilted ever so slightly at the use of my phrase.

"Oh, Kate. You and I are going to get along wonderfully or kill each other."

Her smart-ass straightened in her seat.

"Don't worry. I haven't used the phrase 'off with her head' once . . . today." I winked and then focused on Leopold. "Leo, take a deep breath and look at me. I've already heard you're a master of strategy. If we're going to destroy the other Houses in field games, I'm gonna need you to be able to look at my face and not puke."

A small throaty chuckle escaped.

"Your High—" Leo cut himself off. "Cassandra." My name came out strangled and awkward in a deep baritone voice. "I am excellent in strategy, not so good with people."

"Neither am I."

"Bollocks."

"Beaux, don't make me ask you to leave the room. Go on, Leo. Until I tell you otherwise, speak freely around me."

My cowboy Jack kicked out his legs, crossing them at the ankles and then dipped under his black cowboy hat. He was a freaking ladies' "come visit Australia" ad come to life. Poor Leo's eyes ping-ponged between Beaux and me.

"Leo," I pressed.

"Sorry. Strategy is my forte. I have no doubt when our battle powers are utilized, we will decimate our opponents. I guarantee it." His words rushed out.

"Good to know. Kate, do you feel the same?"

"Leo is good at what he does." She pulled her arms in tight like the compliment pained her.

Silence settled between the two. Leo spared Kate a quick glance, but not quick enough. Kate pounced on the look, threw it back at Leo with enough disdain that would make Shakespeare sit up and say, "The lady doth protest too much." Palpable tension arced between the pair. The kind of tension that only dared to surface between two people who loved to hate or hated loving each other. Kate was the dominant one and Leo was terrified of her. No wonder Yayati had suited them. Once Leo's testicles decided to drop, he'd give Kate a righteous run for her money.

Beaux's chair scraped against the wood floor as he stood. The black t-shirt that seemed to have shrunk two sizes since we entered the room climbed up his stomach, revealing a tan stretch of skin and jeans that hung low on his hips.

Too low.

Too much skin.

Too much Beaux.

My gaze skittered like Leo's. Unsure where was safe to look and knowing in any direction that had Beaux and his lickable abs on display was disastrous.

My hormonal awestruck eyes finally settled on Beaux's cat-getting-ready-to-obliterate-the-canary smile.

"See something you like?"

"Not hardly," I countered.

"A.J. was right, the tips of your ears do turn red when you lie." Beaux chuckled, grabbing his backpack and swinging it over his broad shoulder as he stalked toward me and right into my space. If the pair of Tens had any questions about who was the dominant in our relationship, the possessive arm that snaked around my waist and pulled me into him was all the answer they needed. "I'm done for the day. There's a bull I need to punish. Head back to your dorm room after class, and Cass?" He pulled back, looked down his slender, slightly crooked nose at me, with eyes daring me to challenge him before the ultimatum left his lips. "No more late night dorm breaks."

The ball of nerves in my stomach sprang loose.

"I don't know what you're talking about."

Beaux bent down, his breath tickling the fine hairs inside my ear. Years of fortitude shattered with a simple release of a hormonal sigh.

Shit, was that from me?

The soft chuckle of air skittering down the length of my neck said it wasn't from Beaux. "You know exactly what I'm talking about. If the Shadows had gotten any closer the other night, me and my mates would have stepped in." The tip of his nose ran along my cheek until we were staring at each other.

"You followed us?"

"No. I followed you." His green eyes burned with a heat that made my knees weak. "Stop looking at me that way, or I'll think you've decided to embrace my fuck buddy proposition."

"Not with comments like that," I hissed, stepping out of his reach and back into reality. Beaux cracked a crooked grin that matched his perfect crooked nose and walked down the steps and into the darkness of the theater.

Kate and her honeysuckle scent stepped next to me, watching Beaux stroll off into the darkness as if it were a sunset on a Hollywood set. "You said to speak candidly with you, right?" Her focus never wavered from Beaux until the shadows of the theater consumed him.

"I did."

Her big copper eyes abandoned the darkness and settled on me. "How the fuck are you going to stay a virgin around that boy?"

"Kate," Leo chastised.

"Wait until you meet my boyfriend." I smiled, even though I know it didn't reach my eyes . . . or my heart.

TWENTY-SIX

WAIT UNTIL YOU meet my boyfriend.

I'd made that bold declaration in this room last week, and I was still waiting for my House heads to "meet" my boyfriend. I checked my cellphone one more time. Fourteen texts, ten voice messages, and a drunk dial that Olivia quickly killed later, I'd still hadn't heard from my boyfriend. I grabbed my backpack from the back of my chair, nearly knocking it over and earning me a disapproving glance from Leo, my male Ten.

The House of Spades and the House of Diamonds had both lost their Field games, but that was only a temporary reprieve unless we won our next game.

My Tens and I had spent seven days reviewing the three minutes and thirty-seven seconds of vicious ass-beating we'd taken—I'd taken. A.J. had won before the first play was called. The hesitation after the buzzer, we concluded, was his attempt to be a good boyfriend and give me a few seconds to get my shit together. Kate thought we could use that weakness next month when we met again. I unzipped my backpack and shoved my notebook and some of the dread hanging from my heart in there. What she didn't know was that A.J. would be on a plane tomorrow (I didn't know when, because he wouldn't return any of my calls) to Malaga. But I was damn certain he'd be back for the second and final Field Game that would determine the tournament seating.

"Cassandra, you sure you want to run a sacrifice play next time?" Kate asked.

I thought about it. Given the way I'd left my position unprotected the last time, A.J. wouldn't see another ballsy sacrifice move coming. Lord knows he wasn't seeing much of anything from me coming. After finishing with Kate and Leo and our twice-a-week strategy meetings, we left the theater and walked toward our next classes. Well, I walked. They glared at each other. Kate switched her backpack from one shoulder to the other, glaring at Leo when he tried to take the hot pink backpack from her. Normally, I'd ask what their deal was.

Were they dating?

Did they date?

Had they ever wanted to date?

I'd wanted to ask half a dozen times, but Beaux and his merry band of self-doubt had wormed their way into my head, making me question every word that came out of my mouth, every gesture. Instead, all I could do was listen to the irritated exhales from Kate, the deafening silence from Leo, and take odds on who would be burned the most by the flames of tension between them. Seeing who would end up the dominant Ten card and who would be the flip would probably be the highlight of my college career.

Gods knew it wouldn't be anything I did.

We rounded the stairs, pushed through the glass doors, and stepped into the sizzling desert sun, headed in opposite directions. The Tens were going to Beam Hall. They would graduate from the Harrah College of Hotel Administration. If the dominant Heart chose to serve, we'd work hand-in-hand running the House of Hearts' assets. If they both chose to serve, they'd be married and the lesser ten would fold into the other. The two-becoming-one part of the marriage ceremony would be taken literally. Their family's line would still serve but only on a peripheral level. They'd wait in the wings to be called upon. There could only be one Ten, one Queen, in any suit. Cara was learning that one the hard way.

"You'll be okay walking across campus by yourself?" Kate spoke up.

"I'll be fine." I shifted my backpack. The added Philosophy books slid around. I was meeting my roommates, The Future Four as Gia had named us, and our Symbolic Logic's Professor, Dr. Davidson, during his office hours to see if we could worm out another clue to the moon and ship riddle.

Kate shifted from one flip-flop to the other. I liked her. Dad always said if a person was willing to let you see their toes, then they didn't have a whole lot of secrets hidden anywhere else. Leo, on the other hand, was covered from head-to-toe in either an SPF second skin or UV-resistant clothing, trying desperately to protect his alabaster skin. He'd have to earn my trust another way.

"I think we should—"

"Kate," the royal edge Mom carried in her voice slipped into mine, "You'll be late and I was pretty serious about our House not being the weakest link. I know trust is earned, but until I've earned yours, you'll have to obey because I am your future queen."

Kate's shoulders straightened, crushing any sense of camaraderie she or I thought we'd had.

"Very well." Kate turned, not waiting for Leo or my dismissal.

Mom said ruling was about choices and demands. I was going to have to choose to not be friends with my Tens if I was going to demand their respect. I made my way across campus. Maybe the weight of my books wasn't the only thing heavy in my backpack. Maybe it was the weight of the crown looming over my head.

The early evening summer sun started to lose some of its bite but not enough to stop sweat beading up along my forehead. I welcomed the quiet of the campus in the afternoon. Most of the classes had let out for the Labor Day Recess.

I pushed through the doors and took the steps three at a time to the floor that housed the professor's offices. The heavy metal door clicked shut behind me as I stepped into the abandoned hallway. An eerie feeling slithered down my neck. I normally didn't let my imagination run rampant when it came to thriller movies, but there was something about the quiet hallways, the way the plate glass windows seemed to hold their breath as I walked by. I swallowed over the bundle of nerves in my throat and pulled out the paper that had Dr. Davidson's office number on it. Jumping at the sound of another door closing, I picked up my pace, my heart pounding in my ears.

Symbolic Logic. Who made up the names of these courses?

I turned the corner and smacked into a cold wall. Freezing hands gripped my back as my backpack splattered, torpedoing my things all over the cold stone floors. With my arms pinned to my side, I had nowhere to look but into the black eyes of Chance Carrington, resident Shadow asshat, dancing with a demented glee.

"Look at you pulling off the college freshman frenzy like a boss." The voice made my insides churn.

"No time for you, Chance." I tried to get my feet under me, but Chance dipped me farther to the floor. "Last I checked, your boss agreed to the U.L.V. Campus being a hands off area. So hands off."

"Cassie, Cassie, Cassie," he cooed. "I figured since you were open to other suitors, I'd throw my hat in your woo-ring."

I felt my eyebrows bunch up. "What the hell are you babbling about?"

"I figured you were a little less cliché—the cowboy and the gentleman, although calling A.J. a gentleman is a stretch, given the way he nearly de-virgined you in the student parking lot last week. But that's not important. At least not to me. I wonder if Midas and God-daddy D. have a wager on you breaking the white wedding clause."

"Fuck you," I wiggled, but Chance's grip tightened, his fingers dug through the fabric of my sundress and into my spine.

A vile grin sharpened the planes of his face. "Is that an invitation?"

Somewhere inside me, a shudder released and died before giving Chance the satisfaction of knowing he was the cause. Dangling above the linoleum floors, with my things scattered about I realized how very vulnerable I was. I had two Jacks sworn to protect me, ignoring their orders to stand down, and here I was in the clutches of the worst human being ever.

"If I'd realized you were going to walk right into my arms, I would have packed my velona."

"I didn't realize Z-Paks cured douchebaggery. Wait. They don't."

"Cute." But the way his nails felt like they were breaking the skin on my back said he was far from amused.

"Chance, I'm going to tell you one last time. Let go of me . . . or else."

"I'd like to see the or else."

"I bet you would." We both knew he was alluding to my Balanter powers. I'm sure Hondo had warned his House, and a secret like that never stayed quiet. Quite the opposite, it spread like herpes on prom night. Not that I would know . . . or needed a Z-Pak.

"You've got quite a mouth on you. Here I thought you only threw your weight around in the comfort of your own dorm."

"What?"

Chance's eyes flared and the world righted itself. Blood rushed back to the places in my arms he'd pinched and bruised. Curiosity filled the room like chum in water.

"You know the penalty for breaching the Dayton Complex is death, right? How would you know what I said in my dorm room?"

Chance stepped away from me. The once shark-like stare now darted around the room, looking for someone to overhear us, interrupt us, someone to save him.

"Answer me." A small flurry of warmth tingled up my spine. I stomped out the warmth and hoped he would chalk it up to adrenaline instead of my Balanter powers.

Inky black strands of hair whipped back and forth across Chances face. "I'd sooner see the depths of Tartarus than face Warren's wrath."

"Rumor has it I can make that happen. Now, tell me." I backed Chance up against the plated glass walls.

"I think I'd rather tell you about your Daddy and face Dionysus's annoyance."

My hands balled into fists, the heat of the Balanter power raged, wanting me to release its wrath on Chance. I took a deep breath, hoping it cooled the heat pooling at the base of my spine. "You killed my father."

A cackle ripped from somewhere deep inside Chance. "Stupid girl. I'm talking about your *real* father. The man who broke the rules and bagged your mom. You really should have stuck around the catacombs the night you freed Malory. He was there. You could've freed him. You could've freed them all, but you chose to save that pitiful excuse of a friend and a boyfriend who cheats on you every chance he gets. I bet you don't even know who he's roomed up with. And Mallory, nobody likes her. She's the last string to your former life, and you're too much of a pussy to cut her loose." Chance turned me, my back pressed up against the cold plate glass window, but he didn't stop. The tips of his toes inched into my space until his body was nearly pressed against mine. "Ask me about your father. I know you're dying to know all the secrets of who he is, who he became, and who sold him out. It's quite an epic romance. And last I heard, you couldn't do those, either." Chance threw my taunt back in my face. "Maybe you should have stuck with your Balanter power. That's the shot of electricity I felt, wasn't it?"

I shook my head.

"You still can't bluff to save your life. I'll remember that when we're in

Malaga."

A snarl of victory snaked across Chance's lips before he turned and left quicker than he'd come.

I slid down the glass window, my things scattered across the floor like Skittles on the ground. Slowly, I gathered my things, catching sight of the top of the Midas Candidates off-campus quarters. I knew A.J. didn't live alone. It never occurred to ask who he was living with. Given the sickening way my heart was collapsing in on itself, I knew his roommate had to be high-ranking—and she probably didn't like me, either.

I skipped Symbolic Logic and headed straight for our dorm room and the lesser of my two problems. If I was right, the Shadows had done a lot more than breach the Dayton Complex lobby, and that was going to piss off my roommates more than my absence.

♥

"CASSANDRA VERA, YOUR lazy ass better have an extraordinary excuse for missing our oh-so-special meeting with Dr. Davidson and Symbolic Logic. We could've used your persuasive powers at the meeting." Olivia's threat penetrated the door before the key turned in the lock. So far, I'd found five extraordinary excuses for missing class. The air changed as the door opened and feet padded across the carpet.

"Cassie?" Gia asked, her slender fingers settling on my shoulder. "What are those?"

"My extraordinary excuses." I tossed one of the pinhole cameras to Olivia. She was our resident cat burglar, so it didn't surprise me when her face paled instantly.

"Where did you get this?" Olivia asked.

I pointed to the white camera that, after a Google search, I found out had an audio function, as well as a rotating lens. "That one came from the smoke detector in your room." I held up its matching counterpart. "This one came from the smoke detector in our room. There was one more in the smoke detector above our heads. This little guy"—I picked up a camera no bigger

than a lithium battery—"this one was in our front door plate. And that one"—
I pointed to the towel hook with drywall still attached—"I yanked off the wall
across from the toilet in our half bath."

"The loo?" Helen gasped before sinking into the chair.

Gia walked around the couch, eyeing the cameras. "How did you find these?"

"Google and a run in with Chance."

The room collapsed around us as my roommates took in the fact that
somebody had been watching and listening to us. They'd heard us plotting our
escapes. Watched us change in our rooms. The front door plate—I could
think of a handful of moments, when taken out of context, could have looked
wildly inappropriate between me and Beaux. And the thought of the one in
the bathroom . . . My stomach rolled.

"Explain," Olivia ordered. One-word commands meant she was a nanosecond
from losing her shit.

"After my meeting with my Tens and on my way to our Symbolic Logic
meeting, I ran into Chance. We sparred. He taunted me with my birth dad's
identity and location but only after he let it slip that he thought I was only
mouthy in the comfort of my dorm."

"We have to tell the Jacks," Helen whispered.

"How long have they been here?" Gia asked. "I mean, if something similar
was here when our mothers were . . ." Her words trailed off, but the impact
still hit us hard.

How long, how many transitions of power had they listened in on?

I sank into the couch. "Oh, god. I hadn't even thought about that. They
shooed Olivia and me out of here and had some sort of bonding moment
before we all came back the day we moved in."

"The key cards. The elixir. That's how they knew where we were the
night before the Hearts' Field Game," Helen leaned forward and grabbed one
of the cameras. "Did you get them all?"

I shrugged.

"So they could be listening in now? On devices we haven't found?"

I nodded. "Oli, you okay?" Olivia wrapped her arms tight around her
stomach like they were the only thing keeping her from splintering. "Gia, go
get the guys."

"You sure?"

I nodded to Olivia, her legs now drawn up to her chest. She may have despised Francis, but he was the best I could do for her because I was going to murder Isaac.

Protect her, my ass.

Gia sprinted for the door while Helen went and made some tea. She swore it would soothe Olivia. Olivia didn't say a word the three minutes Gia was gone. I doubted she'd be saying much. Whatever Chance and his minions did to her at prom still had the ability to send her spiraling into a near catatonic state.

I'd expected the Jacks to storm the room, with mythical weapons drawn and a shoot-now-ask-questions-later mentality. Instead, they walked in like we'd thrown five snakes on our coffee table and asked them to grab the TV remote.

William walked over to the coffee table, bent down, and inspected the cameras from afar. "Gia said you found these?"

"That's right?"

"How?" Hondo asked. He stood behind Helen, hand planted on her shoulder and tension recoiling between the two of them.

"Chance tipped me off."

"Tipped you off?" Beaux asked. He'd barely walked into our dorm room before assuming his cowboy stance. Legs shoulder width apart, arms crossed over his chest, and a black cowboy hat shielding any telling emotion his face could give away. But I knew those eyes were trained on me. He didn't need to see the cameras. He wasn't here to protect the cameras. He was here to protect me.

"I ran into him after a meeting with my Tens. Don't get fidgety. He was just as surprised to run into me as I was him. I think it was a bit of Lady Luck shining on us."

"You do, do you?" Beaux's Australian lilt was harsh and void of any emotion.

"Yeah. I don't think we would have known about these unless he was caught off guard."

"This is why we activated ourselves," William started. "Gia, I know you think this is supposed to be an adventure, but when you let Cassie pull stunts like three nights ago and these things are in play . . . " William grabbed one of the cameras and shook it like I figured he was imagining it was my neck, "Cassie, you have to stop."

"Cassie, didn't pull me into anything," Gia started.

"Wait a minute," A.J.'s voice interrupted from the door. "Cassie wasn't the only one who pulled the dorm room Houdini."

Butterflies fluttered in my belly but were quickly doused. Why was he here? Where had he been? Who had he been with? Zee? My heart dropped. And why didn't I want him here for this discussion? The sinking feeling that everything was being reported back to Midas slithered up my spine.

I bit down on my lip.

It was happening. We'd reached that threshold Mom had warned me about. His gestures were too little, too late. Why was he even here? Building a life was more than the grand gestures, it was the mundane moments. It was everything he was sacrificing to be with me without ever being with me. Something switched in me. My heart knew what had to happen long before my brain would ever catch up and accept it. I couldn't do this anymore. With everything going on, I couldn't be the girl on the side hoping for another crisis for A.J. to come and save me from. I wanted a boyfriend but not at the cost of sacrificing myself. I wanted to be worth the fight. And clearly I wasn't.

Beaux nodded his head like he'd been listening in on my thoughts. Maybe it was in my eyes or maybe he'd just been paying attention to me every waking minute the last few weeks, and he knew how to read me.

William left the table of cameras and took up his stance behind Gia. "It's not a stretch to think Cassandra was the catalyst."

"Actually, it wasn't Cass," Gia spoke up.

"Excuse us," I muttered to the room. My gaze caught A.J.'s as I crossed the room, nodding to the door. "I need to speak to you, A.J." The words tasted sour in my mouth and from the look on his face, sounded just as bad in his ears. "Alone." I shot Beaux a look but only found the brim of his black cowboy hat. The door latched behind us, sending my heart thrumming against my rib cage, thundering in my ears.

I couldn't believe we were doing this.

I couldn't believe I was doing this.

Me.

It was so . . .

I ran my hands through my hair, grabbing the ends and twisting them into a bun. I couldn't do this anymore. I couldn't be the only one vested in this relationship. I wouldn't be the wimpy, clingy girlfriend who sat at home wondering what my boyfriend was doing. Who he was doing it with. I had to be more than just a duty, just a save in the nick of time.

I deserved more.

"That bad?" A.J. leaned against the wall. Worry fixed in the crease between his eyes; the skin crinkling around the edges set off how tired he really was. How worn down he was from playing both sides of the game. Protecting me and serving his House. Olivia was right. There was no way to rule with your heart and protect your House. I was a fool to think it was even possible.

I leaned against the wall across from A.J. Opposite sides. Since he saved me on Fremont Street, we'd been on opposite sides. I knew what I had to do. Not just for him—I wasn't a martyr—but for me.

"My first few weeks in college and I really am not enjoying the lessons I'm learning."

A.J. hung his head. My heart spasmed, the rebellious strands of hair he always combed back fell forward and his shoulders slumped. He knew it was coming. He knew I was ending this and still he wouldn't fight for us.

Wouldn't fight for me.

"Is this about the field games?" he asked.

"So you remember you kicked my ass and humiliated me in front of . . . everyone?"

A.J. rammed a hand through his hair, his head leaning back against the wall. "I had a job to do."

"I did too, but afterward"—the words jammed in my throat—"you never even bothered to see if I was okay. Your candidates knocked me out. I woke up in my room and you never even bothered to call. Two weeks, A.J. You haven't returned—" I choked on the words. It'd been hard each time he ignored me, but adding it up, presenting it to him in a perfect little box of failure? He could profess his feelings for me all he wanted, but his actions clearly said something else.

I meant nothing.

A.J. stood still, his silence speaking for him and his eyes avoiding the truth in mine.

My lip trembled. "I was foolish to think this could work."

"No, you weren't," A.J. offered, but there was no conviction in his voice. I didn't know when he'd left our relationship, but he was long gone.

"You kicked my ass two weeks ago, and you couldn't be bothered to see if I was okay." I held up a finger, cutting A.J.'s rebuttal off at his lips. "I know you're playing two roles, but if I learned anything these past few weeks, it's that I need someone who is there for me. Chance said he wished he had his velona."

A.J.'s head snapped up, a fire burning in his eyes that I hadn't seen in months. "He didn't, did he?"

"No. He really wasn't expecting to run into me." I assured A.J., kicking at the small tear in the carpet. These halls and all their ghosts, all their pasts, were nothing compared to the uncertain future in front of me. If I was going to survive, if my House was going to survive, I knew what I needed to do. I met A.J.'s eyes.

"Velona is Greek for needle. That's the needle he needs to claim my power for the Shadows, right?"

A.J. nodded.

"Chance is an asswipe, but he did help me see something today. Two halves don't make a whole. Wait." I held up a hand, cutting off another of his objection. "I won't make you choose between your House and me. And Beaux's tiptoeing on the outside, waiting to swoop in when you can't."

"Like the other night? He told you I wasn't there?"

My heart sank. "No, he didn't say anything. But I've come to expect you not to be there, and that's what I'm talking about. You said I needed to trust you." The bite of tears clawed at the memory of A.J. with Zee on Fremont Street. The way he slipped his arm around her, pulled her in close to his side like he used to do with me.

"Everything you've missed . . . and you think a few hot and heavy make-out sessions will buy you enough time to get to the next crisis." I watched my words hit A.J. He was either an incredible actor or relieved this was finally coming out. "I can't be pacified with stolen moments and sweet nothings. I can't be your secret, A.J. I can't stand that no matter how much my heart loves you, my mind knows you'll be forced to choose your House or me and it will always be your House."

"You think Beaux will choose you?"

"No. I don't think anyone will choose me. And the one person I wanted . . .

was never available for me to wait for." Tears blurred the hallway until A.J. was nothing more than an outline of a boy I once loved. "I need a Jack. I need someone, even if their heart doesn't want me. I need someone to have my back. And you can't do that. You never could."

A.J. stepped forward, but I could see goodbye glinting in his eyes. He was going to let me go. He was okay that I was breaking up with him, and that hurt more than knowing he probably regretted saving me in the first place.

"I know you think this is the right choice for us, but Cassie, I do love you. I meant every syllable when I told you I wanted to marry you. I've never stopped fighting for you." A.J. cradled my face with his hands. It would be so easy to let him waltz me down this road again. I could sit here in Las Vegas while he and Zee went off to Malaga. I could wait and hope that every moment, every look I had watched between them didn't exist. A.J. skidded his thumb along my cheekbone, willing me to comply.

I wanted to give in.

I wanted him.

But . . .

I just couldn't be his dirty little secret anymore.

A.J.'s fingers stilled on my face; he knew I was already gone. "Cassie, please. Don't do this. I know you don't—"

"Why haven't you ever taken me back to your apartment?" I cut off his declaration. The sickening feeling only intensified as A.J.'s eyes widened.

"Don't do this."

"Chance said you were keeping secrets. I'm guessing this is only one of many." I stepped out of his touch. "Say it. You know I already know. Who have you been sharing an apartment with? Say her name so we can end this. It's Zee. You're sharing an apartment with Zee."

"It's not like that."

"It was the moment you hid it from me." I walked across the hall, my hand gripping the doorknob like it was the exit from a bad nightmare. The cold brass spun in my palm, but before I could leave, there was one more thing I needed to do. The last string to cut. And Chance was right, I was a pussy, but more than that, I was pathetic for ever believing love could conquer all.

"I relieve you of your duties. I'll have my Ten, Kate, send word to Midas. His heir is freed of his duties to the House of Hearts. Good bye, A.J." I shut the door behind me and leaned against the frame, not ready to let go of the doorknob or the dream just yet.

Beaux's body shielded me from the others. He was always protecting me. Always fulfilling his duty. "You okay?"

"Walls are that thin?"

"No. A.J. may know your ears turn red when you're lying, but I know your lips." Beaux ran the pad of his thumb across my bottom lip. "When you chew on the bottom one, someone's about to have or has had their arse handed to them."

"I relieved . . ." The word tripped on the lump in my throat. "I relieved A.J. of his duties. You still want the job? It's all yours."

"I never wanted the job—"

"I know," I cut him off. "But now it's yours, so cowboy up." I pushed past Beaux and his insult, my focus trained on William. "Are you done persecuting me? How about you, Hondo? You got any more impertinent digs to send my way?"

Gia stepped toward me. "Where's A.J.?"

"I relieved—don't." I stepped away from her attempted hugging. "We have bigger things to worry about than my love life."

"Cass." Olivia winced at the way my look cut her down.

"So the cameras." I pushed the words past the shards of my heart stuck in my throat. "How do we make sure this is the lot?"

Silence filled the room. The Jacks snapped looks at each other, while my friends, the future queens, stared at me. Helen didn't know my history with A.J., but she did know my heart belonged to him. She knew the story of how he saved me. She may have been from halfway around the world, but her heart and mine, we both believed in the happily ever after. At least mine did.

"I've notified Zee," Beaux finally spoke up, breaking the palpable quiet in the room.

"I'm sure you have."

"She's the House of Midas's second in command. I figured you didn't want the heir running point on the cleanup."

"And you thought the second would be a better choice? Is there not a third?"

Beaux stepped into my space. His fingers wrapped around my arm, pulling me into him and whispered, "I get you're hurting, but don't say something that you'll regret. Pain has a way of bringing out the worst in people."

"You would know, wouldn't you? Did you know they were living together?"

Beaux winced at the question.

"You did. Why doesn't that surprise me? Do your job and make sure this place is free of bugs." I grabbed my backpack I'd flung against the wall when I'd raced in here and walked out the door.

TWENTY-SEVEN

I WANDERED THE campus until the pink skies turned purple. When the walkway lamps kicked on, I left campus and hiked up Flamingo Way toward the vibrant glow of the Las Vegas Strip. A few minutes or maybe a few hours passed, I couldn't tell anymore. Time seemed to be a dull ache that only reminded me how bad everything was. Construction forced me across the street. I waited at the stoplight on Flamingo and Swensen, staring at the Grand Apartments, the Midas candidates' off-campus housing.

I knew where A.J. lived.

I could have walked over here half a dozen times in the past few weeks. I guess the chicken-shit girl in me was too afraid to throw pebbles at the glass castle façade. I should have known something was up. A piece of me did, I guess. I never pushed the issue. I was fine to let him feel me up in the front seat of his car. I kicked a rock off the pathway. I was willing to take any tiny piece of affection A.J. threw my way, as long as it was attached to the boyfriend label.

There wasn't anything special about the Midas apartments. They didn't glitter in gold or have neon signs flashing "Future protectors live here!" Quite the opposite. A few girls walked past me, one sparing me a look as they headed down the street and into the lobby of the apartment building.

If their floors were organized like ours, the corner unit with the warm light pouring out onto the balcony was where A.J. and . . . and Zee lived.

Zee stepped out onto the balcony, her long legs pouring out of tiny shorts and all that gorgeous brunette hair piled high up on her head in a messy bun. She lifted the barbeque lid and slapped two pieces of meat on to the grill.

My heart cramped.

Two pieces.

He'd gone home and now was eating dinner. Probably relieved that he was rid of me. I felt the pain of betrayal lodge in my throat before I stepped off the curb and walked closer to the apartments. I wasn't pulling an ex-stalker move, construction had me crossing . . .

Oh, hell, who was I kidding?

I was totally going psycho-ex on him.

My phone buzzed in my backpack. I reached around and pulled the phone free as another round of vibration went off in my hand. That made at least eight.

Beaux: **Haven't offed yourself, have you? Get your ass home.**

He'd keep texting until I answered.

I shot one last glare at the lovebirds' balcony and hurried up Flamingo Road. White curtains fluttered out of the open slider door, shooing me away before I was caught looking pathetic on their surveillance cameras. Nothing would give Midas greater delight in seeing me misty-eyed and longingly staring at his grandson's veranda.

There were eyes everywhere in Las Vegas, and if Midas wasn't watching, Dionysus would be.

I hustled up the street, letting my anger flame the small embers of hate and disgust I'd had over the cameras in our dorm room. The Shadows would be preoccupied with their hidden cameras being discovered. The girls were too rattled to help me search for my elixir. I swiped through the last seven text messages, all from Beaux, ranging from wanting to know where my sexy ass was to threats of getting my red-tipped ears back to the Dayton Complex before he set the hellhounds on me. Normally, I'd laugh at the mythological demon pooches, but these days, anything was possible.

I shot a text off: **Walking. Don't worry. I have a disguise . . .**

I grinned, knowing that that incomplete sentence would tick Beaux off more than anything else. His imagination was almost as dangerous as mine. I Googled direction to the Paris Hotel and put my earbuds in, hoping to blend in with the rest of the summer tourists. By the time I turned right on to South Las Vegas boulevard, sweat trickled down my back. I was two water bottles into a poorly thought-out plan when the smell of clove burned my nose. I didn't have to turn around to know Isaac was behind me. I pulled the earbuds out and listened for the heavy thud of boots falling behind me and the sticky scent of clove cigarettes permeating the air.

"Rough night, Princess?"

"How many cameras do you guys have in our complex?"

Isaac fell into step with me. "Five less than we did before tonight."

"For a guy who claims to love Olivia, you sure have a sick and twisted way of showing it. How many disciples did you let watch us? Watch her?"

"Cassie, ye of little faith." He shot me a sideways look. "I disabled all but the hallway and the living room. You're welcome."

Hope blossomed. "Really?"

Isaac tipped his head, and the dichotomy of who he was and how he acted continued.

We walked in silence, dodging tourists and dudes paid by the pamphlets they pushed until we stopped at the light across from the Paris Hotel.

"This is where I leave you, Isaac."

"I don't think so. We have this place staked out, waiting for a run on the Arc. Turns out Livi's minion was smarter than you. He figured out Midas's switch."

"What are you babbling about?

Isaac's black hair danced along his shoulders in the breeze. Humor lit his eyes, making them iridescent blue. "Look at Livi pulling a fast one on you. She didn't tell you what her run with Francis the Failure produced?"

"I think you've spent one too many nights in the catacombs."

Isaac rocked back on his heels. "Still, you're her family. I figured she'd break rank and tell you where to find your elixir."

"She doesn't know," I quipped, but a sickening pain gripped my gut.

Isaac crossed his arms over his chest, and my heart constricted. He and A.J. were so alike.

"Why are you so willing to help us? Last I checked, your position as second wasn't quite so secure. Chance nipping at your heels and now Warren trying to wow his daddy."

"Warren doesn't know how hot the fire he's playing with burns," Isaac muttered under his breath. "It'll scorch the Earth."

"Tell me. I can't help protect Livi if I don't know all the facts."

Isaac's lip ticked up in a grin that said, *nice try, but not happening.* "You let me worry about Warren. Now that Livi's safe, get your ass in gear and figure out where Midas hid your elixir."

"In case you haven't been watching, I've kind of been focused on Olivia, or did you forget the shower room visit you paid me?"

Isaac's eyes turned cold and hard, and I felt naked all over again. "Cassandra, think outside the box. Take a minute, have some *tiramisu* and *reflect* on what I'm saying. Midas wants to keep you all *close* and *under his roof*." Isaac's blue eyes drilled the words into my brain before he held a finger up to his ear. Was he listening to an earpiece? "You better get back to campus. Your boy's getting ready to hunt you down."

"I. . . I . . . A.J. and . . . we aren't . . ." The words tangled in my throat.

"Oh, I know about you and A.J. I said there are five fewer cameras in your dorm room. Didn't say how many were in your halls. I didn't think you'd have the spine to be the one who ended it. You had doormat down to an art form."

"Thanks."

"I'm talking about your boy, Beaux. He's a strapping fine Aussie. You should explore that. I knew my baby brother would blow it. Always trying to please everyone. Letting the things he loves the most slip right through his fingers."

Now I knew he wasn't talking about me. His actions the past few months proved it. And if they hadn't, the fact that he was shacked up with a girl and didn't feel I needed to know . . . I let anger override the pain of the last thought.

"Not sure I'll be taking orders from the Shadow's spawn."

Isaac flagged down a cab and opened the door. "I'm not a Shadow, Cassie. Dionysus isn't a Shadow, either. We're their keepers, or haven't you wondered why you can't get flashes of my former life?" He nodded for me to get in and I did. "Know your enemy, Cassandra Vera. Know your enemy." Isaac slammed the door shut and ordered the driver to take me to the Dayton Complex at U.L.V.'s campus.

I pulled out my phone and sent a text to Beaux that I was headed home. The drive back to campus was quick and Isaac had been right: Beaux was pacing the front lawn of the Dayton Complex, waiting for me. He paid the cab driver before letting me out of the car and then tucked me under his arm while he hauled me into the lobby and then the elevator of our dorms. His jaw clamped down, fist ready to level anything that came through the elevator doors.

"What's wrong?"

The elevator leapt up.

"The teams swept your room," Beaux finally said. "You found all the cameras, but not the listening devices. There were three more in your bedrooms and the living room. Security just finished their sweep of the top floor. Cass, they found forty-two cameras and seventy-eight listening devices. Six in the bathroom you and the girls use."

My mouth gaped. Isaac hadn't said anything about listening devices. What if he didn't know? What if they heard him helping? Beaux freed my bottom lip from my teeth. The touch of his thumb on my lips sent a jolt of unwanted heat through me.

"Lots of gossip happening in the girls' bathroom?"

I snapped my eyes up to his. "You know us girls."

"I know you girls have secrets. Secrets you don't want us to know."

I bulldozed over his statement with my own. "Gia and I have got to get our elixirs. Not just to save our lines, but to protect our hides."

"Right. About that."

My heart plummeted. "Gia left, didn't she? She knows where her elixir is?"

Beaux dipped his head.

That was it. Emotions thickened my throat. It was every ruling line for themselves. The weight of being the last unsecured line, the single focus of the Shadows, disappointing my mom and my sister, sat on my chest. Then there was A.J., the thought of him stuck in a cramp of my lungs.

Beaux's thumb wiped under my eye, catching the tear I didn't know was falling. Everyone would be activated, and all I had was the help of a Shadow, a reluctant protector, and a cheating boyfriend. Ex-boyfriend. A shudder ripped from my lungs as I threw my arms around Beaux. His musky scent filled me in more ways than I could ever know.

"Tell me you want my help now." The pain in Beaux's voice was so rich, so fresh, it cut me open all over again. I wasn't supposed to have these feelings. I wasn't supposed to have a boyfriend who cheated on me. "Cassie, I can help you. You don't have to do this alone."

"Why doesn't anyone want me?" I sobbed. "Am I that hard to love? Am I that dangerous? Just an abomination, right?"

"You're not any of those things." His whispers fell into the crown on my hair and found their way into my heart. "Tell me you want my help, Cassie."

I nodded my head and dared to look up. Beaux's gaze captured mine and lit something inside me.

The elevator doors pulled open to the top floor of the Dayton Complex. Cara and the rest of the spares were on the couches. Her gazed locked with mine, uncharacteristic worry furrowed her brow.

Are you okay? she mouthed.

My heart stuttered while I nodded yes.

Beaux leaned down, his lips brushing the tip of my ear. "Your ears are red."

"I appreciate the flirt, but it's not necessary. Enjoy your freedom while you can, Beaux." The air cooled around me as I walked down the hallway, and I knew Beaux wasn't following. I shut the door behind me. They were so two-faced. Saying we were all in this, but then when it really mattered, each and every one of them had no problem leaving me.

"Cassie," Olivia called out from the kitchen.

I walked past her and Helen, shooting looks at them that I hoped rooted them in fear. They'd both found their elixirs. Both had activated their battle powers. Neither had been loyal enough friends to tell me. House before heart meant before friendship and blood as well.

"Cass?" The fear I'd hoped for was in Olivia's voice, but it did nothing to quench the ache of betrayal.

I shut my bedroom door, glaring at Gia's side of the room. I knew where she'd gone. We were supposed to do this together. Be a united front, but William had gotten to her, too.

My bedroom door opened.

I ignored it.

I needed to amend the "don't knock" rule.

"Cassandra?" Olivia questioned. She leaned into the doorway. "Do you want to talk?" I shot her a look, and any more questions she had died on her lips.

"When were you going to tell me?"

Olivia shifted in the doorway. "Tell you what?"

It dawned on me. How many other secrets was my cousin hiding from me?

Her cellphone rang—"Heartbreaker." Olivia fished out the phone from her pocket. "Do you want to talk to him?"

"I hardly want to talk to you."

Her eyes flared, but she took a moment to ignore the call and send off a message before looking back at me. "What's wrong with you?"

"When were you going to tell me?" I asked again. The fabric of my comforter bunched up in the palms of my hands. A warm tingle shot up my spine. I could let the Balanter power loose, should let it loose. "You found your elixir two weeks ago."

Olivia stepped inside and shut the door. A small crease wedged its way in between her eyebrows. "How do you know that?" she whispered.

"Why didn't you tell me?"

She searched my face for the answer, and when I wouldn't let her off the hook, she searched the corners of the room and then the ceiling. Her big, emerald, betraying eyes fell back on me, looking for some sort of forgiveness.

"Isaac told you?"

"You should leave my room now." I wrapped my arms around my middle like they were holding me together. Power surging under my skin, so close to the surface that at any minute, I could lose my shit and rain down a Balanter ass-beating on my roommates, starting with my cousin.

"Cass."

"Leave. Now." Warmth raced up my spine, and this time, I did nothing to beat back the influence. The power was as intoxicating as it was terrifying. Olivia's eyes glazed over, the small piece of her she still controlled fought for my attention and then disappeared. "I don't want to hear your excuses, Olivia. I get it now. I may be your cousin, but I'm not in your house. I don't matter." My phone rattled on my dresser.

"Stay put," I ordered and walked over to my phone. A.J. and another message. I spun on my heels, walking right up to my cousin. Her eyes flared, but that was all the response I would allow her body to give. She was under my control, and as long as I didn't leave a mark, I could do whatever the hell I wanted. A small piece of me warred against the power raging in me, fighting for control and reason.

Olivia whimpered.

"I'm going to let you go, and you're going to leave my room. You're going to tell the others that I know they've all betrayed me. The three of you found your elixirs and have been activated." I swallowed over the hurt in my chest. "You're going to call A.J. and tell him I know he's sleeping with Zee and he's to never call me again."

I stepped back, rage or tears—I couldn't be sure—pricked at the edge of my vision and released my cousin. I'd expected her to scamper out, but she stood her ground. Defiantly walking up into my space. Heat raced up my spine. I pulled in a deep breath, not trusting the power.

"I get you're pissed, Cassie, and you have every right to be angry. But you do that shit again and I will clock your ass. You got me?" She pushed a finger into my chest. "Be mad. Be hurt. But understand, you're still my cousin, and while I may be obligated to my House, I'm your blood." She turned on her heels but wasn't done. "It's Labor Day weekend, so I'm taking the others to my mom's house. Get your shit together or move out. Your choice."

I sank back on to my bed. My phone buzzed again.

A.J. and yet another "we need to talk before I leave tomorrow" text.

I was done talking. I was done with everything otherworldly.

TWENTY-EIGHT

FIFTEEN TEXT MESSAGES in thirty minutes. Boys were so damn confusing. I couldn't get him to pay me a minute of attention when we were together, and now that I'd dumped him, I couldn't get him to leave me alone. I handed the cab driver a wad of money and thanked him for the three swigs from his flask and for taking me to the wildest country bar he knew of. I didn't even mind when he started toward Fremont Street.

I waded through the two rows of Harley Davidson motorcycles flanking the entrance. The warmth of the cabbie's whiskey settled in my knees. Country music shook the old siding, and an extremely large and intimidating bouncer stood with his arms folded over his chest. I stepped up to the door, knowing full well I had no business being here. The security guard's eyes rolled over my body, taking in every inch of me. When I thought he was going to send me away, he smiled and stepped aside, letting me in. All my friends may have been underage asses, but we were royalty. There wasn't a bar in town that didn't know we were to be catered to. Even the bars I knew A.J wouldn't think to find me in.

And that was okay by me.

I stepped into the darkened entrance, pulled forward by the noise and music.

The shockwave of music washed over me. Girls danced on a bar that went the length of the room. Bodies filled the dance floor, and a girl screamed into a blow-horn, "Do we serve water?"

The room screamed back, "Hell, no!"

I giggled and made my way to the bar. After a few minutes, a barstool cleared. My mind raced with empty thoughts while I dragged infinity symbols through the mixture of peanuts and . . . oh, god, I didn't want to know what else was in here.

"Want a beer?" a husky voice asked over the noise, sending every nerve in my body into spasms.

Beaux.

A.J. may have been high enough on the patrol to not have to step foot in a country bar, but Beaux . . . Beaux was everything A.J. wasn't, and tonight that seemed to be exactly what I needed.

"Do you want a beer?" Beaux asked again, irritation picked at the edge of his words.

My nose wrinkled with disgust as I stole a quick glance over my shoulder.

"Figured." Another newly scabbed cut over his eye pulled as a chuckle died in his throat.

I spun on the stool and leaned my arms up against the bar. For some reason, it felt right and that was why it was all so wrong.

"They don't sell umbrella drinks here, so . . ." He searched me, looking for the balk. "I'll order you a coke. Diet?" He pulled up his eyebrows like he had me all figured out.

"What's that?" I pointed to the dark amber liquid he held in a shot glass. A daredevil grin pulled at the corners of his lips.

"You can't handle this."

"Try me."

"Already did."

The double entendre pushed my wannabe bravado into action. I snagged the glass from his hand and tossed it down my throat. My eyes flew wide open then pinched together as the alcohol seared a path to my stomach.

"What else you want me to prove tonight?" I asked.

The burning sensation in my belly warmed, and it had nothing to do with the toxic liquid. I handed him back the empty shot glass and a bring-it-on smile. His eyes held mine, tempting me, daring me to go over the edge with him. I had just enough anger, and with the right amount of alcohol in me, it could be a damn good idea. He pushed the shot glass back to the bar keep.

"Well, pour us another round." Beaux dipped his white cowboy hat at me.

Challenge accepted.

I took a pretzel and pointed it at Beaux's head. "I thought only the good guys wore white hats."

"Who said I was bad?" He handed me another shot glass. The air stilled between us and I quickly threw back the amber liquid, cringing as the alcohol bit at my insides. Beaux's grin was like a slow-pulled match, smoking just beneath the surface—then BAM, it lit my insides on fire.

"Your sexy little cowboy smile doesn't work on me."

"You think I'm sexy?" His rough, calloused hand covered mine, wiggling the shot glass from my fingers.

"Wh-what?"

"Sexy." His eyes leveled with mine as his arms trapped me against the bar. "You think I'm sexy."

"That's not what I said." My voice caught on the thrill in my throat.

He appraised me, sending a warning skittering down my spine. "You said my smile was 'sexy.'"

"You heard me wrong."

Beaux leaned on the bar. His face inches from mine sent my pulse racing as his eyes searched for something in me. The bartender slid two more shots next to us, but that didn't break the spell Beaux held over me. He leaned forward, his lips so close to my cheeks, my skin tingled.

"Your ears are red," he whispered; his nose skimmed my earlobe and I couldn't help but curl into him. "Drink up. You deserve a night out." He put the shot glass in my hand, a smile played at the scar on his lip. A scar that was as fascinating as the lips it marred.

I slammed back the amber liquid. My phone bounced on top of the bar. I didn't need to flip it over to see was summoning me. Shoe pinched when it was on the other foot, didn't it? I held up two fingers at the bar keep. Four more shots slid in front of Beaux and me. I tossed my two-shot back rapid-fire, and the ache that had taken a permanent hold on my heart seemed to loosen. Warmth swirled around in my belly, traveling up my arms and down my legs. Every uptight nerve in my body seemed to give way and abandon whatever worry it had carried. I giggled. Beaux gave me sideways glance. The skin around his eyes crinkled and became the most interesting thing I'd ever witnessed. The room swayed and my belly dipped like it was on a rollercoaster.

I rubbed my fingers along my teeth.

"What are you doing?"

"My teeth feel fuzzy."

Beaux snorted, taking the new shot of whiskey from in front of me. "I think we've determined five to be your limit."

My head jerked like it wasn't attached to my body, swimming in a sea of delightful disconnect. I kept my eyes on Beaux, throwing my hand up in the air. "One more for meee." The words slurred and mixed with another giggle. "Three more for him."

The bartender glanced at Beaux.

"Don't look at him," I scolded. "Do you know who I aaam?" I giggled at the last word.

"You're pissed already."

"Am not." I leaned into Beaux's shoulder, or he caught me from sliding off the barstool. I'm not sure which, but the crinkled skin around his eyes had nothing when it came to his muscles. "You're really strong." I looked up and watched Beaux's eyes soften. A liquid heat broke loose in me, pooling in between my thighs. "Why do all of the good-looking guys have beautiful gem-colored eyes and I have shitty brown ones?"

Beaux chuckled again, sitting me back on top of my barstool. He lowered his head until his eyes were level with mine, and I couldn't help but lean my forehead against his. The room spun again.

"Your eyes are far from shitty brown. They're beautiful slicks of honey and the most captivating, the most tempting things I've ever seen."

I snorted. "I love when you talk. Say supercalifragilisticexpialidocious. Wait." I put a finger to his lips and lost myself in the soft, plump skin.

Beaux smiled.

"Helen says we should shag and be done with it."

Beaux rolled his eyes. "You know why you can't shag, right?"

"Because I'll get knocked! Up!" I sputtered. "Same as my mom. I wonder if she even tried to use birth control? Zero percent effective when you've been tapped by the gods to be of breeding age." I snorted. "But you're a Club, and we could do it because then I wouldn't curse my kid like my dad cursed me." My vision blurred. "I have to pee." I started to push away, not wanting to cry and also kind of serious about the peeing thing.

Beaux snagged the belt loop of my jeans pulling me in between his legs. His arms wrapped around my waist, while his chin nuzzled into the crook of my neck. The sweet scent of whisky danced on his breath, but it was the warmth radiating off him that was almost as intoxicating as the drinks.

"You know you're not a curse. You're sexy as hell, and any bloke would have to be a wanker not to count himself lucky if he had the chance to bury himself inside you."

My thighs warmed, and I fought the urge to turn in his arms and plant my lips on his face. It was the crudest, sexiest thing I'd ever had said to me. And I adored him for it.

"You're saying that because you wish I was Zee."

Beaux pulled the lobe of my ear in between his lips, his arms tightened around my waist as my knees went out from under me. "I'm saying that because you're not Zee." His grip around my waist loosened and then left when he was sure I could stand on my own. "Go pee and I'm going to take you home." He swatted me on my butt, sending me on my way.

♥

RAYS OF EVIL pain seared my eyes. I tried to pry my eyelids open but quickly shut them when I realized the rays of evil were coming through the living room window. I stirred and immediately wished I hadn't. I'd lost count of shots after the three I'd downed post pee break.

Six?

Eight?

It hurt too bad to think. I rolled over, regretting the movement as leftover liquor sloshed in my head. The pillow next to me sighed, and instantly all that leftover alcohol evaporated. I peeled open an eyelid.

"Oh shit," I muttered. My palm splayed against Beaux's bare chest. I'd expected a patchwork of hair and pecs.

Right about the pecs.

Wrong. God, so wrong about the hair.

Beaux's wide, chiseled chest rose and fell with a heavy breath. Thick ropy lines divided the muscles of his chest in half, then disappeared under a washboard set of abs. I tried to look away but couldn't. It was like Adonis had touched him and then decided to make him even more gorgeous just to mess with all the girls by giving him a small patch of blonde hair that started just under his belly button and disappeared under the covers.

Beaux chuckled, eyes still shut. "You done gawking?"

I jumped at his voice, heat singeing my cheeks and traveling up into my hair. "I don't know what you're talking about."

"Cass, I'm hungover, not dead. I can feel the heat from the tips of your ears radiating all the way over here."

He was right, but there was no way I'd admit it to him.

"Psh." I kicked off the blankets, relieved when I saw he was still wearing his jeans—although they were unbuttoned, struggling to hold back a morning bulge that did right things to wrong places my nightshirt covered. "You want to tell me why I'm on a makeshift bed in my living room?" I asked.

Beaux hitched his arm under his head, and he looked even more sinful with his arms flexed. "Your bed was too small."

"I'm sorry," I sputtered.

"I tried putting you in your bed, but you kept stumbling out here and falling asleep on the floor."

"I did not."

He cocked his head, the sun catching in the waves of his blonde hair. "Right, you did."

Silence crept into the room, and I wasn't quite sure Beaux hadn't fallen asleep.

"Not that I'm ungrateful, but why'd you spend the night?"

"No fucking good deed goes unpunished." Beaux rose up on his elbow, grabbing the blanket and pulling it back up over his pants. "I stayed because you asked me to."

"I . . . I . . . wha? I mean. How did you take that?"

Beaux shook his head and rolled over, his back as well-defined as his front. "I took it to mean you didn't want to be alone. You also handed me your phone and told me not to let you text A.J. Don't worry, Princess, your drunken confessions of still loving A.J. are quite safe with me."

"Thank you," I whispered, unraveling myself from the blankets. The room still felt like it was sliding out from me. I eased up onto all fours and used the coffee table to finish my attempt to master standing while hungover. I gripped the edge of the table, staving off the urge to puke and then I saw it. A handwritten note. I recognized A.J.'s penmanship immediately.

"Anybody come by last night? Anyone leave me a note?"

"No," Beaux huffed. "Sleep. I need sleep, woman."

My stomach pitched again, this time having nothing to do with the shots of whiskey I'd pounded last night.

The bold block letters sliced across the page. Anger dripping from the simple period. Four words: **See you in Malaga.**

I had four words and three months to wonder what A.J. thought he'd found when he came to say good-bye.

TWENTY-NINE

"TELL ME AGAIN you didn't do the nasty with Beaux," Malory teased, walking back in from her kitchen. I'd left a few minutes after I was certain Beaux had fallen asleep. It wasn't my finest moment, sneaking out with a hot Aussie passed out on my floor and no idea when my roommates would be coming back. I figured all parties deserved a few moments of cheek-searing embarrassment. They'd all been more than willing to let me dance blindly through the last three weeks. Secrets and elixirs and don't-tell-Cassie's galore.

I held the ice pack up to my head. "I didn't do the nasty with Beaux."

"How do you know? I mean you show up on my doorstep hungover and smelling like sex and rock and roll. Or was it sex and country?" She giggled at her own joke.

Okay, it was kind of funny.

"Still a virgin, Mal." I moved the ice pack to the back of my neck, bracing it between the couch and me. "You're sure this will work?" I asked, taking the anti-hangover concoction she'd made me.

"Have you ever seen me hungover?"

"Never . . ." My thought was swallowed by another wave of nausea.

"You puke on my mom's carpet, you're getting the cleaning bill." She took my hand and wrapped my fingers around the glass.

I sniffed at the brown and white liquid; the scent of more alcohol gagged me. "What is this?" I tried to hand it back.

"Bourbon Stout Flip." Malory pushed the glass back at my lips.

"It smells like alcohol."

Malory's head danced on her shoulders.

"You want me to drink more alcohol to combat the effects of an alcohol-induced hangover?"

"Don't question the methods, just drink."

I pulled my head away from the lip of the glass. "Can I question what's in the drink?"

"It's better if you don't."

"Oh, now you need to tell me."

Malory blew out a big breath and started ticking ingredients off on her fingers. "Bourbon, coffee liqueur, spiced rum, egg white and . . . stout."

"Stout?"

"Beer. Lager. Guinness is in yours." She pushed the glass to my lips. "Better to take it all at once. Don't want to hit you with a cleaning bill." She wrinkled her nose as I let the cool rim of the glass touch my lips. The smell of coffee, beer, and egg assaulted my nose.

The cool liquid, the consistency of a milkshake, slid down my throat. My eyes flared meeting Malory's shit-eating grin.

"Don't do the crime if you can't do the time, Princess."

I wiped the remnants from my lips. "Don't call me that."

"Why? Because of your Dad, A.J., or Beaux?" She took the glass from my hand. "Yeah, I've heard Beaux call you Princess. It's not the same as A.J., but there's a similar heat behind it. A.J. had every right to be worried about Beaux as your Jack." Malory disappeared around the corner and into the kitchen.

"A.J. was my Jack, too," I called after her. "He decided being a servant wasn't as glamorous as being the master."

Mid-morning sun filtered in through the sheer fabric curtains. Mal had muted the episodes of *COPS* for me, but that didn't stop me from watching a set of policemen take down a drunk and disorderly girl. Could've been me last night.

"How would you know that? Not like you all spent too much time talking over the past three weeks. Aside from the few hot and heavy petting sessions you told me about, you were more friends-with-benefits than you were a relationship." Mal walked back into the room, steam billowed from a bowl of soup.

"You put beer in that, too?"

She brushed off my statement and handed me the bowl of chicken soup. "Seriously, Cass. You make it seem like A.J. up and abandoned you."

I shrugged my shoulders.

"I broke up with him last night." I swirled the soup around in the bowl, afraid to look at Malory. "I had a run in with Chance, and he let it slip the Shadows were listening in on us and that A.J. was living with Zee."

Malory sank back into the cushion next to me. "He's living with her?"

"Yeah."

"He told me things were dubious between you two. I never figured him to shack up with another girl while he was giving you the goo-goo eyes."

"Dubious?"

Mal shot me a sideways glance. "English teacher's handing out a full grade bump if you email him five sentences a week with words he's chosen. Figured it couldn't hurt."

"And when did you talk to A.J. about us?"

"The third time he broke a date with you." She moved away from the couch, uncomfortable she'd been found caring.

My heart swelled at the thought of Mal hunting down A.J. and demanding he man up. The hum of the air conditioner kicked on. Even in September, it was still crazy hot during the day. Mal said the weather wouldn't start cooling down until October or November. I sighed. October and November seemed years away. Forget about Thanksgiving and Malaga and . . . A.J. No, it was better this way. If we'd stayed together, this would have been my future. Me sitting on a couch contemplating all of the *dubious* things A.J. was doing. I could rock a college word, too. No grade bump needed. An ache rolled through my heart. Maybe if I said breaking up with him was the right choice enough times, my heart would catch up with what my head already knew. A.J. would never be free to love me.

I spent the rest of the day on Mal's couch. Her mom was in Malaga at Mom's hotel overseeing the arrangements for the Thanksgiving Poker Tournament. Word was starting to circulate around the poker world's regulars about the extravagance Carina Corazon would bring to the circuit. It'd been four years since the House of Hearts hosted the tournament. The tournament was on Mom and Cara's shoulders. Getting Mom a good seat at the Royal's table fell on me.

Later, I walked back to campus, the sun helping with the eradication of alcohol from my body by way of sweat. A glutton for punishment, I took the long way home, stopping at the Midas housing complex. Yesterday, the place was bustling with people, candidates. Today, the place was all but deserted. Most of the high-ranking candidates went to Malaga with A.J. and Zee.

A.J. and Zee.

I tried to push the image of them frolicking (yes, frolicking) on a beach out my mind. Azure seas and white beaches. Zee's long, tan, legs kicking in the white-wash while A.J. spun her around in arms that used to wrap me up and promise me forever. Another nauseous wave rolled through me. I shoved my hands into my shorts, turning my back on their perfectly vacated balcony and made my way home.

The elevator doors slid open on the top floor. Early evening on a Saturday, I figured most of the people were either just waking up, already out, or home for the last long weekend until Thanksgiving.

I tiptoed past Beaux's room and pushed open the door to my dorm. Gone was the makeshift bed. The blankets, nicely folded, sat at the edge of the couch. Nothing but silence greeted me. I wrapped my fingers around A.J.'s note in my pocket. I was going to show Malory, but then decided the less she knew, the better. It was a crappy thought, but if I learned anything from my future queen friends last night, it was to keep everyone at arm's distance and trust no one. I walked in and sank into the couch, grabbing my phone from the coffee table. I had seven missed calls, three missed texts, and not one of them was from A.J.

I spent the rest of the weekend bouncing off the walls, researching where in hell my elixir could've been hidden and avoiding Beaux. Morning-after guilt seemed to happen even when nothing went down.

Monday night, my roommates finally showed back up. They walked in giggling and suntanned. When I asked how their weekend went, what they did, Olivia answered with a glare that could peel a fake tan off a showgirl. Gia hightailed it into our room and then to the bathrooms.

By Tuesday afternoon, I got the message loud and clear: they weren't talking to me.

Two weeks into the cold-shoulder treatment, I gave up trying. When I was home, I was in my room or the common area.

We ate separately.

We walked to classes separately.

The three classes we had together, they'd stand and walk to the opposite side of the room if I sat next to them.

They did weekends at Olivia's compound, off-campus.

We lived separate lives.

After years of friendship, I knew when Gia had moved past pissed and into hurt. I'd have taken pissed until our senior year over one day of knowing I'd hurt her. But she had to realize that she'd hurt me, too.

For three weeks, Gia would wait for me to fall asleep before she went to bed and then be gone before the sun rose. The purple smudges under her eyes said this was taking more of a toll on her than it was anyone else.

Ms. Maddox split our class time. She worked with the Queens who had solidified their rein on Mondays while I was being normal in my Computer Science Class; I'd learned to hack a server, way cool. Ms. Maddox worked with me and my "limited innate powers of persuasion and bonding" every Tuesday. We'd abandoned the formal training last week and concentrated on deciphering the riddle and Isaac's helpful hints of me "having some tiramisu and reflecting" on something and wanting us all "under his watch." It was gibberish three weeks ago and even more so now that I had a week until midterms. A week until my elixir's solution expired and my family's rule ceased to exit.

Cara picked up on the rift among the Queens around week four after I spent a couple of afternoons with her. When her roommates came home, well, lines apparently were drawn, and I fell on the persona non grata list for the spares, too. I fully expected her to take their side, but after hearing how the future Queens had broken the pact and found their elixirs and I still had no clue where mine was, she and Olivia had an all-out war in the commons. It should have made me feel better, my half-sister being on my side, but . . . it didn't. It was just another catastrophic repercussion of my presence.

Week five started like all the others. I made my way to my weekly strategy meetings with my Tens, checking my phone for some sign from A.J. There wasn't and hadn't been since I lost my shit and went ass-over-shoulders drunk. The only thing going my way in Vegas was the weather. The air was cooler and I'd abandoned my sundresses and flip-flops for my Converse and jeans. At the beginning of October, Beaux started to sit in on the strategy meetings. We'd come up with four deadly offensive maneuvers. The numbers were already practicing them in the game Cara had created; this weekend, the week before midterms, we had access to the field and we could practice them live.

That decision to live practice was split at my war table.

"You run the plays live in that arena, you have no idea who's watching." Beaux's voice was deadly, more so now than ever before. A shadow from the brim of his hat played across his face, hiding the deep worry lines I knew were etched in his forehead.

"If we don't run them, then how will we know they'll work?" I placed my elbows on the table and cradled my chin in my hand. I knew he had a point but I was starved for interaction, craving a fight for an excuse to unleash five weeks of pent-up aggression.

"He's right, Cass," Cara's voice came from the back of the theatre. "The Numbers have been running the plays flawlessly. Kickin' ass with the new formations, actually." She walked up the stairs to the theatre stage, holding up the recent data the games creator, our tech-genius Eight, had printed out. "They've got this."

I ran my hands through my hair, gathering the ends and twisting them into a nervous bun. "Helen and the House of Diamonds played their last Field Games yesterday and lost miserably. The House of Diamonds has their battle powers." I let the implications that I'd yet to find my elixir hang in the air. "If these plays aren't executed flawlessly . . . I overheard Olivia last night. My gut says she's mastered her battle power, and I don't even know what the fuck ours is!" I swiped all the books off the table and stood. The books clattered to the floor, echoing off the acoustic walls of the theatre.

Eight sets of eyes bore into my back, adding to the mounting pressure I felt suffocating me with every breath I took. I was no more qualified to lead a bar crawl than I was a field game. My mom should have never claimed me. I'd only disappoint her, my House. I was the definition of disappointment.

Cara came and stood next to me. She didn't say a word, but her support meant when I failed to win the last field game, when I failed to secure our line, I'd be disappointing her most of all.

"Let's call that an adjournment." Beaux's Australian lilt cut through the awkward silence. Chairs scraped against the floor, Kate and Leo picked up the remnants of my temper tantrum.

"Cass," Cara threaded her fingers through mine. Our eyes met. Where contempt should have been, I only found concern. Not for our line, but for me. Yayati would've been proud of her.

I was.

"We all have faith in you. Trust your House and concentrate on the elixir." Her gaze held mine. "They won't let you down."

Her eyes searched mine, willing all the power I knew she possessed into my inept body. She would've been an amazing Queen of Hearts. She was strong, unyielding, bold, loyal, and everything I wanted to be.

"Okay," I conceded. It was the least I could give her. "They were your warriors before they were mine. You believe in them and I believe in you."

Cara's eyes filled and shimmered. "Let me know if you need my help." She squeezed my hand. We were far from BFFs, but we weren't enemies. That was something.

I didn't move as the footsteps of my subjects left the room. The quiet I'd come to hate closed in around me. Beaux was still here. I'd become so conditioned to his boots clacking on the ground, I could hear him coming up the quad sidewalk while I was in my bedroom four floors up.

"It's good they see you have trust in them," he finally broke the silence.

"If I don't find the elixir by Halloween, then it will all be misplaced faith, won't it?"

Beaux's chair scraped across the stage, boots punished the wooden floors as he marched over to me and wrapped me up in his arms. His warmth seeped into every fiber of my being. I hadn't realized how much I'd missed the contact until just that moment. Soap and a scent distinctly Beaux swirled around me. I couldn't fight him anymore and leaned my head back on his chest.

"That wasn't so hard, was it?"

I chuckled. "Downright painful."

"You haven't heard from him?"

My body jerked at the thought of A.J., but Beaux tightened his grip on me. "Off-limits."

"Fine," he said. "You leave the arena empty this weekend; Midas will think you can't handle two projects at once. He'll leave the A-team in Malaga. I overheard Hondo on the phone with Helen. They didn't lose because of the

Diamonds' battle powers, which is to freeze time, by the way."

I turned in Beaux's arms. "You know their battle powers?"

Mischief glimmered in his green eyes. "Right. You've been off sulking. I've been doing what I do best."

"Riding bulls and seducing girls?"

"Thank you for both compliments, but no. Lulling people into thinking I'm a dumb spare." He tapped his temple. "Those boys could no longer keep a secret than I could keep my hands off a pretty girl." Beaux pulled me closer into him; a noticeable thickness below his belt grew between us.

"Keep it PG, cowboy." I tried to sound affronted, but embarrassed was more the octave I'd reached. "Battle powers."

Beaux smiled down at me, his arms tightening one more moment to drive home the point that the wind could blow and he'd be ready to bed a girl. He lowered his mouth to my ear, his breath sending delicious shockwaves down the side of my body.

"House of Diamonds can freeze individuals. Helen can freeze people and time. They lost because she never got a chance to execute a play. She choked, and that was Midas's B-team. House of Clubs can see almost a minute into the future. Gia needs her black opal and a safe spot, but when she's mastered her power, she can become invisible."

"What? Invisible, really?"

Beaux nodded, the tip of his nose ran along the edge of my cheek. "House of Spades' lower cards have greater use of their innate ability of influencing people, but it's Olivia's battle power that's going to make all sorts of sense to you. She can control people's minds. Possess them. Sound familiar?"

I rested my head on Beaux's chest. His heart thrummed under my ear, and I totally got how girls could lay their head on a guy and be lost for days. The steady beat did something calming and intoxicating to me and my girly parts.

"Not complaining, but you good?" Beaux asked.

"Do they know what my power is?"

Beaux pulled in a deep breath, his chest expanding under my cheek.

"I didn't think so," I whispered.

"You need to make up with your friends, Cass. Gia's running her last Field Games tonight against the B-team; we could go and watch."

I shook my head. "They'd think I was spying on them. I'm the evil Balanter, haven't you heard?"

"You had one slip—two slips." Beaux quickly corrected himself. "I'd like to see them handle that much power as benevolently as you've done. I'd have tied them to a barrel and let a bull take a few licks after the stunt they pulled. You'd agreed to work together, and they let their Jacks run right over your alliance."

"You think that's what happened?" I pulled in another calming breath of the cowboy who had me wrapped up in his arms.

"It's exactly what they did. I'm not just good-looking, I'm quite devious when I need to be. These blokes don't realize how powerful the four of you are together. The world's going to need you united, which means one of you is going to have to bury the hatchet in something besides the others' backs."

I snorted. "And you think it's me?"

"I think you've got a week until Halloween, and then it won't matter."

My stomach dropped. He was right. I had a week to mend fences and find my elixir. If I didn't, then it wouldn't matter what I, Cara, or Carina did.

We'd be exiled.

THIRTY

ANGRY, HIGH-PITCHED VOICES and threats laced with exotic accents filled the top floor of the Dayton Complex. The spare Diamond Queen held the common's room TV remote high in the air in one hand and the Spades' spare Queen's face in the other. Both girls' protectors rolled on the floor, trying to punch the other. All of it was over a soccer game and a missing bottle of body wash. Clearly, I wasn't the only one having issues with roommates.

Beaux tucked my hand around his forearm, maneuvering us through the gawkers laying witness to two potential royals behaving badly. It was refreshing to see I wasn't the only one with "issues" needing to be dealt with. I pulled in a deep breath, nerves and butterflies ramping up their flutter inside me the closer we got to my room. I'd always been the passive person growing up. Never one to make a scene because it would surely end up on a website or gossip show. I'd flown below the radar for so long, I didn't know if my social wings knew how to carry me through this kind of storm.

Beaux stopped us in front of my room, his stance widening as he crossed his arms over his chest. The brim of his cowboy hat cloaked us in a shadow that I wished had Gia's invisibility awesomeness.

"Deep breath," Beaux whispered, the pad of his thumb freeing my bottom lip from my teeth. "They were your friends before they were your enemies."

"You stole my line."

"I altered it for the occasion." He nudged my shoulder. "If you mean it, say you're sorry. Ask for their forgiveness. That's all you can do. Maybe wish Gia luck for tonight."

My heart rattled my ribcage. "You make 'sorry' sound so easy."

"It is. Righteousness tends to muck it all up." Beaux turned the doorknob; the door gave way, letting the sounds of my roommates spill out into the hall. They didn't know or didn't care what was happening in the common room.

Sweat pooled in my palms, my head floated on a rush of adrenaline as I walked over the threshold. Beaux slapped my ass and disappeared behind the closed door before I could be outraged.

"I'm coming!" Olivia stopped short in the kitchen. Foam from the root beer floats sloshed over the rim of the three mugs in her hands. Her shoulders rolled back, the iron bitch façade dropping into place.

"Can I talk to you?" I pleaded. "All three of you, if possible."

I don't know what she saw in my face. Maybe it was my mousey voice, the defeated way my shoulders hung, or the pathetic way I was wringing my hands; whatever it was made my cousin stop the cold-shoulder glare. But it didn't stop her from putting the mugs on the counter and walking into her bedroom.

My lip trembled, tears welling up in my eyes. Maybe it was too late. Maybe five weeks was the expiration date on I'm sorries. A silent sob shook my shoulders as I turned and started back to the front door.

I'd leave.

Nobody deserved to live this way. Malory was commuting from The Eclectic, I could, too. It'd be like old times, and the other girls wouldn't have to walk on eggshells around me. Mom would be disappointed we couldn't—

"Where you going?" Olivia called out.

I spun around, the three of them standing in the sunlight like mirages of a future I didn't know I needed.

"I . . . I. . . I thought you . . ." Warm tears skidded down my cheeks. "I thought you didn't want to hear my voice."

Olivia hitched her hands on her hips. "You said you wanted to talk to the three of us. Two sentences in five weeks, you better be damn sure I'm grabbing the others to witness the event."

I chewed on my lip. I guess I had been marching around on a high horse, but so had they. Glaring at me and—I cut the thought off. There was that righteousness Beaux had warned me about. I wasn't here to prove my point of right or wrong. I was here to apologize.

"I just wanted to say I'm sorry. I'm sorry I unleashed the B on you, Olivia. I'm sorry I judged all three of you without listening to your side." My hands flopped like defeated fishes out of water, out of time. "I have excuses and you have reasons, but in the end, we're not talking and most of it, all of it, is my fault." I bit down on my lip again, wishing my apology was enough but knowing it was probably too little, too late. "I'll move out. I don't want to ruin this for you." I spun on my heels, tears blurring my vision.

"That's it?" Gia huffed. "You're just going to give up?"

I stopped mid-step. Yeah, I guess I was giving up. If I stopped long enough, all the reasons why I should came rushing in like a tidal wave.

"What's the point? I don't have my elixir. My family's line is about to be exiled. Two boys who don't want me shattered my heart. I'll wait out the four years and choose to forget all this on my twenty-first birthday."

"The Cassandra Vera I knew was much more badass than this." Olivia waved a judgmental hand up and down my form.

"I agree," Helen chimed in. "Any bitch that can make me shut up and then has the bollocks to come and apologize clearly deserves a second chance."

"Francis told me Beaux knew where the elixirs were." Olivia folded her arms over her chest. She tapped a toe on the floor, her tell of being nervous. "I thought you'd already been activated, that's why you were so calm that morning."

I shook my head. "Why would you think that? Why would Francis say I was activated?"

"I don't know." The heated look in her eyes said she'd damn well would be finding out though. "But you haven't found it yet, your elixir, have you?"

I shook my head again.

"We can tell you where it is, but it won't be easy. Not now," Gia said. "I barely got mine, and that was five weeks ago. I made William go with me yesterday. The Shadows are crawling all over the fountain like ants on honey." Gia's gaze found mine across the room. All the weeks of silent hostility evaporated like water on a hot sidewalk. "They know your time is about to expire. They think you're going to be desperate enough to be stupid."

I rounded the chair and sank into the cushions. "Why are you being so nice to me?"

Olivia glanced at Gia. Gia stole a look in Helen's direction, and Helen finally spoke for the trio. "We're not. We haven't been. I certainly haven't." Helen caught Olivia's mocking glare. "What? I can admit when I was wrong. I'm growing up." She wiped at an imaginary wrinkle in her Capri pants.

We jumped at a knock on the door. Gia pulled a quick look at her watch. She was dressed in all black, her blond hair tied up in a ponytail. My stomach flipped. Field Games.

"That's William." Gia held a hand to her stomach. Her nerves matched mine. "Cass, grab the door for me. Knee William in the balls if he gets out of line. He's been pissing me off with his holier-than-thou routine." She stomped across the hall and disappeared into our room.

I opened the door and let William in. He didn't give me a second look as he walked in and picked up her bag. Gia came out of our room with black Converse on her feet and an air of confidence I'd never seen her possess. She marched across the room, pulled me in for a hug despite William's disapproving grunt.

"It's in the Fountain of the Gods at the forum shops in Caesar's Palace. When I get back, I expect a hint of a plan." Gia pulled back, her blue eyes sparkled with badassery.

"Gia!" William reprimanded.

Her shoulders bounced. "Ladies, I'll be back shortly. William, we need to talk."

William's face paled at the phrase that sent most men's balls up into their stomachs.

Two hours later, Gia walked in the door with stitches over her right eye and her left hand in an Ace bandage. William carried her things to her room, came out and made her soup, then pulled me aside. "I'm sorry I assumed you were the one putting Gia in harm's way. She seems to be doing a fine job of that by herself." He stole a glance at our bedroom door.

"What happened?" I asked.

"Ten minutes and they swarmed the castle. They were ruthless, Cassie.

I've never seen a B-team have such disregard. And yes, I've seen Field Games before. We watched tapes of Gia's mother. The secondary Midas candidates acted like they had something to prove. I . . ." His words trailed off as he pinched the bridge of his nose. "It was the weirdest thing. We were the enemy instead of the sparring partner." William shook the thought off, his stance widening. "I'm supposed to say sorry."

I felt my eyebrows crawl up my face. "Supposed to?"

The harsh lines around his mouth softened. "Fine, I was an ass. I know most of the crap Gia's found herself in since the semester started was her doing, not yours."

"Still missing two words, William," I teased, loving every second of his two-minute grovel. It did very little for the years of crap I'd put up with, but it was something.

He rocked back on his heels like the words were going to knee him in the junk. "I'm sorry."

"Forgiven." I threw my arms open. "Shall we hug it out?"

William's eyes flared, and the soft giggle from my bedroom door said Gia had witnessed everything.

"C'mon, William, one hug won't kill you," Gia said through fingers covering her grin.

The poor guy squirmed under his Queen's order. It was perfect, and had I not just done the groveling act, I'd have let him squirm a while longer. Beaux's Australian lilt rumbled through my brain with one word: Righteousness.

I took the higher road. "You'll owe me one." I patted William's chest and turned to face Gia. "Should I ask how the others fared?" I pointed to the bandage covering the stitches over her eye. Gia gingerly touched the spot, wincing at the contact.

"I wish. You mind if William stays in your bed tonight? He's supposed to watch me for signs of concussion." She shook her head.

Gia may have thought she'd convinced us everything was fine, but the way her knuckles turned white gripping the doorframe said otherwise.

"That's fine. I'm used to doing time on the couch."

♥

A SLIT OF sun shot across the darkened room. Blooms of dust bounced in the sunlight. I rolled over, grabbing my phone from under the piles of paperwork that me, Olivia, and Helen had put together last night.

Eleven A.M. and still nothing from A.J. Five weeks later, you'd think my heart would have given up on the stupid rejected feeling.

I yawned, stretching like a cat that had finally been pacified but feeling none of the contentment. After William convinced Gia we'd be fine plotting without her, I had received a text from an unknown number.

Your rooms are clear.

It took a few minutes for me to reverse search the number and find it was registered to a pawn shop just off Fremont Street. Thank you Computer Science "hacking" class.

Isaac.

Olivia was safe. What did he care if our room was clear or if I ever found my elixir? If anything, he had the most to benefit from turning me in. Maybe that was his plan. Lull me into this trusting web of deceit and then personally hand me over. I couldn't imagine Chance standing down, and with Warren in the mix, Isaac had to be scrambling to secure his position.

The Isaac variable had sat in the back of my mind while me, Olivia, Helen worked until three-thirty in the morning. At a quarter to four, the sky started turning the color of cotton candy, and we were no closer than when we'd started. Somehow we had to get me into Caesar's Palace, to the Fountain of the Gods, over the railing, into the Fountain of the Gods, shimmied up the rocks, and to the top of Zeus's spear. My elixir was in the orb at the top of the slickest, most public fountain in the world. Okay, not the world, but it might as well have been.

I'd used some of my newly learned computer skills and hacked into the Palace's surveillance system. Olivia had been impressed as hell when we found the camera monitoring the Shops in the Forum had a dedicated live feed for the fountain. Our triumph was short-lived. Dodging the Shadows would be one thing, but evading Vegas security would be another. There was no way I wouldn't be arrested.

"Time?" Olivia grumbled now.

"Eleven."

"I thought we were going to get an early start of it?" Helen answered from the makeshift bed she'd made out the couch's cushions.

My stomach did a little flip remembering Beaux half-naked body and me drunkenly sprawled across him. I shook the thought from my head. I had so much to do before the end of the week, tripping over memories of bare-chested Aussies had to take a back seat.

The girls and I spent the rest of the morning and the next two days monitoring the Shadows from the Caesar's Palace's live feed I'd hacked. They moved in two groups of three around the fountain in four-hour shifts. It was depressing as hell to know there were so many indebted souls. The gods were right to have one of their own oversee the Shadows. If they ever had a uniting factor, the world would be easy pickings.

"Looks like lunch time has the smallest infestation of Shadows." Gia tapped her pen to her lip and then the TV screen, not catching the tiny cringe from Olivia. She was in love with Isaac, and I was pretty sure she didn't know he wasn't a Shadow.

He was an anomaly.

A secret weapon Dionysus had kept hidden in plain sight. For what purpose? I was still trying to piece that one together.

Helen grabbed the pen from Gia, shooting her another annoyed glance. "Pretty sure it's the lightest Shadow time because it's teeming with tourists. And stop with the pen tapping. I've told you, it's driving me batshit crazy."

Olivia and I giggled. Things were slowly getting back to normal.

"Okay, I say I make a go of it on Friday when the weekend wave of tourists descends on Vegas. Olivia, you think you can handle a spectacle?"

Her eyebrow arched over a beautiful emerald eye. "Have you met me?"

My shoulders rose. "You make a scene in Jimmy Choo—"

"Ooh, let me make the scene," Gia interrupted. "It's Jimmy Choo. I can so create a scene with the god of shoes."

"God of shoes was Hermes," Helen offered.

"Hermes is the god of shoes and scarfs." Gia laughed. "Get it? God of shoes and scarfs, because he's got wings on his feet and fashion houses." She doubled over, clutching her stomach.

Olivia tossed a pillow at Gia, but her emerald-eyed gaze settled on me. "Friday's cutting it short, Cass. Midterms start with Saturday classes. You sure you don't want to try this bait and switch tactic tomorrow?"

I shook my head. "We won't have the element of the awestruck tourists snapping shots of my asshatery."

Gia rounded the couch and plopped down next to me. "You want the tourists?"

"Yeah, if they're busy snapping pictures of me in the fountain and you're going Fashion Diva on a Choo rep, hopefully the pandemonium will create a vacuum of safety for me."

Helen brought a tray of teacups, saucers, and English tea and placed it on the coffee table. "When you get to the top, you insert your key card into the seam of Zeus's orb. It takes eight seconds for the card to read and the latch to give way. Your hands will be wet when you reach the orb, take that time to wipe them dry. You're going to have to take the elixir then and there, and the elixir vile is bloody childproof." She muttered off a string of curses in Hindi. "They still treat us like—"

"Focus," Olivia interjected.

Helen's gaze landed on mine. A fire I liked seeing burned in her eyes. "On the plane to Malaga, you're going to have to fill me in on who's treating you all childlike." I caught Olivia waving me off the subject. "What else do I need to know? What does it taste like? Did you feel your powers activate instantly? What did it feel like?" I stood up and started pacing the living room. Tourists and taste buds, it was enough to send a girl to the crazyhouse.

"It tastes like cucumber water, and no, you don't feel anything," Gia said.

"Mine tasted like strawberries," Helen interjected. Resting her hands on her knees, she looked at Gia, then Olivia, and finally settled on me. "I didn't feel anything magical or mythical. It was more like a relief washed over me, and time seemed to bend to my will."

"You know I'm going to be mad as hell if my battle power is the ability to create a giant love fest."

Gia cackled, Olivia threw another pillow at me, and Helen snorted, which sent us all into a fit of giggles. It was the most normal moment I'd lived in all of my life, even if it came about because of mythical potions and shimmying up gods in fountains.

Friday morning, I woke up and wandered out onto the balcony. A cool breeze whistled through the trees. The wind was changing, winter was coming, and the morning felt like it was the last few grains of sand running through a timepiece. I heard the slider open behind me and caught the scent of fresh brewed coffee.

"Can't sleep?" Olivia asked, handing me my cup of coffee.

"Thanks." I blew into the cup, releasing more Columbian aroma into the air. "No. Keep running the day through my mind like a speed freak." I pulled a sip of hot heaven through my lips.

"I hear ya." Olivia leaned onto the balcony, her eyebrows pinched together. "It's been keeping me up all night. I have no idea what costume I'm going to wear for tomorrow night."

I spit out my coffee, laughing loud enough to wake everyone in the Dayton Complex, as well as the Shadow dorms across the quad. "I'm worried about this afternoon, Oli."

"You shouldn't. Your elixir's going to be a walk in the park compared to tomorrow night." She turned and leaned her back against the balcony railing. "Fremont Street and Halloween? The two go together like good times and bad decisions." She waggled her eyebrows at me. "You and Beaux have any ideas on a costume."

I shook my head. "Not a couple, Oli."

"I hate that nickname almost as much as the other one. I think you should call me V."

"I'm not calling you V and stop trying to distract me."

She settled down in the chair behind me, and early morning sounds picked up our conversation. I'd never really listened to the birds on the quad or the way the wind whistled through the walkway before catching in the branches of the trees. I sighed.

"Beaux thinks we should leave the practice arena empty tonight. He thinks Midas will leave A.J. in Malaga and let the B-team take me on." I stole a quick glance over my shoulder.

Olivia's eyes caught mine over the rim of her cup, and I already knew she agreed.

"You too?"

She nodded.

"So the arena stays empty." I leaned on my elbows, the ends of my hair dangling over the railing. Four stories of dorm rooms were all that separated me and my children's children from a normal life. I could still forget everything. Let Cara run the show. How hard would it be to leave myself a note, a journal, something that would explain the inexplicable urge that would surely draw my loved ones here?

"Aphrodite," Olivia interrupted my thoughts. "You go as Aphrodite and Beaux can rock an Apollo costume," she snorted. "I'd like to see some Aussie abs."

"Why Aphrodite?" I pushed her out of the drool fest Beaux tended to create with the mention of him or his abs.

Olivia pulled another sip of coffee through her lips, though the lust swirling in her eyes said she'd rather be running her lips across Beaux's obliques instead of her coffee mug. "We're going down to Fremont Street dressed as Greek gods. You could be Aphrodite."

"Who's we?"

"Everyone. Dayton Complex. Kind of our way of giving the gods a 'we're not just your servants' eff you."

"Mature."

"We're dressing up in costumes. Pretty sure mature was never a factor," Olivia chided.

"My last field game is tomorrow." A small bundle of nerves exploded in my stomach. "If I—"

"No," Olivia cut me off. "Cass, look at me."

I turned and met her emerald eyes.

"You get back what you send out into this world. You were destined to lead the House of Hearts. The fates have thrown every obstacle in your path, and your heart has seen you through. I have no doubt you will secure your line this afternoon. When you do, you'll kick A.J.'s ass back to Malaga and make him rue the day he ever chose to cross you. Now go get dressed. We've got some chaos to create." Olivia pushed out of her chair, taking all the certain determination with her.

There was nothing to say, no way to argue with such strong conviction.

I almost believed her.

Almost.

THIRTY-ONE

A WAVE OF tourists rushed past us, snapping pictures on their phones as if the selfie were a life preserver. My own wave of personal hell swelled up in my stomach. The Fountain of the Gods in the forum looked manageable on closed circuit TV, but like everything in Vegas, it was larger than life in person. Water rushed down the mammoth marble statues, making the stone breakneck slick. I swallowed over the bundle of nerves in my throat.

"The orb's gotta be like thirty feet up in the air," I exhaled.

"Thirty-two," Helen's voice answered from the cellphone.

"Oli, give me your 'give 'em hell' speech again." I leaned back on the marble Corinthian column. I was losing it if I was naming the types of columns I wanted to bash my head against. Maybe I should have brought Beaux. He could have. . . I let the thought get swallowed up in another rush of tourists. Beaux was about to mount a bull, the same bull who'd abused his head the first time I'd met him.

Revolution.

I guess we all had scores to settle today.

My heart scurried up my chest as another dose of adrenaline dumped into my bloodstream. It was better this way. He still thought we were making a late night attempt at the elixir while everyone was at Fremont Street doing the Halloween thing. After Beaux had stopped laughing at my idea of us dressing up as Aphrodite and Apollo this morning, a glimmer rooted in his eyes, and an hour later, he'd found costumes and hired two kids to dress up as us as we made a play for the elixir.

His bait and switch plan was good.

Mine was better.

"Ladies," Gia asked over her teacup and bug-eye sunglasses. "I'm thinking now might be the time."

I peeked around the column and found what she'd seen: a group of kids and their frazzled parents pooled at the entrance to the forum shops. Lady Luck was definitely on our side. Caesar's Palace was housing the Youth Basketball Championships. Six hundred young men from eight- to fifteen-years-old from across the country and their families were calling Caesar's Palace home for the weekend. Six hundred young men that both created and admired spectacles.

"I'm going. This group is going to love you, Cass. They're the perfect mixture of hormonal teen boy and fascinated gawkers. I'll see if I can snag a few of those Shadows with a hip wiggle I've been working on." Gia stood, adjusted her mini skirt, and picked up the Jimmy Choo bag. A wicked smile pulled at her lips. "I've waited all my life to do this."

"Return a pair of broken shoes?" Olivia asked.

"Create a spectacle," Gia answered, sashaying across the cobblestone floor of the forum. *Five minutes,* she mouthed back at us. Her hips swished and swayed, catching and holding the attention of three Shadows.

"Gia's hips don't lie. I count seven Shadows. Wait, six," Olivia ticked off.

"Good Lord," Helen crooned over Olivia's cellphone. "How long's she been practicing naughty rich girl?"

I chuckled.

"Remember," Helen continued. "Key card goes in the orb, then wipe your hands; don't want you tumbling from Zeus's arm. And please tell me you've been practicing opening bloody childproof caps." Helen's voice hitched.

"Yep, all week long." I wiped sweaty palms on my board shorts. Again, Lady Luck was smiling on us: Caesar's peripheral pools were still open this late in the season, which meant me in board shorts and wave walker shoes wasn't too far out of place.

Olivia and I jumped at the screech skittering out of the Jimmy Choo shop. I choked on the laugh about the same time Olivia's eyes widened.

"Two more Shadows are on my side of the fountain, ladies," Helen said. I looked back at the massive wave of teenage boys now craning their neck to see where the damsel-in-distress noises were coming from. A few broke away from the group and inched forward. They pulled the other boys from the group until a dozen or so teens with cellphone cameras at the ready trickled into the forum. Their parents followed, and after a few heartbeats in my throat, the wave of tourists started to crest on the shops.

"Go!" Helen and Olivia said at the same time.

Adrenaline dumped into my bloodstream, nearly stopping my heart. I scurried across the walkway, catching sight of the last Shadow disappearing from my side of the fountain.

"Ma'am," the restaurant's hostess tried to stop me, but I rushed past her. Surfing through the empty tables to the fountain, I used the chair and table to hurtle over the rod iron guardrail. Gia's wail crested over the fountain as my feet splashed down into the water. I sucked in a mixture of spray and hotel air. The cold water slapped at my knees, punishing me for breaking the rules. Gripping the base of Poseidon's triton, I hoisted myself up into his lap, catching the flash of several cameras. Thank God they were on the other side of the fountain. Whatever Gia was doing, she was keeping me safe from discovery. I slipped and slid across the marble rock formations. Water from the outcropping above crashed down on me as I looked for a way to the next level. With each slippery step, Zeus's orb seemed to move farther and farther out of my reach.

"I didn't break them," Gia's voice screeched. "Do I look like I'd return something broken? I want to see a manager. Now!" Her heel stomp echoed in the forum. I snorted as I found dry hand and foot holes in the marble to raise myself up to the level of the fountain.

Zeus's marble eyes looked down on me, judging me, wondering if I was worthy enough.

I wasn't.

I never would be, but my family was, and he'd just have to cough up the elixir so I could secure their line. I gripped his calf, grabbed hold of his lightning bolt, and said a quick sorry for using his who-ha as a foot hole.

"She's in the fountain!" A boy screeched. I didn't look back to see who said it, but given the voice-changing crack, my cover was blown by a ball player and not a Shadow. I focused on the orb and kicked off Zeus's penis to launch myself to the crook of his elbow. My wet feet kicked and slipped against wet marble until I finally hooked my leg over Zeus's arm and swung myself up. A wave of black hoods jumped into the fountain. The hostess screamed for security. I pulled the key card out of my pocket, nearly losing it, my fingers were so numb from the frigid water and spotted a hooded boy clearing Poseidon. He mercilessly grabbed Zeus's genitalia. I quickly pushed the key card into the orb and started counting.

One Mississippi.

Two Mississippi.

Three Mississippi.

I tore open the zip lock bag.

Four Mississippi.

Five Mississippi.

I wiped my hands on the dry washcloth.

Six Mississippi.

Seven Mississippi.

Cold fingers wrapped around my ankle, and a brief flash of the Shadow's history jolted through me before I kicked him free.

The orb opened. I'd fully expected a gold light to explode. Instead, a simple vial with a heart stamped into the bottle top sat nestled in a bed of red satin. I carefully picked up the elixir; my family's line was nearly secure.

Cold fingers wrapped around my ankle again; this time, the Shadow and his memory weren't so easy to kick free. My spine snapped straight. The cold memory of the Shadow beat back any warmth I could muster from my Balanter power until it took hold . . .

Black hair flopped in my eyes again. She'd left me. She'd promised she'd be there when I got home from school, but I should have known better. Everything in my gut told me she would take the money and try to double it.

"We make our own luck, Seth." Her voice had cracked around my name this morning. The lie was too much for her vocal cords to handle. The eviction letter fluttered in the breeze as I pushed open the front door. Suppressing the bile that churned as the cockroaches scurried away from the summer sun, I flipped the light switch to finish sending the roaches back into the walls. I always thought you needed food to bring them out. A roach squashed under my foot.

"Gross."

I walked over to Mom's closed door and knocked.

"Mom." I double-checked the wall for cockroaches before leaning on the frame. "Mom?" My knuckles rapped on the door again.

Silence.

Too much quiet.

Worry mixed with the ache of hunger in my belly.

No way could she have fallen off the wagon again.

One more knock was gobbled up by the silence. My hand shook as I placed it on the doorknob. I'd found her lifeless body once before. I was twelve. I'd cut school and found her in time. A trickle of cold sweat dribbled down my spine, preparing myself to find my mom's unconscious body again. The door swung open and everything was wrong.

Everything was gone.

"What the fuck?" I stepped into the empty room. We didn't have much, but what we did have, what she had . . . it was gone. The dirty outline of where her mattress sat and a note taped to the wall were the only evidence she'd ever been here.

I punched the wall, welcoming the fire raging up my arm. It was my pitching arm, but that didn't matter anymore.

This place was a shit hole.

My life was a shit hole.

I whipped my backpack in front of me.

Coach was full of shit. I pulled out the college recruitment letter.

"U.L.V." I crumpled up my future and dug around for the other card. The smooth black card—

"Cassie!" My name bounced around my brain. The memory of the Shadow clawed at my conscience, but Olivia's voice sounded again. "Cassandra! Snap out of it!" Olivia screeched. The Shadow shook the fog from his eyes. One, two, three kicks to the face from my free foot and the boy let go. He grasped at air. The same wide-eyed shock look filled his eyes as he grasped at the air, finally hitting the marble floor of the fountain with a sickening thud. My heart stopped. I couldn't take my eyes off his lifeless body. His name was Seth. His mom had abandoned him and I'd . . . I'd killed him.

"Drink it, Cassie!" Gia screamed. I looked at the base of the fountain and found three more Shadows had taken up Seth's cause, more determined now than ever.

I fumbled with the vial's cap. God, my hands were slippery. The ridged edges chewed up my palm. Panic clawed at my throat. My heart thrashed against my rib cage as I pulled my foot out of the reach of a fourth Shadow. I was never going to get this open.

"Take a deep fucking breath, Cassandra. Push and twist!" The Australian lilt of a cowboy, my cowboy, yelled from below. Beaux yanked the foot of the Shadow beneath me, sending him tumbling down the face of the mountain. Despite myself, in spite of the Shadows behind me, I smiled. Took a deep breath. And felt the calming warmth of my Balanter power surge up my back. I pushed down the cap, feeling the difference already as it twisted effortlessly under my palm. Another Shadow briefly touched my shoulder before falling from Zeus's arm. I tipped the vial back, pouring the cool liquid into my mouth, letting it rush down my throat.

Peach Bellinis.

I smiled at the memory of Sara, my adopted mom, and me on a beach in Fiji with virgin Bellinis. Cold forearms wrapped around my throat, splintering the memory as I slipped off my perched position on Zeus's arm. The world tipped upside down. Air whistled past my ears, my hands fished for something, anything to grab hold of. Several different variations of my name launched from my roommates trying desperately to stop my death fall with their will. But nothing could stop me from splatting on the slick marble rocks below. At least my sister would have her chance to rule. My world froze with a spine-jarring stop. I dangled like a fish on the end of a hook a few inches from Seth's lifeless eyes. A small blink and I knew he wasn't dead but close to it. Bile turned in my stomach. He'd had such a shit life. No one deserved the cards life had dealt him. He sure as hell didn't deserve this. Warmth danced up my spine as hot palms burned into my ankle. A wave of Australian swear words rained down on me.

"Fuck me, Cassandra. You've got to lay off the pastries, lass!" Beaux lowered me next to Seth. The small rise of his chest had me scurrying up right.

"Call 911 now! Olivia," I hollered. "He needs an ambulance."

Water sprayed around me as Beaux landed next to me. A sick thud of flesh meeting flesh sounded behind me. I looked back in time to see another

Shadow meet the lethal end of Beaux's fist.

"Let's go."

I yanked free of Beaux's grip around my arm. "He needs an ambulance."

"He needs to be put out of his misery." Beaux's eyes pulled from me, landing over my head. "Right, mate. Look at your feet. That's an empty vial and she's no longer available." Beaux cracked his knuckles. "But we could always dispute the evidence."

The Shadow he threatened quickly turned.

"Ambulance is on its way. So is security, Cass," Olivia called out. "Let's go."

I hated the visions. It would have been easier not to know this guy was all alone. No one would mourn him if he died. Seth's chest rose and fell under my hands. A warm tingle danced along my spine. I didn't want this boy to be alone anymore. I didn't want him to have to suffer by himself. He deserved to have someone give a shit about him. He deserved . . . happiness. Heat shot through me.

"Go," Seth the Shadow whispered.

"I can't leave you alone."

A smile pulled at his lip. "It's alright. I'm used to alone. Go."

Beaux snagged the empty vial, wrapped his arm around my waist, and this time, I didn't fight him. We jumped into the water at the base of the fountain, Seth's eyes still firmly fixed on me as Beaux climbed up and over the railing. He wrapped his fingers around my wrists, hauling me up and out of the water.

"I'll send someone to the hospital if you want," Beaux said in my ear as he lifted me over the iron railing.

I nodded. "Do it."

"You're starting to sound like a Queen, Cass." Olivia wrapped me up in a towel as we hurried down the corridor and out of the Shadows' view.

THIRTY-TWO

"I STILL CAN'T believe you missed last night. Halloween? On Fremont Street?" Malory walked her feet up the wall next to my bed. "It was crazy. I've never seen the place so packed. It was . . ."

"Epic," I finished for her. I'd been hearing about the epic Halloween party all day. Epic was securing your family's ruling line, epic was knowing you had access to your battle power—even if I didn't know what that meant—epic, as sick and twisted as it was, was knowing the Shadow who'd nearly sent you plunging to your death had made it through surgery and looked like he wasn't going to be paralyzed.

"You mock, but you didn't see the hotness I hooked up with last night. All dark and devious." Malory wiggled her eyebrows at me. "He'd have made you contemplate all your virtuous ways."

"Yeah, well. Only thing I'm contemplating now is how to kick A.J.'s ass and secure an awesome seat for my mom in Malaga." I tugged at the triple knot in my shoe. "You're coming to Malaga, right?"

Malory twisted up right on my bed. "You want me to come?"

"Carina texted me from Malaga. Your mom's not going to be home over Thanksgiving. You think I'd leave you here by yourself?"

"I . . . I . . . just thought . . ." Malory pulled at the hem in her t-shirt; her big eyes swam with doubt and frustration. "Wouldn't be the first time you left me for the Wonder Kids."

"If you're referring to last year's spring break, you left me. For Florida and your dad." I winked at her and the smile pulling at her lips.

"Yeah, I guess I did. You really want me to come?"

"Wouldn't have it any other way." I stood, zipping my jacket over my black t-shirt with the flaming red heart. Butterflies skated around in my stomach. I hadn't seen A.J. in nine weeks. No calls. No texts. Not even a random butt dial. The small piece of my heart that still hung onto a sliver of hope ached. This was exactly how it would've been if we'd stayed together.

"Wish me luck." I headed for the door before Malory could see the protective smile slip into place. She'd have killed A.J. for that alone, and I needed him good and fit so there were no excuses when his castle fell.

"Kick his ass, Cassie." Malory slapped my ass as I left.

"KICK HIS ASS," I muttered, skating around the perch of my castle. I shot another pissed-off glance at the House of Midas perch and Zee skating around the top. "He'd have to have shown up for me to kick his ass."

"Let him underestimate you, Cass." My little sister Cara chimed through the speaker in my helmet. "Let 'em all underestimate the House of Hearts and see what happens when they do!"

The stadium shook from the House of Hearts' Warriors' deafening cry of approval.

"You've claimed our line. We all felt the power surge through us. It's time to show everyone the badass side of the House of Hearts. Let them know all the way in Malaga we're coming!" Cara hollered as another primal roar erupted from my house's warriors. Cara skated over to the side of my platform. "Run your plays, Cass. She's scared shitless. Look at her."

Across the arena, under the harsh downlights highlighting the House of Midas's perch, Zee paced the platform on her skates. At first glance, nothing looked different, but as I watched closer, there it was. The worried way Zee worked her lip. The constant scanning of all the Hearts skating above her. We'd rattled the Third in Command and even better, she knew it.

And so did the man who loved her.

Beaux skated up to the front of my perch, casually folding his arms on the wood. He didn't fool me. I rolled forward, kneeling so we were eye-to-eye. His green eyes like cold chips of emeralds said he'd shut off any emotion, but the way his muscles rolled under his forearms, the minute tick of his jaw, and the way his pulse pounded along his neck said he'd have given anything to be anywhere but here.

"You ready for this?" I asked.

He stole a quick look over his shoulder. "I'm a man of my word, Cassandra. Right now, my word lies with my House."

"Just what a girl wants to hear."

His eyes met mine, and for a brief second, I felt the anguish, the betrayal he felt going against Zee. So this was my future? It was almost as bad as my past with A.J.

The static from a microphone silenced the arena. The hiss of skates slowed, then stopped.

"Good evening," Midas's voice filled the arena. I kept my focus on Zee. There was no one in the viewing box who concerned me. And watching Midas's Third squirm was far too entertaining. "Let's make this quick," he continued.

I could hear the chuckle in his voice. I'd be making this quick, all right. My House had fallen in three minutes and thirty-seven seconds. His would fall in under two. Zee would carry the humiliation back to her suited match, and A.J. would know how costly it was to underestimate me.

"Welcome to the final meeting of the House of Midas against the House of Hearts. As it stands, only the House of Spades has beaten the House of Midas. Should this trend continue . . ." Midas paused and we all knew he fully expected the trend to continue. "Remaining seat selections will be determined by each House's combined recorded time. House of Hearts, you will need to take the Midas castle in five minutes seven seconds to out-seat the House of Spades. You will need an unprecedented two minutes fifteen seconds to take top seat from the House of Midas." The snicker in his voice made me want to scale the stadium walls and shove a gold-plated heart down his throat. "Games will commence at the sound of the buzzer." Midas had barely finished his words when the buzzer sounded.

Skates clacked against plywood before slipping into a melodic hiss. Red lights from my warrior's skates lit the path of the arena. Around the top, dipping down one side of the House of Midas's platform, shooting across the floor and up into the rafters again. The whipping gates were up, but I wasn't planning on using them.

"Cass," Cara's voice had a bite like a bitch slap as it came across the speaker in my helmet. "Offense Seven."

Vindication spread like ripples on still water: slow at first but gaining with each beat of my heart. I could get used to this girl as my sister. I double-clicked the button on the side of my headset.

"Offense Seven," I said calmly. The tingle of warmth at the base of my spine surged. "And Hearts, I want it done in under two."

A wave of sound crested into a roar of approval. Zee's eyes locked with mine. Pure panic flared her pretty brown eyes, and if I were a betting girl, I'd have wagered my House that a few gray hairs were woven into Zee's beautiful chestnut mane.

I pulled my eyes from Zee's to the scoreboard. The second clock flipped numbers faster than my mind could register them.

"One minute. Where are we on executing?"

"Thirty seconds, Princess," Beaux's voice was hard and he'd called me by my official title. He was mad as hell. Welcome to my love life. I smirked while counting the gold lights above me. No way was I going to get leveled like I had last time. A.J. and Midas had made a serious error underestimating me. A bead of sweat dribbled down the side of my face, my pulse raced in my ears. How thirty seconds stretched into forever was beyond me. Three more passes above; the red lights on my warrior's skates showed they'd moved into formation. The scattered gold lights said Zee and Midas had no idea what was coming. Another surge of heat raced up my spine as Zee's wide eyes filled with terror so apparent they glistened from across the arena. Her eyes locked with mine and only fueled my resolve. She could have the two boys' hearts. I'd take her castle.

"Storm the castle," I calmly issued the command. Red lights attached to House of Heart Warriors shot like arrows from a bow down the ramp behind me and from the arena floor opposite me. House of Midas had no option but to skid to a halt where they were and watch as Beaux subdued Zee.

Beaux hung his head, then looked back at me. My heart tripped over my conscience. We all had prices to pay. Roles to fulfill . . . no matter the cost. He'd proven himself, even if it did slash him to his core. I bit down on my lip, willing any feeling of remorse back to the pit of my stomach it'd climbed out from. The Queen of Hearts would have been proud. My mothers would have been devastated.

The air stilled around me, holding its breath. I couldn't bring myself to look at the clock. If I hadn't proven my worth, vindicated my house . . .

The microphone crackled to life.

"House of Midas's castle has fallen. One minute fifty-two seconds." Midas voice fell flat.

A hush tumbled across the stadium. How could they all be so quiet when we'd won?

Beaux stood and turned toward me. What was wrong with them? I wiped the sweat from my upper lip.

"Cass, you okay?" Cara asked. Her big eyes searched mine like I was a wounded animal, not sure if I was going to lash out or . . . "You're bleeding, Cassie." Her words tumbled together, her face spotting at the edges, the world tipping, and then . . . nothing.

THIRTY-THREE

THREE WEEKS AND nobody had uttered a word about my bloody nose or my victorious head-over-ass fainting spell. I'd come-to on the platform in Beaux's arms and Cara's pale face hovering over mine. I'd always pegged my little sister for the one to be counting down the seconds to my demise, not panicked I was leaving it all to her. Not even Ms. Maddox had spoken about the Hearts' overwhelming victory—well, not to me, at least. Mom called Cara to our hotel in Malaga a week ago, and with her gone, it seemed like I was open for all sorts of observation and intrigue. I may be in line for the Queen of Hearts' crown, but my little half-sister still wore the Princess tiara. After she left, the whisper and hush treatment seemed to spread like an epidemic on campus. I'd walk into a room, and the words would scamper away into hidden corners.

"Stop worrying." Olivia knocked my knee with hers. "You're going to do fine."

I forced a smile.

"Still fake," Olivia huffed. "Now pick up your cards."

My nerves started kicking into overdrive when the pilot of our private plane announced we were making our final descent into Spain. Every second, the cabin seemed to be getting smaller. When Olivia asked what was wrong, I'd made the mistake of telling her I'd abandoned my online poker lessons. But that wasn't what was sitting like day-old pizza in my belly. It was the tournament itself. I wasn't afraid of playing. There was no way the Heirs would play until we were on a throne. It was more a nagging feeling, something I couldn't put my finger on. Over an oatmeal facial and couple of shots of Fireball, I'd let my worry slip. Helen said it was a fear of the unknown. It wasn't. Our oatmeal facials, Gia walking in with a pizza box, and Olivia shuffling cards and telling me it was winner's remorse, I'd been on a nonstop déjà vu thrill ride the last three days. They were part of the vision I'd seen in Yayati's cave in May. The same series of visions that included A.J. dying in front of my eyes. Even the plane ride had my heart tripping over each beat.

"Cass, your Mom is going to have best pick of the table because of you. You should at least know what the hell is happening." Olivia searched my eyes. I know what she was looking for, realization that I'd done something right. She was almost willing the acceptance into me, but the thing was . . . that was my parlor trick. And for some reason, I couldn't shake the feeling that all the whispers, all the side-eyed looks—hell, even the fainting spell—had something to do with my parlor trick of doom.

I grabbed the cards, resisting the urge to swipe the whole deck and start shuffling. "I don't see the point of this. It's not like we're playing."

"You don't know that," Malory chimed in. "What? I pay attention," she huffed when eight heads swiveled and pinned her with varying forms of shocked and awed looks. Malory kicked her new stilettos up onto the coffee table, arms triumphantly behind her head like she had waited all her life to revel in this moment. The moment she'd stunned not only a plane full of people, but also royalty and their protectors.

Beaux cut through the silence first. "She's right." His gaze lingered on Malory. The muscle tick along his jaw was something I'd learned meant he wasn't buying her sudden interest on Royal Poker protocol lightly. "Top-seated House picks what game is played and who will be representing the Houses. That happens only if a previous side wager that'd been won isn't cashed in."

"I know," I whined, sucking in a breath of air at my awesome card hand. "But the Royal Tournament has played Texas Hold'em since our parents and family came to power. You really think that'll change?" I stole a quick look at Malory. "What? I pay attention, too."

"Cass," Gia interrupted. "You remember how every year in California, we'd watch the football draft with your dad?"

I ignored the sharp twist of hurt around my heart. It'd been almost a year since my adoptive parents were murdered. Everyone kept saying to give it time or that the hurt got more manageable. Everyone was wrong. The soul-shattering ache that I'd caused their death hadn't diminished and wasn't even close to being manageable. I relished the pain and hated the sting of tears in my eyes. Beaux's hard glance knocked me out of my pity party, and I stuffed the hurt back into the corner from where it'd leaked out.

Gia's gaze bounced from Beaux and back to me. Whatever she saw, she was kind enough to ignore. "House seating is like that; you may have the number one draft pick, but it doesn't mean your owner hasn't traded down for a better deal and more money."

"I know my mom. She wouldn't trade down."

"You won." Olivia grabbed the cards from hand, shuffled, and started dealing again.

"I didn't—"

"Yes, you did," Beaux cut me off.

"Cass," Olivia's tone said she'd caught on to the tension between me and Beaux. "What they're trying to say is, you don't count on your seat until your ass is sitting in it." She nodded to the five new cards in front of me. "Now pick up your cards. The game is Royal Hold'em."

"I only know Texas Hold'em."

"Same concept, only you play with ace through tens. Royal flush is the best. Then four of a kind, full house, straight and two pair; you get the idea."

Picking up the cards, I watched for Olivia's tell. A good hand, her eyes would pin me to my seat. A bad hand, well, her eyes would pin me to my seat. I hadn't really figured out her tells. I knew when she was serious about picking a lock, she'd wrap her hair up in a bun and mumble to herself, but for poker, she was like reading a granite tabletop. Hard and unforgiving. My tell was apparently way too easy. If I had a good hand, I sucked in a breath of air. If I had a bad hand, a small crease would Harry Potter its way between my eyebrows. Helen went as far as snapping a picture of my crease and Harry's scar, then blew them up to poster board size and spent a night of mud masks and pizza comparing the two. She was right: the mud mask did moisturize and I did pop a Harry when I had a bad hand.

I flipped over my cards, sucked in a quick breath, and heard Oli's aggravated huff.

"Royal Flush," Malory called out. She laced her hands behind her head with a shit-eating grin.

My cardstock House stared back at me as our plane's wheels touched down. Malory was right: Ace of Hearts through Ten of Hearts. I handed the cards back to Olivia and ignored Beaux's piercing eyes. Yeah, I was going to love Malaga as much as I loved getting a pap smear.

Humid, salt-scented air rushed past my face as the car made its way from the airport to the center of Malaga. The sun was setting against the azure sea, and white lights twinkled to life as we made our way down the hill to the Costa Del Sol. Another wave of déjà vu swept over me.

"You okay?" Helen asked.

Gia twisted in the front seat.

Olivia wedged her body between the third row and me fishing for the windows' down button. "You're not carsick, are you?"

"She's not sick." Gia stuck her hand back, patting my knee. "It's Catalina Island, isn't it?"

I focused out the window, relieved that something had clicked. Gia had put the out of focus feeling into place.

"It is," I whispered.

"Sara and my mom used to take us to a small island off the coast of California. Catalina Island. They'd rent out the house on the top of the hill, and we'd spend all of July up there swimming in the infinity pool and . . ." Gia's words trailed off like she was having her own déjà vu moment.

"And playing cards," I finished for her. "They both really knew, didn't they?"

Gia nodded.

The car slipped back into an uncomfortable silence as we drove through town. The car bounced along the cobblestone drive, through pale pastel stucco buildings and vivid purple fuchsias, toward the glittering lights of my mother's hotel. I knew it was hers. It was in the middle of town where everyone could see the ostentatious structure standing three stories taller than every other building.

A few moments later, we were in the hotel and ushered up to our private suites. I stopped the bellboy and had him unload my bags at the door and leave. The heavy door clicked behind me, the silence deafening. The setup was similar to the penthouse suite I'd first found in Las Vegas. Rich wood floors bled into don't-touch-anything rooms, but the scent of simmering spaghetti sauce was the smell of my new home. I wandered to the right and found the kitchen, a pot simmering on the stove, and a note taped to the fridge.

I'm sorry we couldn't be here when you arrived. Cara and I will be out late tonight with the other Families. Fridge is stocked with your favorites. Cara cooked the noodles, and there's sauce on the stove. Don't worry, I tried a bowl of pasta before we left. Consider me your official Royal Taster.

I snorted. A few months ago, Mom's joke wouldn't have been so funny, but now . . . now everything was different. I had a sister and she didn't seem to be interested in anything but my happiness. I grabbed a bowl, dished up some noodles and Sassy sauce, and wandered out onto the balcony. Inky night skies left little to see of the coast, but the grounds of the Hotel Bella Mar were lit up and on display. Three pools, one waterfall falling into the next, set the stage for the outdoor entertainment. I sat down and listened to a band blend pop hits into traditional flamenco music while waves crashed off in the distance. Hotel balconies framed the tropical courtyard below. Each balcony had terra cotta planters filled with carnations perfuming the air. I hated carnations at home, but here in Spain where everything felt familiar and out of place all at the same time, they fit. I pulled off a bud and ran the petals through my fingers. Somewhere in the hotel, on the grounds, maybe down at the pool, A.J. was here. My heart flopped at the thought of him. It'd been three months since I'd seen him.

Was his hair longer?

Was his skin tanner, and what did that do to the blue in his eyes?

Did he know I was here? The hairs on my arms stood straight up as a heavy dose of terror and anticipation dumped into my gut.

Did he even care?

I polished off my bowl of noodles, a glass of wine, and when the wind turned chilly, I padded back into the house. After dropping off my bowl in the sink, I grabbed my bags and headed back to my room. The hall was exactly like the one at home: a double door entry at the end of the wood-paneled hallway was Mom's. The door on the left was Cara's, I could tell by the Chanel No. 5 still clinging to the frame, leaving my room behind the door on the right.

Adrenaline dumped into my bloodstream. The last time I was home in Vegas, A.J. and I had had a fight and he was behind my door, abs ready to apologize. The knob twisted in my palm, my heart beating with a rare thrill of anticipation as the door edged open.

And . . . nothing.

No A.J.

Just a dark and empty room. My heart twisted. Me alone with my thoughts was a dangerous thing.

"You broke up with him, Cass. Remember?" I chided myself, feeling up the wall for the light switch, hoping to chase all the memories of that last night back into the shadows.

Gold light rained down from the recessed lighting in my room. My room. I swept over the luscious brown carpeting that reminded me of Malibu Beach sand, up the four-poster bed draped with heavy red and gold fabric. I followed the ostentatious fabric as it climbed up my headboard and all but jumped into the wallpaper, wrapping around the room to the closet, past the private bathroom. My gaze stopped at the spot where the secret passageway would have been at home in Vegas. Yeah, me and my thoughts should never be left alone. I hesitated a moment and finally gave in. Thick carpeting scrunched under my toes like sand on the shore as I mumbled my way across the room.

"This is stupid, Cass." I stared at the wall, contemplating all the other things I could be doing, should be doing. Like practicing poker or making sure Beaux wasn't fantasizing about licking Zee's tonsils. Tomorrow morning was the seating; we all needed to have our heads screwed on tight.

Screwed.

The image of A.J. and Zee, you know, screwing . . .

"Shit," I muttered watching my hand tremble inches away from where the sweet spot on the panel would be. "Fuck it." I pushed the door, heard the click, and stepped back from the hidden door in my wall.

Just like home.

"You?" I jumped, stumbling backward. "Dionysus?"

"Cassandra." Dionysus' thick fingers wrapped around my arms, stopping my fall. The man smiled down at me, but it wasn't a man. It was a god, and I hadn't seen him since I'd cost him a minion.

He was even more beautiful than I'd remembered. His shoulder length blonde curls were cut short, and the piercing blue eyes seemed more like sapphires plucked from a quarry than pigmentation floating in his eyes.

"What are you doing?" I shook off the godly haze Dionysus always produced, and cleared my throat. "You know what would happen if I just screamed?"

Dionysus chuckled. My threats were nothing to him.

"I wondered how long I'd stand here waiting for your curiosity to kill something." He ran his hand through his hair, and the locks grew to his shoulders under his touch. There was the god I remembered from the quarry. "Off to wander the hidden hallways looking for A.J.? Young love. I should learn to always bet on such a thing." He chuckled. I knew that laugh was at my expense. "Or maybe not."

I straightened my spine. "What are you doing here?"

"There's my girl." Dionysus reached out to touch me again, but I stepped out of his reach. "Sassy."

I eyed my door, the only way to leave, knowing I'd never make it out alive. Standing in the presence of a god on a good day was intimidating. Standing in the presence of a god who had wagered on your death was get-the-hell-out-of-dodge menacing.

"You had two mothers full of spirit. I'm not surprised you ended up with such moxie."

"You knew my mother?" All that need to flee settled, rooting me to the ground. I knew Sara and Mom were tight. So tight they and my dad were the only ones who knew I was alive . . . and a threat.

Dionysus's stance widened. The amused look dancing across his face said I'd tipped my hand. He didn't give out free information and I just told him I was interested.

"Sara, you knew her?" I pressed, trying and failing to hide the need in my voice.

"Everyone knew Sassy Sara." He leveled me with a look that made my skin crawl. "Who do you think gave her the name?"

I felt the cool façade my Hollywood adoptive parents had taught me slip into place. There was so much about them I didn't know. Probably would never know. But the god in front of me, he would know that my last breath would be spent making sure he paid for killing the two people who died protecting me.

"I'm assuming the same person who ordered her death."

The smirk slipped from Dionysus' face, rage flushing his cheeks as he cleared his throat and leaned into me.

"There's a song, 'Wanted: Dead or Alive'. You know it?"

I nodded.

"You should hold it close to your heart, because you may be the heir apparent." He bent down and picked up Carina and Sara's diamond hearts from my chest. "But to me, you are an outstanding debt that will be collected." His eyes searched mine as he let go of the pendant, the diamonds significantly cooler from his touch. "Dead or alive, Cassandra. I'll let you decide which one I'd prefer." Dionysus stepped back into the hidden passage, humming the Bon Jovi tune as he walked into the darkness.

THIRTY-FOUR

DESPITE DIONYSUS'S FINAL threat tossing around in my head all night and the fact that my ex was wandering the halls of the hotel I would someday run, I was totally going to move to Spain after I graduated. Costa del Sol was the key to my heart. I kicked my feet up on the iron railing of the balcony. Pink skies danced across the azure ocean. The blue waters stretched out in front of me as far as I could see. Down below, the sounds of the ocean mixed with the chords of a guitar and rhythmic click of castanets. And, hell, even the red carnations everywhere I turned were starting to grow on me.

The whole place was starting to take root in my soul. All those years of wondering where I fit in, where I belonged, why I felt like such an outsider, this place answered them. I was home.

Despite the chilly weather, the sun-bleached pastel terra cotta planters, the purple bougainvillea climbing the walls, and the salted sea air screamed summer warmth. I snuggled down into my cardigan, ignoring the buzz of my cellphone's text. Beaux. Checking on me again. Probably reminding me that the minute I left the safety of our penthouse, it was game on. Don't give anything away. Don't show any emotions. Don't let my emotions get the better of me. Don't. Don't. Don't. Warnings tap-danced down my spine with a shiver.

"Buenos días, Mija," Mom's voice floated out on to the balcony.

I smiled. I didn't know much Spanish, really could only ask where a bathroom or a beer was in the language, but I knew Mom's voice and I knew she was calling me her daughter. I turned in my seat. "Morning, Momma."

Carina, my mother (I rolled the word around in my mouth, waiting for any remnants of bitter taste, but it was long gone), was stunning, statuesque. All the words that could describe a goddess, Mom made them her bitch and then showed those audacious words they never knew their own meaning until she'd entered a room. Carina smiled, the warmth in her honey eyes a stark contrast to the cold white shell crown sitting under a sheer black veil. A black choker dangled the biggest diamond heart I'd ever seen around her neck. Another breeze swept through the balcony, fluttering the edges of her red skirt, and I wondered how she wasn't freezing in the black and red form-fitted dress. She looked like a flamenco dancer who belonged on *Dancing with the Stars*.

"You look beautiful, Mom."

"Just another day at the office, darling."

I snorted. "Well, where's my flamenco girl get-up then?"

"In your closet." Mom slipped into the chair next to mine, fiddling with the strap on her stiletto; a cool, ocean breeze drifted through our balcony, picking up the ends of her skirt. Mom leaned back, pulling in a deep breath. Like the ocean air was vital to her existence. I guess we really were more alike than different. I doubted I'd ever really know all of Mom's hidden facets.

"What's that?" I nodded to the white envelope in her lap.

She handed me the sealed envelope. "Our wagers. Each House's player turns in their sealed risk, what they want should they win."

"And ours is?"

"Not to be discussed until we win."

I ran my hand over the intricate Heart, our Houses' crest, stamped into the red wax. "And what if we lose?"

"Our sealed wagers are burned immediately, the winning risk is opened, and that wager is collected at the stroke of midnight of the New Year."

"My birthday?" I said around a strangled chuckle. "You really picked a shitty day to make my debut."

Mom forced a smile. "You were worth it."

I bit down on my lip, knowing this was the wrong place, the wrong time, but the question of who my dad was sat in between us like a giant circus elephant. The way Mom pulled in a deep unsteady breath said she knew it, too.

"Are you ever going to tell me about my father?"

"No." she fired, watching the slap hit me squarely. "He'll only lead you to heartache, Cassandra."

Another set of heels clicked on the tile behind me. Mom's lips pulled up, and I knew the conversation about my father was over—again. I turned in my chair. Cara was dressed as beautifully as our mother. The only difference was that her shoulders were covered in black and red lace, and where my mother had a crown, Cara's auburn hair was pulled up and over into a bun behind her left ear, accented by a giant red carnation.

"Morning, sis." Cara bent down and kissed me on both cheeks. "Seating is in an hour. You should start getting ready."

"Is that a carnation in your hair?" I felt my eyebrows climb up my forehead. "Wait, you were serious about that dress you brought in last night?"

"Of course I was." She scoffed and then pulled me into her. "Have you seen A.J.?" she whispered.

A familiar pain cut through me as I shook my head.

I'm sorry, Cara mouthed, then said aloud, "You think you can be ready in thirty?'

"Years? Maybe."

"C'mon." Cara extended her hand. "What are little sisters for?"

Twenty minutes later, I looked like a carbon copy of my sister, only where her bun was on the left, mine was on the right and a small tiara (*peineta,* Cara had corrected me) sat on top of my head. No veil, thank the gods.

We marched through the lobby. People stopped everything they were doing as we made our way across the white tile flooring and toward the ocean room. The clack of our heels echoed up into the stained-glass rotunda. I tried not to stumble as I took in the lobby. Being ushered in the side door last night, I'd missed the beauty.

"Stop fidgeting," Cara scolded.

"Yeah, I'll remind you of that when you're about to see your ex and his girlfriend for the first time after your breakup."

Cara snorted. "Don't worry. You've definitely got the upper hand in the wowza department."

I tossed a thank-you wink my sister's way.

Down two corridors, both overlooking the Costa del Sol's blue waters, we finally stopped in front of a set of heavy driftwood doors. A faint heart pattern ran along the veins of the doors, much like the gold vein did in the wallpaper at A.J.'s house in Vegas. My heart dropped to my toes. He was behind that door, and I prayed his heart was doing the NBA slam-dunk the way mine was.

Cara leaned in, noticing I'd spotted the hearts. "Poseidon's always had a soft spot for the House of Hearts."

"Not who I was thinking of."

"I know, but sometimes it's nice to know you've got a god or two rooting for you."

"You ready?" Mom asked, straightening her gown before she turned and inspected us with a warm smile. She'd changed so much since the first night I'd met her. I'd taken all her hard looks, disapproving glares, and judgments and made them mine, made them about me, when really, they were hers. I was just the mirror bouncing back all the rotten and horrid choices she'd had to make . . . alone. The nagging questions about my biological dad floated up to the surface.

How could he leave her?

How could he leave me?

Did he even know I existed?

And if he did, why?

My world always circled around that one little word: why?

Cara threaded her fingers through mine, answering Mom's questions for the both of us with a nod. I was anything but ready. Upstairs, Mom had taken a phone call. The Houses were already assembled and Midas was waiting. She hadn't rushed me, but the worried little line that creased her forehead said there was something bigger than a tardy bell hanging over our head.

"Before we go in, I've been informed there's been a formal protest lodged against your last win." Mom grabbed both Cara and my hands, her warm honey eyes hardened. "Before the seating, Midas will hear the complaint and rule. Cassie, don't say anything, okay? You don't need to defend your actions. Whatever happens"—she swallowed hard over the next words lodged in her throat—"whatever happens is nothing compared to losing you."

I didn't have time to ask what Mom meant before she pushed open the doors. Rays of sunlight so bright I thought I was walking through the gates of Heaven lit the room, but there was a heaviness that hung in the air. A weight that assured me I was far from Heaven. It was like the room knew it was holding not just royalty but royalty appointed by the gods of Olympus, and at any minute, those same gods could smite us from the face of the earth. I swallowed hard over the knot in my throat as I followed Mom into the room. People pulled back, forming an aisle as we walked forward. On the right, I spotted Helen and her mother, as well as the rest of the House of Diamonds. Our house, the House of Hearts, stood farther toward the front of the room. On the left, I spotted the House of Clubs, Gia and her mom, standing next to Olivia and the Queen of Spades. I scanned the rest of the room, my gaze landing on Beaux. He shifted from one foot to the other, looking sinfully handsome in a black suit accented with a red tie. And when he swiped a few stray strands of blonde hair from his face, I knew every girl's heart fluttered. My heart was clacking about in my chest as well, but for an entirely different reason.

A totally different person.

There were four hundred of the gaming communities' most powerful people assembled, but the room shrank to just me and him.

A.J.

He stood so still that if he hadn't just pulled in a deep breath, I couldn't be sure the man in front of me wasn't a statue or a wax figure. I resisted the urge to look away and met A.J.'s gaze head on. He wore a black suit with a gold tie, his jet black hair was combed back, but where the edges used to curl at his neck, they now danced rebelliously along his shoulders. My insides tingled with memories as A.J. licked his lips. Cold blue eyes took in every inch of me from the top of my head to my well-polished toes. Inspecting all the ways I didn't know I'd changed until I was under his scrutiny. My shoulders pulled back, challenging him to take me all in. See all the things he'd missed. My chest filled with all the ways he'd disappointed me.

"Keep your cool," Beaux's lilt came from behind me, sending shivers down my arms. "I've seen that shit-eating grin on his face before."

"A.J.'s not smiling."

"No, I'm talking about Midas."

I turned ever so slightly, catching a glimpse of the man with a golden touch's grin.

"My job, Princess, is to watch your back even when you're making goo-goo eyes at the enemy."

The need to protest swelled and died as Zee stepped up the stairs, taking her spot next to A.J. and snapping the world back into place. Watching her hand snake around A.J.'s arm . . . something inside me ached. All those fissures he scored into my heart suddenly scorched to life then died. I could see it now, how Mom had walked away from it all.

This was what she was talking about, my heart turning to stone.

I caught Cara steal a glance my way, but I stood still. Even though my heart ached for him, A.J. would never know just how deeply choosing his house, his grandfather, and Zee over me shattered me. A.J. and I, we were doomed from the beginning and no amount of love could have ever saved us. We were love-struck fools to believe it ever could have. And I'd never make that mistake again.

"Carina," Midas said, stepping forward. I hadn't even seen the man with the golden touch standing next to A.J. or Zee. But wasn't that just like A.J., commanding my attention until it was too late to see anything, anyone, that could harm me? He may have wanted to protect me, but clearly the only thing he could ever do was distract me until death claimed me.

Midas cleared his throat. "Do you have anything to say about the accusation, Cassandra?"

Ladon Midas's words caressed my face like barbed fingers secretly searching for a weak spot to latch onto and tear.

Mom, stealing a quick glance over her shoulder, steeled her spine. "I'd like you to repeat the accusation for all the court to hear, Ladon." She thought she was buying me time, probably hoping I could spin together a plausible defense for the charges laid against me. Problem was, I didn't know what I could possibly have to defend myself against. Couldn't fathom what someone could say I did. Instead, all the extra time was letting the panic swirling in my gut to settle and mix with the shoe-dropping feeling I'd been feeling the last three weeks.

Midas bristled at Mom's use of his informal name while a murmur rippled through the room like a shockwave. Quickly recovering, Midas smacked his ivory cane against the marble flooring. The ominous sounds of displeasure echoed off the high ceilings like lashings from a whip. The room fell into a tomblike quiet, all too afraid to say anything, all too pleased they weren't the focus of Midas's wrath.

"Very well, Carina"—Mom's turn to prickle— "Cassandra Vera, Heir to the Heart line, you have been formally charged with tapping into forbidden powers in order to acquire your only victory in the Field Games. What have you to say?" Midas flexed his fingers, then gripped the edge of his cane like it was my neck.

"I say bullshit."

"I see we're keeping it classy," Zee spoke up, earning a stern sideways glances from both A.J. and Beaux.

Midas pulled in a deep breath. "That's your answer?" Despite a smile on his lips, the skin around his eyes crinkled. "You do realize there was an arena full of witnesses, your House's players, your appointed Jack, as well as the Appellant."

I shot Zee an irritated, disappointed look. This was how she was going to play this hand? Zee was going to be the damaged damsel in distress? Someone needed to hand her a modern day kick-ass heroine and a dose of grow-some-lady-balls before she hurt herself. Zee wouldn't be satisfied until I was destroyed and Beaux along with me, even if it sent the women's movement back two hundred years. You know what? She was perfect for A.J. He had no problem throwing me to the mythical wolves any time I wandered into the gods' gray area. Why would I expect anything less from the woman the gods had him hooked up with for all eternity?

"I didn't use forbidden powers. My House's Warriors won that match fair and square. If your girl's feelings were hurt because she let *your* castle fall in record time, then you've got bigger problems than me and a bolt of heat that shoots up my spine—"

Gasps ripped through the room. My gaze darted to Beaux, but he shook his head like he'd done in the plane. The soft lines of his face hardened. Too much information. I'd done it again. I'd given away too much. Fuck, I really couldn't play poker. And . . .

Oh, god. The memory of the field games, the rush of heat racing up my back. I couldn't have. I turned and found my answer in my mother's eyes. I had cheated when it came to the Field Games. Midas's eyes glimmered when the realization of my admission sunk in. I hadn't won the game; I'd whammied my opponents into submission. I didn't know it at the time, but I'd broken the rules.

Mom cleared her throat. Her shoulders squared making her head tilt in that royal way that sent chills down my spine. "I don't see any rules being broken."

By the way Midas's paper-thin wattle bristled, Mom's tone and head tilt did the same things to the immortal king as they did to me.

Mom held up a hand, stopping any objection Midas could have formed. "I'm sorry, but Cassandra claimed the Heart's elixir, and she is the offspring of the House of Spades. No one was out of play or harmed."

I listened for the whispers to ripple the still waters of silence. The near admittance of my being the Balanter should have made at least one head turn, one whisper sound like a shout, but there was nothing. Either no one cared, they'd all gotten comfy and cozy in the knowledge that I, the person who could end their way of life, was walking among them, or I wasn't quite as big a threat as everyone had thought I'd be. A pleased smile spread across Midas's face. He cut the distance between us in half with two steps.

"Since my House was the victim of your daughter and her forbidden powers, I say she was out of play, and Carina"—Midas tossed a deadly look at Mom, her shoulder slumping under the criticism—"she did harm people. Ask the Queens of the House of Spades and Diamonds. You still don't see the abomination you and Dante created."

"Dante?" I whispered. Mom's shoulders snapped back like she'd been whipped. My dad's name was Dante? Midas turned his gaze to me. The tips of his lips lifted. He knew what he was doing, I knew what he was doing, but I couldn't avoid the golden carrot he dangled in front of me. Not a second time. He knew my father. He knew . . .

"Where is he?" I asked, my voice so low I couldn't be sure he heard me. But the smile blossoming across his ancient face said he'd not only heard me, he'd found the weakest link in the House of Hearts: me and information about my dad.

"Ladon, is there a point to all of this?" Mom interjected before Ladon Midas could answer. "Or do you merely want to make a scene?"

"The point, Carina, is that I have a grievance against the House of Hearts. All Houses are present, and seeing that your daughter has admitted to using her forbidden Balanter powers to advance her House's position, I see only two courses of action: House of Hearts forfeits their right at the table or I have the right to impose a remedy."

He'd done it. Midas had always been looking to up his position at the Royal Poker Tournament. And with my stupidity, I'd just handed him the opportunity. I worried my lip and fought back the painful sting of tears.

"As the House of Midas Heir Apparent, I agree with my grandfather and his necessity to remedy the violation." A.J. stepped forward, his cruel blue eyes still trained on me. "You went too far, Cassandra."

The sharp-tongued response I'd readied for Midas fizzled and died on my lips. A.J. agreed with Midas? The all-out smack of betrayal cut deep, hurt more than I could have ever imagined, and drew the very essence from my soul.

"Any objections?" Midas asked the room, but only a fool would have voiced one. It was every House for itself, and I couldn't blame them. "Seeing none, my remedy is to add a new lineage to the table. I welcome the Shadows to our coterie. To even out the Balanter's power, of course." A hushed whisper filled the room while Midas strutted down the aisle, opening the driftwood doors.

I didn't have to look to see who was there. A.J.'s eyes said it all. Dionysus, Warren, and Isaac were now welcomed into the realm of the Cards. The gods were now at our table. The balance of power had shifted, and I had helped in giving it back to the creators. What little control over our destiny we had, had been damaged, if not destroyed.

A.J. closed the space between us. The musky scent of him filling my senses.

"I need to talk to you."

"You can kiss my ass, A.J."

"There's something bigger happening than you losing your cool and the Shadows joining the game. I need to talk to you." A.J. widened his stance, the edge of his shoe touched mine, and despite his Benedict Arnold impersonation two seconds ago, I swear my heart tripled its beat.

"No."

"Cassie."

I ignored the playful tone in his voice and all the things it stirred up in me.

"Go to hell, A.J."

"Where do you think I've been the last three months without you?" The soft fabric of his suit brushed up against my bare arm. I fought against the shiver his touch produced.

"Too late. Not all the sweet words in all the pages of time can get you out of this. Go talk doom and gloom with Zee, I'm not interested."

A small chuckle rumbled in his chest. "Use your keycard and come see me tonight at eleven. I'm in the west wing, second floor, third door on the left in the corridor. And Cass?" His blue eyes warmed, sweeping over me from head to toe and pausing at all the places I remember he liked, all the places that craved his touch. "You look fucking amazing."

Despite my head screaming "hell, no," my heart fluttered.

A.J. left my side. The chill of his absence made the vice that should have long since disappeared squeeze my ribs, wrench my heart. A.J. followed Isaac, Warren, and Dionysus up to the front of the room, stealing one last glance my direction. Heat swamped my face, every cell in my body rattled with confusion and . . . aw, hell, straight out lust. The boy was hotter than any model or actor I'd seen in L.A. And the new look, the rebellious curls dancing along the tops of his wide shoulders, it tempted a girl to forgive him, but I'd gone down that road once before. I so wouldn't be repeating my mistakes.

I pulled my attention from A.J., focusing on Mom, who looked like the poster child for cool and collected, even though the dancing vein along her forehead said otherwise. I scanned the room, checking to see if anyone else, any of my friends, had caught the awkward moment between me and A.J., but everyone looked a little flustered with having the three worst beings in the world in our presence. I'd had my meet-and-greet with the Shadow god last night. Midas went through the seating ceremony, which was nothing special: names on a bracket that were handed out to the heads of the Houses. Midas sauntered up to the front of the room. This was his show. Our hotels were merely the host.

"Ladon," Olivia's mom, the Queen of Spades, said. Her use of Midas's first name was a giant eff-you in support of Mom. "There's a mistake."

Midas's stride never faltered. "No mistake, Genevieve. I assume we've done away with the formalities of titles, yes?"

Genevieve's eyes narrowed. "Apparently we've done away with a number of formalities. Our proper names and titles being the least of the concerns."

"Why are the Heirs listed as players?" Mrs. M, the Queen of Clubs, asked.

A smirk played at the corner of Midas's mouth. Seconds turned into minutes as the room fell into a deep and tangible silence. I craned my neck, peeking over Mom's shoulder to see the tournament brackets. My heart pounded in my ears as my name in the fifth seat came into view. The heirs weren't supposed to play until our reign began. A slick film of panic-induced sweat trickled down my back.

"Remedy." Midas scanned the room, daring someone to speak up, question him, but everyone, even the Queens, seemed to be resolved to obeying Midas's will.

"Don't," Beaux leaned forward. Heat and soapy man scent wafted over my shoulders.

But I didn't listen.

"Ladon," I broke the silence. "Sorry, obviously I'm new at all of this, but wasn't your remedy inviting the Three Little Shadows to the table?"

Warren's lip snarled, Isaac cracked a deadly grin, but Dionysus stood perfectly still. In my dealings with the overseer of the Shadows, I'd just moved up the last few notches on his hit list to occupy the number one slot.

"Cassandra, as your mother so wonderfully pointed out, you represent the House of Hearts and the House of Spades. Two Houses wronged my players. Two remedies were called for." Midas closed the distance between us; behind him, I could see A.J.'s hands fist until his knuckles were white, and I could hear Beaux stop breathing behind me. "Learn the rules, little girl. Learn them quickly, or Sara and Steven's death won't be the only blood on your hands." He stepped back and addressed the rest of the room with his booming voice, "A.J. will collect your new Houses' wagers and opening bids as you leave."

Beaux's arm snaked around my waist, pulling me back before I could do anything. He didn't have to worry. Midas was right. People were going to get hurt under my reign. Starting with him.

THIRTY-FIVE

I'D BEEN THE last to leave the seating room. Cara had moved on to a crisis at the mortals' poker tournament. The House of Midas's goon squad escorted Mom and the other Queens out before the last syllable of A.J.'s name hit the air. Four would-be queens were left to decide who to attack and what asset of their enemies would cause the greatest pain. Once a target was named, our parchment was taken and dipped into a shell-shaped cauldron in the middle of the room. After a few moments, a block of ice with our House's emblem floated up and hovered over the cauldron. Helen and Olivia made their choices quickly; Gia hung around until A.J. called her out on the time. A house was given five minutes from the second the last drop of ink hit parchment to submit their wager. If they failed to do so, all your House's assets were at stake for your opening bid, and nothing was gained if you won.

I couldn't think of a single thing I wanted from any of the Card families. I guess my mind was still stuck on the name of my father. That's when it hit me. I scribbled down my opening bid and neatly printed my wager. I didn't want a penmanship slip to keep me from the prize of freeing my father from his Shadows' debt. I sealed the bid with the wax and heart emblem before taking it over to the Han Solo-inspired freezing step. A.J. dropped the paper into the solution, but his gaze never left mine.

Through tight lips, he whispered, "Eleven o'clock, Cass."

"You keep thinking that's going to happen." I crossed my arms across my chest, certain he'd be able to see the cheerleader hurky jump my heart was perfecting.

A.J. smiled, his charming dimple attempting to seduce a yes out of me.

"Not if my life depended on it." I turned and left the room.

Cara and I spent the rest of the morning, afternoon, and evening locked in our penthouse studying, practicing, and playing strategies for every type of poker game that could be thrown my way. When we'd gotten back to the room, I'd tried to forfeit my claim to the throne; shoved the shell tiara on top of my head into Cara's hands was more like it. Cara was more prepared to lead than I could ever be, but she'd been the first to tell me—shout actually— that she wouldn't let me. Even worse, she told me she believed in me, and that morsel of confidence sat in my gut like a day-old tuna sandwich.

When the sun started setting, lighting the sky ablaze with reds, pinks and purples, Mom excused herself with a quick kiss on top of my head and a muttered prayer to Sara to watch over me.

Everyone but me was in my corner . . . and A.J. An old ache let loose from deep in my heart. An ache I'd thought had long past, but this morning, after seeing A.J., I realized it hadn't gone away. It'd only lied dormant, like a volcano waiting for the perfect conditions to erupt.

I tapped the R.P.T. play again icon on my computer and went on to lose poker game thirteen. My only shimmering moment of triumph came when I was certain I'd eaten my weight in cookie dough. Yes, I secretly hoped salmonella would kick in and I'd be too sick to participate. Desperate was placing all my cards on enacting clause thirty-two in R.P.T. rules and bylaws: letting Cara step in as my second. I knew there was more than the raw cookie dough and threat of House extinction rotting in my gut. A.J. and his *find me, something's wrong* comment wasn't sitting well, either. Normally, I'd think the whole thing was A.J.'s gambit to get me to tiptoe the secret halls. See how utterly ticked off I was at him. But there was something in the way he waited to tell me things weren't right, an urgency, a secrecy.

Oh, he was a shit.

The king of shits, really, and I'd wasted too much time playing his "trust me" games. I tossed the last of the cookie dough wrapper into the trash, grabbed my laptop, and padded down the hall to my bedroom.

About an hour later, Cara poked her head into my room. "Mom needs my help setting up in the ballroom." She eyed the tornado-like state of my bedroom. Comforter on the floor, sheets thrown back, clothes piled into colors, whites, and darks on the floor, with me lying in the middle of it all. I'd either had a passionate romp in my bed, ending up on the floor with my lover buried under a pile of need-to-wash whites, or I was an overzealous laundry sorter. Cara didn't have to jump too far, seeing how all my gettin' busy prospects were interested in another girl.

"You going to be okay?" She nodded to the pile of sheets puddled at the edge of my bed. "Need me to call in housekeeping reinforcements?"

"No." I sat up, eyeing the mess from an upright perspective. "I clean when I'm nervous."

"And what's this?"

I snorted. "An artistic interpretation of my inner-psyche."

"You're gonna need to work on it." The normally barbed comment held no bite. "You want to come down with me, or shall I leave you to your artistic Freudian analysis?"

"I was going for a Van Gogh or Picasso vibe."

Cara tilted her head, and squinted her eyes. "Maybe Jackson Pollock?"

"Oooh, I loved his *The She Wolf.*"

"I was thinking more along the lines of *The Deep.*"

I wrapped my arms around my knees, hoping to keep the ache pulsing in my heart from showing. "Someone's been busy studying their art history book."

Cara reviewed her manicure with a knowing smile. "Solid A on my midterm." Her gaze found mine, her knowing-smile falling just a bit. "Don't let the seating get to you. If anyone can handle this, Cass, it's you." She pulled the door shut behind her, leaving me and Pollock wondering what I'd done to deserve her change of heart.

I grabbed my computer and logged back on to the R.P.T. website. Twelve hundred world-famous and up-and-coming poker players started their quest for a seat at the two-day tournament on this site; surely it could get me and my poker shit together in two days.

"You lose," the busty computer dealer—Busty Betty, I'd named her—called out, then collected my chips. "Play again?" she asked.

I clicked *yes.*

The Royals started their tournament on the third day at the stroke of midnight, playing until the sun rose or the chips were gone. Whoever was left standing with the most chips had the right to wreak havoc on a losing House's assets.

"You lose." Busty Betty bent over again, collecting my chips. "Play again?" she asked, and I clicked *yes*.

Wait, was she smiling at me?

I wrung my hands. They hadn't stopped shaking from when I handed A.J. my wager. I was hoping Mom wasn't too attached to the Fiji island Poseidon had gifted her. I hoped it was a big enough carrot to dangle to throw off the scent of my blood in the water.

With Midas and now Dionysus in the game, if either of their Houses won, it was a clear-cut guess whose House they'd be coming after.

The House of Hearts' world assets were pretty impressive. It was no secret Midas was desperate to get his hands on The Eclectic and expand Caesar's Palace's grounds. Mom had once said in passing that Dionysus wanted the small casino she had in Fiji. Something about being in Poseidon's backyard. But assets included people, and the asset both were interested in, both had killed for, was me. If they could control me, own me . . . the world would be—

"You lose," Busty Betty interrupted, nearly spilling her tits over her top, laughing at me. "Play again?" she asked.

There was no way either the House of Midas or the Shadows could win, not if free will had a chance of surviving a godly temper tantrum. I gripped the edge of my computer, my head floating like a balloon attached by a small string of sanity. Either the salmonella was kicking in, or Busty Betty had pushed me into a full-blown panic attack.

"There's something bigger than you losing your cool." A.J.'s words crowded out any further contemplation of poker and Busty Betty. *"You look fucking amazing"* sent me over the edge. My palms slickened, a dribble of cold-sweat trickled down my spine, and, yep, there it was: the first itchy signs of a hive on my face.

I pushed down the panic, grabbed my purse and a jacket, heading for the secret door in my bedroom. Free will, that's what A.J. meant by something bigger than me. It had to be. My fingers trembled a moment, but curiosity and the need to head off the two dearly decrepits who wanted to control me pushed me forward. The dark, hidden hallway in direct contrast of the bright white light of my room, and me in the middle of both, sent a chill down my spine. Cara, Pollock, *The Deep,* and a hidden passageway, what could go wrong? I closed my eyes and slipped into the darkness, pulling shut the trap door behind me.

"Because all sane people go slithering around in secret passageways hunting down their ex-boyfriends to confirm their assumptions of mythological beings' obsessions with you." The bare lights flickered on in agreement. I opened my eyes and started navigating the maze of hidden passageways to A.J.'s room. One thought driving me further into the dark abyss of the passageways: if something really was up, then I couldn't let my pride, my hurt heart, cloud my duty to my House or humanity.

It didn't take long to find my way to A.J.'s room. It was like he was a magnet and my body couldn't repel him no matter how hard I wanted to hate him. Not that I'd ever let him or anyone else know A.J. Vasillios was my ultimate weakness. Gold light bled through the tiny outline of the secret door, and I held my breath. Not sure if I should knock or—

"A.J.," a muffled voice asked.

A girl's voice.

Zee.

My heart dropped. All those confident, save-the-world feelings I'd started with withered up and floated away on the stale dust plumes in the secret passageway.

What the hell was I doing? This had all the makings of a Lifetime stalker movie. The fate of mankind might have been a big enough cover to get me here, but really, someone should just tattoo Psycho Ex on my forehead, because I'd give anything to know why Zee was in A.J.'s room. Maybe even wager humanity's free will to know how comfortable she'd made herself.

"What's up, Mom?" A.J. asked.

I seriously needed to dropkick myself in my fake lady balls.

"Zee wants to know if you're hungry."

Of course she did. Probably had a few stakes left over from stabbing my heart.

"I'm good. I grabbed food after the seating."

There was a pause. I could all but feel A.J.'s mom, Miranda, reach out and slap her adopted son.

"You didn't stand up for her, did you?"

I strained to hear A.J.'s response even though I'd lived through yet another A.J. betrayal. I knew the answer.

"There was nothing I could do."

I gaped at the trapdoor. *There was nothing you* would *do.*

"I think I'm going to have to teach you how to reassess your priorities."

"Anything else?"

"She's a good thing, A.J."

"I know. That's why . . ." I held my breath but couldn't hear the muffled words.

"A.J., that girl has been through too much. She doesn't deserve your betrayal, too."

"Trust me, Cassie's going to get everything she deserves."

I stumbled back, a nail head from a bare stud dug into my spine. I'm going to get everything I deserve?

There it was.

The truth hanging out there like granny panties in the wind, big and undeniably wrong. I was going to get what I deserved. How could he say that about me, unless I really never meant anything to him? I was so stupid, forever thinking someone could want me without anything in return. I'd abandoned every self-preservation instinct my parents had taught me for a tempting smile and a moment of attention. I'd dared to imagine a forever with A.J., even wrestled with guilt-riddled nights when I weighed following my heart over the bloodied up image of him Yayati had shown me. Afraid that I'd be the reason he died. My stomach fell. He'd never felt the same.

I winced. Harsh light sliced through the darkness as the trap door opened.

"Cass," A.J. whispered. He stole a quick glance over his shoulder before stepping into the passageway, pulling the door closed behind him. Like magnets reversed, I stepped away from him, but there was nowhere for me to go. Nowhere for me to hide. Not standing this close to him. Not when those blue eyes begged me to ignore everything I'd just heard. My fingers curled into my palms. The way his eyebrows knitted together, he didn't think I'd come. A.J. really didn't have the first clue who I was, who I'd become while he was away.

And I didn't know him.

"You came," he whispered. His fingers fished a stray strand of hair from my face and tucked it behind my ear.

My heart tripled in beats at his touch. I couldn't tell if there was amusement, relief, or regret in his voice. I wasn't even sure if he'd asked me a question or stated a fact. I guess he'd changed, too. Not just physically, either. The big, bulky, gym-induced muscles had leaned out, turned into a massive ropy display of strength that touched every aspect of his body. A.J. looked more like an Olympic swimmer than the well-lifted boy he'd been in Las Vegas. With wide shoulders and the way his jeans hung low on his waist, it was only now that I realized he didn't have a shirt on.

I blushed, swallowing hard over the lump of lust that had loosened. God, I hoped he couldn't see what his proximity did to me. "You asked me to come," I whispered, my eyes holding onto the gold button of his jeans, afraid to look in his eyes.

A.J. pulled in a deep breath, making his jeans slip lower on his waist. The muscles in his stomach made a tempting V any girl would want to chase after. That was new, too. I crossed my arms, refusing to give into the need to run fingers over all the physical changes. Wondering if I had the same effect on him. My gaze darted back to the amused quirk of his lips.

The smile pulled at A.J.'s dimples, but the muscle that quivered along his jaw said he wasn't amused. Not yet.

"I've asked you to do a number of things. This is the first time you've actually listened."

"Then I guess I'm getting what I deserve."

A.J.'s smile faded. "You heard that?"

"The walls have ears as well as eyes. Mom taught me that."

His hand rammed through his hair. Dark curls bounced around his shoulders. How many times had Zee run her hands through his hair? How many times had her hands skidded over the planes and curves of his body? And worse, how many times had A.J. done the same to her?

"Cassie."

"Cassandra," I corrected. "You can call me Cassandra."

He ignored my amendment and continued, "I wanted to talk to you about this morning."

"There's really nothing to say."

A.J. stepped closer to me. Heat radiated off his body, pummeling my face with all the reasons why I fell in love with him and all the ways he'd broken my heart.

"Cass." He crossed his arms, muscles undulating under his sun-kissed skin.

Some things didn't change. I knew this stance. This was the "we're going to get this through Cass's thick head" position.

"Think back to the beginning of the year. I told you this was going to be hard. That you were going to have to trust me even when everything in your gut was telling you I'm lying. Midas and Dionysus are up to something and it's not just finding another way to collect on a centuries-old bet. There's something more."

My stomach turned knowing ending my life was the centuries-old bet. Now he had my attention. And by the glint of hope shimmering in his eyes, he knew it.

"Dionysus sent Chance to meet with Midas here in Spain about a month ago. My morning class was canceled. Midas didn't know I was home. Chance said the Shadows had failed to get your line removed from the throne. And Beaux saved your life?"

I nodded, thinking back to the way Beaux snagged my foot to keep me from spilling my brains all over the fountain. And Seth. The glimmer of freedom in his eyes.

"I'll have to thank him." A.J.'s large hand cradled my face, held me so gently, it hurt.

"Not your job anymore, remember?"

A.J.'s eyes hardened. "Nevertheless. He saved you."

"Chance?" I pushed him forward, pulling my chin from his touch.

A.J.'s lips puckered with annoyance, but he continued. "Chance said everything was in place: that you were in position to fall, they just needed to push you hard enough. Make any sense to you?"

I thought back over a semester's worth of run-ins with Chance. Every needled comment, every heated prompt to get me to lose my cool, until it finally clicked. "Chance wasn't at the last Field Games."

"No, he was here in Spain."

The reality of all the random pieces of my first semester started locking into place. I'd turned and bowed and folded to every whim of Dionysus, and if A.J. was right, Midas and the weight of all my mistakes, A.J. included, sat on my chest. "Looks like I took the bait then, didn't I?"

"Something tells me this is bigger than the seating."

"Bigger than giving the Shadows a seat at the table?"

A.J.'s shoulders flinched, so he knew the magnitude of inviting them to the table.

"A.J., if the Shadows win, they'll have access to a Houses' assets. Assets! Finances, places, people . . . people, A.J. People like me." I hated the way my voice broke around the hysteria, like it was all sinking in that my complicated life was about to become fatal.

"Not going to happen." His eyes burned with a ferocity I'd only seen one other time. The last time he'd risked everything, defied his House, and saved me. A.J. closed the distance between us. His hands ran up my arms, their heat burning a path to my soul. He pulled me up to my tiptoes, licked his lip like the words sitting there were burning him. Tension arced between us, making my body go languid. All the familiar feelings of being protected, cherished, worth a damn, were here dancing between us right now. Finally, the boy I'd fallen for was standing in the man before me.

"The Houses won't let that happen." A.J.'s grip loosened, shattering the spell, and then he was gone.

Something inside me broke. My life wasn't his to protect. I'd relieved him of his duty and he'd gladly taken the opportunity. He'd all but sprinted back to his life before me. I bit down on my bottom lip, hoping to stop the quiver. Praying he hadn't seen the small tremor. This was my getting what I deserved. No matter how many promises, how many gestures, I would never outrank the duty to his House and family.

"Why did you ask me here, A.J.?" I didn't give him time to answer. "I saw you with her. Long before I knew who Zee was to you, I saw you. The two of you. Together."

A.J.'s eyes flared like the guilty man with an exposed secret he was.

"I saw you holding her hand. You pulled her into you like you'd done with me on Fremont Street. You were coming out of the Golden Gate Hotel. You'd probably shown her the phone and wall trick. Explored the hidden tunnels and wound up in a janitor's closet." I swallowed back the bile in my throat, but my stare never left his. I wanted to memorize each shocked line crinkle his forehead, each surprised fleck of gold in his blue eyes glitter to life. I needed to watch it all unfold across his face, feel each infidelity lance my soul and remember the burn of betrayal. "You . . . you kissed her."

A.J. leaned back against the bare walls, letting the silence stretch between us. Time ticked by, each second guiltier than the next.

"This is why you pulled away from me? Because you think you saw something?" No crinkle, no spark in his eyes.

Heat singed my cheeks, and for an instant, I wondered if I was wrong. If I'd jumped to the wrong—

A small huff, maybe a chuckle. "Were you spying on me?"

And there was my answer.

"If you only knew what we were doing," he muttered, raking a hand over his face.

"I'm the bad guy? I'm not the shit who was holding someone else's hand . . ." I stayed rooted to my spot, willing the tremble of my lip to stop, the tears burning my throat to stay put. "I'm not the one who cheated. I saw you, A.J. I saw you kiss . . . I saw you kiss her with my own eyes!"

A chuckle ripped from somewhere deep inside A.J.'s chest. He leaned forward, his forehead touching mine. "Says the girl who's already slept with her Jack." His eyes darted back and forth across my face, surely taking in my shocked expression. "That's right, I saw you, too."

"I never slept—"

"The morning I left," A.J. stepped into me, so close I could see his pulse jump under the skin of his neck. "I came to say goodbye. I'd hoped you'd cooled down and changed your mind. You'd changed all right. All snuggled up with a naked Beaux. I'd be surprised if you weren't already carrying and hiding his child." His hand singed the skin of my belly. "Like mother, like daughter," dripped from his lips.

I slapped his hand away from me and welcomed the burn of my palm across his cheek. The sting of heat and pain tore up my arm, mixed with the audacity of hurt pooling in my eyes. "I know you were there; you did leave me a note. I know what you think you saw. And now I know how much you think of me."

I prayed he couldn't see how I was shattering inside. I would never give him the satisfaction. "What I don't know is whether you're mad about what you think you saw or that you think you lost to Beaux." Every muscle in me begged to release years of anger on him. But what good would that be?

I stepped away. "I thought you knew me, A.J. Saw the real me. Silly me, here I thought you were different. Your brother was right, you really are a wannabe. Thing is, I don't need a *wannabe* when I've got the *real thing* in Beaux." Sobs banged against my soul, begging to be released, but I backed away from A.J. His hardened face growing fainter and fainter until . . .

He was gone.

THIRTY-SIX

"YOU SUMMONED ME?" Beaux said, stepping out on the balcony. I hated how his voice had turned hard and cold. It had to be as hard for him to see Zee with A.J. as it was for me. But Beaux never let it show. He never let loose, let go, unless it was on the back of a bull and he had the reigns. I admired and hated that about him.

"Cassandra," he prodded when I didn't answer immediately. "You woke me up at four in the morning. What do—"

"I need your help."

Beaux rolled his eyes. I couldn't blame him. I'd run so hot and cold with him, but I did need his help. And he was my Jack—that tenuous bond between his to protect and mine to keep ebbed and flowed like a muddy river. Friendships and more had started on less.

"I need you to teach me how to play poker."

Beaux rocked back on the heels of his boots. "You have your computer for that."

"You and I both know it isn't working. I'm losing every hand I play, and Busty Betty doesn't teach me how to bluff. I need to know how to bluff."

"No." Beaux started to turn and leave.

"I could order you as your Queen, but I'm asking you as your friend. Help me."

He shot me a look over his shoulder, brilliant green eyes considering me, really observing me, like they were taking me in for the first time. I'm not sure what he saw, but after a few moments, he took off his cowboy hat, swiped back the renegade locks of blonde hair, and tossed the hat on to the table.

"Whatever you've got planned, Cassandra, it's not going to work."

I fought back a smile, the guy knew me too well. "I don't know what you're talking about."

"You do, too." He grabbed the other chair like he would the reigns of a bull and sat. "And did you call the computer, Busty Betty?"

I leaned forward in my seat, fighting the urge to take his hand but not wanting to muddy our waters any more than we had. I needed his brain if I was going to get this to work, preferably the one north of his belt buckle.

"Yeah, I did."

He shot me a sideways look, a smile pulled at the jagged scar spidering from his lip. "Her tits are quite amazing."

"You know they're fake?"

"Right, but somewhere, someone inspired those . . ." His voice faded into a teenage boy's dream.

♥

WE SPENT THE first four hours on the computer, me learning the basics of all the games. Royal Hold'em still seemed to be my hang-up. Whatever hand I played, the Jack would seem to be my downfall. When Forest Gump said life was a box of chocolates, he was wrong; it was a card game and the Jacks would always end up sticking it to you. They were the card that could go either way: win you your hand or cost you everything. It depended on the fates as to how they were going to treat you.

Beaux disagreed. He had a thing for quoting Rick Warren, a pastor in Southern California. "Play the hand you're dealt. A wise player can play a weak hand and win the game."

I knew there was something there, but I was still hung up on a pastor comparing life to poker and not being a descendent from a card line.

Mom and Cara woke up around eight to find me running card scenarios and practicing my tilt (that'd be my frazzled, "holy crap, I don't know what

I'm doing" look). Cara may have enjoyed Beaux's learning tactic—pelting me with Fruit Loops when I was wrong—a little too much. Mom joined in for another hour, until she had to get ready for the opening ceremonies. She didn't push when I declined to attend, sending Cara in my place.

"You know if you're not there, not just the House of Midas will be talking, all the other Houses will think you're weak. You're putting blood in the water, Cassie."

I nodded.

A moment passed between us before she kissed me on my forehead and started for the door. "I'm not sure if you're terrified or if this isn't the wisest pre-game maneuver in the books."

"What does your gut tell you?"

Her honey eyes warmed and a rare smile pulled at her temple. "I think you're brilliant."

The next forty-eight hours were a blur. At one point, Malory stopped in, wanting to make sure I hadn't boarded a jet, leaving her here stranded with her mother.

The thought of Mal's mom in Malaga, sent a shiver through my body; her gestures usually came at a price. She thought Mal would be homesick and flew over to be with her for Thanksgiving. I was already looking over my shoulder with the Shadows and Midas, I didn't need Malory or her mom adding to the drama. My stomach flopped. I'd slept most of Thanksgiving barely nibbling on the turkey the staff had cooked. Tonight was the official start of the Suits tournament. My counterparts had gone quiet after the opening ceremonies.

Beaux wouldn't let me refer to them as my friends. His brows would furrow and his green eyes would dull. "They're your opponents until Saturday."

I leaned on the railing of the balcony, breathing in the last sweet scents of the day before the sun dipped into the ocean.

"Not going to jump, are you?" Beaux's voice drifted from behind me. I didn't have to turn around to know he was leaning in the doorframe, thick, muscular arms crossed and any telltale look hidden by the brim of his hat.

"You could only be so fortunate to get rid of me that easily." I turned, watching Beaux's eyes flare slightly at the potential peril me leaning on the iron railing could bring.

My Jack.

My protector.

His lips thinned out as he contemplated all the worries, warnings, advice he should give me the night before the competition. A small muscle ticked along his jaw, his tell he was holding something back. The way his pulse leapt from beat to beat up his neck said something was wrong and he'd fix it before he'd tell me there was a problem. Beaux was full of tells. He was also a good man, and he deserved happiness. He deserved a girl who loved him so much, she'd throw her legs around him in the middle of church and not care if she made God blush. I was sad I wasn't that girl. A small twang let loose in my belly. I was a little jealous of whoever that girl was.

Beaux pinched the bridge of his nose, another tell of his that he was tired. "There's four hours until midnight. You should probably get a rest in." He pushed off the doorframe, his long legs eating up the space between us.

"You really think I'm going to get any sleep?"

Beaux wrapped me up in his arms. My head fit perfectly on his chest, his arms wrapped comfortably around my waist. Anyone walking by or watching would think there was something going on between us. They couldn't be farther from the truth. Beaux was my protector, and overt forms of public affection made people uncomfortable. We were friends, but my body missed being held, missed being special, being cherished. My body craved for the one thing I would never give it.

Love.

"Remember the plan." Even though Beaux's voice was a whisper, his words rumbled to life in his chest. "You lose the first ten hands. That'll give you enough time to watch everyone. Look for sloppy chips, shuffled cards, any changes in what they normally do and then remember it in that beautiful brain of yours."

I wrapped my arms around his waist and pulled him tight to me, smiling when I felt him come to life below his belt buckle. Pressed close to him, I could hear the stuttered beat of Beaux's heart; felt the extra breath he pulled into his lungs. He didn't love me, not like he did Zee, but knowing I could make a man feel something meant I wasn't truly damaged. I closed my eyes and pushed the vision of A.J. from my mind.

"You go rigid when you think of him," Beaux said. A piece of me wanted to hear a hint of jealousy in his even tenor. "You'll have to remember that when you're head-to-head with him on a flop."

"I know," I whispered.

"He knows your every move, every breath. He's watched you since the day you came into this life, Cassandra. The Shadows and the House of Midas might be your greatest threat, but A.J. will always be your biggest weakness." Beaux shifted. "Even if you have to fold a great hand, don't go head-to-head with him until the finals."

"Your faith in me is epic."

Beaux pulled back, his gaze locking with mine. "You're epic all on your own. I'm just trying to make you legendary."

A smile pulled at my lips as I thought of all the one-liners I could lob his way, but there was something in his tone, the way his fingertips pressed into my back that made me believe he meant every word of what he said.

"Thank you," I finally offered up.

"Wasn't so hard, was it? Accepting a compliment."

I leaned back, enjoying the view of Beaux from within his arms, taking in the underbelly of the rough and tumbled cowboy who hid behind the harsh exterior. "I'm learning."

"Try to get some sleep. I'll wake you at eleven." Beaux's grip loosened, letting all the nerves and insecurities of the evening rush back. "I'm serious, Cass. Sleep."

I waved off the final warning and padded down the hall, grabbing my cell from the dresser and scrolling through the messages: Two virtually word-for-word texts from Gia and Olivia, a good luck and an "I'm scared as shit"; a smiley face from Helen; and a simple "trust no one" from what could only be Isaac's disposable cell. It wasn't hard to crawl into bed and hide away from the world behind my eyes.

♥

WARM FLESH TRACED the planes of my face. I curled into the palm of a hand, loving the way the rough calloused flesh gave just enough bite to wake up the woman in me.

"Cass," a low voice rumbled. "It's time."

I wrapped my arms around Beaux's wrist and pulled him closer to me. The hint of cinnamon whisky still clung to his breath.

"Cassie," he cautioned, his voice so close to my ear, goosebumps sprang to life. "Your mom's here, pretty sure you're on the verge of making her blush."

"No, she's not," Mom chimed in.

I pulled open my eyelids, wiping the sleep from the corners before realizing Cara and her boyfriend were also in the room.

"This the part where you tell me I'm Dorothy and Malaga was all a bad dream."

"Not even close, sunshine." Cara shot me a quick wink. "We're going to head down and make sure the room is set up."

"Who won the regular tournament?" I asked, hoping it was the college underdog Mom had mentioned during a Fruit Loop pelting.

Mom smiled. "Molly Lee."

"That's awesome. First female unseated player to win. I guess Thanksgiving miracles do happen."

"Concentrate on making your own miracle. Side bets are running crazy, so even if you lose the tournament, people can lose a lot more than just their worldly goods. Your Mum and I, we've made enough maneuvers to keep you safe. I think." Beaux brushed back the strand of hair from my face, tucking it behind my ear. The weight of his body on my bed rolled me close to him. "Don't worry." He ran a finger down my nose.

Mom cleared her throat. "Cassandra, I've met with the other Houses. They don't agree with the way Midas brought the Shadows to the table. This tournament has always been about the Suits handling their disputes without the interference of the gods. With Dionysus at the table . . ." Mom crossed her arms, her spine snapping into place. "With a god at the table, everything's changed."

Cara continued, "The Kings have all decided to fold with in the first hour. If it's you and a King and you have a bad hand, take the bet. If we can stockpile your chips, then you'll have a shot at outlasting Warren, Isaac, Zee, and/or A.J. I don't know anything about Warren or Isaac's tells." Cara's eyes darted to Beaux and then back to me when he didn't speak up about Zee. I didn't expect him to. I would never ask him to betray his heart if I wasn't directly in danger.

"Don't worry, I've got Warren," I hissed, remembering all the ways I've wanted to hurt him since he nearly cost my best friend her life.

"A.J.'s not so bloody hard. Not when it comes to Cassandra," Beaux finally spoke up. "He sucks in his bottom lip when you've got him on the run. When he's got the upper hand, he blinks twice as fast. And Cass, the bloke is always going on about the first night you met."

Heat rushed through me, settling in my cheeks. I knew exactly what he meant and I knew exactly what I was going to wear.

As if reading my thoughts, Mom stepped forward. "Dress comfortably. Don't worry about a fashion statement or anything you've seen in Sassy's movies. You're going to be there all night, into the early hours. You have two ten-minute restroom breaks. If you're not at your table when time expires, your winnings are thrown into the next pot."

"Got it, no meeting in the ladies' room."

Mom snorted. All eyes landed on her, making sure their ears hadn't mistaken them.

"What?" Mom giggled. "That was funny." Just as quickly, her royal demeanor slipped back into place. "Beaux will bring you down. You have an hour, but Cass, be there with plenty of time to spare. Arrivals are so revealing."

Mom, Cara, and the two others left my room. The door clicked shut, and it was only me and my thoughts. I sat in the sea of silk luxury, wondering if I was even a thought in A.J.'s mind, shuddering at the notion I was probably all Warren could think about. Arrivals were so revealing; yeah, so were departures. I tossed back my bedding and headed toward the closet. I knew what everyone would be wearing tonight. Saw the black and silver sex on a hanger dress Gia packed. Helen had a red dress shipped in from Abu Dhabi. I knew what everyone expected, but there was only one person I needed to affect. I grabbed my U.L.V. hoodie from the closet; the faint scent of gasoline and death still clung to the fabric. Yeah, I wasn't planning on playing fair tonight.

Slipping on my skinny jeans, black converse, and U.L.V. hoodie, I almost missed the small knock on the paneling. I tiptoed over to the panel, my fingers trembling at the thought of A.J. on the other side, and unhinged the secret door.

"Ready to kill 'em, hot stuff?" The Shadows' second in command stood in the darkened passageway.

"Bite me, Isaac."

"I love it when you try to talk dirty." Isaac poked his head into my room as I pushed on his chest to keep him in the corridor. "Beaux from Down Under teach you the potty talk?"

"Shut. Up," I huffed, pushing the door shut. Isaac's body stopped the movement.

"What? You don't want some inside tips on how to win tonight?" The slight twitch of his long black lashes said he was dead serious, and if I'd missed that tell, the way his familiar blue eyes were like ice chips said this was far from a social call. He was dead serious about me winning.

"No, not from you. And you're like the millionth person to tell me I have to win the tournament tonight. I figured you'd be on the hope-she-loses bench."

Isaac feigned a jab to the heart "That hurts, Cassandra."

"I doubt you've felt anything in that organ in quite some time."

The planes of Isaac's face hardened, his lip thinning into a menacing line. "Now that was uncalled for."

And for some reason, I believed him.

"Follow my brother's lead: he's an ass, but trust me, he'd never put you in harm's way."

A strangled laugh left me.

"Here I thought the cowboy taught you how to play. Rumor is you and Royal Hold'em still don't mix."

"Why do you say that?"

"Someone in the Suits doesn't like you very much."

I stepped into the corridor, pulling the door shut behind me. "That doesn't really narrow down the list all that much."

Isaac chuckled. "You and I are more alike than you'd ever like to think, Cassandra Vera. Both filled with good intentions, surrounded by bad people and impossible choices."

He was right, and that scared the shit out of me.

I pushed forward. "Why the Boy Scout good deed, Isaac? You hoping to redeem yourself?"

This close, I watched his eyes go stormy.

"There's no redemption for me, Cassandra. I'd have thought you figured that out by now."

"I guess I'm a sucker for the misunderstood."

"I'm not misunderstood." He started to say something else but stopped. "Zee is not an ally, neither is Warren."

"You're telling me shit I already know."

"If you'd let me finish," Isaac stepped farther into my space, so close he could count the freckles on my cheeks. "The King of Clubs isn't going to throw his game. He's mad you never told him you were the Balanter."

"Bash? I didn't know there was anything to tell him. Wait, how do *you* know?" I leaned back against the bare walls, watching the harsh lights get lost in the severe planes of Isaac's face. Hoping I'd see him balk, lie, but there was nothing. He was totally telling the truth. "Gia'll kill Bash. Last time, Isaac, why are you telling me this?"

Isaac quirked an eyebrow. "More than ever, the House of Hearts needs to win this tournament." A knock from my bedroom door found its way into the corridor. Isaac looked at the door, then leveled his eyes with mine. "I know you don't trust me. Take the advice or don't. But understand there's a lot more riding on this game than just your House's assets."

"I know. My life."

"More than that." Isaac pushed me out of the corridor and into my room. The secret passage clicked shut as my bedroom door opened.

"You ready?" Beaux asked, confusion lacing his voice.

No, I was far from ready, but I'd play the game anyway.

THIRTY-SEVEN

THIS CLOSE TO midnight, with the tourists' poker tournament finished and a rare celebratory bullfight at La Malagueta, the hotel was virtually empty. The hallway I'd walked down with Mom and Cara two days ago was abandoned. Beaux stopped in front of the doors to the seating room. His blond hair slicked back made his green eyes look like fresh cut grass. Beaux stepped closer, so close I could see the definition of his pecs through his white tuxedo shirt. I craned my head, hoping he couldn't see the blush staining my cheeks. He ran his arms up and down my hoodie, probably hoping to relax me but having the opposite effect.

He nodded to the hallway window. The makings of a massive storm whipped the tree branches up against the floor to ceiling windows. "Looks like Poseidon knows this is about to happen."

"Not too happy, it would seem."

"Makes you wonder what he knows and we don't."

A chill slithered down my spine.

"You ready?" Beaux crossed his thick arms, muscles undulating, waiting to know how to react: whisk me away or do battle. With Beaux, it was always my decision; he'd tell me when I was headed down the wrong path, but he wouldn't stop me. Just the opposite, he'd lead the way and listen for my next command. I didn't know if I loved him or hated him for the faith he had in me.

"Probably not, but that's never been a factor before."

He let lose a smile that would make a lesser woman shirk her responsibilities and jump him in the hall. My heart was broken; it wasn't dead.

"Before we go in," Beaux started, then stopped. His Adam's apple bobbed like the words were stuck in his throat. "Zee wraps her fingers on her right hand when she thinks she can win, and chews on her nail when she's in trouble."

We stood in the hall, waves of guilt rolling off my Jack, my protector. Wrapping my hands around his neck, I pulled Beaux close to me, his forehead resting on mine. "Why are you telling me this?"

His green eyes locked with mine. "I may not look the duty bound type, but I am. Your mine to protect."

I let his declaration sink in. I'd never doubted his loyalty to me. I just never knew he'd be willing to gut himself to keep me safe. "Thank you."

"It's only a nugget, Cassie. You're still doing all the hard work." Beaux kissed my cheek, leaving the scent of cinnamon whiskey on my skin. "Now walk in there like we practiced. Tilted and scared."

Beaux turned and pushed in the door, stretching the fabric of his tuxedo taut against his shoulders. We walked through a fine mist and into the grand ballroom. The room was darkened, more intimate. There were only four lights illuminating the oblong driftwood poker table. As my eyes adjusted to the dimly lit room, the bodies outside the reach of the light's glow were like shadows peeling away from the darkness. At the table, Zee stood behind a chair to the left of the dealer's seat. He didn't give it away, he'd never betray me that way, but I could feel the tension coil in every muscle of Beaux's body.

I couldn't blame him. Zee's strapless gold gown clung to every curve her body wanted to share, showing off all the right places, hiding the ones that trouble most girls. The fabric was like liquid gold and seemed to horde any spare light.

Selfish bitch.

Isaac walked past Zee, nodding to the seat I was approaching before he stopped next to the boy who could stop and steal beats from my chest simultaneously. I swallowed hard over the nerves, willing my feet to move forward. A.J. stole a glance at me over his shoulders. His eyes widened, his body seeming to turn of its own free will. The four lights flickered as his eyes locked with mine. My pulse churned in my ears, head swimming as we shared a raw moment. I tripped over my converse, earning me a hint of a dimple, but it was gone so quickly, my soul ached. Beaux grabbed my elbow, catching me before I ate the floor.

Beaux spun me around, draping his arms on my shoulders like a manager would a boxer before a fight——or a boyfriend would his girlfriend the moment before he stole a toe-curling kiss. "Everyone's using all their best tactics tonight. Concentrate on the cards and their holders' ticks. Ten hands, Cassie. For ten hands, these people are test subjects. Win the game and mend fences with your boyfriend later."

A strangled laugh died in my throat. "You say that like I have a chance of winning."

"You have the *best* chance. You only have one weakness. A.J." Beaux placed a small kiss on the top of my forehead, and I could feel my back burn under A.J.'s gaze.

He was right. A.J. was my weakness, but there were no fences to mend. We were done.

Beaux let me go, surveying the room like I'd seen bodyguards do for movie stars all my life. Mom said arrivals were everything; she wasn't lying. The room was filled shoulder to shoulder with Suits and Shadows alike. Everyone was here to see the transition of power officially begin. A volatile current hung in the air, the smell of discharge of change as the new generation of Royals took the reigns to their respective Houses. One by one, the royal heirs stepped to their chairs. Despite my rule breaking, I was seated across from Midas, our dealer. His chair sat empty, but even empty, it felt like I was sitting down to dinner with the devil himself.

Olivia pulled out the chair next to me, breaking protocol by taking her King's position, as well as not waiting for the official signal to sit. Her king was dismissed to her left. He was a non-descript boy who was only an echo of power when he stood next to Olivia.

"You look like shit, Cass."

"Thanks, Cousin."

She tossed me a smile. "Sit the fuck down."

I eyed the symbolic empty chair on my right. A reminder that the House of Hearts' King didn't exist, and a warning to all future Hearts that our house had already sacrificed so much.

"I think I'll stand."

"You look like you're about to hurl chili cheese fries. Sit down and put your game face on." She kicked out the chair next to her. "You want me to hold your hand?"

I snorted. "That bad?"

She eyed Beaux. "You two were locked in her room for almost two days, what the fuck did you teach her?" A naughty smile pulled at Olivia's lips as she stole a glance at A.J.

Heat swamped my cheeks.

"Let's hope she bluffs better than she denies shenanigans, right, A.J.?"

"If I sit down, will you stop?" I pulled the chair out and sank into the lush leather.

"Probably not." A wicked smile played at the corner of her lips. I'd have been mad if me completely flustered wasn't part of the plan.

House by House, formalwear-by-formalwear, the table filled. Each Queen with a King on her right and a Jack watching her back. I signaled for Beaux; a second later, his warm breath skidded down my neck. Inches apart, I could see every new fine line of worry I'd etched into this man's face, each line a direct tie to his heart. He was a good man, and I ached that I didn't feel for him the way I did A.J. I mourned that he'd never know love, but that was our life.

This was our duty.

"You rang?" Beaux pushed me out of my head.

"This is like chess. The Kings are the figure heads, but the Queens hold all the power?"

"By golly, I think she's got it." Beaux smiled, then for good measure and because he knew it would send Zee through the roof, he kissed me on the cheek. A quick wink and he was back guarding me.

Warmth rushed through me as I traced the hint of moisture he left on my cheek. My gaze met Olivia's disapproving glare. She arched an eyebrow, and I knew we'd be mending fences over this well into the New Year.

The room hushed as Midas walked in. Dressed in another Bespoke suit, his white hair cut close to his head, he wasn't as decrepit as I remembered him. In fact, he seemed years more youthful than he had three days ago. A plastic smile marred his face as he greeted the room, his gaze finally settling on me.

"I see you dressed for the occasion, Cassandra."

I smiled, not trusting my voice to not give away how truly scared I was.

A.J. took his seat to Midas's right with Zee to Midas's left. They were the perfect couple. Sitting here, at the table, it all fell into place. I would've always been opposite the two of them, always watched and never fully fitting in.

Mom cleared her throat. The rustle of expensive clothing shifted her direction, but Midas kept his attention on me and I returned the look, glare for glare. Seconds stretched into minutes, until I rolled my eyes and dismissed the king with the golden touch.

Mom was beautiful. It was the first time I'd seen her tonight. She wore the same red dress she had the night my life changed. The night I found out the Queen of Hearts was my mom.

My stomach crawled up my throat at the memory of the night. The car accident, the smell of clove cigarettes, and the black work boots I was certain belonged to Isaac or Chance. Winning the card game may have been high on everyone's to-do list for me, but I still had unfinished business with the Shadows' secondary command.

"Welcome to the annual Royal Poker Tournament," Mom began. There was an odd shimmer in her eyes. Almost like the magnitude of the evening was just hitting her. With Cara standing next to her and me in the heir apparent's seat, I guess it was hard to miss. We'd grown up.

"Wages have been made by the Houses' Representatives and sealed." Mom pointed to the space above us. In clear blocks of what looked like ice suspended in the air, each House and the Shadows' signed and sealed white envelopes dangled.

"The mist you passed through incapacitated your god-gifted powers for twenty-four hours. Chips have been equally dispersed, and like always, the game will continue until there is a victorious House representative. At the stroke of midnight, the game shall commence. At four a.m., the game will halt for a ten-minute break. A second break will be given when the final three players have been determined. Should a Houses' representative fail to be in their seat at the end of a break, his or her winnings will be pushed into the pot for the next win. A single card is being dealt; highest card calls the game of choice. May fate smile on your House, may the gods be merciful with your wager." Mom stepped back into the darkness; only the glint of dim light off her diamond heart broach let me know she hadn't left.

She never really had.

My entire life, she'd always been there, hidden in the darkness, making sure I was safe. Sacrificing everything she was, every ounce of happiness she should have had, for me. My eyes adjusted to the darkness cloaking her, and for the first time, I really saw the woman who was my mother and everything shifted. The room shimmered. As if she knew what I was thinking, her hand trembled as she raised it to her heart, light catching a tear tumbling down her cheek.

I love you, she mouthed.

I smiled, biting back the tears as another piece of my world slipped into place.

The rush of cards broke the spell, focusing my attention back to Midas. He flipped over the first card, a King of Diamonds. A smirk pulled at his lips. Midas eyes locked with mine before he haphazardly started dealing the cards, first to Zee, then Isaac and Warren, then Helen and her Diamond King. He skipped the empty chair next to me, pausing a moment before tossing me my card. His faded blue eyes locked with mine again, only this time, he produced no fear. If anything, he only fueled my anger for the way he'd treated both my mothers the last eighteen years.

Olivia cleared her throat and Midas moved on, dealing her, and then her King cards. Gia and then Bash. Given Bash's cold glare, Isaac was right. Bash was good and pissed. A.J. reached out and grabbed his card. Palms slick, I shifted my focus back to the playing card in front of me. This was it. Let the games begin.

Midas flipped his hands, palms up. I didn't have to see his face to know he was rocking the smug, mightier than a human, less than a god look on his time-weathered face.

Everyone turned over their cards.

My stomach sank. The two of Hearts sat in front of me. Olivia had the Queen of Spades card. Her King flipped over the two of Spades. Gia had the nine of Clubs. Bash leaned back, triumph rolling off him in audacious waves. He scanned the table, making sure everyone noticed the Ace of Clubs card sitting in front of him. I couldn't see A.J.'s card, he shielded it with his hands. Were those fresh scabs on his knuckles? The urge to examine Beaux's face for any newly acquired wounds was quickly replaced with a wave of nausea rolling through me.

Zee's card.

Her shocked gaze locked with mine. There it sat, the Queen of Hearts card. In front of her. Olivia pulled in a small gasp of air. I knew instantly it wasn't because of Zee's card. She wouldn't give the girl the satisfaction, nor would she betray me by being shocked. Only one person could evoke that reaction from her.

Isaac.

The King of Spades card sat in front of him. He looked as comfortable with the card as I would with a cobra in front of me. He pulled his stare from the high-ranking card and found Olivia. Electricity arced between them making the air heavy and almost tangible with all the unresolved moments they shared. I guess we all brought more to the table than the weight of our Houses. I started to reach for her, but Beaux put his hand on my shoulder. She was a weakness I couldn't afford to let the world see.

Not if I loved my cousin.

Not if I honored my House.

Warren grumbled, flipping over the four of Clubs card. Helen had the Queen of Diamonds and her king held his suit's Jack card.

Bash had the highest card. If Isaac was right, my stomach cramped, there were a million ways Bash would know Royal Hold'em was my weakness.

All eyes turned to A.J. He again held my future in his hands, only this time I wasn't quite so sure he'd keep me safe. A.J.'s blue eyes met mine. Ever so slightly, he sucked in his bottom lip and I knew he wouldn't be a factor in my future. He pulled his eyes from mine and flipped over his card.

If I thought my heart had broken before, I was wrong. So wrong. I stared at A.J.'s card, completely unaffected on the outside while everything inside me shattered to the core. If the gods hadn't been clear enough, fate had. The King of Hearts sat in front of him. A match to Zee's Queen card. I fought every instinct to push away from the table, run, and find the next flight to a deserted island.

Fiji. I could go to Fiji and be certain to never have to be in the presence of A.J. Beaux squeezed my shoulder, reminding me I was on display.

I swallowed every bitter taste of hurt and steeled my spine like I'd seen Mom do a million times before. I'd always hated her for the move I was mastering right now. I'd thought it made her cold and calculated, when really, she was suffering a million deaths inside.

Midas took in a few more triumphant browses of me and A.J. Even if he lost the game, he'd won the battle, if not the war. A.J. and I didn't belong in the same state, let alone the same sentence. I'd released him of his duty. And the only thing it really cost him was his one-time, get the girl out of trouble card. I honestly couldn't be too sure if that wasn't by design, either.

"Sebastian, heir to the King of Clubs line, has won the draw." Midas folded his hands in front of him. "The game is yours."

Bash didn't spare a second. "Royal Hold'em."

Gia opened her mouth, wincing when William put a hand on her shoulder. She knew better than to object at the table. A House divided was open for attacks both at the table and for the term of their reign. Gia shrugged off William's warning, leaning into Bash. She whispered something in his ear, but Bash's gaze never left me. He shook his head once, but his fingers whitened.

"The game is Royal Hold'em," Bash reiterated.

"That game is for six players." A.J. interjected. "How do you propose we solve the thirteen sitting at the table?"

I didn't wait to hear his answer before offering my own. "We draw again. Bottom six are eliminated."

"Cass," Olivia murmured.

Helen shrank into her seat, but Gia leaned forward, ready to draw again.

"And the winnings?" Midas asked.

I leaned back in my chair, not sure if the feeling rushing through me was confidence or fear. Maybe it was a byproduct of accepting I had only what was in front of me. My House's line and Beaux watching my back. Either way, the tingle of adrenaline dancing along my skin was more bearable than the hurt I was sure I'd pay for later. "Push 'em into the pot. First round should be amazing," I answered.

Midas leaned forward, resting all his weight on his steepled fingers. "You seem awfully confident, Cassandra."

"Welcome to the new age," Helen blurted out. I couldn't love her more than I did right now.

The old man shot her a disapproving look, but the future Queen of Diamonds met him eyelash for censuring eyelash.

Midas cocked his head. "Let us begin."

THIRTY-EIGHT

MIDAS'S EYES NEVER left mine as everyone else tossed their cards back to the center of the table. I wondered if I was the only one who noticed the slight tremor in his hand as he retrieved the cards. My presence did tend to send the centuries-old asshats into fits. The room hushed. Midas tapped the cards together. The arrogant bastard loved the control. Loved how the room hung on his every movement until he allowed the cardstock to rush together, breaking the silence.

Bend, rush, break, tap.

Bend, rush, break, tap.

It was methodical and so reminiscent of another time . . .

One-Mississippi.

Two-Mississippi.

Three—

I'd learned to count the seconds between Mom's card shuffles like it was lightning waiting for the clap of thunder. Three seconds to shuffle a deck meant I'd be sitting on the top step well into the night and Dad had much bigger things to worry about than a day's worth of missed meals. Something had Mom spooked. My thoughts tumbled back through the day to Julia's funeral. The beautiful redheaded actress lay in a white satin coffin, with a red rose in her hand. She was like a Disney princess waiting for her prince to break the spell she was under.

But there would be no prince.

Julia was dead.

And she was only a year older than me.

Midas cleared his throat, "Again, we are waiting on the House of Hearts." I scanned the table; every player had a card sitting in front of them. Unlike before, they were waiting to turn over their future, not quite ready to be one of the seven asked to leave the game.

"Turn them now," Midas ordered.

I flipped over my card and let the sweet breath of fate rush into my lungs. The Queen of Hearts winked at me both on the card stock and in real life. Olivia let out a curse and shoved her pile of chips to the center. A two of Spades all but guaranteed she was out. The Spades' King didn't fare any better with a two Clubs. Dude was as weak on cardstock as he was in person. But worse, the House of Spades' fate would not be in their hands. Bash spun his card in front of him. The same supreme smile plastered on his face meant I didn't have to see the Ace of Clubs. Gia's stared at the Queen of Clubs card sitting in front of her, a blush staining her cheeks. It stung of betrayal to notice her tell.

"Mend fences later," Beaux's advice echoed in my ears. I looked to the other side of the table, not ready to deal with A.J. and his card.

Warren held a ten of diamonds card up. "Am I in?"

Dionysus's hands were fisted behind his son, while Helen and her King pushed their three and six cards to the center of the table along with their chips. Murmurs rippled through the room as the six spaces filled with players.

Isaac tossed his King of Spades card across the table. The card landed in front of Olivia for a moment before she flicked it back to the center of the table. I choked on a giggle. God, I loved my cousin, and gods help me, I loved the fire Isaac brought out of her.

That left A.J. I didn't have to look to know he was one of the six. I could feel it in my bones. The way my heart dropped and my stomach flipped when he was in my orbit. The way my palms went sweaty when I knew A.J. was looking at me, waiting for me to look at him. Isaac and Olivia weren't the only ones who entertained the gods, they determined we were going to play this game all the way to the bitter end.

Bells chimed in the distance. One after the other, until twelve echoes hung in the air.

"Our players have been chosen," Midas spoke up. "The House of Clubs, Sebastian and Gianna. The House of Hearts, Cassandra. The House of Midas, A.J. Finally, Warren and Isaac will represent the Shadows."

A.J. pushed his card, facedown, to Midas.

"You don't want her to know?"

The black curl I'd fallen for shook across A.J.'s forehead.

"Very well. Your King of Hearts' card is safely tucked back in the deck." Midas shuffled the cards his gaze, like the room's, darting between A.J. and I.

"Royal Hold'em, it is." Midas began dealing the cards.

I'm sure everyone was thrilled Bash picked Royal Hold'em—everyone except Warren, given his, "Royal what?" outcry that earned him an audible sigh from Dionysus. Warren should've concentrated on exceling at more than sweet-talking virgins to give up their v-card.

At least I had a general knowledge of Royal Hold'em. After my thirty-six-hour crash course with Beaux, I knew Royal Hold'em was like the normal Hold'em game, with a twenty-card deck created by removing all the cards except for the Tens, Jacks, Queens, Kings, and Aces. Each player was dealt two cards facedown. These were the players' hole cards and were played by that person alone. This was followed by a round of betting. After that, a flop was dealt with three community cards. These cards were available to all players. Another round of betting, and then a turn card was dealt. More betting lead to a final community card, called the river, being dealt. There was a final round of betting and then everyone showed their hands and the winner took the pot. The best five-card hand won. A royal flush (Ace, King, Queen, Jack, and ten cards from the same suit) trumped all cards. If there were two royal flushes in a hand, Spades undermined Hearts. Beaux had tried to explain the reason behind the cards' order and ranking, but it was like explaining the difference between Ravenclaw and Hufflepuff to a Muggle. Cards and poker were lost on me; the awesomeness of Harry Potter was not. Four of a kind (four tens or four queens, four of anything) was the next highest winning hand, followed by a full house, then a straight (three cards of the same suit in order). The most common winning hands were three of a kind, two pair, and one pair. If you were really desperate, you could play a high hand of one card, usually an Ace.

I flipped over my cards and watched for my opponents' tells. Three hands in, I had Warren's down. His lip would twitch when he had a good hand, he'd scowl at his cards when he had a bad hand, and when he was bluffing, he'd lock eyes with the person calling the shots and wouldn't back down. Not even when he lost. After an hour into the game and seven lost hands, I had a Royal Spades Flush in my hand, and I almost scrapped the plan.

Almost.

Four bells chimed through the room; it'd been three hours since my awesome Royal Flush hand I'd folded. I wasn't quitting college and joining the pro circuit, but I was faring much better than Warren. I knew when to fold. I knew when to push a hand, and I most certainly knew when to bet the house. I organized my chips, eyeing the table. Gia was ahead of me on chips but not by much. Isaac and Bash had several piles of chips in front of them, and A.J. wasn't too far behind. Another rhythmic shuffle of the cards was quickly consumed by the spectators' murmurs, while Isaac caught me checking out his chip pile.

A sly smile pulled at his lips.

"Warren," Isaac said, a chip flipped with ease from one of his knuckles to another. "I heard you had a way with the ladies."

Warren grumbled, his eyes darting between the pot and the last few chips in front of him.

"That's a yes?" Isaac pressed.

"What?" Warren pushed all but three chips into the pot. "Yeah, I guess."

I felt Beaux tense behind me. He knew I had plenty to say about Warren and his women abilities, especially when it came to Malory. But my comments would have to wait. I was working on a three of a kind, Aces high. I needed the flop card to treat me nice. Holy shit, when had I turned into a poker player?

"Warren, darling," Gia called from across the table. "Don't be modest. You talked Malory out of her hymen and marched her to the edge of her grave."

The room gasped. My mouth fell open as I pinned Gia with a look of admiration. Beaux placed his hand on my shoulder, snapping me back into player mode and killing all the ways I'd dreamed of eviscerating Warren Michaels for what he'd done to my best friend.

"Or did I get that wrong, Warren?" Gia pushed a sizeable stack of chips into the pot. "I call."

Warren glared at Gia. "I don't have enough—"

"I'll cover you," Isaac cut off Warren. "What?" he answered Olivia's glare. "I'm out and I love a good verbal ass-whipping, you know that."

Olivia raised an eyebrow, moving around the table to stand behind Gia. She tolerated Malory because of me, but when it came to Warren Michaels and what he did to Malory, Olivia and Mal were thick as deflowered virgins.

Midas flipped over the river card. I stamped down the squeal. I had four of a kind. The only other hand that could beat me was a Royal Flush. Heat swamped my cheeks as I searched the table, trying to remember who went first. Gia broke protocol showing her cards. She thought she was the strongest hand. With a three of a kind, Jack high, she almost beat my four of a kind. Bash folded immediately. My stomach flopped, wanting to know if I won, afraid I would lose it if Warren disrespected Malory.

"Malory?" A blue vein popped along Warren's temple, saying otherwise. "Not sure who that is, she must not have been very good in the bed."

"Maybe you weren't that memorable, either," I added.

"Everyone remembers me, Cassandra." Warren's lips snarled. "I remember you."

Seconds seemed to stretch into eternity. The room, stunned by the slap of Warren's implication we'd been together, hung suspended before time caught up and everything spiraled into a cacophony of chaos.

A.J. nearly crawled over the table to get to Warren. The room spun. Beaux lifted me from seat, shielding me with his body from the thuds of violence protecting my virtue always brought.

My virtue.

That was all A.J., all anyone, really had ever cared about. Keep her a virgin until the gods saw fit to make her a mom. My uterus must have been lined with gold. I twisted in Beaux's arms, never seeing if A.J. got his hands around Warren's neck.

Beaux's eyebrows furrowed together. "I'm going to snap his fucking neck," he ground out. His grip on me loosened, allowing me to slide down the length of him.

"I'm good."

"No, you're not." Beaux's heart hammered under my palms. I stole a quick glance to see if A.J. had beat him to the throttling.

"At some point, the world is going to stop obsessing about me and my virginity. When that happens, you all are going to be disappointed. I'm just a girl. Nothing special. And certainly nothing worth risking your life over."

Beaux scanned the room over the top of my head before his gaze settled back on me. "This isn't about some bloke getting the first poke in your pants, Cassandra. You're the Balanter——"

"I'm just a girl."

He nodded to the poker table where all our Houses, some of our very lives, dangled in the balance. "And this is just a game."

I pulled my hoodie down, catching A.J.'s disapproving glare.

"Cassandra," Midas interrupted. The malicious twinkle in his eyes turned my stomach. "Are you forfeiting your seat?"

I stole a quick glance at Mom. Her hard-to-read face had slipped. Concern marred her porcelain skin. We both knew what position Midas was maneuvering me into. I either abandoned my seat, forfeiting the tournament, or I acknowledge that my House, Cara, wasn't capable of providing protection. I'd already taken so much from my sister, I wouldn't take her honor, not when my mine was used to taking hits.

"You wish." I slipped into my chair, ready for the retorts.

Midas's lips parted, but Isaac spoke. "I'm sorry about my colleague, your Highness." Isaac twisted in his seat, his eyes holding onto Olivia's long enough to make a statement to those who suspected they had a history. "Warren's apparently lived too long among the common."

Mom recovered before the rest of the room. "Thank you," she inclined her head. "We're not used to such rudimentary behavior."

We were Royals, hypocrisy with a side of an apology seemed to always be on the menu. It was, however, rare for the delicacy to be served by a Shadow and one as high-ranking as Isaac. Whatever game he was really playing, it was far more complex than the one at the table.

"Shall we continue?" Isaac asked Midas.

"The House of Hearts' cards have left the table——"

"I'm sure Cassandra is good with forfeiting the round and not the game," Gia spoke up, earning her a quick look from William and Midas. "Cass?" she continued.

I looked at the three Aces in my hand and the Ace of Clubs on the flop. Four of a kind, Aces high. "That's fine," I said, knowing the likelihood of seeing that hand again was damn near impossible. I tossed the cards onto the table.

"Oh, Cassandra," Midas clucked, turning my cards over. "That was quite a hand." His eyes locked with mine. "The finite rules seem to get you every time."

A.J. grunted, flipping over his hand of two pair, ten high.

"Win to Gianna." Midas signaled her to take her winnings.

Mom cleared her throat, "Very well. That's four a.m. We'll take our first break. Players have ten minutes."

Beaux slipped into the empty chair next to me. "There's a resting room for you behind your mother—"

"No. I'm gonna stay here." The space between us seemed to crackle with tension. "You think they're buying the floundering damsel act?"

"Right," Beaux scanned the room behind me. "You're down to four players."

"Three," I corrected. "Gia won't betray me."

"You hope for the best, I'll plan for the worst, Princess. That's why we work so good together."

"Is it?"

"Right." Beaux leaned into me until our foreheads touched and his long hair curtained us in privacy. "We've both been bit by love's bad fortune. I gave up and you're still fighting mad."

"No, I'm not."

"It kills him that you don't look at him the way you used to."

My heart thrashed against my rib cage. "I don't know what you're talking about."

Beaux's green eyes darted across my face. "You're a horrible liar. Remember that when you go to bluff. You're sure you don't want to go to the resting room?"

"No."

"I'll check Gia isn't being *swayed*." He kissed my forehead before he stood, leaving me face to face with A.J.

I thought I'd seen every emotion play across A.J.'s face during the eight months we'd been together. I was wrong. The normally soft edges of his face hardened, solidified. He never thought it was possible to be replaced. I could see all of the second chances he thought we'd have dying right before me. I wanted scream, "This was what I was talking about!" He'd pushed us too far, counted on too many next times. There was nothing between me and Beaux. Nothing but mutual respect and even that was a foreign concept when it came to A.J. and me. I was always some treasure to protect, some toy to make sure no one else played with. He loved me like a kid loved his Transformer. A.J.'s eyes glistened before turning cold. The last portal to his heart seemed to close permanently.

It was done.

We were . . . over.

And the ache nearly consumed me.

THIRTY-NINE

MIDAS TAPPED THE deck of cards on the table, eyed his watch, and then tapped the deck again. "Is your King joining us, Gianna?"

Gia shrugged her shoulders.

Disdain rolled off Midas like heat shimmering off the hot Vegas asphalt. "Your mothers must be so proud of the etiquette you two—you four—are exhibiting tonight."

"We are." Our mothers all answered in unison.

I bit my lip, trying to stop the smile. I'd always had my parents, Sara and Stephen, in my corner, but this was different. These were people who knew nothing about me except that I came from Carina, from the House of Hearts, and they'd support me both because and despite that very fact.

Mom stepped out of the shadows, and the room stilled in her presence. Feared and revered, she was exactly how I wanted my reign to be. She was the missing piece to the puzzle of me.

"House of Clubs," Mom said. "Nine minutes. Should your King fail to be in his seat in the next sixty seconds, his winning will be forfeited."

"We have been warned," Gia said, folding her hands like I'd seen Mrs. M, the Queen of Clubs, do so many times when me and Gia were growing up, getting into trouble.

The memories rolled through me, yanking at the frayed and damaged strings to my heart. Growing up, there'd always been a missing piece of me. Sara and Stephen never made me "feel" adopted, but the facts had been that I was adopted. There was always a piece of me wondering, searching the shadows for a clue to who I really was. I'd spent forever looking outside for answers when I should have looked at my parents and my best friend.

I shifted in my seat, trying to get Gia's attention, then fought the urge to signal for Beaux. Had he done something to Bash? Everyone was playing Bash's absence so cool, so calm; something had to have happened.

What if it was traced back to me?

To Cara?

Were there consequences in offing your opponent?

My heart jack hammered in my chest as the seconds ticked away on the game clock Midas had moved to the middle of the table. Thirty seconds out. I scanned the players in their seats. Gia was studying her manicure. Isaac was watching Olivia circle the room like a shark waiting for the first drop of blood. I'd gotten used to Midas's weathered eyes always destroying me, but the same look from A.J. was new and devastating. A feeling I'd become quite accustomed to feeling when his name was mentioned.

"Time is up," Midas said. No pomp. No circumstance. A matter of fact that the King of Clubs was missing and his House had lost their power position on the game. Gia pushed her fallen King's winnings into the table. And another rip of the cards tore through the thickened air.

That was it? No one was going to look for him?

Midas dealt the cards and the tournament resumed and I was the only one stunned that someone was missing.

"Cassandra?" Midas nodded to the cards in front of me. "Ante up."

Bash's fortune wasn't anything that would tip the balance in one House's favor over the other, but it was sweet as hell winning the hand.

Nobody said anything for the next hour. Hand after hand, the table descended further into an uncomfortable silence. Hand after hand, Gia's pot dwindled. One hand she raised an ungodly amount, knocking Isaac from the round. I'd nearly folded as well, until I caught the small twitch of her eye. She was bluffing. She was staring right at me, bluffing, knowing I knew her bluff.

I pushed in most of my earnings pile. The room gasped and then cheered when I flipped over a pair of Queens, Hearts and Clubs. The room settled. Gia was one round from being eliminated and me neck-and-neck in winnings.

The clock chimed five as Gia bet her last hand. She fell to Isaac and his three Aces, courtesy of the flop. Isaac was good. As Mom stepped forward and excused us for our ten-minute break, it dawned on me: I was a pawn in a much bigger game. While the Queens had their agenda, Isaac and A.J. had theirs. Me in the finals was a given. How the finals went down, that was where the game actually started. Everything else up to this point was a necessary dance to entertain the spectators. I glanced around the table. All plastic smiles and game faces. Bile swirled in my gut, climbing up my throat. I pushed back from the table, trying to maintain a calm, but there was no way to hide my shaking hands. Beaux stepped in front of me. His wide body blocking out the spectators' view of me falling apart.

"Keep it together for two minutes while I get you to your anteroom." He turned and calmly tore a hole through the onlookers. I counted steps and kept my attention on the back of Beaux's black tux, the way the fabric gave around his muscles as he opened the door, the ripple of tension through his biceps as his hand fisted. I forced my brain to focus on how he was everything a girl dreamed of and nothing this girl wanted romantically. Despite all that, at some point, we'd be expected to love each other enough to make a child. An heir to secure the Heart's line. An arranged marriage and forced fornication seemed so much easier to handle than the events at the table.

I snorted.

"You checking out my bum?" Beaux teased. "You only snort when you're checking me out."

"I do not."

The door closed behind us and my knees gave out.

"Easy there." Beaux caught me in his arms before I face-planted the floor. "Sit down, tell me the hottie." He walked me over the leather couch, giving me a minute to take in the masculine room.

Warm cherry paneled walls melted into deep, emerald green carpeting. A bolt of lightning from outside lit up the decanters on the bar cart next to the window. Rain hysterically pelted the beveled glass, like Poseidon himself was trying to get my attention. Everyone, every god wanted something from me, and I had nothing left to give, nothing but my mere existence.

A hysterical giggle ripped from deep inside me. I hung my head in my hands. "I can't do this."

"But you have been." The cushions gave under the weight of my protector, pulling me closer into him.

"I've been a pawn pushed from space to space. Not once was I in control out there."

Beaux brushed back a lock of my hair, hooking it behind my ear. "Don't buy in to your own tilt."

"I don't know what I'm doing."

"I've seen the hands you've worked. The winners you folded." His green eyes softened. "You just have to believe in yourself for another hour."

The weight of the evening settled between my shoulders, leaving an ache that would last long after the night. "The last rounds go that fast?"

"Right, you're that good."

I pushed back into the leather cushions, half-tempted to curl up and let my time expire. The other half filled with ire that everyone out there was betting against me. Even A.J.

Time ticked by. Beaux always gave me time. He never rushed me into getting out of my head and into my responsibilities. He had faith that I'd get where I was supposed to be and time would wait for my arrival.

"What's the strategy?" I finally asked.

"Kick ass and take the winnings." Beaux stood up and walked to the window. Grabbing a bottle of water, he turned and tossed it to me. The man was equally stunning in a tux as he was in cowboy boots and jeans. "A.J.'ll come out cards and chips blazing. He has something to prove to not only you but his brother as well. Isaac'll sit back and watch A.J. throw his sack around."

I choked on the water.

A wicked side-smile blossomed on Beaux. "Win the first hand and don't look back. This is an all-out sprint. A.J. should be the first to fall. You take his chips the first hand, and he'll have something to prove. Isaac's going to think your confidence is a façade."

"It isn't?" I screwed the cap back on, hoping Beaux didn't notice the tremble in my hands.

No such luck. His long stride ate up the space separating us before he bent down, eyes level with mine. "We spent two days for the next sixty minutes. Both Vasillios blokes think they know you, Cassandra. Isaac thinks he can manipulate you. A.J. thinks he can control you. It all comes down to you. Is it a façade, or is it the dawn of a new age? Your reign?"

I didn't know how to answer him. Lie and tell him I wasn't scared, or own up to what I've always known, that I was nothing special and so far from spectacular, I made ordinary look extraordinary.

A small rap on the door saved me.

"Five minutes," a muffled voice cut through the heavy wood door.

"I'm going to go sweep your seat. Wait for me here." He cupped my face in his hands, eyes searching mine, willing every ounce of courage that coursed through his body into mine. "You've got this." Beaux leaned forward, placing a small kiss on my forehead before he stood and took all the confidence in the room with him.

I wandered over to the window; watching the storm outside seemed to be more soothing than the calm inside the casino. So many people hoping I'd win, betting I'd lose. Beaux was right, it really did come down to what I believed, what I wanted. Problem was, despite all the "growing" I'd done over the last year, inside, where it really counted, I was still the scared little girl waiting for someone to tell me what to do. And I didn't want that to change. Given my track record of standalone decisions, I clearly needed someone to direct me. I wrapped my arms tighter around my waist, hoping to wring out a hidden ounce of courage.

"You're as beautiful as the day I fell in love with you."

My heart stopped, then tripped outside my rib cage. A.J.'s reflection pulled in the watery lines running down the window. He crossed the room, the musky scent of spiced apples and man assaulting my senses, attacking the place in my heart that would always belong to him.

Words clogged in my throat, fighting with the stupid giddy girl who wanted to smile and pretend the last four months had all been a bad dream.

. A.J. cocked his head, a rebellious black curl dancing on his forehead. He really thought it was that easy. He could come in here, spout sweet nothings, and I'd fall into place. I'd follow *his* plan.

"What do you want?" I whispered. The air stirred, vibrated like molecules heating to the point of exploding. Chemistry was never an issue with us. Trust and respect—

"You. But you've always known that." A.J. pushed the ends of my hair over my shoulder. My skin hummed with the electricity the two of us this close together could produce.

"And Zee?" I played along, knowing this was a last ditch maneuver to get into my House. "You two . . ."

A.J. nuzzled into my neck, sending all my thoughts, all my rebuttals to the wind. Habit and a hopeless romantic streak that could get me killed rolled me into him, my body flushed with old memories. Our bodies ebbed and flowed, dancing, tracing every give and take of our physiques. A.J. pulled in a deep breath, his lungs pressed deliciously against my breast. A guttural hum came from the back of his throat. I knew he felt the connection, felt how our bodies had missed each other. But we'd moved past physical attraction and died a slow, painful relationship death. God, I could give in and slip back into my role of naïve girlfriend, pretend he didn't belong to someone else. Pain gripped my soul. How could people be more perfect together physically and such a hot mess in every other aspect?

"You have to stop," I muttered, but there was no force to my words, and by the pull of A.J.'s lips against my cheek, he knew it.

"God, I missed you." He murmured. The right statement, the wrong time, and a history full of lies and broken promises didn't stop him. "I missed the way your nose wrinkles when you want something but won't allow yourself to give in." He kissed my nose, the tangy scent of wine clung to his breath. "I missed the way your eyelashes splay across your cheeks when you're afraid to look at me, afraid I'll see every secret you think you have hidden." His lips seared their way from one lash to another, curving into a smile when my body released a traitorous shudder. "I missed the way your body comes alive when I'm near."

God, I loved the way his lips felt, but I knew what came next. All the explanations on why he continued to break dates, break promises, break my heart. I deserved better than this. My brain demanded more, but my masochistic heart would always trip and fall for A.J. I tried to step out of his embrace, but loving arms snaked around my waist, holding me in place.

"We're two fucking magnets, Cassandra. Why are you fighting me?"

"Because you don't belong to me."

He leaned in, the hint of stubble grazing my cheek. A.J. whispered, "I will always belong to you. Body, mind, heart . . ." His words trailed off as he pulled my earlobe between his lips.

I jumped, but A.J. held me rooted to the floor. Heat, desire, adrenaline dumped into my body, waking up all the places I didn't want to admit were his, only his. The urge to push my body into his was overwhelming. Everything in me wanted this declaration to be true.

But I knew better.

I'd lived through all his kisses and ditches. I'd been so blind before, ready to accept every lie he tossed my way. A long neglected heat ignited in my belly, one that had nothing to do with the way A.J.'s lips skimmed across my neck. Was I really this gullible? Did he really think he could send me reeling with a few stolen kisses? The thought rose from the ashes of all the other times A.J. had kissed me into forgiving him. And I'd let him slide. All the other smiles of triumph he'd grinned because I was too busy dreaming with my eyes shut too tight.

Not anymore.

Not with this girl.

"This is how it works?" I stepped away, severing the connection and really seeing my ex and all the ways he played me. His heart thundered under my palms, the weight of his body against my fingers, begging me to forgive him. His face paled. He knew he was too late. I may have been in the room, but I was already gone. "I was slow to the table, but I get the game now."

"What game, Cass?" A.J. stepped closer to me, like he had Prom night when I told him I wouldn't go to the dance with him because he'd lied to me. I had mistaken his chivalry for loyalty. I wouldn't mistake this passion for love. Not love for me, at least.

"It's not about poker chips and playing cards, is it?" I took two steps away from him.

"Cassie." There was a soft condescending undertone to his voice. How had I missed it before? A.J. closed the distance between us, wrapping me up in his arms, trying to scramble all my senses.

"No!" I pushed out of his arms, certain his touch was as deadly as any venomous creature that slithered the world—more so because his toxins went straight to my heart. "Tell your grandfather you taught me well. Too well. This"—I held up a hand to stop him—"Me. Us. We . . ." I swallowed over the painful shards of my next words. "We were nothing more than a game."

Time ticked by again, only now it wasn't patient. It wasn't given to me like it had been with Beaux. This time, it fumed and smoldered in A.J.'s eyes until the hurt turned into rage.

"You think you were a game?" A.J. mocked. "You pushed me away. And I'm the one playing a game?"

"You let me go. You let me go without so much as a fight or an argument or a question crossing your lips. A.J., my entire life has been lived never being trusted, always being second, and never worth the fight. You have no idea." My words pushed through the tightness in my throat. I would never let him see me cry. Not for him.

"Yes, I do. I've known it every day we've been together and every second we've been apart."

Hurt seemed to shudder the air between us.

"I never made you feel—"

"I'm not going to relive the past with you, Cass. All you had to do was accept me for who I am."

"But that's the problem. I know exactly who you are. You're heir to the House of Midas, and you were *never* mine to love."

A.J. rammed his fingers through his hair. He'd done that so much with me, how was he not bald? "You have to know I'm walking a thin line. Fuck, Cass! This is the same conversation we had four months ago. We're really going to start this all over again?"

"No." I felt the words harden in the pit of my stomach. "We aren't going to start all over again, because every path we could ever take would lead us right back to where we are now."

A wicked smile pulled at his lips. "Stolen moments, hot kisses, and my hands branding paths on your body that no man has ever touched before?" A.J. stalked forward. "I heard your plea for more in your bedroom. Your whimper when my tongue flicked your nipple," he whispered. "I felt the way your body came to life—comes to life when I'm near you!"

My face flamed with all the memories. A.J.'s charm was potent, but there was too much between us now. Too much doubt and deception. We'd reached that point where enduring stolen moments and forbidden highs weren't enough. I pulled myself out of A.J.'s arms, and for the first time, he realized we'd crossed over the no-return threshold. We circled the room like two sharks waiting for the chum to drop where it had before. The problem was, the chum had always been my heart and he wasn't going to get to it so easily this time.

His eyes widened, black pupils nearly consuming all the blue I'd fallen for, trusted in. "Don't do this, Cass," he warned.

"I didn't," I whispered. My ribs constricted more, hoping to stop the next words from leaving me, but it was too late. "You have Zee."

A.J. flinched like I'd struck him with my hands instead of my words. "And you have Beaux."

"Exactly." I nodded, knowing I had no one. I was the future Queen of Hearts, and despite the title, I'd never know lasting love. "Now if you'll excuse me." I crossed the room, proud that my steps didn't falter. Amazed they didn't give away all the ways I was dying inside. "I have a poker tournament to win." I shut the door behind me, fighting the urge to collapse and cry.

But what good had that done me before?

Not a damn lick of good. I straightened my hoodie, pulled my hair into a tight ponytail, and ignored the pain in my heart. The pain that had to be my heart dying.

I nearly ran into Beaux outside of the tournament room. I didn't respond to his reprimands for wandering the halls without him. He'd resorted to grunts and snarls by the time I took my seat at the table.

Beaux sat in the chair next to me. He pulled my chair into him. His long, strong legs caging me like a wild animal about to run. "Your head alright?"

I kept my gaze focused on the chips in front of me.

"Cass."

"Never better."

My spine locked into place as A.J. sat down. His eyes were clear, hair perfect. Even his hands were calm and steady. Beaux shifted next to me, eyeing A.J. and then me.

"You're a fucking liar," he whispered so no one could overhear.

"Anything else? No?" I rushed, not giving Beaux a chance to respond. "Then make yourself useful and grab me a grog and stay out of my personal life."

"You need more than alcohol to get you past this, and let's not forget what happened the last time you got good and pissed."

"Lovers' quarrel?" Midas chimed in. His ancient skin folded into a smile. "Such heat and passion. Have you seen anything like it before, Atticus?"

"Deal the cards," A.J. answered.

Beaux's hand fisted a second before he pushed away from the table.

Midas reached forward, grabbing the new, sealed pack of cards from the center of the table. "Time has yet to expire."

"We're all here," I pushed. "What's your problem?"

"The rules, Cassandra. You have to know the rules." A soft chime echoed from the game clock on the table. Midas's folded smile blossomed, revealing yellowed teeth. "When will you learn?"

"You should worry about that day. Lose sleep over what will happen when I do figure everything out." I folded my hands on the green felt table. "Now deal the damn cards."

Midas's glared at me, but I noticed the slight tremor in his hand and better yet, so did A.J.

I settled into my seat, watching the cards fly to the three remaining players. Beaux was right. A.J. bet big, Isaac sat back and watched, while I won the first hand. A.J. came back strong on the second hand, betting nearly half his chips. But it was the slight pull of his bottom lip through his teeth that had me calling his bluff.

A chortle came from Isaac as he glanced my way. "I didn't think you had it in you." Isaac threw a handful of chips into the pot. Even I knew it was an applaud to my audacity instead of a call of my hand.

"Turns out I actually am the dark horse everyone's been so afraid of." I turned over my hand of Aces. I had this round without the river's help. Just how I liked it.

A.J. sank under his grandfather's glare.

I collected my chips amongst the whispers and murmurs of how the House of Midas was poised to fall. As always, I was on display in my gilded cage. It grated on my nerves and patience. I could feel the tiny rope of restraint snapping cord by cord. Each link tied to my heart, a bond to a broken promise: a future I had no business investing in, let alone counting on.

"Ante up, Cassandra." Midas prompted, shuffling the cards.

I gauged the table. A.J. wouldn't look me in the eyes, Midas had already moved past me—always counting me out before I was even down, but Isaac's blue eyes widened, something pulled at the side of his lip. Admiration. He knew what I was going to do long before the thought formed in my brain.

I was done playing this game. I was tired of being on display. And it was long past time I made a statement to all those who doubted me. I pushed all my winnings, every single chip, to the center of the table. The room gasped.

"You sure that's the play you want to make?" Isaac's question caught both A.J. and Midas's attention.

I nodded.

"You haven't even been dealt your cards." Isaac pushed.

"A wise player can play a weak hand and win the game."

Beaux set down an amber shot in front of me, a hint of approval pulling at the corner of his scarred lip. The scent of cinnamon teased my nose.

"I'm in." Isaac pushed in his winnings next to mine. "So, little brother. Are you man enough, or do you need me to dive into this one headfirst, too?"

A small twang of regret plucked loose from my gut at Isaac's obvious dig. I felt the words burning the back of my throat to speak up, wanting to remind Isaac that A.J. was a kid when the accident that thrust their car over the bridge in California happened, killing their mother.

"Fuck you, Isaac." A.J. pushed his chips in. Midas grabbed his wrist. The disapproving look mixed with a caustic grunt that didn't stop A.J. or his chips. "I'm in."

Midas hesitated. A strand of white hair pulled free and dangled in his eyes. He dished out the cards. One by one, the murmurs and whispers of the crowd faded away until the room was blanketed with an uncomfortable silence. Since we'd bet our Houses, literally and figuratively, Midas laid down the four flop cards, his fingers twitching to flip over the fifth.

I pulled my two cards up from the table. Two Queens, the Queen of Hearts and the Queen of Clubs, already winked their support at me from the flop. My stomach turned. In my hand were the Queen of Diamonds and the Queen of Spades. Damn if the gods didn't have a sense of humor.

I fought every urge to throw my hand down and tap-dance on the table. How Queenly would Midas think me then? I swallowed over the ball of nerves in my throat, catching Olivia circle the table. I stifled a laugh as she rounded behind Isaac and he tilted his cards so she could get a better view. They were perfect for each other. Besides Isaac being a Shadow and Olivia being the heir to the Spade's throne, they were a match through and through.

"You find this amusing, Cassandra?" Midas asked. "Making a mockery of our traditions?"

"Pretty sure you nailed mockery when you invited the Shadows to the table." I smiled. "No offense, Isaac."

Isaac adjusted his cards like the insult never came close to hitting its mark. "None taken, Cassie."

"Don't speak to her," A.J. spat. His knuckles were white from the stranglehold on his cards.

Isaac pushed back in his seat, eyes rolling so far into the back of his head, I thought he'd tumble out of his chair. "If she was so damn precious, then why the fuck did you let her go?"

A.J.'s lips thinned to a white line. If he wasn't breathing as hard as he was, he could have been mistaken for a corpse.

Isaac slapped his cards on the table. "You never could understand that the big picture comes with a cost."

"You don't think I know that?" A.J. hissed.

"I know you like to think you'd lay down on a sword, take one for the team, but the truth is, it's just not in your heart. You gave up a fucking gem of a girl, a chick who got you and all the loads of shit you came with and still loved you. You gave her up for an old man and a sense of perverted duty."

I wanted to throw my arms around Isaac's neck, squeeze him, and thank the gods that at least one of the Vasillios brothers understood me, but then I remembered . . . this was all part of the game. It had to be, because the alternative was Isaac Vasillios, second in Command of the soul-sucking Shadows had not only a conscience but also a moral compass that actually pointed true north.

Tension pulled so tight, it threatened to bring down the four walls of the room.

"Four Queens." I said, laying down my cards.

"What?" Midas asked.

"I have Four Queens. Turn the river card and I dare anyone to beat me."

Before Midas could turn the river card, A.J. shoved his cards into the deck. "I'm out."

Midas leaned in, whispering, "What were your cards?" But A.J. ignored him

My heart thundered in my ears. There was only two hands that could beat mine, a Royal flush or Aces high. With the two Spade cards, the Ten and Queen, showing, the odds were pretty even. Midas flipped the river card, an

Ace of Spades. Olivia straightened, her face paled, and I knew I'd lost. With very little flare, Isaac carefully laid down the two cards that sealed my doom. Ace of Hearts and Ace of Clubs. The Shadows had won the tournament. Just how much my gutsy call would cost me was left to be seen.

FORTY

BEAUX WAS RIGHT. Everything went quickly after I lost.

After the Shadows won.

The ice blocks holding the losing Houses' wagers were obliterated immediately. Five puffs of smoke were sucked up into the ventilation like they never existed. Isaacs' wager fell to the table, the ice shattered, and the image of an island with my House's heart emblem floated above the playing table.

Mom let out an audible sigh when she realized it was her favorite resort in Fiji. Dionysus nearly snapped the back of Isaac's chair, he was so angry. Golden curls that hung to his shoulder blades hardly shielded his cherub face turning purple. Could a god bust a vein? Given Isaac's initial bid of all-access to Catacomb data the odds makers figured he and Warren would have tagged me as their winning wager. I was too busy watching Isaac and Dionysus, I missed everyone else's reaction. Gods help me, I was kind of worried about the Shadows' Second in Command. My mind tripped over the why of the night. Isaac could have wagered anything, why tag Fiji? There were so many whys when it came to Isaac, it made my head feel like it was caught in a rip current. Really, the why didn't matter to Poseidon. The god of the sea was less than pleased with the outcome. Dionysus having access to Fiji, you might as well have handed him the keys to Poseidon's kitchen and archives.

After we left the gaming room, the storm outside turned ugly. Mom shook her head as she hustled me upstairs. Anxiety rolled off her like sideways sheets of rain. I prepared for a massive ass-chewing. I'd been so damn cocky. Silence chased us down the hallway and crashed into us at the door of our suite.

"Get packed. We have to leave." Mom's eyes were wild. I could see a million emotions rise and fall. Something was wrong, something that made her calm exterior crack.

"Are you okay?"

"We will be. I need to get you back to Las Vegas."

"Why?" I choked on my question when Mom fished her room key out of her bra.

"They found Sebastian tied up in a closet."

The window at the end of the hall rattled to the point of shattering.

"I didn't have anything to do with that."

Mom nodded. "I know, but the Kings of the other Houses, they're already unsure about your powers, and the Queens can only hold them at bay for so long."

"I'm sorry about Fiji."

"I don't care about the island. It's nothing." She took my cheek in her palm. "Poseidon is angry about Dionysius in his backyard, but it's Zeus who's always wanted you dead. That was the only thing he and Midas ever agreed on. The other Houses always aligned with us." Lightning lit up the hallway before the lights flickered. "Get changed. Our plane leaves in an hour. That should calm things down here."

Mom opened the door to our suite; it bustled with people. Our bags were packed and already being taken down by bellhops. Mom changed while I went to the bathroom, and was ready to leave before the toilet stopped running. Cara stayed behind to oversee the cleanup and press, but that didn't stop Mom from having Cara's bags packed and a car ready to take her to the airstrip four hours after us.

An hour into our private flight to Geneva, Cara called with word the ocean swells had breached the wall and water was pouring into the Bella Mar. When we boarded the House of Heart's private jet in Geneva for New York, the hotel guests had been relocated and the Bella Mar's first floor would be hosting mermaids for the next year, possibly two.

"I'm sorry," I whispered. It was hard not to take the damage personal. My go-big-or-go-home attitude was probably what Isaac had been counting on. We'd had enough run-ins in Vegas, he knew A.J. falling to me was all I'd be focused on. If I'd just played it safe. But I'd been so sure of my hand.

"Stop." Mom slipped her cellphone back into her clutch. "The guilt-whipping you're giving yourself. Stop. It was an unbeatable hand."

"Except I was beat." I cinched the seatbelt tighter.

Mom's warm fingers wrapped around my wrist, stopping me. "You bested five Houses and lost to a Shadow."

"Bested or lost, it still means I cost you something you loved." A realization filled the cabin. Mom's expression changed, and I knew she could see it too. I would always be a cost to her. Everything she loved would be damaged because of me. "Why did you declare me heir?"

"Why wouldn't I?"

I let loose a strangled laugh. "Because Cara has this world—"

"Cara knows her duties."

"Cleaning up after my messes? Let's face it, my whole life is a train wreck."

Mom swiveled her chair around; elbows planted on her knees, she leaned forward and grabbed my hands. "Feeling sorry for yourself will only take you on a journey of your worst mistakes and bring you right back to the very moment you're trying to escape. What's really going on? I love the hotel. I adore Fiji, but I'd give it all up if I knew it would continue to keep you safe."

"You shouldn't have to."

Mom's eyes softened and went distant, like she was tripping backward through years of her own memories. "I know, but I'm a mother." She held up a finger, cutting me off. "I don't expect you to understand, but one day, you will."

"Don't remind me." I pinched the bridge of my nose.

"You're talking about the consummation ceremony." Mom's cheeks flushed. Good to know this was seven shades of awkward for her as well.

I nodded. "The whole thing is so medieval."

"Yes, it is."

"That bad, huh?" Something churned in my stomach. I had a hard time wearing a bikini, and now I was going to be expected to let everyone see me naked and gettin' busy. I pushed the visual of me and Beaux and the nasty out of my head. "I know you loved my father, but Cara's dad . . . I mean, did you love him?"

"No, not at first." She brushed imaginary wrinkles from her slacks and leaned forward again. "I didn't love him when Cara was conceived. We were fulfilling an obligation." Mom grabbed her glass of wine and tossed it down her throat like a shot of whiskey. "You should ask all your questions now. I'm certain neither of us will have the gall to go for it when we aren't captive in an airplane twenty thousand feet in the air."

I squirmed in my chair. God, it was like having "the talk" with Sassy all over again. Only no Hollywood visual aids or show tune moments. "Midas watches?"

Mom nodded. "He and the other Houses' Royals have that right."

"Did they watch you?"

Mom chuckled. "Only Midas. I was the last one to consummate my relationship with my Jack, Hector. Cara has very little of him in her. Her loyalty. Her loyalty is from Hector. Midas . . ." Mom's words trailed off as the crinkle of skin between her eyebrows deepened. "I think Midas always suspected you existed. He just never had the proof. He could never quite put all the pieces together on the same page."

The hum of the engines filled in the awkward moments. I wanted to ask where she and my father had conceived me. How did they find the time to be alone? When had she given up on me? But what good would diving into past sins do?

"Did Cara know her dad?" I finally asked.

Mom shook her head. "It's hard to tell what she remembers and what she's made up." Mom combed her fingers through her hair before pouring herself another glass of wine. "She gets her imagination from me. She gets her loyalty from Hector." Mom's eyes glassed over like she was going to fall asleep.

"So you said." I fished the glass from her hand. "You should get some sleep, Mom."

She didn't listen to me.

"I loved them both, Cass. People say you can't, but . . ."

"I know."

"You love Beaux." It wasn't a question, and if it was that clear to Mom, what had A.J. picked up on?

I shook my head. "Not that way. I mean, he's handsome. He sends my stomach on a roller coaster, but it's not love. He gives me room to make mistakes and is there to clean them up, but—"

"He's your Hector."

"Don't say that. Hector died for you." I pushed up from my seat and paced the tiny airplane aisle. The cold bitch exterior Mom had perfected, it wasn't out of conceit and entitlement, it was a protective armor from losing two loves of her life. "What happened? It would kill me if Beaux died for—"

She shook her head. "He died keeping you a secret, Cass." Mom leaned back in her chair, crossing her long legs. "Cara's father knew about you. I sent him to warn Sassy and . . . " Her words trailed off. Mom pulled her honey-colored eyes from me and focused somewhere in the past. "When you were seven, your father led a team of rogue Shadows to find you. Your father had figured out a way to reclaim some of his soul. He'd figured out how to somehow keep that part of him from Dionysus's control."

"Why do you say that?"

"Because Dionysus wouldn't have sent a recovery team to get you. He'd have killed you on sight and brought back your body to collect from Midas and free himself form Zeus's exile."

My stomach dropped. We still didn't know what Dionysus had wagered for my life. It could've been as simple as a piece of property, or it could have been as grand as the Shell of Clarity. I was an outstanding debt. I pushed the thought from my mind.

"Tell me about my dad".

"No."

I recoiled from the single-word slap. One word that stung. The hard look in her eyes softened.

"I'm sorry. Nothing good could come from that."

I sank into the chair next to her. "I came from that," I whispered.

"Cassie." She reached for my hand. "You are the only thing good that came from him." She pulled back her hands, folding them in her lap. "Cassie, your father . . . " The word seemed to stick in her throat. "Your father and I loved you."

"But you kept him from me?"

Mom seemed to be physically injured from the question.

"I did." Mom polished off her glass of wine. "He was willing to risk everything for you."

"And that was a bad thing?"

"It was." She let the two words hang in the air. No explanation. There were a million reasons puckering her lips, desperate to be free, but Mom reigned over them like she did everything in her life—with no mercy.

I thought back to when I was seven, trying to remember a faceless person in a crowd of memories. I needed my parents' wall of pictures. They chronicled my life—the thought cut short.

"We used to have my birthdays at a park on the bluffs," I started. Mom rolled her head my direction. I'm pretty sure she was feeling no pain physically, emotionally was an entirely different story. I needed a few answers, and in this state, she might just give them to me. "My parents, Sara and Stephen." I reiterated for no reason than to buy some time. "I loved the bluff, but after my seventh birthday, we stopped having them there. I couldn't figure out why. Maybe it was something I'd done." I pulled at the only loose thread in the perfect plane, wondering if I pulled too hard, the whole thing would go down in flames. I had that effect these days. "It wasn't until I went back after Sassy and Stephen were gone did it all make sense."

Mom sat up in her chair, eyes clearer than a kid on Christmas morning. "Go on," she pushed.

"Gia and I were Disney Princesses that year. She had a special blue Cinderella dress, but it wasn't as pretty as my yellow Belle dress. I remember the dresses because of the swings and the way the fabric would fly up and then rush forward. Sara said it was the wind bringing our pretty yellow and blue fabric to life, but I told her it was magic. I was certain I was an enchanted princess, and on my birthdays, I had so much magic, I could make the wind blow and the world move." I paused, remembering how Sassy's eyes had bugged out like a gerbil squeezed too tightly.

Mom smiled but it didn't reach her eyes.

"I remember Dad came running over to the swing set, whispered something in Mom's ear that made her eyes wild—kind of like yours were back at the hotel—and her face looked like she was going to throw up.

"She yanked me off the swing set, screamed Aunt M's real name, and was headed to the car when I'd finally wiggled free. Aunt M had run across Bluff Park and scooped Gia up. Aunt M running that alone should have been a hint something was wrong."

Mom chuckled.

"Aunt M's eyes were as wild as Mom's. They were darting everywhere, but you could tell she wasn't finding anything. They wrangled me and Gia to the car. I kept screaming, 'We haven't even sung happy birthday!' Somehow I wiggled free again and threw myself to the ground, ready to pitch a fit. I'd done it earlier that week when Mom put her hands in the cement at Mann's Chinese . . ."

It hit me. All the pieces of a puzzle I never knew I needed to solve seemed to slip into place. Mom knew it, too; her face paled to the color of the creamed seat.

"Your last message to Sassy said, 'they found her.' Hector delivered the message and the 'they' was my father. He'd come for me? He found me because I threw a temper tantrum and the tabloids caught it. They ate it up. Sassy went behind the camera after that event."

I sank back into my seat, bile churning in my gut. "What could possibly be so special about me?"

"Did Sassy ever tell you fairytales?"

I did a double take. "What?"

"Fairytales. Once upon a time—"

"In a land surrounded by sand," I cut Mom off, "there were four kingdoms." Mom nodded.

"You were the Princess helped by the Northern winds? My father was the Prince who went to the Shadows and . . . disappeared?"

"And you are the Balanter," Mom finished.

"There never was a happily ever after in my future, was there?"

Mom slipped her fingers through mine and let the silence answer me.

FORTY-ONE

THE WONDERFUL SCENT of books and knowledge permeated the air of U.L.V.'s library; now all I needed was that scent to translate into words. Three weeks after my disastrous showing in Malaga, the library was the only place I could hide and not be found.

I stared at the cursor blinking on my computer screen. "My Decree" was all I'd been able to write for my final project in Queens' Class, aka Government 101a. I leaned back in the library chair, wishing the warm leather would release words, sentences, and paragraphs from others who'd sat here. My decree wasn't the only thing keeping me from heading home for the winter break. The meeting I just finished with Dr. Misch warning me that if I ever used my "talents" in computer hacking like I had at The Forum, I'd not only be suspended but expelled, was certain to have gotten back to Mom. I'd been her everyday daughter for almost a year; I'm not sure how social deviant would sit with her, even if my dastardly deed had been to secure our House's line. I wouldn't bring up the other computer I hacked. Dionysus hadn't figured out or been alerted that I'd been wiggling around in his mainframe, looking for my dad. If Isaac knew, he wasn't saying. I hadn't seen the Shadow with a conscience since he took Mom's favorite casino.

I held down the return bar, watching the blank pages scroll past. A lasting decree. My one and only chance to leave something, a change for the future members of the House of Hearts; it shouldn't be hard, but it turned out I had very little to say and everything I'd want to change. The consummation ceremony being the first. Arranged marriages, the second. The elixir hunt, third. I'd started bold and determined, ready to rally my counterparts to take back whatever they'd turned in and rewrite everything. An overwhelming movement of solidarity. They weren't quite as enthusiastic. Olivia was stunned into silence, Gia did her best guppy impression, but it was Helen who finally said, "Pick one thing. One vital thing that will enhance your line and focus on that." My sisterhood of solidarity took a flying leap, and the inability to pick anything set in.

Olivia was certain my writer's block was location induced. It wasn't; two continents and about a thousand locations could bear witness. Gia thought it was a defense mechanism because of the tournament loss three weeks ago.

My stomach cramped at the memory.

Cara said the Bella Mar was nearly destroyed. Poseidon's wrath against the coast of Malaga lasted three days. Mom's hotel took the brunt of his fury. Helen had her own opinion on why I couldn't write my only paper due.

"You self-sabotage, Cassandra." She'd kicked her foot up onto the table and shook a bottle of hot pink nail polish. "You're afraid to succeed more than you're afraid to fail, so you'll take failure and blame everyone but yourself."

The words stung. Olivia had thrown a pillow at her head and knocked the hot pink nail polish onto the white carpet. I appreciated Olivia's loyalty, but Helen seemed to be onto something. When I met with Ms. Maddox, she'd blended Helen's sabotage theory with Gia's self-defense idea and ended up giving me an incomplete in the class. I had until the start of spring semester to turn in the paper or get an F in the class. My first semester at U.L.V. was less than stellar, depressing actually, on the grade front. I blamed—I pushed the thought from my mind, angry that Helen and her self-sabotage theory seemed to be edging out all the others. It didn't matter whose theory won, an F would all but seal my fate for academic probation and open a whole new can of pain in my butt. Maybe there was a little bit of truth in all my roommates' theories, but Olivia's simple, "Your heart is broken," seemed to bite the most. If I'd learned anything my last year in Las Vegas, it was this: if it hurt, then it had to be true. I raked my hand over my face, hoping to chase away the face of the boy who'd led me down to the realization that love hurt and truth was a convenient play on words.

A.J.

I closed out of my word document, making sure to save my precious title before procrastinating on the school's social media site. A.J.'s student profile picture filled my screen. It had been easier to move on with him half a world away. Having A.J. here, my heart scurrying around my chest, was like living the lies all over again. I'd turn a corner and stumble into old memories, a familiar scent of him. All those pathetic moments created a mosaic of a person I didn't want to be. I didn't want to be the ex-girlfriend staring at his and Zee's balcony, ducking into darkened classrooms at the sound of his voice, and all but nose-diving into a bush when he came out of the Dayton Complex. Isaac had fished me out of that fine moment. After plucking twigs from my sweater, whatever reason Isaac had come looking for me was quickly forgotten with a pitiful head tilt and an offer to buy me a round at the Coyote Bar. I'd thought about taking Isaac up on his offer longer than I should have, but finally excused myself. I'd seriously lost it if Isaac, Shadow de douche, looked like a damn good answer to a broken heart.

I stuffed the memory and my computer into my backpack, slung it over my shoulder, and set off for location one thousand and one. Maybe the Field Games arena would jar something. I pushed open the heavy library door with my butt, turned, and smacked into the boy I was trying to avoid.

I fumbled to catch my backpack while A.J. fumbled to keep me from smacking the cruel linoleum floor. Traitorous tiles could've at least let loose an echo or moan to give a girl an ex-in-the-hall hint.

"Dammit, Cassandra," A.J. complained as I scampered out of his grip. I shifted again in his arms, face close enough to the linoleum that I could see a faint vein of gold snaking through the white tile. A.J. wrapped me up in his arms, muscling me to his chest and finally setting me on my feet. I thanked the gods when he bent down to manhandle my backpack, giving me a moment to compile myself, or at least to bargain with my pulse to slow down.

"What are you doing here?" he asked, nearly shoving my backpack into my chest before grabbing my elbow and hauling me down the long hallway. Three class doors passed before I could yank my arm free.

"I could ask you the same. And don't maul me. You gave up that privilege."

A.J. ran his fingers through his hair, stance widening into a parental patronizing shoulder width. "I didn't give it up, you took it away."

"Tomato, tomahto."

"What are you doing here?"

"Not that it's any of your concern, but I had a meeting with my Computer Science instructor."

A.J. grunted, which meant he knew that was only part of the reason. The rest was that I was full of shit. I was hiding.

"What?" I pushed.

"What did your CS professor have to say?"

I turned on my heels, too chicken to lie to A.J.'s face. "I'm brilliant at hacking impenetrable servers."

"And lousy at lying."

I stopped in my tracks. "Why do you care, A.J.?"

The air thickened between us like a storm surging all its strength before letting loose an ungodly fury.

"I never stopped."

"Sounds like you found your Achilles heel; you should put a Band-Aid on that before it gets infected and spreads." I couldn't turn around. Couldn't see what emotion played across his face. Whatever it was, it would cut me to my core. Cut me so deep, there would be little chance of me putting the pieces back together. Moments stretched like knots of lies pulling tight between us. The only sound was the rustle of his jacket.

"You always have been, always will be, the chink in my armor, the soft spot in my heart, the key to my soul." The cold was gone from his voice, replaced with the lulling cadence of hope.

My stupid heart ached. He was always good with one-liners. Heat seared the fabric of my shirt. He was always so stealth, so quiet. I should have known he'd always MacGyver his way back into my life, into my heart.

"I get you don't want me in your life right now, but understand, I am yours. I always have been. I always will be. You can push me away, you can believe what everyone is certain is fact, but Cass . . ." The palm of his hands skidded down my arms, and I fought every urge to lean into him. A.J. lowered his head, his chin finding its resting place on my neck like no time, no lies had ever passed between us, before his lips pulled up into a grin. "Cassandra," he purred. "We write our own futures, and your name is the only word I'll ever pen."

My eyes closed, ridged muscles in my shoulders loosened. The memories of last New Year's Eve and the days after rushed in like a tsunami. Harsh and unforgiving, every moment, every look, every simple breath I took involved this boy. His devotion at the treaty line when he defied his House and dared Midas, thrashed against all the reasons I had to not trust him. A flash of A.J. lying in a pool of blood danced across my eyelids. He may have written me into his future, but my conscience would be the eraser. His soul may sing of our tomorrows, but his lies ruined their todays. I'd worn too many loved ones' blood on my hands, and while A.J. may not have deserved my love— and gods help me, I still did—he did deserve my mercy. I pulled in a deep steady breath and stepped out of A.J.'s arms.

"Leave me alone," I whispered and walked away, yet again.

I turned the corner and stumbled up the stairs to the roof. Afraid to run into someone on campus, desperate to be alone, I willed the door to be open. I'd Bruce Lee the thing if it wasn't. I easily tumbled through the door and into the cool Las Vegas breeze. Gravel from the roof bit into my palms as I fell, pulling in a deep breath.

"Son of a blanket," I whispered, rolling over and eyeing the rip in my jeans.

"I thought Olivia was going to work on your cursing skills this year." A shit-eating grin spread across Chance's face like he'd just polished off a fresh plate of gotchya.

"Yeah, well you should hear me talk about you when you're not around."

"I thought you'd be home for the holidays." Chance cooed from an iron bistro chair. He leaned his elbows on the matching table, grabbed his drink, and nodded to the empty seat next to him.

"I am home."

"No, you're on campus." Chance pulled in a sip, eyeing me over the rim. "Curious girl, what are you searching for now?"

I stood up and dusted myself off, afraid he'd see right through me. I was all open-book these days. "Who said I was searching for anything?"

Chance rose from his chair, closed the space between us, and violated my personal space. "A.J. and your stolen moment in an empty corridor?"

I took a step toward the door, afraid he could read every raw emotion crossing my face. Chance was a careless Shadow, but that didn't mean he wasn't cunning.

"No, no. Don't go. We should chat." He reached behind me, taking my hand off the doorknob.

"I have nothing to say to you."

He caged me in with his other arm. "But I have all sort of things to say to you." This close, the tainted smell of rot clung to his breath. "I've enjoyed watching you two do the avoidance dance now that you're both back on campus. Diving into bushes. Such a fine act for a future Queen."

Heat flushed my face. "Nobody's on campus, actually."

"You are. I am."

I raised my eyebrows, watching my point slam into Chance's face like a well-placed fist. We were both nobodies in this world.

"Cute, Cassandra. But one of these days, you're going to see the nobodies are actually somebodies you should have kept close."

"Like my enemies."

A smile pulled at Chances' lips. I'd never noticed how yellowed his teeth really were.

"Merry Christmas, Chance." I started around him, but the sinewy muscle of his arms flexed, careful not to touch me. I guess the rumor about my ability to see the Shadows' prior lives was making the rounds.

"Did you see him?" he whispered.

"What?" My heart sunk. Call it intuition or heebie-jeebies, I knew the "him" Chance referred to wasn't A.J.

Chance stepped even closer, mere inches separating us. A rotten musk cloaked by cheap cologne wafted up from him. "Did you see him? He was in Malaga. At the tournament."

I pulled back. Chances eyes searched mine, hoping for a hint of recognition to root.

"Who?" I finally whispered.

A small twitch toyed with his lip, and I knew who he was going to say long before the name left his lips. "Your father."

My world tilted as I fought to keep my composure. "Dante," I choked out.

Chance nodded.

"You're lying."

"And you were too focused on A.J. and Zee's matching hand to notice daddy dearest standing behind Warren. Your mother didn't miss him." Chance circled around me, the chill from him repelling every cell inside me. "You didn't feel the air tense between the two of them? Didn't see their eyes lock? The hushed breath race into your mother's lungs like she'd broke the surface of a horrid nightmare?"

I shook my head, playing back the night, but all I could remember was Isaac calling out my ex-boyfriend, flipping over his card, and winning the tournament. Everything besides that hadn't mattered.

The Shadows were taking over and destroying Mom's favorite hotel in Fiji in over a week, and it was my fault. Given the massive storm and tidal surge that had damaged the Bella Mar to point of closing for a month, Poseidon had heard who his new neighbors were, and wasn't too happy.

"Second chances, Cassandra. Your entire life is always hinging on second chances." A nasty little sneer flashed across Chance's face. "Ironic, don't you think?" Pencil thin eyebrows climbed up his face. The irony wasn't lost on me—his name, his possible second chance. Chance stepped away from me, sizing me up as if he were the only one who held the key to a question that I'd been asking almost my entire life. Who was my father? What had he wagered? And why couldn't I let go?

"Questions is," Chance interrupted my thoughts, "if you could recognize a second chance, would you be ballsy enough to grab it?"

"Try me."

FORTY-TWO

I WAS DOWN to my last fingernail and my last nerve when Olivia tossed an overnight bag on my bed. "Enough, you've been moping around since we got back from Spain. Either make up or let him go."

"Real tactful," Gia said, slapping Olivia's tush.

Olivia shrugged her shoulders. "I know what I saw."

It was a carrot she'd been dangling for the last week, and not a very tempting one. Since we'd come home from Spain, Olivia was firmly in the make-up with A.J. camp, Gia not too far behind. There was nothing they could say that would budge me. Not after his last attempt to seduce me at the poker game, not after he accused me of sleeping with Beaux.

"Seriously, Cass," Gia picked up the conversation, "your sulk has turned funky and depressed in the last two weeks. If you keep it up, you're going to be sporting a black bob-cut like Malory. Trust me, you don't have the attitude to pull it off." Gia winked. "What's changed?"

Olivia interrupted. "Cassie, you know he threw the game."

"No, he didn't." I answered.

"Olivia shrugged her shoulders. "Like I said, I know what I saw. He had you beat. He had Isaac beat with a Royal Flush."

"Then he's not only a liar and a cheater, he's a coward, too."

Gia barked out a laugh. "Disobeying Midas is far from a coward."

She was right, but I was too chicken to admit it. I was too afraid to admit a lot of things.

What's changed? I pulled my pillow into my lap to keep from spilling all the details of my chance meeting with Chance. That's what had changed. Chance not only knew who my father was, but where he was. He'd all but dangled a treasure map getting me to bite at the bait of my father's whereabouts. I'd held it together, walked down from the roof cool and composed on the outside, but his words, they'd haunted me through Christmas and the week leading up to New Year's. The thing that bothered me the most wasn't that I didn't know where my father was, but that I would have if I hadn't been so fixated on A.J. and Zee's *moment*. I was always focused on the wrong thing. That stopped now.

Olivia nudged my mattress, demanding an answer without having to ask.

"What changed? I changed," I finally answered. "And Oli, I need you to back off. I like Isaac, all he wants to do is keep you safe, but you don't see me shoving him down your throat."

Olivia took the comparison like a smack to the face, but she got my point

Gia nodded. The room filled with the awkward silence we'd been able to avoid all semester long; everyone had changed. Halfway through the year, and we were nowhere near the starry-eyed girls our mothers had dropped off in August.

"I guess we've all changed this year." Olivia finally broke the silence. "Still not a good enough excuse to ditch us on New Year's Eve. Your birthday?" she pushed.

"I think I'm going to sit this one out. Sleep until the spring semester."

"You turned your paper in?" Gia asked, wandering over to my dresser. A sheepish grin took over her face as she pulled open my jeans' drawer. I wasn't going. She could pack a bag for me, but I wasn't going with them. I was staying right here. Not even chubby baby New Year himself could waddle down from the heavens and convince me otherwise.

I shook my head. "I'll sleep until the day before spring semester."

"Cass," Olivia sat down, eyes fixed and determined on getting me past tomorrow's anniversary of my parent's death and my birthday.

"I know. The best way to honor their memory is to live a full life. I'll do that next year. Scout's honor."

"You weren't a girl scout, Cass," Gia reminded me.

"No, but I can play one."

Gia's eyes welled up at the line Sara used all the time. She quickly turned and stuffed my folded pair of jeans into the overnight bag.

"Besides, I told Carina I'd come home tomorrow night, ring in the New Year at The Eclectic."

"And Malory?" Olivia asked.

"Malory's been M.I.A. since we got home from Malaga. After finals, she texted me her mom was taking some vacation time. They were spending the holidays in Europe."

Gia stilled. "That's new."

It was not shiny pretty new; it was hold your breath and pray you're far enough from the fallout new.

"I guess you're right, Olivia. Everybody's changed." My phone buzzed on the nightstand. "It's Beaux, we're meeting before his dad lands tonight."

"Dinner with the in-laws." Olivia cackled.

I knew Gia couldn't help her eyes from rolling any more than I could my stomach. I'd met Bash and Beaux's dad twice; once was all the frightened fifteen-year-old girl inside me needed. I'm sure Bash's "abduction" and how I was involved would be the main topic of discussion. I pushed the thought of the night from my mind, hugged my friends, and padded off to the showers.

Olivia and Gia were gone when I got back. A note and a key to the Red Rock sat on top of my packed overnight bag:

Bail on Beaux, he'll be no fun tonight.

Carina'll understand about tomorrow night.

G.

Four hours and a disastrous dinner later, I navigated the hidden passageway of The Eclectic. Bash and his dad's dirty looks and snide remarks had me tiptoeing my way into the oversized bed in my room at Mom's house. Gia was totally right that I should have bailed. I needed another judging once-over from the current King of Clubs like I needed a lobotomy. A lobotomy would've been more fun. I knocked off the receiver of my landline, muted my cellphone, and stared at the lights dancing across the ceiling of my room. A forgotten ache pinched my heart. This time last year, Sara and Dad were kissing me good-bye, promising they would be back from New York before I knew it. I'd promised to stick close to home.

They'd lied.

I'd lied.

The three of us had been lying to each other for years. If they'd only trusted me with the truth, I would have made a different choice. I rolled over, staring at the outline of the hidden door, wondering. My eyes fluttered, fighting off sleep. I wasn't ready to deal with tomorrow and if I went to sleep—A yawn cut off the thought long enough for my body to take over and force my eyes . . .

♥

"HAPPY BIRTHDAY, SWEET girl." Mom's voice eased past my sleepy haze, completely ruining my plan to Sleeping Beauty away my birthday.

"Here I thought I was being all clever sneaking in last night."

"Eyes everywhere, Cassie," Mom said as a ray of sunlight light sabered my eyes. I knew she wouldn't stop at one blackout panel, she'd make sure my room was bathed in sunshine before I wiped the sleep out of my eyes.

"Right, what was I thinking?" I let the sarcasm drip, knowing we both knew there was no bite to my bark. I pushed myself up, sliding along the red silk sheets and back against the headboard of my four-poster bed. She floated across the floor like a Disney princess, picking up my shoes, putting my landline phone on the hook, searching the room for my cell. I didn't have the heart to tell her I'd stuffed it under the mattress after Beaux texted me twenty times in a row making sure I was okay.

"Looks like someone left you a present." The way she emphasized *someone* meant she'd hoped A.J. and I had made up. I feigned a smile, hoping the conversation I'd had with A.J. yesterday not only pushed him well into the not-from-him category but also landed him firmly in the when-hell-freezes-over line. Mom handed me a jewelry box-sized package before leaving. She stopped in the doorway, auburn hair catching the rays of sun fashioning a flaming halo around her head. She was beautiful. If I had even an ounce of her poise, her beauty, I'd count myself a lucky girl.

Who was I kidding?

I was already lucky. She loved me. She'd always wanted me. If nothing else in this world went my way, knowing that one fact, knowing in my soul that I was wanted by not just one but two moms, was all I needed. Hell, I was beyond lucky. I was blessed. And I needed to stop focusing on what I didn't have and appreciate the hell out of what I did.

"Happy birthday, Cassandra. May all your wildest wishes come true," Mom lowered her eyes, her tell that they were filling with more than emotion, and shut the door behind her.

Silence tiptoed into the room. Inch by inch, it seemed to crowd in, its focus the same as mine. If A.J. didn't leave me the box and according to Beaux's last threatening text, I was meeting him later tonight for a proper birthday dinner, then who had tiptoed into my room last night? A shudder racked my body. Who'd been in here while I was asleep and left me the box? I examined the red shiny wrapping paper, my reflection bouncing back. A thick black ribbon wrapped it up like some sort of Nightmare Before Christmas gift with a bow on top. I pulled the edge of the ribbon, unwrapping the package to find a white box. I hesitated a moment, remembering Sara's playful warning: *If it isn't Tiffany blue or jewelry store black-velvet, it's nothing you want.* She was probably right. I lifted the top off and found a black keycard. This one was different than the others; it was made of wood, like my Pithos box. But that wasn't what had my spine snapping iron-rod straight, it was the note inside.

Second Chances, Cassandra.
Bring the key, the shell, and
unlock yours tonight.

Midnight.
Your second,
Chance.

I flipped over the card, finding an address.
Ice slipped down my spine.
Déjà vu.

I knew this address. It was an abandoned pawnshop across the street from the entrance to the catacombs. I'd gone down this rabbit hole earlier this year and barely escaped with my life. Odds were, I was about to do it again.

"Happy freaking birthday to me," I muttered.

Later that afternoon, I climbed into the car Chance sent for me. Either something had crawled into the cavern where Chance kept his cojones, or he thought no one was watching. Knowing the worm the way I did, there wasn't new courage in his bold move, someone was protecting him. When we passed the first barricade on Casino Center Boulevard, I was certain it was someone very powerful in our world. We inched along the boulevard, navigating the hordes getting ready to ring in the New Year. Revelers tried to catch a glimpse into the car, what "special person" was allowed to drive past the barricades. A shiver raced down my spine as we turned right onto Stewart Street and then right again on Main Street, away from the party at the Fremont Street Experience. I played with the loose black string at the edge of my sweater, careful not to tug it too much. You never knew which string would unravel something. My heart sped up as the car pulled to a stop. The divider between the driver and me lowered.

"He's waiting for you around the back."

"You're not going to open the door?"

"I'm not that kind of a driver."

"But you'll be here to take me back."

The divider started climbing back up. "You can hope," he muttered.

I pulled in a steady breath, and opened my door. The noise of the freeway rushed in, nearly screaming at me to shut the door and leave.

But I couldn't.

If Mom wasn't brave enough in the past, then I had to be now. Last year, I couldn't save Sassy and Stephen, but I could try to save my dad. I had to know. Where was my father, and could I free him? Dust from the unpaved parking lot kicked up on a gust of wind. I straightened my black jeans and sweater, anchoring my House's broach over my heart. My finger went to twirl my designator ring, but I'd left it and its tracking bug at home. As far as anyone watching my ring signal knew, I was at home in my room and had been all day. And given the white I-lost-my-phone lie I told Beaux last night, he'd be watching the ring.

"I'm not that kind of driver, so if you're waiting on the door," the driver said again.

"Yeah, try waiting your whole life." I muttered, opening the door. The black sedan pulled away from me the second I shut the door. I swallowed hard over the lump of fear.

I'd read about this place last year during committee finals. It was one of the original Shadow strongholds. Somehow it had survived the government's eminent domain when the freeway expanded. Now it stood all alone, literally overshadowed by Highway 95. My hip pocket vibrated. I fished out my phone and read the text:

Not having second thoughts about your second Chance, are you?

I wasn't ready to even begin wrapping my head around how he got my cell number. Given the listening devices I found earlier in the semester in our dorm, I didn't put any stock in privacy.

I slipped the phone back in my pocket and started toward the back of the building. The front door was nothing more than plywood and wood planks, making it impossible to use. Gravel crunched under my feet as I made my way along the side of the abandoned building. The rusted iron arm holding three chipped gold balls from the eaves like a flagpole and the faded letters of the words "Silver Exchange and Loan" warned I was at the right place. This place had to be one of the earliest pawnshops in Las Vegas. How it was still standing here spoke to the strength and influence the Shadows had. Spoke to how crazy I was for being here. But not knowing about my birth father, wondering if every Shadow I saw in this town was somehow a genetic match to me . . . it was driving me insane. The questions of who he was and why he thought the Shadows were their only option for me were all-consuming. What had he wagered, and who had failed?

I had to know.

I jumped at the whine of wind whistling through the boarded-up windows. It was my birthday, and I was marching right back into the lair of my enemy. Someday I'd listen to the sensible girl inside me, but not today. Not when I was so close to knowing both sides of my parents' history. I willed my heart to slow down as I rounded the back of the building. Another iron arm with three balls dangling jutted up and out like a sick child's mobile taunting the world. Did anyone recognize the symbol of the early pawnshop?

Chance climbed out of two metal cellar doors attached to the foundation of the building. His hair had grown a little longer, less product holding it in place, adding to the feral vibe rolling off him. I waited for some Wild West showdown tune to play and a tumbleweed to cut between us. Chance folded his arms across his chest and threw a smile at me. How could anyone not appreciate evil when it smiled and tempted you?

"Are you coming or what?" Chance asked, nodding to the open doors. "You've made it this far, why not walk all the way into the lions' den?"

I closed the distance between us, my eyes trained on his, but my heart thrashed, begging for me to turn and walk away. "You're no lion."

"And you're far from the savior, aren't you?" Chance plucked a strand of my hair from the wind, and something chilling rocketed through my body.

I'd never consciously stood this close to a Shadow before. Aside from the paled skin and lifeless eyes, there was no real way to distinguish a Shadow from a mortal. Except one. One I'd missed until I was digging around in Dionysus's cloud of information. My attention fell to Chance's left hand and the missing piece of him.

Chance followed my gaze. "You are a nosy thing, aren't you?" He stepped closer, making every cell in my body run the opposite way. "Question is, where have you been nosing around to find all your knowledge?" His eyes darted across my face, looking for an answer that there was no way in this hell or beyond I would give. Not if it meant certain expulsion from school.

"I don't know what you're talking about." I stepped past him toward the open cellar doors, not glancing back, knowing for certain my ears were flaming. "Are we going to do this, or stand around talking about all the ways it's a blessing no one can put a wedding band on your ring finger?"

"You can't lie for shit, Cassandra Vera." He was so close to me, I could feel his lungs expand with each breath he drew. "Some things never change." His icy voice slid down my spine. Chance stepped around me and started leading me down the steps into the darkness of the cellar.

I'd done this last year, with a different Shadow. Somehow, Isaac and the catacombs seemed all kittens and rainbows compared to tonight. I rubbed at the hair pulling at the back of my neck.

Listen to your hackles, Sara would say when I was a girl. All those random thoughts of wisdom—she'd been preparing me for this life since the day Carina gave me up. Two moms and neither of them could give me the answer my soul needed: Could I save my father? I pulled in a deep breath and followed Chance into the darkness.

Stale, musty air pulled me deeper into the cellar. Chance stood near the glow at the bottom of the stairs. He stole a glance at me, probably to make sure I'd followed. Although, the way my heart was thundering in my ears, he was probably making sure I hadn't died on the steps from a heart attack. He stepped down and rounded the corner at the bottom of the stairs. I followed, letting my eyes adjust to the dimly lit room. I could barely make out the walls or the person standing in the corner. I could tell by the slouch that it wasn't Isaac. The only other thing I could make out were his black work boots.

A cold chill ripped a memory from my soul. A memory I'd thought I'd long since dealt with —or buried with my parents . . .

I'd dangled from the roof of the car, strapped safely into my seat belt. Mom and her sunshine yellow dress were gone. She was gone. Dad was in her place; the giant bear didn't move. God, why wasn't his chest rising and falling?

"Daddy?" I called to him, already knowing I wouldn't be hearing the rich and husky grumble. I released my seatbelt, falling to the floor. Dad's eyes, vacant orbs, stared right through me. The crunch of glass under foot sounded from outside our mangled car. Someone had hit us on purpose. I found black work boots casually walking toward our wrecked car. My moment of relief was quickly chased away by the icy feel of dread slithering down my neck. The black work boots annihilated the remaining shards of glass as they passed by my window. Instinctively, I held my breath, bit back the scream in my throat as the smell of clove cigarettes assaulted the remaining molecules of clean air.

I tried to shake free of the memory. My heart ached as the scent of clove cigarettes permeated the air. The glow from the bare lightbulb danced off a plume of smoke the person hidden by the shadows released. The smell took me back. I was in the hospital, recovering from the accident last year.

The sweet scent of clove cigarettes wafted into my nostrils. No sound, just the sweet stench of smoke. I tried to peel back my eyelids, willing them into compliance. Slowly they opened, letting in a small glow of yellow light around the sleep sand threatening to seal them shut again.

A figure stood close enough to my bed that I could make out it was a man, but far enough away to distort his face and keep him shrouded in the shadows of the night.

The Shadows! I heard the monitor next to my bed kick-start as I thought about the boys in the black hoodies chasing me, the black work boots that had cruelly sauntered through shards of broken glass.

A harsh light from the hall blasted into my hospital room. My eyes slammed shut in protection, but I wanted to see this man's face.

"I'm sorry, sir," a nurse whispered. She'd been chatting to me all day, pep talks on why I needed to wake up. How so many people I loved were waiting for me. The handsome young man who would only leave my side when my mother entered.

"Visiting hours are over," the nurse continued. "I'm going to have to ask you to leave."

There was no answer besides the beep of the machines.

"Are you a family member?" she pushed.

The loud thud of boots on linoleum finally answered for him. My hospital door shut before I could hear the man's voice, if he spoke at all.

I stopped short. "Who is that?"

"The grand prize." Chance nodded to the figure in the shadows. "You're going to be shy?" he barked into the darkness. "All I've heard about for a year is how beautiful she is. What a spitting image of her mother she is. Get your ass out here so she knows what she's playing for."

The man shifted in his boots. A minute step forward, a larger stride back. The rock of a hesitant man, maybe a guilty man. My mind tried to wrap around the fact that the man nervously shifting from foot to foot in the shadows—

No, I pushed the thought as far from my mind as possible. There was no way the man responsible for my parents' death, for almost killing me, was my biological father.

"Dante," I whispered.

Chance rounded the table, reaching into the shadow and pulled my father into the dim light of the musty cellar.

He shied away from Chance like a dog beaten one too many times. An old, threadbare sweater hung from his arms. I swear his shoulder bones threatened to poke through the fabric. Dark jeans—they were so dirty, they looked black—were held up with a weathered belt cinched so tight around his waist, it nearly cut him in half. The harsh, razor sharp lines of his jaw and cheekbones looked like they'd slice through his paper-thin skin at any moment. But beneath it all, there were hints of the boy he'd been in the beaten down man standing before me. I could tell by the way he clinched his fist, there was fight left in him. The way he worked his jaw when Chance wasn't looking. The small spark of life in his cold eyes flickered when his captor was too busy showboating. I inched forward, hoping to find something familiar. His hairline had obviously receded on the sides, leaving a small strip of hair: an old man's Mohawk

"Dante?" I whispered, but he recoiled from his name like I slapped him.

I looked nothing like him. My eyes were my mother's. My movements, mannerisms, every one of them belonged to her; there could be nothing of this man in me. I'd wondered my whole life about this moment, and now it was here. Silence crawled in around us, anxious to witness this . . . reunion. I searched for something in common with the man but found nothing. It could've been a trick. I wouldn't have put it past Chance, except every fiber of my body knew this shell of a man was the other half that had made me. I swallowed hard over all the questions lodged in my throat. Where had he been? What happened to him? All the questions I wanted to ask disappeared when I looked at Dante's left hand and his missing ring finger. Whoever this man was, he'd sold his soul to the Shadows and lost. Something fierce and loyal ripped through all the questions I had, stripped me down to the primal need to protect one of my own.

To protect my father.

"What did you do to him?" I couldn't pull my gaze from my father.

"I didn't do anything to him, you did."

My attention snapped to Chance. His arms crossed as he smugly regarded the scene he'd orchestrated.

"I'd love to give you the rundown of daddy dearest's fall from glory, but we'd wind up right here"—he smacked the table, making the edges of the red fabric float up—"with wagers to be made and games to be played." His lip ticked. "He's not much to look at; I can't even promise he'll clean up nicely, but . . ." Chance let the words die on his tongue.

"Yes, I still want him," I whispered.

Dante's focus found mine and there it was. The flash I'd thought I'd seen earlier. He was still in there. He'd been beaten, nearly broken, but Mom and I could put all the pieces together again. Chance was right about one thing; this had been my fault, which was why I was the only one who could fix it. I may have been too late last year to save my parents, but not this year. I stepped forward, pulling the chair from the covered table. Chance mirrored my movement, rolling up his sleeve and signaling someone else from the Shadows. Warren stepped forward, along with a woman. I rolled my eyes; of course Warren would be here. I searched for the Cheshire cat grin, but . . . something was off. A blank stare, lifeless eyes, his movements—they were like a marionette. But the master holding Warren's strings was nowhere to be seen.

"Why's Warren here?"

"He's backing our little off-the-books bet."

"You don't have the authority?"

"Better to beg forgiveness than ask for permission."

I gripped the iolite shell in my pocket. If this was off the books and he'd done something to Warren, then all the odds in Vegas said I was about to get screwed. I glared at Chance, a familiar warm tingle humming at the base of my neck. Chance would pay for every minute of pain Dante felt, and maybe a little for what he'd done to Warren. If he thought he was going to get away—

"Warren," Chance interrupted my thoughts. "That buzz of electricity you feel is the Balanter's power. Exciting, yes?" The play left his eyes. "Every jolt I feel is another lashing for Daddy. Do *I* make myself clear?"

"Crystal," I answered.

"Good." Chance gripped the edges of the red cloth and yanked. I wasn't sure if he said anything else. I couldn't think about being screwed over by the demoted Shadow. I couldn't really focus on anything except the gun pointed at my head.

FORTY-THREE

THE WORLD FADED away, everything except the four guns strapped to what had been a traditional roulette table. The barrel of a gun pointed at me, another at Chance. I swallowed over the rock of fear in my throat. There was nothing traditional about this roulette table now. The colored number slots were gone from the spinning section of the roulette table. At the opposite end of the guns were metal U-shaped chin holders. It looked exactly like the medieval contraption my optometrist strapped me into when he puffed air into my eye and lied it wouldn't hurt. Given the dangling buckle, this contraption didn't use the honor system for you to keep your head still; they strapped you in and it was definitely going to hurt.

"What's this?"

"Russian Roulette, Vegas style." Chance sat down in the chair across from mine and spun the wheel. I jumped at the tick, tick, tick of the wheel.

"Cassie, you really thought you'd waltz in here, get all electric with your forbidden power, and then sashay out of here with your dad?"

I fought to find my voice, to peel my eyes away from the roulette table of death. "First, I don't waltz. Second, you don't get to call me Cassie. Third, answer my damn question. What is this?"

Chance lifted an eyebrow at my tone. "You know what Russian Roulette is?'

I nodded. Who didn't know the jackass game of putting one bullet in a revolver spinning the barrel and then taking turns at pulling the trigger? You had a one in five shot of splattering your brains before the other guy.

Chance grabbed a package of playing cards and tossed them at me. "Vegas style means we add cards. Double check the package hasn't been opened." He pointed to the deck I'd snatched out of the air. "Each player is dealt five cards. At the same time, the players flip over a card. One card at a time. Highest card wins. Looser pulls a trigger."

"Like War?" I checked the deck; the blue seal hadn't been broken.

"Exactly like War, only you can choose any of your five cards to flip."

"That makes it better."

Chance motioned to the cards, asking for them back. Without hesitation, I tossed them at him like a bad game of hot potato.

"It adds a little more room for the gods to smile on their favorites."

"Awesome," I muttered.

Chance chuckled. "What's the matter, Cassandra? Not sure who's lower on their shit list?"

I pulled out the chair and forced my body into the seat. "Shut up and deal."

"Ante up first."

I pulled in a deep breath, wrapping my fingers around the smooth iolite shell: Poseidon's Shell of Clarity.

Crap.

Dante had done the same for me. Risked everything. One of us had to come out a winner. Poseidon was just going to have to deal with my risk. Chance's breath caught as I laid the shell on the table. He leaned forward, eyes glazing over as if the mirage he'd been searching for suddenly materialized on the table. With fingers crossed under his chin like he was praying the shell wouldn't disappear, he studied the way the dim light bounced off the swirls of blues and greens.

"They thought for sure it was still in the cave," he murmured to himself.

"I know."

Chance pulled his gaze from the stone, a smirk disfiguring his lips. "I thought you were there. The forbidden smell of teen sex has a way of lingering."

I shifted in my seat, not ready to discuss the status of my hymen with him.

"Still a virgin." Chance teased, leaning back in his seat and snapping his fingers. "And you still can't bluff to save your life."

Warren walked out of the shadows, his movement still so unnatural, and unrolled a scroll. Carefully, he placed it in front of Chance.

"I lose, you get Daddy dearest. I win, I get the shell."

I nodded.

"Words, Cassandra. The universe needs to hear your words, and I'll need you to seal your bet with your blood."

I cringed. "I win, I get my dad. I lose, you get the shell."

A full smile blossomed across Chance's face. "So be it." He signed the paper Warren had unrolled and then grabbed a wood box, something Mr. Bones probably had fashioned. I don't know what I expected, but four silver pens with sharp spears and four empty vials weren't it. He handed the paper and two vials to Warren, then passed the other two vials to the woman standing next to Dante, my father. I pushed away the hope of freeing him. The Shadows never played fair. Never.

Warren placed the paper in front of me and handed me a box with four silver pens. Clearly, Ms. Maddox needed to upgrade the binders she'd handed out in high school. These pens were far from your average ballpoint pen. A sharp silver tip glinted where the roller should have been. A wave of nausea rolled through me at the sight of one tip already freshly stained with Chance's blood.

"This is far from hygienic."

"You pick a fresh one, Cassandra. They've been sanitized. Although, a disease really is the last thing you should be worrying about."

My heart beat so fast, I was certain Chance could see the thump-thump through my sweatshirt. I pushed down the growing basketball of fear in my throat and grabbed the pen. I hated blood. I hated needles. I hated that this was the only way to save my father. Carefully, I pricked my index finger and pressed the fresh droplet of blood into the spot next to my name.

Chance smiled, the kind of smile that made your insides know you'd all but sealed your fate . . . and it wasn't the happily-ever-after Disney fate. I sucked on my wounded finger, hoping Chance would slip up under the delusion he was getting everything he wanted. He was a fool if he thought he was walking out of here with anything that belonged to me.

The woman took Warren's place next to me. She waited like I knew what she wanted, and when I didn't seem to comply, she turned to Chance. No emotion, no irritation at my lack of compliance, nothing but a slight shrug of her shoulders. She'd probably wait for all eternity for him to answer her.

"She's going to need your arm, Cassandra."

"Why?"

He nodded to the silver syringe in her hand. I jumped like a snake had just appeared next to my face.

"I gave you my word and my blood next to my name."

"Yeah, I'm gonna need a little more. Two tiny vials of blood, that's all that stands between you and your second chance with your parents. Your real parents."

My heart stuttered for so many different reasons.

"You stole my real parents from me last year. I'm making sure you don't do the same with my biological father."

Chance leaned forward, eyes wild. "You still think it was me? I wonder. . ." He let his words trail off and my imagination take over. With every dart of his beady eyes, I knew what twisted path he wanted my mind to dance down. It was a familiar worn-out path I'd already darted down and back a million times since I saw Dante's heavy work boots. I'd replayed the crunch of glass from our wrecked car, but it was the thump of heavy boots on linoleum that released a memory that wouldn't quite materialize. Yes, Dante wore heavy work boots, but so did Isaac.

And so did Chance.

I pushed the thought from my mind and stuck out my arm. The sooner we got this over with, the quicker I could leave this round of mind games.

The woman worked quickly despite missing her ring finger. How had I not noticed the missing digit before? Every Shadow, every single one had a missing ring finger. Her latex covered hands wrapped the rubber tubing around my arm and waited for my veins to pop to the surface. Cold blue eyes, clouded over and lifeless, stared right through me. Apparently the thin barrier was enough to keep me from accessing her memories, igniting some sort of spark from her life pre-Shadow.

"Everyone pays a price to sit at the table." Chance held his bent arm close to his chest. Two vials of blood rested in the wood box in the middle of the roulette wheel. "Even for the infamous Cassandra Vera."

The woman pushed a tiny ball of cotton into my elbow and bent my arm toward me before collecting the two vials of blood. She carefully placed them into the wood box in front of Chance.

"Gotta say, didn't think you had the balls. Good to see not all bull Midas shovels is shit."

"You spoke to Midas? About me?"

"I speak to everyone about everything." Chance's eyebrows climbed up his face. "Advantage me, it would seem."

"In your dreams."

His lanky body leaned onto the table; the white ball of cotton soiled from his blood fell to the surface. "My dreams are so bravura, it's best you keep to envisaging about freeing Daddy and making babies with A.J."

"Bravura and envisaging, I see Malory's not the only one shooting for extra credit this semester."

Chance's eyes measured me, hints of frenzy mixing with swirls of trepidation, like he'd said too much and was hoping I hadn't picked out the pieces.

But I had.

There was something bigger happening here, something larger than me patching up my parents, or mending past mistakes. Chance had slipped. He had an agenda. The scary thing was, would I be able to figure it out before it was too late?

"Ready?" he interrupted my thoughts.

I nodded and accepted the first of five cards.

Chance moved the cards around, arranging and then rearranging like they were shells from a carnival game and I was supposed to figure out under which one my father's freedom lay. When Chance noticed I was only watching, he smiled. "Align them how you see fit, but you can't pick them up. No cheating, Cassandra."

"Said the Shadow who's probably still breaking rules by even having this off-the-books bet." I eyed the cards in front of me. If this was all about fate, and if the gods really did have a hand in the outcome, then the way they were dealt should've been the best order. I just had to convince my heart that my head knew best. I leaned back in the seat, biting down on my lip until I was certain it was bruised permanently and waited to see if my heart or my head won.

Chance spun the table. The hearts symbol and gun landed in front of me. A silver bullet rolled back and forth in the slot. I picked up the bullet, noticing the spades symbol in front of Chance.

"You have a fucking grand sense of humor, Zeus! Grand!" Chance picked a bullet from the table. "You've loaded a gun?"

I shook my head, catching a glimpse of the man who'd helped make me.

He stood still but not like the girl who'd drawn my blood. Dante's stillness was forced, not by the gods or by the Shadow across from me; his calm was self-inflicted. If I wasn't sure before, the bead of sweat dribbling down the side of his face confirmed it.

Just how free was Dante?

I watched my father from the corner of my eyes as I popped open the chamber, slipped in the bullet, and gave her a spin, just as Chance as commanded. My heart was beating so loud, so hard, I was certain that was the reason Chance was smiling.

"How many times have you done this?" I asked, trying to ignore the cold steel barrel under my fingers.

Chance's lip ticked. "More times than you."

"How many?" I pushed.

"I don't want to brag." Chance flipped over his first card, the King of Clubs. "But let's say double digits are involved."

I stared at the card in front of him. Only an Ace could beat his king. My stomach dropped to my toes, taking all the blood from my head.

"This is where you flip your card, Cassie."

A bullet of adrenaline shot through my veins as I flipped over my card. "Only my friends call me Cassie." I kept my eyes on Chance's face, hoping to see defeat in his eyes. But they were cold and lifeless. Seems he only had two looks: cold and lifeless or creeper grin. Either one chilled me to my bone.

"And it seems only I'm the one with enough pluck to know who won this round." His bushy eyebrows danced on his face. "This can be quick and dirty, or long and agonizingly slow, Cassandra. I always took you for a q and d girl."

"Funny, I always took you for a douche." I stole a quick glance at my card. A two. It didn't matter what suit, I'd lost the first round. My heart sloshed in my ears. "So what do I do now?"

"Chin in the holder," He nodded to the metal u-shaped thingy in front of me. "Show me what a brave girl you are, and pull the trigger, Cassie. If you don't, then we use the straps. And what sport is there in that?"

I leaned forward. Black spots of fear and adrenaline pricked the corners of my vision. I was moments from passing out or throwing up, but the cold metal on my chin chased away the mental fog. I reached forward, my hand wrapping awkwardly around the butt of the gun.

"Look at you all noble and whatnot." Chance folded his hands under his chin, but his gaze pulled from mine toward the table. "Red button, Cassandra. Just like a video game."

My stomach dropped as I leaned back.

"Pull away again, Cassandra, and you'll leave us no other option than to utilize the strap."

"I was looking at the button you failed to point out the first time. Really, for someone whose done this in the double digits, you sure suck at explaining the rules."

Tangible anger rolled off Chance.

"You sure you weren't just a spectator?" I pushed. "How would Isaac feel about you claiming his wins at the table as your own?" I jumped as Chance's palm slapping the table. Even the passive phlebotomist girl looked startled.

"Are you refusing to play?"

"No."

"Then put your chin in the holster and push the trigger." His words were slow and enunciated, but they carried a rushed undertone that told me Chance was totally doing this against all Shadows' knowledge. So who was he working with? And who had convinced him the wrath of Shadows and the gods were worth the risk?

Chance slapped the table again, chasing away any more questions.

I pulled in a ragged breath, wiping away the sweat of my palms on my pants, and put my chin in the padded rest. My hand trembled, hovering over the red button.

"Any day now, Cassandra."

Three quick breaths through my nose, my pulse screaming in my ear, I dropped my hand on the button and listened . . . Silence screamed as time slowed down the click of the hammer easing back. The rush of air as it sprang forward. Metal on metal clacked through the air and more importantly, an empty chamber. I jerked back in my seat, grasping at my heart as it thrashed around in my body, no longer contained by my rib cage.

"You're still here," Chance said, studying his cards.

I wiped away the tears running down my eyes and found Dante standing in the same place, with the same expression on his face. The only indicator he'd even grasped his only daughter had almost died was the tight clench of his fists. Maybe he wasn't as free as I'd thought. What if Mom was right and he really was gone?

"Ready to go again?"

I nodded, hoping to unearth the seed of doubt taking root in my gut. Maybe Dante wasn't worth my life. I flipped over another card, not waiting for Chance's authorization.

The Queen of Hearts smiled up at me.

Chance flipped over his card, a Ten of Clubs. Without pause, he leaned forward, pushing the button as he said, "Winner goes first, Cassandra." The clack of an empty chamber reverberated. Chance leaned back in his chair, flipping the next card in front of him. "Rules apply to you too, Cassandra." He tossed his Four of Hearts at me. "Flip and pray you don't come up with a two or a Joker," he ordered.

"You only have a four showing."

Another creeper grin pulled at his lips. "Silly girl, a two or Joker means automatic war."

I licked my lips, hating how the knot in my gut only seemed to be growing, "You really do suck at explaining this game," I reiterated, flipping over my card, a Five of Diamonds. "Any other rules you want to tell me before you pull your trigger again."

Chance leaned forward into his chin rest. "Like what?"

I jumped as he pulled the trigger, another empty chamber down. I wiped my palms on my pants. The realization someone was going to die started to settle. "Are there any Jokers in the pack?"

"Are there Jokers in our world?"

I nodded.

"So then there are here." Chance pulled his third card from the table, holding it close to his chest. "I say we go at the same time."

Oh, crap.

"Or not," He added. Throwing his Queen of Spades at me.

A flash of Olivia raced across my vision. I refocused on my cards. I hated the way my fingers trembled as I gripped the card stock. With a quick flip, it was my turn to pull the trigger. I laid down the Three of Clubs, catching a glimpse of my father. He hadn't moved. I was risking my life for him and he hadn't moved. Either by his own will or the will of the Shadows, it really didn't matter. Whichever force rooted him, my peril was nothing against the power over him. Slowly, the fear in my gut dissipated. How many years had the Shadows been manipulating families? How much longer would we put up with it? I put my chin in the rest and slapped the red button. The hammer hit an empty chamber. Instead of jerking back with relief, anger swelled. Warmth rushed up my spine, not Balanter heat, but the heat of unfiltered rage. If my father was free, why had he stayed? And why weren't Mom and I enough to fight for?

Chance let lose a chuckle. "It's good we're only playing War. If it were poker, I'm certain your father's life as a Shadow would never be in jeopardy." He looked at Dante. "How does it feel to know she's wondering if you're worth it?"

Dante didn't flinch, not even a blink.

Chance's wicked gaze fell back on me, hands folding up under his chin. "He never was, just like you never were."

"What?"

"Carina never told you? She had the same chance to free him as you did. She'd come waddling down to the catacombs, demanding Dionysus let her baby-daddy free."

"How do you know that?"

Chance didn't answer, "All Carina had to do was give up the shell and you and daddy dearest would have been free." Chance stayed still; waiting for me to move, take the bait, something. "The shell has always been the end goal, Cassandra." Chance clucked his tongue. "Aw, how sweet, you really thought you were special? You really bought into the Balanter/free the world hype? How sweet."

I turned another card, a Joker. My heart sunk even further. Instant war. The gods were laughing at me, and I'd given the Shadows exactly what they wanted. My life was just dessert, a cherry on top of a shit sundae.

"What happens now?" I asked, not sure if I meant the game or my life.

Chance nodded to the remaining deck of cards in the center of the wheel. "Deal five cards to me and then pass me the deck and I deal five to you. Highest card wins. Unless you were asking about something else?"

I swiped the cards, dealt him five, then slapped the deck back onto the middle of the table. "I know how to play War."

"Cassandra." Chance grabbed the deck; his dismissive look stopped me cold. "Nobody is special enough to die for. Sure you're a little more powerful than the rest, but nothing the gods, nothing Dionysus couldn't handle. You're just a silly little girl who still believes in black and white, right and wrong. The sooner you realize that the world is ruled in the gray, the longer you'll live . . . or not." Chance methodically dealt me five cards. "No peeking," he said, adding insult to injury. "On three?"

I nodded. What I'd come here for wasn't what I was fighting for now. I had to get the shell back. And while the world—the gaming world- may have been ruled in the gray—I lived in the blacks and whites and I fully planned to right the wrongs my birth caused.

"Three," I whispered, flipping over the last card in my deck.

"Cassandra!" Carina screamed from behind me.

I spun in my seat, catching the Five of Hearts sitting on my war pile as I jumped up like a kid caught doing the nasty. I rushed over to her, taking her arm and pushing her back up the stairs. "You need to let me finish this."

Her fingers dug into my arms, eyes frenzied. "Cass, whatever you wagered, walk away. Leave it."

"I. Can't," I forced out.

"You wagered the shell." She pulled me up the first stair. "It's not worth it."

"It is. I can get them both back."

Her eyes searched the room behind me widening when they landed on Dante. "He wouldn't want this."

"But I do." I stumbled out of her grip. "I have to fix this, all of this."

"You can't." Mom followed after me, reaching for my arms. "Dante!" She screamed.

Dad stepped out from the shadows, eyes as wild as Mom's, but his body clearly still under control of whatever force the Shadows had over him.

"Carina." Each syllable ripped through from his throat. The deep timber was so reminiscent of my father's, of Steven's.

"My card's been flipped; doesn't anyone want to know who won the war?" Chance called out, but I couldn't tear my gaze from Dante. He was in there. He knew who we were.

"You can't do that, Carina."

My heart skittered up my throat, the hairs on the back of my neck standing straight up. I knew what she was doing before I turned around. I'd lost the war.

I spun around. Mom's chin rested in the metal u, her hand hovered over the red button.

"Mom!" I screamed. I lurched forward to stop her, but time stood still. Everything slowed, motion stopped except for Mom's hand pushing down the red button. The hammer pulled back, and this time, I knew it wouldn't fall on an empty chamber. I knew it like I knew Carina was my mother the first time I saw her. Like I knew A.J. could never be trusted. Like I knew I would never escape blood on my birthday.

Bright white light lit up the room. The explosion of gunpowder pierced my ears but did nothing to quiet the guttural scream from Dante, from me. Mom's eyes flared, her head snapped back out of the harness with enough force that she looked like she'd been in a car wreck. Sara and her yellow dress morphed into Mom and her red turtleneck flying through the air, both of them landing crumbled, broken, and . . .

"Mom!" I screamed again. "Mom!" The room shrank, sweat poured down my back, blood trickling from my nose from the inferno racing up my spine, willing her to live. Demanding she be okay.

Blood pooled under her face on the table where she fell forward. Her eyes blinked once, twice. That had to be a good sign.

"Momma," I fished a piece of hair from across her face.

"Cassie," she whispered, blood bubbling from her mouth. "Cassandra."

"Don't talk. I'm going to get you help."

Mom worked her lips, forming words with no sound. I was losing her. I ripped a piece of cloth from my shirt, pressing it to the hole in her head. Blood, her blood, oozed from the cloth in between my fingers.

Drip. Drip. Drip. It fell to the table.

"Mommy," I whispered, "you can't, you can't leave me, too."

"Cassie . . . " She swallowed, nearly choking on her own blood. Her body twitched like a fish out of water. "You were every good choice I should have made but was too scared to." A bloody smile blossomed across her lips. Porcelain white teeth now stained a vibrant red. "Every good choice I should. Made." Her eyes fluttered. "Too scared to."

Three patronizing misplaced claps shattered the silence that had filled the room. Chance clapped one last time. "Aw, sweet sacrifice, but it doesn't count. *You* have to hit the button, Cassie."

Rage ripped through me. I was so going to make him pay. I slammed my chin in the holder, hit the button, and withdrew my face before the hammer slammed down.

My blood ran cold as Chance tilted his head to get a better look at the fallen Queen of Hearts. I was wrong about Chance, he had one more look: murderer. His eyes sharpened like daggers, gone was the crazed boy who would do anything for the Shell of Clarity, for Dionysus's approval. In his place stood a man in full possession of every move he'd made, every maneuver he'd played, and with a crooked little twitch of his lip, he whispered with enough evil to rob a person of their soul, "Long live the queen."

"Cassandra?" A.J. gasped from behind me. "What have you done? He barely stood in the entrance, eyes judging me, shocked at the scene of my mother dying on the table.

"Help her," I ordered, pushing up from the table. The Shell of Clarity was gone. The spot where Dante had been rooted was vacated, and whatever heat I'd had from the Balanter power abandoned me too. Everything I was had been stolen by Chance Carrington.

FORTY-FOUR

A WHITE SATIN coffin, a red rose in her hand, and the crown she'd died protecting on her head. The Queen of Hearts, my mother, was dead. I stared at the casket, willing her to come back to me, but the winter wind answered *no* for the universe. It picked up an auburn tendril of her hair as an exclamation mark. Cara had been adamant about how and where Mom be laid to rest. Even down to the distant haunting sounds of "Auld Lang Syne" played by a lone bagpiper who wasn't allowed to be seen. Cara had threatened to impale the poor Scot with his bagpipes if she saw him, then she'd turned her feral eyes on me and I watched them shatter into a girl who just wanted her mom to be alive.

"It's her favorite," she choked out. Turns out that all the harsh and cold Carina Corazon had wished for was friendship, pledging that whatever changes life brought, old friends would never be forgotten, at least not by her.

I wanted to take her back to California, but Cara—her eyes went wide and filled with hurt and tears—Cara wanted her here in Las Vegas, with the rest of the Hearts' Royalty. When we met with the Woodlawn Cemetery mortician, Cara's calm exterior—chinked and cracked—completely crumbled when he suggested Mom be cremated, given the extensive nature of her . . . wound. While there'd been a sizeable entrance, it was the exit injury that had nearly taken off the back of Mom's head. I pushed down the guilt and let it mix with the bile churning in my gut.

This was *my* fault.

I'd never seen someone, let alone Cara, move so fast around a desk. She'd had the mortician by the neck with murder in her eyes. Jordan wrapped her up in his arms, whispering in her ear, while Beaux pried her white-knuckled fingers from the mortician's jugular. Beaux and Jordan finally walked Cara out to the car while I tapped the power of the Balanter and not only suggested the mortician apologize, but that he contact the Woodlawn Cemetery in Santa Monica for help.

He did.

And Cara seemed satisfied, as satisfied as a daughter could be burying her mother.

"Are we ready?" The priest asked.

I nodded. The funeral was small, a simple ceremony with nothing to write about, nothing to report on. I couldn't bear Mom's face split-screened with Sara's, both my mothers dead because of me and my choices. No church service, no royal gawkers, no mortal media. Four of us who, one way or another, were related or relegated to Carina Corazon, the Queen of Hearts, by fate.

But that didn't mean we were alone.

A tear dribbled down my cheek as I laced my fingers through Cara's. I let the salty bauble trickle a path down my face, ignoring the pain and the million other tears being held back by sheer will. We swore we wouldn't cry. If I learned anything from my mother, it was that there were eyes everywhere. Privacy was a luxury that no longer extended its privilege to Cara or me. I squeezed my sister's hand, watching her shoulders pull tight and her spine lock into place. Neither of us would give the Shadows the victory of knowing they'd plucked our very souls from our bodies. They'd never know taking the one thing we both loved brought us together, made us a united front . . . for now.

Another gentle winter breeze fluttered through the bare trees. It reminded me of the fairytale Sara would tell me when I was little. About a magical princess hidden by the winter winds. I didn't know it at the time, but it was the story of my birth. Somewhere out there, the fallen prince of the House of Spades, my father, was being held for a debt my mother had been too afraid to pay but ultimately gave her life for. I swallowed over the vision of her dead and the Roulette table. A.J. had used every hidden passage to get me back to The Eclectic. As far as anyone knew, Carina died without me involved, and no one knew what she'd wagered. Another wave of guilt swelled up from my stomach, lodging in my throat.

"Do you want to say anything?" the minister asked, interrupting my thoughts.

I shook my head before he continued. I jumped when Beaux put his hand on my shoulder, and the ache in my heart only intensified. He was too good, and I didn't deserve his loyalty.

"I failed you," was all he'd said at the mortuary. The grit of his jaw said he'd never let it happen again. But he hadn't failed me. I'd failed him. I'd failed Cara. A sob rattled my chest. I'd failed Mom. She'd done everything to protect me. Midas was right; I was the person who caused her demise.

Cara abandoned my hand, wrapping her arm around my waist, as if she knew what I was thinking. She'd eventually hate me, blame me, or both. It was only a matter of time before I lost her too.

"Not going to happen," she whispered.

"What's that?"

"Whatever you're thinking. A.J. and Beaux weren't the only ones watching you this semester." Her honey-colored eyes looked up at me. "I know your every tell. When you go calm as stone, it's usually when you're preparing to let go or close off a piece of your heart. Whatever or whoever you just gave up on, I won't let you."

Something rattled in my chest, shaking me from my very core. I tore my gaze from hers, searching the gray skies for something that didn't exist.

Forgiveness.

Forgiveness I didn't deserve. I knew Cara meant every word now, even if she would regret it later. We were sisters who would never change. How much she loved me, how much she'd hate me when she found out what I'd lost, is what would eventually change.

"Bow your heads," the priest instructed.

I did as I was told, hoping to find solace in his words, but we'd asked for a moment of silence. No words, just memories. Memories of Mom and the night we met rushed through me. Cara and her New Year's Eve tiara, before we knew we were sisters. A.J. . . . God, so many moments with A.J. My parents the moment before the car accident. Mom pelting me with Fruit Loops and Cara helping me get ready. We hadn't had enough time. Not nearly enough. Not with any of them.

I raised my head as the priest said, "Amen." He blessed Mom and closed her coffin.

"Will you be staying for the internment?" the priest asked.

"No," Beaux answered, turning his focus to me. "You and Cara have been summoned to The Council Chambers."

"Why?" Cara asked. There was no more fight in her voice. Not today.

I wondered how long it would take. A cold chill ran through me. I knew I couldn't trust A.J. to keep my secret. His duty to his House would always outweigh anything he'd felt for me. I'd sacrificed the Queen of Hearts, essentially killing our House's existence.

"I'm too young to rule, according to the gods." I stepped away from Cara and Beaux, taking in the last moments of them looking at me like a friend instead of a murderer. The skin around Beaux's eyes crinkled, like he was trying to pry open my mind and see what was going on inside. It was better he didn't know. I didn't think I could bear seeing on Beaux the disgusted, appalled look that crawled across A.J.'s features the night Mom died.

My protector nodded, his shoulders pulling up in a way that said, *don't give up, not yet*, but reality was setting in. Actions had consequences and my actions . . . I couldn't finish the thought. I was standing next to one of the consequences of my actions, and I had the nauseating feeling that my mother's death wasn't the biggest price I'd pay for believing I could change fate.

Cara's hands flew to her hips. "And?" she pressed.

"Midas?" The name came from my lips like a question. Like a plea that maybe A.J. would surprise me.

"Let's not get ahead of ourselves," Beaux interjected. "This could merely be a formality of assigning a regent."

I cocked an eyebrow. "You know he'll appoint himself. Midas has waited eons to get his hands on the House of Hearts, on me."

Beaux's hands fisted.

"The other Houses will never stand for this. They'll fold our line before they let that happen." I finished, hoping they would and I could take my secret to the grave.

"You think Midas is going to make a play for Mom's crown?" Cara asked. "You don't?"

Jordan stepped forward, wrapping Cara up in his arms. "Then we fight."

"No," Beaux said. "We go. We hear what Midas tries to pull. We see if your boy A.J. steps up, does what is right——"

"He's not my boy," I interrupted, terrified he *would* do what was right and tell everyone what actually happened to Carina.

Beaux folded his arms across his chest, his tell that the matter was closed. "And if he doesn't, then we fight to the bitter end. Yes?"

"To the bitter fucking end," Cara parroted.

"She really is your sister, Cassandra," Beaux muttered, his fingers flying across the face of his phone as we walked to our limo.

❤

FIFTEEN MINUTES WAS all I was given to go from grieving daughter to embattled future leader of the House of Hearts. Beside the fact that I'd killed my mother, I wasn't old enough by the gods' law to lead the house, which meant a regent had to be assigned. Assigned by the House of Midas. The pit in my stomach grew, threatening to swallow me whole. The black limousine pulled up in front of The Plaza Hotel. Thirteen floors were all that separated me and the fate of my House.

Beaux's phone chimed four times in a row. A smile pulled at the scar on his lip.

"Who is it?" I asked.

"The other Jacks. None of the other Houses knew you were summoned."

"That makes me all warm and fuzzy."

Beaux shot me a sideways look. "They're on their way."

"Who?"

"Everyone." Beaux slipped his phone into the breast pocket of his suit. "You're mine to protect. I won't fail you again." He tweaked my nose before slipping his hand in mine. Beaux glanced over his shoulder. "To the bitter fucking end, mate. You hear me?"

Jordan smiled, clasping Beaux's hand. They'd battle to the death for me and a lie I could never fess up to. Not if I wanted to keep the House of Hearts alive.

I forced a smile Jay's way as we entered the Plaza's private elevator. Over the past year, this elevator seemed to always be leading me to moments of life or death. Today was no different. Las Vegas would always be me dancing on the blade of peril and pleasure. I guess I really wasn't any different than a tourist. Beaux stepped in front of me as the doors slid back at the thirteenth floor. I knew heavy black doors waited for us at the end of a white marble hallway. What I didn't remember was the ominous way our shoes echoed off the marble. The way the hallway seemed to elongate, making each step a futile effort to reach an end, any end.

Beaux stole a quick look over his shoulder at me. His muscles rippled like a dog's hackles before the first bite of a fight.

"Cass, you listen to what Midas says. You offer no answers. You make no apologies. Force his hand. Let's see how far this fuckwit will push with the council scrutinizing his every move."

Cara giggled. "Fuckwit?"

A smile pulled at the scar on Beaux's lip. The scar he'd earned protecting me and my reign. Cara had been wrong about him. It wasn't that Beaux didn't care about anything before me, he just hadn't had anything to care about before me. Nothing to protect. Nothing his that wasn't his brother's first. My heart ached. He'd always been second best, and I'd made him feel the same way. I threaded my fingers through Beaux's, noticing the slight start at my touch. He was a good man. If this was the life I was cursed to live, then it could have been a lot worse without Beaux by my side. Still, the consummation ceremony for the House of Hearts would be altered in my decree.

The heavy black doors opened before I could fish out my card. The same butler from the last time I was here, in the same black suit and white gloves, stood guard.

"They've been expecting you," he purred.

"Who is they?" Cara asked.

No answer. The butler kept his eyes trained on me, waiting for me to announce my House and my entourage. Cara shifted on her heels, her own set of hackles bristling at the disregard to who she was, who she had been. It was bitter to fall from grace, worse when it was nothing of your own doing. She'd lost out on the birth order lottery. I promised the gods she'd never feel this way again.

"My sister asked you a question, I suggest you answer her now."

The butler's cool façade cracked, his left eyebrow drawing up in a subtle affront. His eyes glistened with an uncanny wash of anger as he stared right at me. "The House of Mid—"

I raised a finger, cutting him off, and then pointed to Cara. "My sister asked the question. You answer her."

White bushy eyebrows furrowed on a stoic face. "That's not protocol."

"Yeah, lots of things are about to change. You should get used to it."

"As should you," he muttered.

Beaux squeezed my fingers. Apparently, the slight tick of the butler's lip hadn't been lost on my Jack.

The Midas kiss-ass turned his body toward Cara, clicked his heels, and answered, "The House of Midas."

A.J. My stomach dropped. I stepped forward, not waiting for the butler to invite me in, certain I'd just added my family to the king of gold's undesired list as well. Given the butler's response, they would never be welcomed here. It didn't matter if they sided with me or not, just showing up with me was enough. My pulse jumped when we hit the hallway with the rich wood panels and the photos of The Houses and their reigning royalty. Had they changed Mom's picture? Beaux threaded his fingers through mine.

"It's empty," he whispered so only I could hear. "You will get through this, Princess."

I forced a smile and started down the hall. My getting through this, that's what I was afraid of. I *would* get through this, but at the cost, at the demise of how many people? How many other lives would be ruined because of me? Mom's empty frame seemed to dance off the wall. The missing image called for me to come back, to pay homage. I stepped into the great room. At the head of the onyx table, with fingers steepled under his chin, sat Midas. To his right stood A.J. Judgment fixed in every hard line marring his forehead.

"You have a problem, Cassandra. I have a solution." Midas pushed away from the table. He seemed younger than I remembered, less ancient. His white hair still hung limp, the ends dusting his shoulders, and his blue eyes were still sharp and deadly.

I willed my feet to carry me to the table, hoping the next-in-line veneer held. "You always do," I answered. Pulling out the chair opposite Midas, the chair with our House's crest engrained in wood on the back, I sat like I'd watched Carina do a million times. Slow, steady, and with a false confidence oozing from me, I lowered myself into the chair designated for the House of Hearts. I could only pray Midas bought it.

"Your House is without royalty."

"I'm royalty. My sister is royalty."

Midas tipped his head. "Eligible royalty."

I swallowed the hard pill of formality.

"May I continue?" Midas asked.

Beaux bristled behind me. Yeah, I felt it too. The air of finality descending on us. We were marching down a path that wasn't going to end well, and it sure as hell wouldn't be ending without bloodshed.

I stayed quiet, knowing any waiver in my voice would be heard, if not by Midas, then by A.J. And I didn't know where my ex-boyfriend's loyalties lay. I didn't know if he'd already chosen the duty to notify his house or the honor of protecting my secret.

"I'm assigning myself regent to the House of Hearts."

Cara rushed the table. "We just buried our mother and you're making a play?"

"If I don't, then the Shadows will." Midas smiled. "Given where your mother's body was found, we don't know what transpired. We don't know what she wagered for Dante's life."

A.J. shifted behind Midas. He hadn't told Midas I was responsible. I was the one who made the wager with the Shadows. It was me, I wanted to scream.

"My mother would never—"

"Cara, she did." Cara and I spun around at Gia's voice coming from the back of the room. "She called my mom."

I felt the pinch of confusion, and when the Queen of Clubs spoke, I knew Mom was protecting me from the grave. I spun in my mother's chair, finding Gia and my mother's best friend stepping into the great room.

"It's true. Carina called my service. She left a message, knowing I'd get it too late to talk sense into her. She was going to save Dante." Her blue eyes found mine, piercing me with a look as if to say *for you.*

"No," Cara whispered, stealing my attention. Jordan caught her. I stood and let him place my baby sister in her rightful seat. "That makes no sense."

"Why?" Midas pushed Cara for an answer, an answer she would never know, could never know the truth to.

"Because she wouldn't." Cara caught herself, her formal training kicked in. "She would never betray her House."

Another sliver of guilt wedged its way into my soul. She may never have, but I certainly did. I'd been willing to sell all our souls for the possibility of an illusion. The possibility that all the fragmented pieces of the people who made me would make me a whole person.

The pronounced thrumming of feet falling on marble filled the room. Beaux was right; they were all here, all the remaining House royalty. My mother's friends, my friends, and the Jacks that protected all of us were here. They would fight to their death to protect me, my sister, and the House my mother died for. If they knew, none of them would forgive me. How could they, when I could barely breathe, let alone utter the words?

"Whether she did or didn't doesn't matter." Midas held up his palm, silencing the room. "The fact remains that the House of Hearts' heir apparent is too young to rule."

Olivia's mom stepped forward, her hands resting on my shoulders. I knew what she had to do. No matter how it pained her, she had to fold my House. Midas was right. If I couldn't rule, then the Shadows would make a play for our holdings, for our people, for our power. And if Midas was regent, the balance of power would tip. The other Houses would be at risk.

"As highest ranking member of the House of Spades, I urge the other Houses to join my entreaty to fold the House of—"

"Wait." A.J. looked through the crowd of royals, something pulled at the edges of his lips. My gaze landed on Zee. Of course. She was dressed in a black sheath dress, like she was the one who was supposed to be in mourning.

He nodded, a smile blossoming across his face. The kind of smile I used to put there. "Let her in."

"Who is it?" Midas pushed.

And unfamiliar voice called out from the back of the room, "Someone who has a word to discuss with you."

FORTY-FIVE

THE AIR CRACKLED with the electricity of a fight and the fragrance of demise. I thought it was the death of my house, but given the way Midas was paling, maybe not.

"Excuse me, lovely." It was a petite woman—no, a lady. This woman was the epitome of elegance and class. She was a lady through and through, even when she dismissively stepped around Zee like she was a column or a tree or a mound of dirt. Grace and poise dressed in a form-fitting black dress that proved you were never too old to be stunningly gorgeous.

"Grandma," Cara whispered.

"What?" I stepped toward my sister, certain I hadn't heard her right. No way would everyone fail to tell me I had family beyond Cara and Carina. They couldn't all keep a secret like this.

Zee cleared her throat. "The House of Hearts' Queen Mother would like to be seen."

"No," Midas snapped.

The woman slightly tipped her head, but the ripples of the minute gesture were like shock waves from a nuclear bomb. "Don't make me call Poseidon. You know I'm his favorite." My grandmother—the word was foreign on my lips—patted her clutch and the immortal king froze.

"Why are you here, Victoria?"

"I am here to minimize our defeats and move forward." She scanned the room, and when no one budged or murmured, she tipped her head like my mother had done so many times before and said, "I have a solution."

"No."

"You say that, but I'm certain the rest of the room would like to hear one more option before they fold the House of Hearts and have to explain to the gods why." The soft lines of my grandmother's heart-shaped face hardened. She was as shrewd as she was stunning.

"I would," The Queen of Clubs finally spoke up, hardly more than a whisper.

"Sarina, my darling." My grandmother strode over to Gia and her mom. "You're as stunning as ever."

Mrs. M curtsied while Gia stared star-struck. I couldn't be sure if it was because of my grandmother or the way her mother had just transformed into a teenager asking to stay out past curfew. Given the subtle way Mrs. M. worked her lip, I had to go with the latter.

"Your daughter is a spitting image of you. The girls turned out beautifully." She glanced over her shoulder at Midas. "Amazing what they did without us knowing, or meddling. Not everyone needs a silver spoon in their mouth to grow up with a sense of nobility and dignity." She glided around the room with an air of aristocracy you could only be born with, an air of entitlement I was sorely lacking.

Victoria stopped in front of Helen and pursed her lips, evaluating the House of Diamonds' heir apparent. "Helen."

Helen's face blanched before she nodded and acknowledged she was put into her place with the simple utterance of her name.

"I'm sorry to hear your mother is ill, but I see she's made amazing strides with you and your . . . decorum."

Helen's eyes went wide at the assessment that found her lacking.

Midas grumbled.

Olivia's mom pressed, "Victoria, you have a solution?"

"I do. It's a bit unconventional, but I think it will suffice." There was a glint in her eyes that made something churn in my belly. "Seeing how forward-thinking you were with Cassandra, I hope you'll take my suggestion seriously."

The Queen of Spades and Clubs' shoulders sagged. My grandmother hadn't known I existed until last year. She didn't seek me out because she didn't care; she didn't come looking for me because she was pissed she'd been kept in the dark. Gods only knew how my grandmother would react when she found out I was the cause of her daughter's death.

A warning whispered in my head. I needed to get Cara out of here and far away from Las Vegas.

Victoria took the silence as a gesture of approval. "I'll be regent until Cassandra's of age."

"Why?" the question bubbled up from me.

"I'm sorry?" Victoria turned to me. The first time she acknowledged my presence.

"Where've you been?" I clarified.

"Henderson."

"Ten minutes away. Why didn't she tell me? Why didn't *you* find me?"

Victoria closed the space between us. Up close, she was even more stunning. Porcelain skin lay flawlessly over a heart-shaped face. She had my mother's honey eyes, and her hair was the same warm auburn as mine. Victoria gathered my hands in hers.

"Not here. Not now. But someday, I'll explain it all. Right now, I need to save our House and your reign."

Victoria stepped away from me, leaving me tucked out of the way at the edge of the table, while she sat in the chair next to Cara. Every logical thought I had said to run, but instinct told me to stay put, play the game, and listen to what she had to say. She was going to use my House to regain her power, but I was going to use her to save my House to fight for another day. Today was the day I started using everything Mom had taught me. *I need you to start analyzing every angle of a problem, even if it doesn't look like a problem. Every statement someone utters to you has an agenda,* Mom's voice cautioned.

"I'm waiting, Ladon." Victoria folded her hands at the table. Back ramrod straight, legs properly crossed at the ankles, not the knees, she was a ninety-pound force to be reckoned with.

Midas's features hardened at the use of his mortal name. Resolve settled into the weathered lines centuries of imprisonment had carved. No matter how opulent the bars, we really were all just prisoners in a gilded cage.

A billion-dollar smile lit up Victoria's face. She already knew she'd won the reprieve for the House of Hearts. She turned her back on Midas, missing the way his eyes turned to liquid fury. While she lobbied the rest of the Houses to support her regency, Midas watched her, vengeance rippling off him in murderous waves. Midas had an agenda, A.J. was right about that, but what was it and how did it play into my mother's death? Midas caught me watching him, and despite the audience, he launched himself at me. His heavy chair clattered to the floor as his frail hands found the strength of an angry army wrapping around my arm and hauling me up to my tiptoes.

I didn't have time to react.

"What did you wager for Dante's life?" His eyes were wild, crazed with obsession.

"I don't know what Carina wagered," I whispered another lie.

Midas grip tightened, pulling me closer to him. "Don't *lie* to me, Cassandra. You should know I can spot a lying, cheating Heart. Ask you mother."

My heart stopped. He was wrong. I had lied and cheated death and my heart would never be the same. My mother's death would have its vengeance. The notion lodged in my gut.

"Let go of my granddaughter, or so help me . . ." Victoria's unspoken threat hung in the air, gaining weight with every second that passed until the room could barely handle the burden. Then, as if she knew the exact breaking moment, Victoria, former Queen of Hearts and my grandmother, leveled Midas with a final blow. "I will notify the gods of your power play."

"My power play?" Midas nearly choked on his words. His crazed eyes darted between Victoria and A.J. and the royalty in the room.

No way. There was no way A.J. would have been, could have been a party to this deception. He knew how I'd struggled with my parents' deaths. Grappled with the notion that all this time, I had a second mother, a second family. He wouldn't . . . My thought was cut off by another shake of my body, this one rattling my senses. Midas's ice-blue eyes glittered with rage. Mere inches from his face, I could see the centuries, eons even, of pent-up anger dancing under the surface of the façade of a man who desired nothing more than to be a full-fledged god.

"I'll approve your regency," he spat, lips snarling like a rabid wolf, "but only if she tells me what Carina wagered to free Dante."

"How dare you." I heard Victoria behind me, so close I could feel her warm breath on my neck and the smell of spearmint. "I don't know your part, Ladon, but I'm certain your hand is as red with my daughter's blood as the Shadow who took her wager. Now let. Her. Go."

Time stretched. Seconds turned into the very centuries Midas had been exiled. Left helpless, I saw the debate to end me now versus taking another order from another royal play in his mind. The deliberation of how bad would it be if he offed me warred with the fear the gods still held over him. Midas let me go as quickly as he'd snatched me up.

I stumbled backward; A.J. caught me before I hit the ground.

"You will pay for this, A.J.," he muttered under his breath, just loud enough for me to know his grandson's demise had been sealed and the result would be resting on my conscience.

"I know." A.J. shifted under my weight. "Do the other Houses acknowledge the new regent?" A.J. asked, while righting me.

Hesitant affirmations sounded from my mother's friends. They'd have to explain their actions to their Kings, and given how tenuous our alliance had been after the tournament, it was going to be a hard sell. A.J.'s hands lingered around my waist, chasing away the chill he'd put there only a few weeks ago. This didn't change anything, I tried to remind myself. He still was the next to rule the House of Midas, no matter what threats his grandfather threw his way. He would still run the gaming commission. He still shared a home with Zee. He still destroyed my heart. A.J. spared me one more look before sliding another nail into his coffin.

"Grandfather?" A.J. pressed.

"Very well." Midas cut A.J. with a look that should have left him dead where he stood. "The House of Midas acknowledges the Heart's regent, now leave." Midas didn't wait for us to acknowledge his demand or his blessing on Victoria's regency before he left. The room exhaled. Houses clumped together. Their muffled whispers bled into shuffling feet until the room was empty except for me, my sister wrapped up in Jordan's arms, and the grandmother I never knew I had.

Victoria stepped forward, arms out ready to usher us out of the chambers like the other families. The others complied without thought, but I was done being blindly led.

"Before we go—"

"Not here," Victoria cut me off. "I know the questions you have, but I won't be answering them here."

"And I won't be going with you until a few of them are answered. Let's start with an easy one: Didn't you want to see me?"

Victoria's honey eyes softened but not all the way. There was still a ferocity in them that made me wonder if I'd ever get a straight answer out of her, one that didn't suit her needs or agenda.

"Of course."

"But?" I pressed.

"Carina told me about you last year. I wanted—" She stopped herself. "I may live in Henderson, but I might as well have been dead to you." She had a wonderful low voice, soft and throaty, with a way of pulling someone in.

I didn't buy it.

"Cass," Cara's fingers wrapped around my arm. "Once a royal's reign is over, they're dismissed. They live on in memories and decrees, but they're never seen."

Cara started at the look I gave her.

"I don't care. I never knew her. I never knew she existed. She could have—"

"Broken tradition? Been banished?" Victoria added.

I turned, taking in my grandmother. "Then why now?"

"Because you needed me." She managed a tremulous smile. "You lost your mother. A mother you only knew for a year." Her eyes searched mine, looking for an answer I could never give. "I lost my daughter."

Cara shuddered next to me, reminding me I had more to think of than myself. I had Cara. I had a House. And I had a fallen Queen to avenge.

I dug deep for the strength Mom always seemed to possess and cleared my throat. "I'm sure you'll fill me in. I need to go to The Eclectic. Meet with the management team."

"I can take Cara home with me." Victoria wrapped her arm around Cara's shoulders.

Cara nodded.

"Fine." I started for the front doors.

Victoria's steps chased after me, stepping in front of me before I hit the elevator.

"Your mother would have prepared for something like this, just like you will now. In her room, there's a floor safe." She reached into her bra and pulled out a slip of paper.

I stared at the elegant woman who'd just felt herself up in the hallway, like Mom had done in Malaga.

"Take it, Cassandra." Victoria pushed the paper into my hand. "I'll take care of Cara. Get your mother's house in order. Do what you need to." She squeezed my hand. She couldn't have known what I'd done, could she?

No.

The elevator doors slid open, and before I could chase after the hidden meaning behind Victoria's *"do what you need to,"* we were headed for the lobby. By the fourth floor, the gravity of Mom's burial and what had transpired in the Council Chambers started to settle, and the more distant Cara became. By the time Victoria's driver pulled up to the front of the Plaza, Cara had gone from ferocious planner to zombie.

I didn't know what Victoria and Cara's relationship was like; they obviously knew each other, but past that—

"I'll take care of her. Do what you need to." Victoria interrupted my thoughts, hesitating like she wanted to say more, but finally resigned and slipped into the car.

My cell pinged in my pocket. Beaux looked at me, eyebrows pulling up, asking who it was. I fished out my phone.

702-555-4722:

We'll find him.

"Wrong number," I quickly shoved my cell back in my pocket. Cold sweat trickled down my spine at the unknown number and Isaac's message. The Shadows couldn't find Chance, for more reasons than the obvious. I had no idea what they'd do to Dante. And worse, they'd know Carina's death wasn't because she was the player. I had to find Chance. I had to fix this or at least repair what I could. I needed my passport and a quiet place. A different kind of guilt started souring in my belly as our car pulled up. I slipped into the back seat before Beaux could press the issue.

"I need to go to the Dayton Complex," I said to the driver.

Beaux slid next to me, cocking an eyebrow.

"I need to pack a few things." It was a half-truth. I couldn't very well tell him I was about to break about a million and one rules and leave without a trace. Silence picked at the already strained car ride to the Dayton Complex. Beaux was a smart guy, too smart sometimes. The way his leg bounced, the way he plucked at the crease in his pant leg; he knew something was up. He knew me.

"We'll only be a few minutes," I instructed the driver. Beaux and all his questions followed behind me, through the quad, into the deserted lobby, and the ride up the elevator to our dorm rooms. The subtle tick of a muscle along his jaw told me he wasn't buying whatever this ruse was.

I slid my key into the lock, but the knob gave way. It was already unlocked. My heart sunk to my toes as Beaux pushed me behind him, slowly opening the door.

Afternoon sunlight bounced off the disturbed dust particles in my dorm room, creating a silhouette effect around the boy standing at the sliding door.

"What are you doing here, A.J.?"

He turned around, hand sliding into his pants pocket like it'd done the first time I'd met him. We were full circle again. Only this time, we both knew my secret.

"We need to talk." A.J. nodded to the couch. Beaux nodded in agreement, long meaningful strides already carrying him to his seat. Both boys in my life eyed the spot on the couch I was expected to take. They already had this figured out. They always had everything figured out when it came to me. I had no say in my life, not when it came to keeping me safe. What they couldn't see was in keeping me safe, they only pushed me to be more dangerous.

Resolve settled in my gut. I knew what I had to do, and I knew I could only do it alone.

"I already know what you're going to say."

"No, you don't, Cass." Even from this distance I could see something shift in A.J.'s eyes. Something telling me to trust him, but I'd gone down that rabbit hole with him once before. His "trust me" always ended up with me in front of Midas accounting for my actions.

"I can't do this with you. Not today. Not right now." I felt a warmth start at the base of my spine. They'd both hate me for what I was about to do, but I needed a head start. I needed to fix this, alone.

"I'm sorry." The Balanter heat swept up my spine, sweat dribbled down my face. I need you to stay put. There's something I have to fix this on my own." My gaze darted between the two boys sworn to protect me. They were both different as night and day. Their reactions were so different from the other the moment before they slipped under my control. Hurt and confusion flashed across A.J.'s eyes before the ache of betrayal seeped into the gold flecks. Beaux's, on the other hand, showed admiration that I'd finally taken a stand, fought for what I wanted. He may not have agreed with the course I needed to take, but his approval was stamped in those bright green eyes. I grabbed my passport and my Pithos box from the bedroom, eyeing the two boys on my couch.

"Don't move until you feel the first rays of morning light from the balcony of your faces." I slipped out of my dorm and locked the door. Twelve hours' head start should give me plenty of time to get lost in the underworld.

❤

MOM'S MANAGEMENT TEAM left with the binder of instructions I'd found in her floor safe. Just like Victoria said she had. The front door clicked shut, and for the first time in over a week, I was alone. A faucet dripped from somewhere deep in the kitchen, echoing off the walls of Mom's house. It seemed like even the house was mourning the loss of its Queen. Grief finally dislodged from somewhere deep inside me. I was too young to have buried two mothers. I swallowed hard, the shard of pain lighting me up from the inside. A dead rose sat on the mantel next to our new family portrait. I'd have to schedule another sitting, one with our grandmother.

I sunk into the white plush carpeting, thinking about Victoria. She was an audacious woman. Maybe that's why she'd been able to stare down Midas in the Council Chambers when I could only bow under his god-like gaze. Cleary, the new Interim-Queen of Hearts knew how to rule the Heart line and terrified the Head of the House of Midas.

It was a new era.

The balance of power was upset because I couldn't control my childlike impulses. My mother's friends—the other Queens—didn't know what to make of The Queen Mother, Victoria, stepping up and saving the House of Hearts. Maybe they were afraid their own mothers would want to relive the past. Maybe they were terrified of how Granny V ruled. I really didn't care how she ruled. She saved the House my choices nearly ruined.

"You were every good choice I should have made but was too scared to."
Mom's dying words bombed my thoughts. The shrapnel of their syllables
lodged in my heart. I doubled over; the agony gripped my soul, shaking me
to my core. Warm tears ran down my face. She was wrong. Chance was right;
I was everyone's worst nightmare. All of this was my fault.

Chance was still nowhere to be found. A second text from Isaac let me
know Dionysus had a price on his head. A figure high enough that would make
the billionaires list turn and take notice. Dionysus didn't have to pay me; I'd
kill the kid myself. I could feel the idea knocking around in my head, fusing
together with the nagging question of why he was willing to turn on Dionysus
and take off with the Shell of Clarity. A ray of light cut through the slit in the
drapes. If I couldn't find Chance, then there was only one person, one god,
who could answer that question.

Poseidon, the very god who'd fashioned the shell and tied it to my life.

And you know, it was about time we had a little chat.

I pulled myself off the floor and headed for my bedroom. The door
bounced off the wall as I headed for my closet, grabbed the carryon bag, and
threw in some clothes and underwear. My overnight bag was in the bathroom.
I fluttered around the room like a fly trying to escape its Venus flytrap. The
binder from high school went in my backpack. If I was going to end up in Fiji,
I'd better read up on the proper way to chew out a Greek god. He was going
to tell me the story about the shell and then he was going to release my dad of
whatever debt he owed.

I'd get a ticket at the airport and text Beaux and A.J before I took off. If
they had even the slightest idea—

The sound of the doorbell followed by a loud knock on the front door
rebounded down the hallway. I knew it wasn't Beaux or A.J. If they had
broken free of my command, they wouldn't have been so polite as to knock.
A.J. would've busted through the secret passage in my bedroom, Beaux not
too far behind him. Another knock, this one not quite as demanding, drew
me closer to the front door. I'd left them both at the Dayton Complex with
the final command not to leave the room until the first rays of morning
touched them. It was a bit dramatic, but that was the Sassy in me. With
everyone still on winter break, no one would be bothering them.

I pulled open the door, expecting to see Olivia or Gia or both on the other side.

"Hello, spitfire." Isaac leaned into the doorway.

My mouth guppied. *Open. Close. Open.*

"Cat got your tongue?" He drawled.

"You?" I could taste the venom of my words.

He looked past me, a devilish smile pulling at his lips when he spotted my luggage.

"Figured you would pull a stunt like this when I saw you tear out of the Dayton Complex like a bat out of hell."

"And that's your concern, why?" The warmth of control rushed up my spine. I knew exactly where to stick Isaac, and I was certain the sun would never shine there.

He threw his head back, a chuckle echoing from somewhere deep and dark inside him.

"Your powers don't work on me." He skidded the pad of his finger along my jaw line. "Don't worry, I'm coming along for the ride. Consider me your chaperone."

My turn to chuckle. "You weren't invited."

"True, but that's never stopped me before." He stepped around me and grabbed my two bags. "This it?"

I nodded, still not sure why my powers didn't work on him and why he was coming along.

"Chop, chop. Our plane to Australia leaves in an hour."

"I'm not going to Australia."

"If you want to catch up with Chance and Daddy-o, you are." Isaac backed out of my house, almost bowing, paying a last homage to my mother.

"And they're going to Australia?"

Isaac ran his fingers through his hair, just like A.J. had done so many other times, before he leveled me with a patronizing look. "I don't need a god to tell me where a dick is headed."

He laughed at what had to be a confused look on my face.

"You're not the only with ancient know-it-all telling you your future. You going to tell me now or later what you wagered?"

"Yayati?" I ignored Isaac's question about my wager.

"We'll have to figure out the meaning of his 'You must acquire the Hearts' island,' together." The shrill sound of an alarm echoed down the hallway.

"Don't be too long. I've got the elevator holding. And Cassandra, Yayati told me you'd fess up about the wager sooner or later." He turned and sauntered down the hall.

I stood in the doorway, one foot in the world I was expected to rule with no emotions, and the other in the hallway, contemplating leaving Las Vegas with a Shadow. Not just a Shadow, but also the ex-boyfriend of my cousin, the older brother of my ex-boyfriend, and the Shadows' second in command. I grabbed my purse, my fingers tightening around the strap, hoping to strangle out a different alternative, but there wasn't one. If I wanted answers, if I was going to right this wrong, then I was going to have to do whatever it took, including leaving Las Vegas with Isaac, the Shadows' Second. I closed the door. The deadbolt slid into place, hardening a place in me I knew I wouldn't be accessing ever again.

My heart was dead, even if my life depended on it.

EPILOGUE

Cass, I've been writing you for so long. I know you're getting my messages. I haven't told the guys you're in Paris. At least, I think that's where you are. That's where you were in August when I broke into Midas' office. Christmas break starts tomorrow. I can't believe you've been gone for almost a year. It's . . . It's not the same here without you. I'm not sure if you picked up on it, but we've missed you.

I've missed you.

Beaux thought your A.W.O.L. routine was funny

up until the third month. A.J. looks like shit. When he isn't searching for you ... He's changed, Cass. And before you add some pissy remark about Zee being there for A.J., stop. She's been looking for you, too. The three of them are almost as desperate to find you as I am. There's a rumor floating around that you disappeared with Isaac.

Olivia's hurt peeled off the screen and bitch slapped me.

Cass, if that's the case, it's okay. I don't know why you'd leave with him, but if you're out there, and you're with him . . . then at least I know you're safe. He'll take care of you, Cass. He's a lying piece of shit, but he knows how much you mean to his brother . . . and to me.

Ms. Maddox said you finished out last year with online classes. She also said you're doing your year abroad program now. She's keeping your vanishing act a secret, but she doesn't think you're coming back. Neither does Helen. Tia's on the fence about your return. Beaux said once he finds you, he's going to throw you over his shoulder and drag you back, something about being his to protect. Cara just sits in your room and cries. She needs you, Cass. We all do.

  Write me.

  I promise I won't share it with anyone.

  Just let me know you're okay.

  Your cousin,

  Livi.

I swallowed over the lump in my throat. She'd started calling herself Livi a month ago. It was a dirty-ass trick, and one day I'd . . . Finishing that thought was getting harder and harder as the days waned on. Warm air billowed the curtains, bringing in the tropical floral scent from the island I'd called home for the last three months.

We'd missed Chance and my dad in Australia by six hours, according to the hotel records. I'd taken a page out of my cousin's breaking and entering handbook and applied it to computers. We waited four days for a hit to come across on anything Chance would use for identification or purchases, but nothing. Isaac had the brilliant plan to bring in Poseidon. After a few weeks of convincing me he knew best and he had a vested interest in bringing me back to Olivia alive, I conceded. It'd taken Isaac and me three months and questionable promises to a couple of wayward demigods to pick up Poseidon's trail in the Canary Islands and follow him to Europe. Once we caught up with him in Paris and submitted our request for an audience, we sat and waited. For two months, Isaac and I would make a daily trek along the Seine to the Fontaines de la Concorde, the entrance to Poseidon's Parisian home, only to be turned away. Until one day, Poseidon's courier showed up on our doorstep, handed us a note that told us to head to Copenhagen, Denmark, and wait. Apparently, I wasn't the only rebellious child on the planet. What little Isaac could dig up said Poseidon's son had fallen hard for Neptune's daughter. Neither of the dads were happy about it. Poseidon ruled the ocean, but Neptune ruled the sea and freshwater. It was symbiotic relationship until Neptune caught Poseidon's son making waves in his daughter's bedroom.

I snorted.

"What?" Isaac asked, walking into the living room from the lanai.

"Was thinking about Neptune and Poseidon."

Isaac shot me a quizzical look before turning and shaking off the last of the ocean from his hair.

"That was two countries and six months ago." Isaac checked the wrap of his towel before he shimmied out of his swim trunks. "Why would you be thinking about them?"

"Can you not do that?" I pointed to the mound of wet swimwear.

I knew what came next. The crude smile, the gross innuendo, then the compliance to do as I asked. Isaac's smile slipped as he kicked the wet trunks out the sliding door.

"What's wrong?" I asked.

"Why's anything got to be wrong?"

The past eleven months of close quarters with Isaac had given me front row seats to his many moods when we were stuck somewhere. He'd start off playful and annoying. Loving every obscene remark that left his lips and relishing their impact on me. By the end of the first month he'd start huffing around, getting antsy; that usually lasted a few weeks, maybe another month. Then he'd get quiet, withdrawn, like he was summoning some sort of power willing Poseidon to see us. Answer our questions. It was usually then we'd get word from Poseidon's royal courier that he'd hightailed it out of the place, and we were given the riddle to our next possible meeting spot.

Three freaky Isaac feelings and three times we were told to move on.

"You think he's gone again?" I asked, pushing away from the computer, from Olivia.

"No, it's something else. Something different."

Before I could form another question, a knock sounded from the door, sending my heart scurrying up my throat.

"Maybe this is it?"

"Don't count on it, Princess." Isaac crossed his arms over his chest, swirling up memories of A.J., as I hurried to the door. More intent on leaving the memory of A.J. that Isaac always seemed to conjure up with a stance or comment, I looked back. Afternoon light filtered in through the gauzy curtains, I couldn't help but think this was how all thriller movies started: A half-naked boy, an inexperienced girl, and an ominous knock on the door.

The cool handle turned easily in my slick palm. I promised myself I wasn't going to scream when Freddy Kruger or Jason from the *Friday the Thirteenth* movies stood on the other side. The door edged open slowly, almost like it was under its own power. My heart thrashed against my ribs.

"Princess Cassandra." The words were just as brutal as the imaginary knives I'd pictured flying at us. I shot Isaac a lethal look over my shoulder as I let the door swing all the way open. It wasn't a mass murderer. It was worse, so much more insidious.

It was Poseidon's courier.

Dressed in a royal blue suit, he clicked his heels together, inclined his head ever so slightly as he extended an envelope my direction. I stared at his white coral cufflink; stamped with Poseidon's seal, not ready to accept that we'd be moving on. My questions still weren't going to be answered. I shook my head, not ready to take the dismissal missal.

"No." I snapped. "You go back and tell Poseidon to stop packing and start answering my questions."

The courier raised his eyes, the irises became fluid, churning like they were being influenced by the ocean before turning zombie opaque.

"What?" he asked. The courier's meek voice altered, deepened. When the courier stood, there was something different about him, not just the freaky eye trick. Something more. His subordinate stance shifted. His chest filled with a confidence that was almost visible. Even his blond ponytail seemed to thicken, turn more voluptuous in front of my eyes.

"Cass," Isaac called out, his footsteps quickening on the tile floor behind me before his hands pulled me back a step or two. "Don't piss off the God of the Ocean." Isaac started to kneel, pulling me with him.

"What are you talking about?" I shook free of Isaac's grip.

"Cassandra Venus Vera," the courier's voice now boomed. Gone was the mousey squeak of the courier, replaced with the tenor of authority.

"Oh, shit," I murmured, stealing a glance at Isaac.

He nodded for me to get down and pay some respect.

"Poseidon?" I whispered, still standing.

"You demand answers?" Meaty arms crossed his chest and opaque blue eyes stared through me. "Here is your answer: Go home. Take back the shell before we have to intervene."

The courier collapsed to the floor. I knew when he looked at us again it would be the subservient messenger. The Greek god who had commandeered his body would be gone.

"Highness . . ." The courier's voice was weak. "Please don't do that again," he muttered before passing out on our floor. I lurched forward, catching his head before it whacked the marble floor.

"You killed him, Cass."

I shot Isaac a look as the courier's pulse thrummed against my wrist.

"I'm not you." The courier's weight adjusted, sending me sprawling to compensate. "A little help here."

"What did he mean, take back the shell?"

"Isaac, later. Help me." I struggled with the dead weight of the round royal messenger, hoping it would preoccupy Isaac from pressing any further. Three people knew about the terms of my Russian roulette game with Chance. One was dead (mom), one was on the run (me), and the other had the Shell of Clarity (Chance).

"Cassandra," Isaac clucked his tongue. "Tell me you didn't wager the Shell of Clarity and lose?"

I didn't have to answer. I'm pretty sure the guilty look singeing my face said it for me.

Isaac paled. "Oh, gods, Cassie. You know this is all sorts of bad."

"I know. Well, I didn't then, but obviously I do now."

Isaac effortlessly picked up the courier. His towel inched lower and lower on his backside as he walked across the room. And before it could fall to the floor, he plopped the courier on the couch and tightened the fabric around his waist. The cool floor seeped into my backside. Isaac stalked back across the room, picked up the note, and opened it.

"You lost the shell to Chance?"

I nodded.

Parchment paper crackled as Isaac took it out of the envelope. His bright blue eyes railed back and forth.

"What is it?"

"For you," he peeled off the sticky note and handed it to me.

"Go home. Take back the shell before we have to intervene." I read back the same words Poseidon had said. "Cute. Anything else?"

"Yeah, but one question: Chance didn't ask for a vial of your blood as part of the wager, did he?

I nodded, thinking back to the evil way his eyes glinted when his phlebotomist pulled out the needle. "Two, actually."

"Oh, Cassandra, you're not going to like this." Isaac looked at me. For the first time, I saw fear roil in his eyes.

"Why?" I scooted closer to get a better look at the parchment. At the top of the page was a foil rendering of the shell my moms had given me, the Shell of Clarity. I started reading and found the exact spot Isaac had stopped. "This is so not good."

"Pack up, Princess. We're heading home." He stood and let the parchment paper of doom float into my lap.

I stood and headed over to the computer—Olivia's email still illuminated the screen—and clicked reply:

Olivia,

We're coming home.

Shit was about to get really bad in Las Vegas.

I hesitated a moment, a slight tremor in my finger, and hit send.

THE ADVENTURE CONTINUES . . .

HOUSE OF CARDS

Curious to know what House of Cards you've descended from?
You're five questions away from knowing.
Visit the link and then connect with other members of your house on
Facebook (www.Facebook.com/MindyRuizBooks).

www.bit.ly/GameOfHearts

Look for the conclusion to The Game of Hearts Series, this winter.

ACKNOWLEDGEMENTS:

First and foremost, to God be the glory. Thank you for continuing to bless me with an abundance of health and love. I hope you're proud of the life I'm living with my second chance.

I've had the pleasure of having so many amazing women come into my life. In elementary school, Irene Takasaki introduced me to the wonders of sushi and growing up on a block full of boys. Middle school brought Meg Valle into my life. She taught me how to lather my eyes in charcoal eyeliner. High school days introduced me to Dawn, Lori, Heather, Angie, and the Cerritos High Drill Team. Their help with decoding boys and the proper ways to get maximum bang height with only two sprays of Aqua Net are some of my happiest memories. College brought another set of ladies into my life, Michelle, Michelle, and Christy. We continued to try and decipher the boy riddle while we were floating on the broken down Theta Chi houseboat in the middle of Lake Havasu. I found my voice, my worth, and my dreams with you three ladies. You showed me having a spine and an opinion wasn't a bad thing and sometimes you had to walk away from a good relationship when the timing was bad. Thank you for Cowboy Sushi nights and discovering our dreams while hitting golf balls off the roof of the U.C.L.A Theta Chi house. To the Bruin Men of Theta Chi, two words: Proper Gentlemen. In the real world, Dina and Rochelle took all those pieces you previous ladies uncovered and taught me how to fight and dream. Each set of friends saw me through heartache and triumphs, bad hair choices and bright clothes. Each of you has had a lasting impression on my life, and there's not a day that goes by that I don't cherish the impact.

Thank you to my darling husband, Mark Anthony, who continues to prove heroes still exist. Thank you for being the example our boys look to when it comes to being a gentleman.

To my sister-in-laws, Kathleen, and Allison: You are two of the most amazing women I know. Thank you for taking on the challenge of loving the Rayburns. We are not an easy family to understand let alone pledge forever and always to, but we are quite entertaining. Thank you for letting me coo over my nephews like the crazy aunt that I am.

To my brothers: Joshua, Patric, Mathew, and Daniel, being your sister is one of the greatest honors in my life.

Mom and Grandma Victoria, thank you for every ounce of you that's in me.

To my three boys: weird is good. When you feel like you're standing alone, look behind you, you come from a loud and large family who will take on the world for you.

No book would ever be finished without thanking Misty Provencher, Amy Evans, Chelsea Starling, Elizabeth Isaacs, Hope Collier, and Megan Allen. Your friendship over the years has meant everything to me. I adore each and every one of you.

To Molly Lee, Rebecca Yarros, and Rachel Harris, thank you for your faith in my words, your friendship, and your overall awesomeness. Thanks for letting a goofy wrestling mom feel like she can create universes that make sense.

Thank you to the United Mastermind group. Every Monday you make me a million times better than I deserve to be.

Christina Marie at LuLoFangirl, thank you for championing The Game of Hearts Series and your friendship.

Heather Lyons, you amaze me.

Thank you to my agent, Italia Gandolfo, for being so patient with me.

K.P. & Jessica at Inkslinger PR, I still pinch myself you agreed to take me on. I heart your faces sooo much.

Janet Wallace, you changed my life. Thank you for StandUp Indies, UtopiaCon, and your friendship. Thank you!

Finally, thank you to the readers who continue to support my imaginary friends.

ABOUT THE AUTHOR:

 Mindy Ruiz lives in a sleepy Beach Town in Southern California. When she's not writing, she spends her time chasing after three boys, making flirty eyes at her hunky husband, watching fantasy television shows, cheering for the Dallas Cowboys, and hanging out at the beach with her very large and loud Italian family.

Her career in publishing started in the 4th grade with a story about a magic, museum-hopping, chair. Now, Mindy writes young adult, new adult, and adult paranormal romance. Her books always include tormented heroes, snarky heroines, and lots of swoon-y moments that will put a smile on your face or make your heart race. Mindy is the lover of a good romance, the underdog and John Hugh's 80's teen movies.

When her toes aren't in the sand or her mind isn't in the clouds, Mindy loves hearing from readers.

Follow her on:
www.Facebook.com/MindyRuizBooks
www.Twitter.com/MindyRuiz

And look for her on:
www.Instagram.com/MindyRuiz,
www.GoodReads.com/MindyRuiz,
www.pinterest.com/MindyRuizBooks.

For exclusive sneak peeks join her newsletter:
http://eepurl.com/bkjTAH